Blood

of the

Assassin

✝

Book IV of the Assassin series

Russell Blake

First Edition

ISBN: 978-1482573367

Published by

Reprobatio Limited

AUTHOR'S NOTES

Blood of the Assassin is the fifth installment in the Assassin series, consisting of *King of Swords*, *Night of the Assassin*, *Revenge of the Assassin*, *Return of the Assassin*, and now, *Blood of the Assassin*. The series chronicles the exploits of *El Rey*, also known by his professional moniker "The King of Swords," who is the most lethal and notorious cartel assassin in Latin America – now retired after a series of misadventures culminating in his being forced to work for CISEN, the Mexican intelligence agency.

Blood of the Assassin can be read as the fifth in the series, or as a stand-alone. It was written so that if it's the first Russell Blake book you've ever read, it's coherent and complete, while if you've followed the *Assassin* novels to this point, it offers another *El Rey* adventure that is, perhaps, among the most satisfying. If you've read the others, skip the background paragraph that follows. If this is your first experience with the *Assassin* tomes, read on.

Blood of the Assassin finds *El Rey* waiting for his next CISEN assignment. The world thinks he's dead, which is just as well, as his former employer, *Don* Aranas, the leader of the Sinaloa Cartel (one of the most powerful criminal syndicates in the world), is testy about his final contract having ended in failure and has put a ten-million-dollar price on *El Rey*'s head as retribution. Captain Romero Cruz, the chief of the Federal Police anti-cartel task force, and the man who ultimately captured the super-assassin and put him behind bars, has been told that the killer received a full presidential pardon for his past crimes, so *El Rey* is now a free man whose sins have been expunged. Cruz's number two man, Lieutenant Briones, who was instrumental in the assassin's capture and who took a bullet from *El Rey*'s gun, is also a key player in *Blood of the Assassin*, as is Dinah, Captain Cruz's young wife (and the daughter of *El Rey*'s former facilitator, who died at his hands).

Blood of the Assassin picks up a few months after *Return of the Assassin* left off.

It has been one of my favorite in the series to write, and I hope that you enjoy reading it as much as I enjoyed penning it.

CHAPTER 1

Sweat streamed down Heinrich Vogel's face in spite of the chill air gusting through the Berlin streets. The crisp wind sliced through his suit trousers, the heavy overcoat he hugged tight against his slim frame of little use. His footfalls echoed dully off the three a.m. façades of the gray apartment buildings framing both sides of the darkened *Obenstrautstrase*, the ponderous branches of the surrounding trees rustling overhead as he made his way from shadow to shadow, clinging to the night like a lover. He felt his mind playing tricks on him – no surprise after twenty-four hours like those he'd just had. At the next intersection, he paused, ears straining for any hint of pursuit. Nothing. It was all in his imagination.

A noise from down the block froze Heinrich in his tracks. Logic said it was impossible that he'd been followed – he had been meticulously careful, except for the one calculated risk he'd been forced to chance in order to get the information. *A risk that may prove to be my undoing*, he thought grimly.

When his informant had turned up dead of an apparent heroin overdose that morning, only hours after their meeting, he'd been immediately suspicious, although the police were treating it as just another dead junkie in a city battling an insidious wave of drug abuse among its former East German population. Unemployment was endemic in whole segments of the demographic, and an entire generation had grown up without prospects after the Wall had come down, leaving Berlin with a lasting legacy of intravenous drug use and crime.

But Heinrich knew that for all his informant's faults, he hadn't been a junkie. Perhaps it had been the only vice the man hadn't embraced. The death had therefore served as an early warning to Heinrich – it was without question a murder, and the timing was too coincidental for him to brush off. After hearing the news, he had spent all day going about his business, filling out tedious reports, the hours crawling past in seeming slow motion in the busy offices of the metropolitan police where he worked as a civilian staffer. When it hit quitting time, he had stayed late, waiting until the day shift disappeared, and then had made his way to a quiet restaurant a few blocks from the huge building that housed his offices, as he did most nights – he was single, no steady relationship, so nobody waiting at home for him with a hot meal and a warm smile.

He'd been pushing the food around his plate and sipping at his Bitburger pilsner for ten minutes when he'd spotted another solitary diner at the far end of the restaurant, who had seemed completely uninterested in him – except for a telltale glance over his book when he'd thought Heinrich wasn't watching.

That had been enough.

Without hurrying, Heinrich had slipped some euros under his glass and gone to the rear of the restaurant to use the bathroom. Once he had been out of sight of the dining room, he'd made a quick dash for the rear service door, surprising the wait staff moving into the adjacent kitchen, but he'd bluffed his way through, holding his phone out as though it explained everything.

Once through the heavy steel door he'd found himself in an alley, overflowing garbage cans stacked by the back exits that lined the sidewalks, and he'd hurried away from the restaurant to the more crowded plaza a block north.

Behind him, the restaurant door had slammed shut again, confirming his worst fears – somehow, some way, he'd been blown, and now they would want to discover how much he knew.

He'd picked up his pace, afraid to look over his shoulder, debating his options. He couldn't chance going to his apartment. It was a guarantee that they would be waiting for him. His bolting out of the restaurant had stripped any veneer of deniability from him – innocent men didn't run from strangers eating schnitzel among a hundred others.

As he'd turned the corner onto the busy boulevard that fronted the plaza, he'd caught a glimpse of the man from the restaurant a hundred yards down the alley. He'd bee-lined for a fast food restaurant where a throng of teens was loitering, and then had slipped out into traffic, jaywalking to get across to the far curb before his pursuer emerged from the alley's mouth.

A VW Passat had almost collided with him, but he'd dodged out of the way just in time, the sleek anthracite bumper missing him by inches, and then he'd been on the sidewalk, disappearing into the milling pedestrians at the plaza's edge. He hadn't waited to confirm that he'd lost his tail, but instead had made his way across the square to a U-Bahn station and descended the stairs before hurrying to a turnstile and slipping through with a swipe of his card.

Standing in the busy subway station, he'd struggled over which line to take, and then decided on whichever arrived soonest. A whistle of air had come from one of the passageways to his right, and he'd pushed past the slower moving travelers to get to the platform just as the train pulled to a stop, its doors opening with a whoosh and disgorging a stream of tired passengers before he stepped aboard.

His mind had raced over his alternatives. One thing was certain – he needed to get the information he'd been given to his control officer sooner rather than later. But the man hadn't picked up the phone any of the times he'd called that day or the night before. He probably wasn't in town. There was no reason for urgency on his part – Heinrich's windfall bombshell of information had come in completely unexpectedly. Normally Heinrich and his control would communicate once every few weeks, which in the current environment of non-aggression was more than sufficient. Nobody had expected Heinrich to get something this hot dropped into his lap, so there had been no emergency protocol set up.

The train had lurched forward and quickly clattered its way to the next station, and Heinrich had used the lull to consider his choices – none of which had been particularly appealing. He'd need to disappear, which would require money – a lot of money, which Heinrich didn't exactly have at his fingertips. But surely the information would be worth a fortune – at least a small one, which would be more than enough to take him to a new town and equip him with a new identity. Maybe even get him out of Germany entirely. Somewhere warm, where he could run a bar and spend his days on the beach.

The screeching of steel wheels had jolted him out of his daydream and forced him back into the moment. Yes, perhaps the information would buy him a ticket to somewhere else, but first he would have to pass it to his handler. Based on what he knew, that wouldn't be easy – people got killed over far less than this every day, and he had no illusions that because he was a low-level police department clerk he wouldn't be targeted. If he was right, the data was pure dynamite. And as with all highly explosive materials, it would have to be treated delicately.

Four stations later he'd gotten out at Wilmersdorfer Strasse and emerged into the night, moving to the pedestrian thoroughfare, thousands of his fellow Berliners around him, buying him a temporary measure of security. He'd fished his cell phone from his overcoat pocket and dialed his handler's number yet again, but it had gone to voice mail. He'd left his fourth message of the day, this one more urgent than the earlier ones.

"This is Heinrich. I was followed from work. I think I've been compromised. You need to bring me in. Like I said earlier – I've got something...big. Really big. Call me. I can't go home. I'm out on the streets. My phone's on."

He'd hung up and stared at the little screen with frustration, and then sighed. It would do no good to get any more agitated. It wouldn't be much longer until his phone rang, and then it would all be over.

That had been seven hours earlier. His control had finally called a half hour ago and set up a meet, sounding more annoyed than concerned. So now, after as many beers to soothe his frazzled nerves, he was alone on a desolate street in the wee hours, and someone who meant him no good was coming for him.

He heard footsteps echoing down the block – at least two men, moving quickly. His eyes swept the street for possible hiding places. He was still too far from the rendezvous point, so there wouldn't be any help from that direction. And he was out of options.

Then he spotted it. A black iron gate, maybe seven feet high, but scalable.

The question was whether he could do so quietly enough that they wouldn't hear him. And if he could, whether there was an escape route on the other side. He peered into the gloom, and then the footsteps picked up their pace, making his decision for him.

Heinrich scrambled up the gate, driven by fear and desperation, and was at the top, hoisting himself over, when his coat caught on one of the faux spear heads that served as flimsy protection against attempting precisely what he was doing. He pulled at it, desperately trying to free himself, the sound of his pursuers now too close for comfort.

The coat gave with a tear and he dropped inside, falling against the cement walkway and landing on his arm, which snapped with a muffled crack, the pain instant and mind-numbing. Tears welled in his eyes as he stifled a cry, and then he forced himself to his feet, his breath stopped in his chest from the agony. It was at least a fracture, if not worse, but the sound of running footsteps urged him forward. He edged down the cramped side passage, a service access way for the building that was primarily used to haul leaking garbage bins, judging by the stink of it.

He was nearly to the rear corner of the building when two men stopped at the gate. He was far enough that they wouldn't see him. Unless they had flashlights.

Heinrich watched them, willing his breathing to a shallow draw, and tried to shrink into the surrounding concrete, pressing himself against the wall, groping, hoping to find a recess he could use for cover. His fingers felt along the edge of the building and had reached the rim of a doorway when his heart sank. One of the two men was pointing at the top of the gate, where a thin strip of overcoat fluttered in the breeze.

He bolted into the inky black at the far end of the walkway, and then a chip of concrete struck his face, ripping a gash as his ears registered the distinctive pop of a silenced small-caliber pistol, followed almost instantly by the tell-tale whistle of a ricochet. Another pop, and then the whine of a slug skimming the wall on the opposite side, only five feet away. He instinctively ducked and threw himself onto the hard cement path, hoping he could crawl to a position of relative safety behind the building, out of range of the rounds his assailants were firing blindly in the hopes of a lucky hit.

Blood ran freely down his face from the cut, but he ignored it – the least of his worries at the moment. He almost fainted from the pain radiating from his ruined arm, but he inched along, using his good hand and his legs to further himself from the danger at the gate. He'd just reached the corner when he heard the iron barrier clatter as one of the men pulled himself to the top, and Heinrich understood that he would only have seconds to find a way out, or die cold and alone from a gunman's slug to the back of the head. If he was lucky. If not, they would torture him for hours first, in an effort to get him to reveal what he knew.

And then he was clear of the passageway and at the back of the building. He drew himself to his feet and stumbled blindly in the gloom, hoping for a reprieve of some sort as the sound of his pursuers moving towards him echoed off the walls, their footsteps bringing with them the certainty of his life ending in moments, barring a miracle.

CHAPTER 2

Two Weeks Earlier, Prague, Czech Republic

The bridges spanning the Vltava River in Prague were quiet at dawn as the sun's tentative rays burned through the clouds that lingered over the city like a fog, an occasional drizzle marring the otherwise tranquil Monday morning. Traffic would begin clogging the arteries into the city center in a few more hours, but for now the roads were largely empty except for an occasional delivery truck bringing produce to the restaurants that ringed the downtown.

A black Mercedes sedan rolled across the Charles Bridge, the sole vehicle on the massive span, moving slowly as it approached the ministry buildings so as not to jostle the passenger, who was sipping coffee and reading the newspaper. His hours were unconventional for a public servant, but Milan Rejt was no ordinary bureaucrat. As the finance minister for the Czech Republic, he controlled the destiny of the nation, and typically worked twelve-hour days – a man consumed by his work. And in the turbulent times of the last few years, his duties had never been more important: to guide the nation through a period of upheaval and change, as lesser economies succumbed to the global malaise that had infected Europe.

A short man in his fifties with an arrogant bearing and hawk-like eyes, his diminutive stature deceived nobody into taking him for granted or underestimating him. He ruled his kingdom with an iron fist, and nothing of any note took place in the financial system without his express approval.

His cell phone chirped, and he punched it on as he eyed the stately skyline. "Yes?"

"Sir, I've taken care of everything for your meeting this morning. The other ministers will be here by nine, and I've arranged with the press to gather forty minutes before the ceremony so that you can hold a press conference," his assistant said.

Milan glanced at his watch – his subordinate was already at work at six, which was unusual. However, today was no ordinary day; it was the culmination of two years of negotiations, struggle, and cajoling. Everyone on his staff had invested the same kind of effort he had, and he expected nothing less from them than absolute loyalty – and the same brutal hours he kept.

A career with Rejt guaranteed lucrative government positions regardless of what party was in power; no matter who was sitting in the driver's seat, they would need money, and Rejt controlled the Treasury purse strings with the tight-fistedness of a medieval money-changer. He had spent the last fifteen years in the government corridors, guiding policy to benefit the interests of the Czech people – and, of course, his own network of rich and powerful associates.

He sank into the butter-soft leather seat and nodded as he listened on the telephone. When he spoke, it was with quiet approval.

"Excellent. I'll be there in a few minutes. I trust you have the paperwork we discussed yesterday for a final review?"

"Of course, sir. I have it prepared for you, on your desk."

"Good. I'll see you when I arrive."

Rejt didn't wait to hear the response, having stabbed the phone off with his last syllable. He looked down at his hand-made Italian shoes, shined to a gleam by his valet, and smiled with satisfaction. Not bad for a humble academic, an economist who had struggled fresh out of school under the Soviet system, and who hadn't known the right people to garner one of the cushy administrative jobs that entailed decent pay, privilege, and little actual work. But when the regime changed and the Russians were suddenly gone, he had been in a perfect position to become a simple administrative assistant to one of the founders of the new government, and once his taste for power had been whetted, he had never looked back.

He took another sip of coffee and closed his eyes.

Today would change everything. He had never been closer. Years of work, and he would be the one who put his stamp of approval on the agreement, which couldn't have been ratified without his backroom jockeying and the pressure that only he could bring.

A pigeon strutted its early morning mating dance, its cooing a rhythmic lament as it swept back and forth across the roof, the shy object of its affection watching from its perch on the metal edge, eyeing the male's bombastic display with approval. Step step step swoop and coo, wings to the side, its chest puffed out, fanning the area in what was surely an impressive avian maneuver.

The man watched the show twenty feet away with dry amusement, and then returned to his errand. The breeze was around twelve miles per hour, and he turned the upper knob on the scope several clicks to compensate. Distance, he knew, was two hundred fifty yards from his position on the roof of one of the Wallenstein Palace buildings undergoing renovation. An easy shot with this rifle. Hardly worth his special talents, although he wasn't going to argue with the million euro fee he would earn for a morning's work.

He had been waiting for two hours, having posed as a workman the prior week in order to get a feel for the best available position for the hit. This was a tricky shot, at an odd angle from his hiding place, but he had pulled off far worse from much greater distances. And at the end of the day, all his client cared about was the final result. The instructions had been very clear: the assassination had to take place this morning, and no other.

Which was fine by him.

Werner Rauschenbach prided himself on his ability to pull off difficult sanctions, and considered himself to be the best. He'd made a small fortune from his career as a high-priced assassin specializing in political and mob-related executions. The former Soviet republics were rife with gangs battling for supremacy, and every few months he got a call seeking his assistance in the elimination of a rival or a non-compliant politician. He had started off at fifty grand a hit a decade earlier, and had worked his way up now to where an ordinary contract drew between two hundred and fifty and five hundred thousand euros; a higher-visibility target, like the one today, could run as high as a million.

At least it wasn't raining hard, or worse yet, snowing. That could complicate matters for his getaway. Ready for the action to begin, he slid back the rifle bolt and chambered a round – likely the only shot he would need to fire.

He shifted on the roof tiles and took another look through the scope. Everything was perfect; now he just needed the guest of honor to show up, and he could finish and get out of there.

His breathing accelerated when he saw the Mercedes swing around the corner and move to the front of the building. He knew the car well – one of his hallmarks was research and planning. Executing the target was usually the easy part. Getting away in one piece was a little more problematic. In this case, it was made doubly difficult because of the location: there weren't a lot of places to hide, and his next best choice had been up on the hill, over seven hundred yards away. Not an impossible distance, by any means, but at two hundred yards he could practically throw a rock and hit the man, so he had erred on the side of caution.

The luxury sedan rolled to a stop near the steps at the front entrance, and the driver got out and walked to the rear door, pausing for a moment before opening it.

Rauschenbach squinted and aligned the crosshairs on the driver's head, which in the high magnification looked like it was only a few feet away. His finger moved to the trigger, and he waited for his target to appear.

Rejt set his paper down on the seat of the Mercedes and took a last sip of coffee before heaving himself out of the vehicle. On the sidewalk, he handed his driver his empty cup, and for a brief moment, as the sun kissed the garden across the street, the palace standing proudly in the background, he was struck by the beauty of the country – his country, for which he had worked so hard.

The slug tore the top of his head off, instantly terminating brainwave activity, already dead before he hit the ground. The driver ducked and watched his boss crumple in front of him, having barely registered the sound of the shot that ended his life – a sharp crack from near the same gardens Rejt had been admiring.

The driver sprang to the car, putting its bulk between him and the shooter, and fumbled for his cell, dialing the emergency number once his fingers began working again. The shock from the bloody killing only a few feet away caused his hands to tremble almost uncontrollably, and it was all he could do to hold the phone to his ear and demand help from the duty officer who answered.

Several police officers, stationed outside the ministry, jogged to the car from their positions by the front doors, and upon seeing the carnage, drew their pistols and scanned the rooflines for signs of a gunman, but decided to wait for backup before they tried to tackle him – wherever he was.

Rauschenbach was already moving off the roof seconds after he'd seen the minister's head explode, and was lowering himself to the ground on the far side of the building with a rope, having left the rifle on the roof. He'd used an Accuracy International AWM rifle filched from the German army, which he could easily replace, and preferred to carry nothing from the hit – he built the cost of whatever tools he needed for a job into the budget, ensuring that there was never a trail back to him.

He dropped to the ground and sprinted to a BMW S1000R motorcycle parked adjacent to some scaffolding, and with a glance at the crumpled tarp that he knew covered a dead security guard, pulled on a black helmet, and started the motor with a roar. After looking around one final time, he slammed the bike into gear and twisted the throttle, tearing up the sidewalk before hurtling off the curb and onto the street.

The wail of sirens in the background was drowned out by the sound of the engine as he raced through the gears, bouncing down the cobblestone streets as he wound his way along the twisting route to the highway that would take him out of town. He was just breathing a sigh of relief when a police car swung out of an alley immediately behind him with its lights flashing and siren screaming, and a male voice blared over the public address system in Czech.

"Stop where you are. Pull to the side. Motorcycle. Pull over now. That is an order."

Rauschenbach considered his options, and then revved the engine into the redline and made an unexpected hard left, flying up a narrow byway barely wide enough for two people. The police car skidded to a stop and reversed, blocking the entrance, and he glanced at his mirror for a split second before pouring on the gas. One of the cops had his pistol out. Werner didn't want to test the police's marksmanship skills – it was those sorts of stupid, unexpected surprises that could get one killed.

The little alley veered left and he ducked down as he urged the motorcycle on, the walls streaking by him in a blur, and then he was out of the passageway and bouncing on a manicured lawn, trying frantically to maintain control of the handlebars as the wheels slid on the slick grass. Another police car came around the corner of a nearby building on two wheels, and he fought to steer the motorcycle to the far street on the other side of the park. A third police car blew down the road he was racing towards, and he gripped the brakes, swinging the bike around. His eyes scanned the perimeter of the park in front of him, and then he made his decision and gunned the engine. The bike leapt forward and he pounded up a set of stone stairs, a squabble of sparrows scattering skyward at his approach.

Rauschenbach darted across the road just as another police car veered onto it, and he swerved to miss the vehicle as he made for the labyrinthine streets only a few hundred yards away. The motor howled as he twisted the throttle, and he disappeared around another ancient building just as one of the officers opened fire at him. Chunks of stone flew off the centuries-old façade, and then he was gone, the sound of his revving engine the only trace of his passage.

Four minutes later he got off the motorcycle in an empty church parking lot and walked to a parked light blue Renault coupe. He stripped off the worker's coveralls he was wearing, balled them up, and threw them into the nearby bushes. His blue pinstripe suit and conservatively striped tie were slightly rumpled but serviceable, and as he eased behind the wheel of the little car he caught a glimpse of his gray eyes in the mirror, the small scar above the right eyebrow an almost imperceptible reminder of a past close call from his days in the military. His salt-and-pepper hair framed a ruggedly handsome face, square jaw, high cheekbones, a slight tan – the picture of a respectable businessman.

He turned the key and put the car into gear, exhaling with relief. The job was done, and he would be in Dresden within an hour and a half, even allowing for some holdup at the border. He was carrying one of his many identities, this time a Dutch passport, and had a rock-solid alibi for his time in the Czech Republic if anyone questioned him. A seller of pharmaceuticals, he'd filled his trunk with samples and literature, and even the most aggressive border agent would come up dry after a few minutes of searching.

He hadn't stayed free, a frustrating rumor for the authorities, by accident. Nobody had any current photos of him, and any old ones would have done no good – extensive plastic surgery had altered his features to the point where his own mother wouldn't have recognized him. He was a cypher, a ghost, who slipped across borders with ease, and carried out the most difficult contracts without drama or complications. He smiled to himself at his professional nickname: *Der Eisenadler.* The Iron Eagle. Indestructible, the ruler of the sky. And now with over fifty hits to his credit over an illustrious career.

Not bad for a simple boy from the Berlin slums and a disgraced ex-cop. A millionaire. Homes in Spain, Germany, and Italy. And a book of business from satisfied customers that ensured he had as much work as he wanted. His neighbors knew him as an import/export executive, always traveling, obviously well-to-do, who kept to himself and never made trouble. Which was close enough to the truth, he supposed. He imported cash into his bank account, and exported death.

A commodity that was in constant demand.

CHAPTER 3

Present Day, Zacatelco, Mexico

A battered Chevrolet pickup puttered down the dirt road on the outskirts of town, springs creaking from the washboard surface's pummeling of its suspension, a red plastic bag taped over its one operating brake light as a safety concession. Raw exhaust belched from a rusting tailpipe, the muffler having rotted out long ago, catalytic converters a silly luxury for the idle rich. Its headlights glowed a dull amber, barely penetrating the two a.m. gloom, the driver squinting as he peered through the smeared bug splatters on the grimy windshield.

Dust swirled in the wind as it roared by the oversized bulk of the stationary black command-center van, *Policía Federal* painted across the side in two-foot-high white letters. From the outside, the vehicle displayed no signs of life, but inside was a hum of activity.

"How much longer until the army gets here?" Lieutenant Briones asked, his voice strained, sitting in front of a flat screen monitor in the rear of the van.

"They said they'll be in position in five more minutes," the man next to him murmured, as though raising his voice might alert their target.

"Five minutes! What the hell have they been doing? They were supposed to be here by now," Briones griped.

"You know how it is. *Mas o menos.*" More or less.

Briones sat back, considering a response, and then decided to let it go. He did indeed know how it was.

"What about our men?"

"In position and awaiting the signal to breach the compound."

Briones nodded and then lifted a two-way to his mouth. "Army's late again. But they say they'll be here shortly," he reported.

"Damn. What else can go wrong today? Did they think that showing up was optional? Who's the commanding officer?" the disgusted voice of Captain Romero Cruz, the head of the Mexico City anti-cartel task force, growled from the speaker.

"Your favorite. General Albacer."

"That explains a lot. I'm surprised he's still awake. Do you want me to scream at him?" Cruz asked.

"Can't see that it will do any good. The compound is dark. Five minutes shouldn't make any difference if everybody's asleep," Briones said.

"Are you ready to go in?"

"Yes, sir. The assault force is standing by."

"Well, thank heaven for small favors. Let's see if we can take these scum alive, shall we? I want a shot at interrogating them."

"I understand, sir. We'll do everything we can to get at least a few survivors."

"Does everyone know what *El Gato* looks like? You circulated the photos?" Cruz asked.

"Of course. If he's still got the fuzz, he'll be hard to miss." *El Gato*, one of the top captains of the Sinaloa cartel, affected a distinctive beard. He was also known for his shaved head – for which, the rumor was, the facial hair was compensation. He was widely believed to control much of the cartel's marijuana, meth, and heroin trade in Mexico City. The *Federales* had received a tip from an informant looking at years of hard time for his role in a drunken bar stabbing a few days earlier, who had alerted them to the location of one of his safe houses. Surveillance had been ongoing since then, and a man who looked suspiciously like *El Gato* had been seen going into the house from a black Ford Excursion early that evening. That had triggered the late night strike on the house – Cruz had been tracking *El Gato* for years, but had always been one step behind him.

Not this time.

Their prey was still inside the house, and the lights had gone off at midnight.

The original plan had been to grab him when he was leaving, but then the opportunity to seize not only the drug lord but also the inevitable stash of weapons, drugs, and cash had been too attractive for Cruz, and he'd given the go-ahead to launch a raid.

There were six people inside that they knew of – five men and one woman, who appeared to be *El Gato*'s seventeen-year-old sometimes-girlfriend. If they could be captured without shooting, it would be another coup in a year of them for Cruz – between capturing *El Rey* and several other high-profile operations, he appeared to have the Midas touch, even if nothing much changed in the criminal underworld besides the names.

Briones sat back, his leg bouncing impatiently, anxious to get the operation underway. Every minute that passed increased the odds of something going wrong and alerting the target – an all-too-common occurrence when the army was involved. Even though all the soldiers on these offensives were vetted and trusted, the truth was that in a world where their pay was three hundred dollars a month, it was all too easy to buy information. He would know soon enough, he supposed. Once the soldiers had sealed off the perimeter he would send his officers in, and then it would be over quickly.

His other radio issued a burst of static, and then a deep male voice cut through the hush in the van.

"Lieutenant Briones. This is Major Gutierrez. We are in position. Are there any changes or additions to our orders?"

Briones shook his head. "Negative. Just seal off the roads and make sure nobody gets in or out. We're going in. Hold your positions unless I expressly tell you not to. Understood?"

"Roger that. We will hunker down. Consider the perimeter sealed. Out."

Briones stood and donned his helmet and Kevlar vest, and over it pulled a dark blue windbreaker with *Federales* emblazoned across the back. He reached down and grabbed an M16 assault rifle and chambered a round, then looked at the remaining three men in the van.

"Time to roll. I'm headed to the first squad. Be there within two minutes. Come on, Santiro. Let's hit it." He gestured to the other man in assault garb, who nodded and slipped his vest on and then gathered his weapons.

They exited the van and trotted down the dirt road to where Briones had twenty crack officers waiting in the dark. He had been through countless similar assaults with these men, and everyone knew the drill.

Hand signals only, fire only if fired upon; the objective to take as many of the cartel members alive as possible.

When the two men reached the others, Briones frowned at the squad leader, a hard-faced sergeant with a decade of assault experience, and gestured to the iron gate in the perimeter wall that sealed the three buildings of the compound from the street. The sergeant nodded and the men moved out, their rubber-soled boots thumping on the dirt as they jogged to the gate. Earlier that day an undercover officer had made multiple slow runs by it and confirmed there were no cameras mounted outside – a positive for the assault force. The sergeant motioned to one of the men, who moved forward with a set of picks and quickly opened the lock. Another man sprayed lubricant on the hinges. Two of the officers pushed it open, and the rest moved into the large area in front of the main house, weapons at the ready.

Briones stood by the perimeter wall, anxiety nagging at him. This was all too easy. Something wasn't right. He debated calling the men back, but then choked down the unease. Sometimes things went well. It wasn't necessary to expect mayhem on every operation. The buildings were quiet, no signs of life, nothing stirring. Perhaps gratitude was more appropriate than agitation.

The group was halfway to the house when a window slid open, and then the night exploded with gunfire, automatic weapons chattering from two of the three buildings. A round caught the officer next to Briones in the chest. His vest absorbed the blow, but the force knocked him off his feet. In the courtyard, a handful of the *Federales* were cut down in as many seconds – a disaster that left the rest without any shelter, sitting ducks for the cartel gunmen.

"Fall back. Now," Briones hissed into his com line, all the officers' helmets containing similar communications gear as well as night vision goggles.

The *Federales* returned fire, trying to buy themselves breathing room, but when they regrouped outside the walls, only fourteen men were left of the original twenty.

"Lieutenant. Do you want to get the soldiers here?" the sergeant barked, panting, watching as his men fired measured bursts at the house.

"I'd rather not. Get the second team here on the double." Briones had ten more men waiting on the far side of the compound as backup. The sergeant murmured into his radio, and forty-five seconds later the additional fighters were crouched with the original team, awaiting instructions.

"They must have motion detectors somewhere inside the yard. Any benefit of surprise is over. Now we need to do this the hard way," Briones said, and the men exchanged grim looks. "I want two teams. I'll get the army here with armored personnel vehicles, and when they roll into the yard, we'll use those as cover. Sergeant, you take the main house. I'll lead the second team to take out the guest house. There's no fire coming from the third building, so I think we can assume it's empty."

"Yes, sir."

Briones keyed his radio and relayed his instructions to Major Gutierrez, and then they waited as the sound of heavy trucks rolled down the dirt road from the larger artery around the bend. Three armored trucks approached and stopped a few yards from where Briones and his men were huddled. The lead vehicle passenger door opened, and a captain stepped out onto the dirt. Gunfire chattered from the house, but had diminished in intensity once the men were out of the line of fire.

"We'll go in together. Let my men open up with the heavy artillery, and then your men can follow up," the captain said. Briones was torn, but then thought about the six men lying dead inside the compounded, and gave his assent.

"Fine. Let's do this."

Soldiers poured from out of the backs of the trucks until there were thirty heavily armed men, faces drawn with determination, prepared for the worst. The captain made a hand gesture and the three trucks eased forward through the gates, the soldiers using the first two for cover and the *Federales* shadowing the last one as the gunfire from the house increased to a barrage. Answering volleys from the soldiers tore through the building's windows, and bullets ricocheted off the vehicle armor and the driveway pavers as the gunmen in the house intensified their efforts.

Briones motioned to his men and they joined the fray, pummeling the cartel shooters with a deluge of fire. One of the men near Briones grunted and dropped his weapon, and then fell towards him, half his face blown off by a Kalashnikov round. Briones' jaw quivered and he took the man's place, letting loose with burst after burst from his M16, enraged at the number of casualties they'd suffered from a supposedly low-intensity home invasion.

One of the soldiers tossed a grenade at the windows and got lucky. The detonation was deafening, and then the shooting from the house stopped. A few more scattered shots emanated from the guest house, and the roar of a big .50-caliber army machine gun silenced them with a three-second sustained volley.

Briones signaled to his men. They fanned out in a loose formation, approaching the house cautiously, crouched, weapons sweeping the area, wary. When they reached the door, the sergeant turned to Briones, anxious for his approval, a thin bead of sweat trickling down his face, grime smeared on it from throwing himself onto the driveway. Briones nodded, and the sergeant gestured to the two assault team members who were carrying an eight-inch diameter iron pipe filled with cement. They slammed it against the door and the flimsy wooden slab tore off its hinges with a crash, and then the nearest officer rolled into the opening, weapon searching for targets.

The interior of the house was a shambles, the grenade's shrapnel having shredded everything in the main room. Bodies lay everywhere, bloody stumps a testament to the explosive force unleashed by the blast. Briones crept stealthily to the rear hallway and pointed at three of the officers. They edged by him and moved down the narrow corridor to where three doors stood intact – the main bedrooms.

Two of the men framed the first doorway, pressing themselves against the wall, and then the third knelt and pressed down on the bronze lever, pausing for a moment before swinging it open. He rolled out of the doorway and they waited for shots. When none came, the two on either side swung their guns into the room and did a fast search of the guest bedroom. It was empty.

Four more men inched down the hall and repeated the process at the next door, with the same results. The rooms were deserted.

The final door stood closed at the end of the hall, and the men listened intently for any hint of movement behind it. Briones nodded from his position, and they threw it wide.

"Nooo. Please. Don't hurt me!" a female voice screamed, terrified and very young. The officers moved through the room and the sergeant motioned to the girl to stand up. She did, shivering from fear, wearing only panties and a T-shirt, and followed their directions to stand against the side wall. It was obvious that she wasn't carrying any concealed weapons, so she wasn't a threat.

Her eyes darted to the bed. Briones froze, and then pointed to the king-sized mattress. The sergeant motioned to two of the men, who fixed it with their assault rifles, and then he spoke softly.

"We know you're under the bed. Slide any weapons out and show yourself, or in three seconds we'll use it for target practice, and you won't survive. One...two..."

A Glock 19 slid from under the bed, and then a man's muffled voice followed. "I'm coming out. Don't shoot."

"Crawl out face down. Once you're out from under the bed, put your hands behind your back and lie on your stomach. Now, or you're dead."

A man slid slowly from beneath the bed and did as instructed, lying face down while an officer cuffed him.

"Turn him over," the sergeant instructed, and when the officer complied, a frigid smile crossed his face.

"Well, well. Look who we have here. If it isn't our friend *El Gato*. Hiding under his teenage *puta*'s bed. Very nice," he said.

The drug lord glared at him hatefully. "You're brave men when I have cuffs on and you can hide behind your helmets, eh? I bet you're praying I don't learn your names," he growled.

"Coming from a man who was whimpering under the bed, the irony isn't lost on me," the sergeant responded, then gestured to his men to pick *El Gato* up. "Make sure this shitbird doesn't hit his head on anything on the way to the lockup van. I want to make sure he's in perfect health to answer for killing the officers outside. Now get him out of here."

Two muscular policemen in full assault gear lifted *El Gato* to his feet and dragged him down the hall. Briones watched them without comment, and then keyed his helmet mike. Cruz's voice came over the channel.

"We got *El Gato*. Everyone but his girlfriend is dead."

"That's good news. He's the most important. What about casualties?"

"We're checking now. It's hard to tell until all the smoke clears. I'd say we lost eight, maybe nine men, and have at least four more wounded. They'll probably make it. But this was ugly. I'm...I'm sorry, sir. They had some sort of early warning system that surveillance didn't spot. Motion detectors is my guess. They cut us down before we could find cover. I should have been more cautious," Briones spat.

"It's always easy after an assault to find fault with your actions in the heat of battle. Don't beat yourself up. You took the objective, captured *El Gato*, and eradicated a key player in the Sinaloa Cartel's power structure. I'd say that's a good day's work," Cruz said.

"Not for the dead men, it isn't."

"Everyone knows the risks going in. Sometimes we take casualties. Sometimes they do. That's the job," Cruz reminded him.

"Their wives and children aren't going to be reassured by that."

"I know. Get me a list of the names. I'll make the calls myself."

Briones nodded silently as the crime scene technicians stepped around the bodies and began photographing the devastation. He had no doubt that the dead cartel gunmen would be replaced by the weekend, if not sooner. And nothing would change except the names and faces. Drugs would still flow like water, and guns and money would work their way into the cartels' hands, to be used against men like himself, who were trying to make the country safer. A thankless job that seemed pointless on nights like this one.

CHAPTER 4

Jean-Claude Bouchard peered at his watch with annoyance and lit another cigarette with a thin gold lighter that had been in his family for generations. His refined features spoke to an aristocratic heritage, as did the insouciant way he sucked greedily on the Gitane and then blew smoke at the ceiling, as if disgusted with it even as the tendrils left his lips.

He should have been asleep at this late hour, or at the very least, been rolling around with one of the young German lasses that he favored with his attentions. Instead, he was waiting for the idiot clerk from the police department that he kept on the payroll – mainly so he could justify to his superiors in French intelligence that he was doing something besides spending their money and enjoying the Berlin nightlife.

At thirty-seven years old, Jean-Claude was in the prime of his career, such as it was – the truth being that even though the French maintained a spy network, there wasn't a lot to challenge him in Berlin. He waxed nostalgic about the good old days, when in his imagination he could have been darting furtively down darkened alleys, meeting Soviet moles, danger behind every door. Unfortunately, he'd been born too late for that, and had to content himself with doing grunt work that was beneath him, running a network of informants who did little more than offer tidbits of gossip and data he had no interest in. Still, as long as the French government was willing to pay to collect it, he would, biding his time until he could return to a nice comfortable desk in Paris once he'd done his obligatory stint in the field, and wait for his father to die, leaving him a nice endowment and a lavish flat in the sixteenth *arrondissement*.

He ran nimble fingers through his thick black hair and then pursed his lips, wondering what the hell the German could have for him that required this ungodly hour for a rendezvous. He stared at his hand, holding the cigarette in the affected way he had seen in the movies, and decided that he would give the clerk twenty more minutes and then leave the little studio apartment he kept for meetings; the ingrate could damned well wait until morning if he wasn't going to be considerate enough to be prompt.

The intercom buzzed at him like an annoyed insect, startling him as he fumed over Heinrich's rudeness – very typically German, he thought bitterly. Not pausing to endure the ritual of asking who was there at four-twenty in the morning, he pressed the black button that unlocked the front door and then paused at the hall mirror to consider his appearance. Thin, handsome, he had been told that he looked like a Hollywood star – Leonardo DiCaprio, although Jean-Claude thought he was better looking than that. DiCaprio looked soft, whereas Jean-Claude in his mind radiated brooding danger, as befitted a master of the clandestine world. He stubbed out his smoke in a crystal ashtray on the side table and sucked in his cheeks, turning his face to inspect the effect on his profile.

A thud at his apartment door pulled him from his ruminations, annoying him even further. Was the man raised in a barn? Couldn't he at least attempt to be quiet? Jean-Claude moved to the peephole and looked out, but saw nothing except for the empty hallway lit by a couple of cheap lamps left over from the industrial revolution. Puzzled, he listened at the door, and then pushed his ear against the wood to better make out any sound in the hall.

He was about to go back and push the intercom button again when he heard it. A scratching sound.

"Heinrich?" he called out softly, his voice betraying his puzzlement.

Nothing.

Another faint scratch. Nails on the door. And then a groan. Almost inaudible.

Jean-Claude swung the door open and practically fell over the German's inert form collapsed across the threshold, blood trickling from his nose and mouth. Jean-Claude's eyes widened in alarm, and he instantly regretted not having brought his pistol – not that there was any obvious threat. He stepped back and kneeled, taking care to avoid the blood.

"Heinrich! What happened? Are you all right?" he whispered, registering even as he asked that Heinrich was far from all right.

The German murmured at him unintelligibly. Jean-Claude stood and then bent down to haul him into the apartment, anxious to avoid any unwanted scrutiny from a light-sleeping neighbor. He got his hands under Heinrich's arms and dragged him in, and then held out his hands, covered in blood, as he moved to the door and kicked it closed behind him. Pausing for a moment, uncertain what to do, he stepped over the wounded man and moved into the small kitchen to rinse his hands.

"Good Christ, Heinrich. You're bleeding like a..." Jean-Claude bit his tongue. Heinrich undoubtedly knew he was losing blood.

He moved back to the German and pulled his overcoat open, and saw a bullet wound high in the chest, and another in his upper shoulder. His arm was twisted at an unnatural angle, broken, and his skin was the color of a shark's belly.

Heinrich tried to speak, but all that came out of his mouth was another gurgle. Jean-Claude knelt and leaned over him, turning his head to better make out whatever he was trying to say.

"What? What is it, Heinrich? Who did this to you?" he demanded.

Heinrich tried to raise his good arm, but then it fell back to his side as he coughed blood all over the side of Jean-Claude's face.

The Frenchman pulled back in horror, momentary thoughts of blood-borne diseases racing through his brain – hepatitis, AIDS, Ebola...

Heinrich coughed again, laboring for breath, and then with a groan, lay still, his chest ceasing its straining, his eyes open, staring into eternity with a puzzled frown. Jean-Claude watched life quit the German's body, and then his arm froze on its way to his face to wipe away the blood.

There was something in Heinrich's hand. Clutched between his dead fingers.

Jean-Claude reached out, trembling slightly from shock, and gently eased the object from his death grip.

A USB flash drive, crimson smeared across one side of it.

Jean-Claude stood, and then his blood chilled in his veins. He heard a sound from the street – the front door. A crash.

Like someone kicking it in.

Mind racing frantically, he pocketed the flash drive and glanced at himself in the mirror, taking in the drying blood spackled on his profile with alarm. Moving to the kitchen he quickly grabbed a dish towel and wiped the splatter away as he calculated his options.

The chances were good that they didn't know what apartment Heinrich was coming to.

Then again, it was only a matter of time until they followed the blood trail to his front door. At which point, whoever had done this to Heinrich would repeat the process with him – an eventuality Jean-Claude wanted to avoid at all costs.

Which meant that he would need to beat them to the stairs.

He threw the towel into the sink, grabbed a butcher knife, and moved to the dining room table to grab his notebook computer before creeping to the door and looking out the peephole.

Nobody.

Yet.

He took a final look at Heinrich's bloody corpse and then eased the knob open. Grateful the hinges didn't squeak, he pulled the door towards him and stepped into the hall.

And heard footsteps on the second floor – two below his.

He debated whether to risk closing up the apartment, then erred on the side of caution and stepped silently down the hallway, passing the central main stairs, up which the sound of the pursuers had drifted, and continued to the service stairwell at the far end. His hand shook as he reached out and gripped the handle, and then he froze when the door creaked as it opened.

The footsteps stopped; then suddenly accelerated.

Abandoning any pretension of stealth, he bolted into the landing and took the steps to the roof three at a time, figuring that it would take whoever was after him longer to climb them than to follow him if he went down – gravity being his friend in this case.

At the steel roof door he stopped again, listening intently. A rustle greeted him from below. Exactly like someone creeping up the stairs would sound, trying to avoid giving away their position.

He unlocked the deadbolt and shouldered the door open, then sprinted across the roof to the next building, which was the same height. He leapt across the five-foot chasm, praying that in the dark he had gauged the distance correctly, and stumbled as his dress shoes skidded on the slick surface. Ignoring the pain from his ankle, he willed himself forward to the rooftop exit and felt for the latch.

Locked.

Shit.

He was halfway to the next building, its roof a story lower, when he heard a scrape from his building. His only hope now was that it was so dark that his pursuers wouldn't be able to make him out. Not a great bet to have to make, he realized, and increased his speed.

He hesitated at the roof edge, and then, hearing the sounds of running steps from his building, he backed up and then hurled himself into space, swearing silently, grateful that he spent a decent amount of time in the gym, but fearing what the landing would do to him. When his feet pounded into the roof he instinctively let his knees buckle and then he was rolling, the notebook shattering as it flew from his hands, another blinding shriek of pain shooting up his left leg as ligaments protested the abuse.

When he came to a stop he was still in one piece. He forced himself to stand; his leg almost gave out, but thankfully it held. Jean-Claude limped away from his landing spot, leaving the notebook, and gimped to the roof door, praying that it was open.

The first silenced bullet thumped into the steel frame a foot from his head. He ducked, wrenching the handle with all his strength. A second shot slammed into the stone doorjamb just as the door opened, and then he was through. He vowed to go to church every morning for the rest of his life as he twisted the lock closed, pausing to take in the heavy steel plate and the industrial hinges.

It would take them a while to get through that, he thought, and then descended the steps as fast as his brutalized leg would allow. As he reached the second floor he heard thuds from above, but they were too late. By the time they got into the building, he would be gone.

Outside on the street, he was the only pedestrian to be seen. At the corner, he glanced around and dared a look back at his building, where a car was double parked outside, partially blocking the two lane street – finding a parking spot was impossible in Berlin, even for desperate murderers. He didn't wait for the killers to make it back to ground level, instead setting off in the direction of the subway, which he could reach in two minutes, even in his condition.

When he entered the station, he briefly considered the torn knee of his two-hundred-dollar gabardine slacks and shook his head, muttering to himself. He fished in his pocket for some change, and his fingers brushed against the flash drive as he dug out the fare.

A tiny bit of innocuous micro-circuitry that Heinrich had paid the ultimate price to protect.

He had never been so happy to see a train come down the tracks in his life, and when he boarded, one of only a few bleary-eyed pre-dawn travelers, he took a seat and exhaled with relief.

Whatever was on the flash drive had to be, in Heinrich's words, dynamite. It had already claimed one blood sacrifice, and Jean-Claude couldn't help but believe, as he fingered it in his pocket, that there would be more where that came from.

The train rocked from side to side as it shuttled down the tracks, and when Jean-Claude got off at the third stop, he had decided that whatever had landed in his lap would require him to be extraordinarily cautious – he would stop at the first open internet café and check to see what was on the drive. If it was as big as Heinrich had intimated, he would be on the next flight out in the morning, so he could deliver it in person to his superiors and hand off the responsibility to others, taking himself out of the line of fire and hopefully landing at least a commendation, if not a promotion, for his expeditious handling of the matter.

Whatever it was.

A creeping sense of dread tickled his stomach. He had a feeling that Heinrich had made the find of his life.

Jean-Claude only hoped that he would live to tell about it.

CHAPTER 5

Associate director Rodriguez sauntered down the corridor to the briefing rooms in the bowels of CISEN, the Mexican intelligence agency that was the south-of-the-border equivalent of America's CIA. When he arrived at the largest, he checked his watch and then entered without saying a word, a file in his right hand. A dozen sets of eyes followed him as he made his entrance and paused inside the door. The long rectangular conference table was cluttered with coffee cups, bottles of water, soda, and pretzels, and most of the attendees had a notepad and a pen in front of them.

A hush settled over the gathered men as Rodriguez moved to the seat at the head of the table, and when he sat down, there was an expectant shuffling, the meeting's star finally arrived. He absently brushed his fingers through his expensively coiffed brown hair and adjusted his tie, a nervous affectation he'd been guilty of since his first job in government service twenty years earlier. Rodriguez looked around at the faces of his subordinates and leaned forward.

"We recently had a disturbing bit of information come in from one of our allies. The French. News that should have everyone in this room on edge."

He had the gathering's attention, and nodded to a man nearest the wall switch. The overhead lights extinguished and Rodriguez flicked on the power button for an old-fashioned overhead projector, waiting as the cooling fan whined into service and the lamp flickered on. He took his time, and then slid a transparency onto its glass top. A grainy black-and-white photograph of a man in a police uniform occupied most of the far wall, with another, sans hat, staring into the camera – obviously some sort of an official ID photo.

"This man is Werner Rauschenbach. He was a member of the Berlin police until ten years ago, when he was forced out under a cloud. His duty record was unremarkable, and he failed to distinguish himself in any way, except for a history of brutality charges filed by suspects he collared. By our standards he would be considered gentlemanly. But the point is that he was unexceptional."

He slid another photo onto the screen, replacing the one of Rauschenbach. A corpse lay on a cobblestone street, a chalk outline around it, blood pooled on the stones.

"This is the first known execution by an assassin known as the Iron Eagle. Tomas Schultz, the number one man with one of Berlin's numerous organized criminal syndicates until he met with his untimely demise. He was coming out of a famous nightclub, a group of bodyguards surrounding him, when a high-powered rifle blew his head off. It changed the lay of the land in Berlin, and enabled his number two man to take the reins – soon after which the Russian mob moved into the city in earnest, partnering with him."

The room was silent, paying rapt attention.

"Rumor has it that Rauschenbach is the Iron Eagle. Apparently, once he quit the force, he took up contract killing and showed a real flair for it. He received sniper training in the army and scored near the top of the charts as a marksman. He's believed to be responsible for a number of the most high-profile executions in Europe and the former Soviet republics, and is at the top of several of the most-wanted lists. In spite of which, he seems to be able to travel without restriction and continue his line of work, undeterred by the manhunt targeting him."

A thin, balding man with bottle-cap glasses coughed.

"Yes, Umberto?" Rodriguez asked. He knew the analyst well enough, and didn't want to have to wait for him to work up the courage to interrupt. Umberto was brilliant but excessively shy, and preferred not to speak unless it was something important.

"Why are we interested in him?" Umberto asked.

"I'm glad you asked. He's considered to be the foremost hit man in Europe. Perhaps in the world." Rodriguez changed the transparency again, and this time a photo of a burning car chassis occupied the wall. "This was the Egyptian ambassador to France. He was vaporized two years ago. Had a complement of serious security professionals working for him. Didn't do him any good." Another photograph. "And this is the Dutch attaché to Spain from six months ago. He was found in his home in Madrid, strangled to death."

Umberto stared at Rodriguez in his vaguely reptilian way, his question still open, and raised an eyebrow.

"The Iron Eagle progressed at some point from organized crime and business targets to politically motivated or sensitive ones. Three days ago, the French came into possession of information that indicates he'll be making an appearance on our shores, sooner than later. A man was killed in an attempt to keep that secret, and another was almost killed."

An older man with a bushy mustache at the far end of the table chuckled.

"Don't we have enough killers here, without having to worry about illegal immigrants coming to compete with ours? I know the global economy is rough, but still..."

Everyone laughed nervously, and Rodriguez smiled.

"Yes, well, I'm afraid this isn't a funny matter. In addition to the information that he's coming, we also got an idea of his target – one that, if he's successful, will permanently alter the future of Mexico...and not for the better." Rodriguez continued speaking for three more minutes, and when he was done, the gathering was somber, any trace of good humor banished. The lights came back on, flooding the room with their fluorescent glare, and he continued in a serious tone.

"Obviously, this cannot be allowed to happen. There's more at stake than our national reputation. There are serious economic ramifications. So as of today, right now, this is our most pressing threat. We have a little over a week. Eleven days to come up with a plan to stop him. On the tenth day, his target will be here, and if we haven't caught him, we'll have a serious problem," Rodriguez finished.

The older man leaned back in his chair and folded his hands behind his head. "Do we have any information on how he's planning to get into the country? Or any more recent photographs of him? Those are, what, over a decade old, you say? He could look like anyone now."

"I've put out the word through unofficial channels to the Germans, but we have to be very careful. It's not impossible that Rauschenbach has contacts in the government there, as well as with the police and the *Bundesnachrichtendienst* – the German intelligence service. Our only advantage at this point is that he has no idea that we know what he's up to. That could work in our favor. If he thinks we're unaware of his plans, then he might let down his guard." Rodriguez nodded at his staff. "I want a working group formed to deal with this today. Any resources you need, you'll get. There's nothing more important than stopping this from taking place. Nothing."

Umberto scratched out an indecipherable message to himself and put the pen down. "What about the *Federales*? We'll need to bring them into the mix. We can't keep a threat to national security like this to ourselves."

"I've thought about that. We'll take it up the appropriate channels and request a liaison. That should satisfy protocol so we're covered. But make no mistake. When all is said and done, this is a Mexican problem, not a departmental one. So let's get to work on it, shall we?"

Umberto wasn't done. "Who was killed? You mentioned that someone died to keep this quiet. Who, and who killed him? Because if they knew that the information was at risk, the German could already be on alert."

"It was a local informant in Berlin. That's all the French would tell us. But I did a search of deaths in Berlin for the last ten days, and found one that fits the bill. Death by shooting. A member of the police department. A clerk of some sort. As to who did it, they didn't have any idea. It's one of the frustrating aspects of the case. But I think we can assume it was someone connected to Rauschenbach, if not the man himself. Although given his reputation, if it was him, I'm surprised anyone got out of it alive."

"What about...what about his security? The target? We'll need to notify them as well."

"I'd rather not just yet. As I said, there's more at stake here than meets the eye, and I'd rather not alarm anyone if we can handle this internally. I'm looking for any sort of ideas, no matter how unorthodox. We can't afford to be conservative in this. I have a meeting scheduled with the president and his chief of staff this afternoon to give them the broad strokes, and I'd like some options before I have to brief them. That gives you" – Rodriguez checked the time – "three hours to mull this over and come up with something. I realize that's short notice, but do what you can. I'll be back before then to hear what you're proposing. In the meanwhile, you can access all the data here, in this file, and on the network. Code name Eagle. Your clearances have all been entered."

Rodriguez stood, and the men glanced at each other uneasily. A cross-disciplinary working group like Rodriguez had proposed was highly unusual, and some of the personalities involved were still smarting from other battles. But he'd been unequivocal. They needed to put their differences aside and come up with something quickly.

Rodriguez moved to the door, took a final look around the room, and then walked out, leaving the group to their ruminations. As his footsteps echoed down the hall, he was struck by a sense of uneasiness. CISEN was good at what it did, but it wasn't set up for this type of a threat. This was more of a security issue than an intelligence one. They weren't in the business of stopping killers. That usually was left to others.

Others...

Rodriguez stopped and stared down the hall, into space, unfocused.

The hazy outline of a vague idea formed.

It was unorthodox.

Then again, these were strange times.

He resumed walking, slower, lost in thought.

At the elevator, when the door slid open with a soft ping, he hesitated before stepping in, as though any movement might jar the fragile construct of the idea and shatter it before it was fully articulated. He punched his floor button, then stepped back with a sigh. It was crazy. There was no precedent. And it would be wildly unpopular with everyone involved in the scheme. The initial resistance would be immediate and substantial.

But that was the least of his concerns. While Rodriguez was politically sensitive, he was also a brilliant tactician, and once his brain latched onto something it didn't let go easily. He was already making a mental list of everyone he would need to get involved.

When the door opened again, he stepped out with a sense of urgency and purpose. He would make several phone calls and float it past his trusted advisors before bringing it to the team. But that was almost a formality. The more he thought about it, the more excited he became. It was either completely crazy, or a masterstroke of genius.

Most importantly, it just might work.

CHAPTER 6

The early morning mist lingered over the canyon north of Urique in Chihuahua, Mexico, the massive excavation of the El Sauzal gold mine a scar on the mountains in the far distance. Dawn had broken an hour earlier, but the morning fog hadn't yet burned off, and the area was still, the town down by the river in the famous Copper Canyon still slumbering.

A solitary figure stared up at the sheer rock face looming almost a thousand feet overhead, lost in thought, and then moved determinedly towards the daunting monolith and reached towards the sky. Strong hands gripped crevices in the outcropping and used them for holds; powerful legs pushed upwards when crannies presented themselves.

El Rey moved with single-minded concentration, fingers probing for the next niche, completely lost in the moment, the sun warming the glistening skin of his bare shoulders as the muscles bunched under the strain. A dark green bandana tied around his head kept the worst of the sweat out of his eyes, which scoured the unyielding stone, searching for an advantage as he powered up the unscalable cliff, driving himself to the peak now eighty stories above him.

His right foot slipped on a slim ledge and a tumble of small rocks skittered dizzily beneath him, dropping twenty stories before finally coming to rest at the base – a fatal distance. His right hand compensated by taking his full weight as he groped with his left, and for a split second he was hanging in space, holding himself with one arm, the endless repetitions of three hundred chin ups every day since childhood yielding lifesaving dividends, the corded muscles of his bicep rigid as he pulled himself to the relative safety of the next hold.

Foot by foot he continued driving himself upward, the black nylon straps of his backpack biting into his skin as he neared the top. When he finally pulled himself onto the summit his arms were shaking. He flipped over onto his back and stared up at the sky, the beginnings of a smile playing at the corners of his mouth. Overhead an eagle soared, riding a thermal as it wheeled into the blue, searching for an unlucky snake or chipmunk, the circle of life constant in this remote region of the country. He considered its graceful flight, the perfect symmetry of its purpose in the heavens, and then his ears perked up at an incongruous sound, gradually increasing in volume – a sound that was familiar, but out of place here, in the farthest reaches of the middle of nowhere.

He sat up as the rhythmic clamor grew louder, and watched the ungainly outline of a military Humvee roar up a dirt trail he would have bet was used only by pack mules and an occasional goat. It drew within twenty yards of the assassin, and then the big diesel motor idled, its high-altitude trek over, at least for the present. The passenger door opened and a rangy man in jeans and a black windbreaker leapt out. He did a cursory inspection of the desolate clearing and then jogged to where *El Rey* sat watching him.

The men's eyes met as he spoke.

"We need to talk."

El Rey considered a world of possible responses, then nodded. "How did you find me? Cell phone?"

"Exactly."

"Ah. But there's no signal."

"That's why we didn't call you. But there's still GPS. It allowed us to locate your position."

"What's the rush?" *El Rey* asked, studying his calloused fingers, still dusty from the climb.

"You'll be briefed on that when we get to headquarters."

"Headquarters," *El Rey* repeated.

"We have a jet waiting on the ground in Chihuahua to take you to Mexico City. Come on. Let's get out of here," the man said, and *El Rey* nodded again. There was no point in protesting the interruption of his outing. He'd made his deal – reluctantly, it was true – but made it all the same, and now he was at CISEN's beck and call.

And his master wanted to see him.

He got to his feet and followed the man to the vehicle, and within seconds of the door slamming shut behind him they were pulling back onto the dirt track. *El Rey* watched as the Sierra Madre mountain range past on either side of him, as rugged and untamed a landscape as any on earth, and settled back into the seat, resigned to being shunted halfway across the country on no notice, no say in the matter, a knight on a chessboard of someone else's devising.

Once they arrived at the little mountain town of Urique, the driver stopped at the edge of the dwellings. In five minutes the rhythmic beating of powerful rotors tore at the sky, the thumping of the gray helicopter a violent intrusion in the otherwise tranquil setting. It landed in a clearing just off the main road, and *El Rey* and his escort ran to it, ducking instinctively as the door slid open and two soldiers beckoned. Within moments they were strapped in and airborne, the entire boarding having taken under thirty seconds.

When they set down in Chihuahua, a Hawker business jet sat near the private aircraft area, stairs down, awaiting *El Rey*'s arrival. He trotted over to it from the helicopter and a pretty uniformed stewardess beckoned from the fuselage door. Once he had boarded and strapped into the seat, the exit closed and the sleek plane's engines wound up in preparation for takeoff. After a brief taxi they were hurtling down the runway and up into the clear sky, the dusty brown of the high desert quickly fading beneath the wings as they climbed and banked south for the hour and a half flight to the capital of Mexico.

As they hit cruising altitude the young woman handed *El Rey* a package wrapped in pale blue paper and asked what he'd like to drink. He opted for water and orange juice, and as she poured him a crystal tumbler he un-taped the parcel. Inside were a pair of khaki slacks and a black long-sleeved button-up shirt – both his size, he noted. The stewardess returned with his drinks and then excused herself and slipped up to the front of the plane, where she pulled a sliding door closed, offering him privacy.

He shrugged out of his tank top and shorts and donned his new clothes, then settled back into the seat, his rock climbing garments stowed in the backpack along with the rest of his gear, wondering what was so urgent that the government had pulled out all the stops to get him to Mexico City as quickly as possible. He took a sip of his juice and then drained the water bottle as the plane hummed along at thirty-eight thousand feet, and then leaned back in the caramel leather reclining lounger and closed his eyes.

It had been almost four months since he had rescued the president's daughter and done his deal with the devil, agreeing to exchange his services for the antidote shots that would sustain him. But this was the first time he had been called. He had spent his newfound freedom in rural locations, choosing to avoid the areas the cartels dominated, in the one-in-a-million chance that he was somehow recognized. Even though he was no longer a wanted man, his sins absolved when he made his arrangement with CISEN, there was still a substantial price on his head. *Don* Aranas had a long memory, and the multi-million dollar bounty he had offered was a powerful attraction for every hired killer in Mexico.

El Rey wasn't really worried about it, but it made matters simpler if he stayed off the radar, so he had moved from place to place, uprooting himself every three weeks, his last home a villa in the colonial town of San Miguel de Allende. He had been there for ten days before he grew bored and decided to explore the wilderness of the mountains around Copper Canyon, preferring the company of coyotes and mountain lions to his fellow man as he bided his time, waiting for the call that never came.

Until now.

He wondered who they wanted him to kill.

His eyes flickered open and he looked around the jet's interior, expensively appointed, all leather and polished wood, lacquered to a high gloss, then reached to his side and found his glass of orange juice. Fresh squeezed, he noted approvingly; then finished it and closed his eyes again.

Whatever the government's errand, he would know soon enough. Which was just as well. He'd been growing restless from inactivity. Truth be told, he would actually welcome an assignment. Whether he liked it or not, he was conditioned to seek out excitement, and the staid civilian life he'd been leading had been almost as bad as a prison sentence – unable to leave the country, inactive, each day the same as the last.

The plane adjusted its course, a minor deviance, and he shifted, trying to get comfortable.

Within an hour he'd be back on the ground, and soon thereafter at CISEN headquarters, being briefed.

Might as well get a little rest, he reasoned.

Things would get interesting soon enough. They hadn't pulled him off the side of a mountain to check on his health.

No, they had something they wanted him to do.

And if they were drawing on him, it was sure to be something challenging.

That was the only thing he could be certain of.

CHAPTER 7

Mexico City traffic was a perennial snarl, cars honking as they brooded in the morning haze, gridlocked on the overcrowded roads. El Rey stared blankly through the tinted windows of the Suburban at the crowds of well-dressed pedestrians milling in the downtown area, trumpeting the city's prosperity with their expensive clothing and designer handbags, a far cry from the wretched poor lining the streets only a few blocks away. The city was a study in contradictions: fabulous wealth lived side by side with squalor, the less fortunate gazing at the wealthy with envy and bitterness and a certain quiet acceptance that was unique to Latin America. Unlike their more fortunate neighbors to the north, the impoverished in Mexico had no hope of ever being anything but poor. It was just the way things were, and it was considered largely pointless to fret over the natural order.

A somber man in his mid-thirties sat in the passenger seat, his crisp blue suit tailored to hide the pistol he wore in a shoulder holster, his gleaming black hair conservatively cut, shining against his olive skin, the white of his oxford shirt in deep contrast with the dark bronze of his complexion. He hadn't said a word since *El Rey* had gotten into the big SUV, which was just as well – the assassin wasn't looking for a new friend.

When the Suburban pulled to a stop at CISEN headquarters, two armed guards peered into the vehicle before waving them through the gate into a parking lot with twelve-foot high surrounding walls that ensured nobody would be seen coming or going from the modern four-story building. They rolled into a stall near a side entrance, and the silent man in the passenger seat stepped out and spoke his first words of the trip.

"This way."

El Rey slid from the rear seat, backpack in tow, and followed his guide to the entry door, which opened as if by magic, pulled wide by another suited man. They entered the building, and two security guards bracketed *El Rey* front and back as they made their way to a ground floor conference room, their footsteps the only sound in the marble hallway.

Once he was seated they left him alone. *El Rey* studied his fingernails, confident that there was a hidden camera somewhere in the room and unwilling to give the observers any more information than they already had.

Five minutes later the door opened and Rodriguez entered, trailed by three men, none of whom *El Rey* recognized. They took seats across from him, and then Rodriguez cleared his throat and slid a manila folder across the table.

"That's the file of a man named Werner Rauschenbach. He's in the same line of work you used to be. German. There are two pages of summary on his exploits and history. Take a few moments to read them," Rodriguez instructed.

El Rey flipped the folder open and glanced at the photos inside, and then studied the documents. When he was done, he took a closer look at the top photograph, then dropped it onto the table and leaned back.

"So?"

"We want you to find him."

El Rey's expression betrayed nothing. "And wish him happy birthday?"

"Obviously not."

"You want me to kill him."

"That would be ideal. But it won't be that simple, I'm afraid." Rodriguez glanced at the picture. "He's coming to Mexico. Might already be here."

El Rey nodded. "And it's safe to presume he's not coming for the beaches?"

"Yes. We've gotten word that he's been hired to carry out a sanction," Rodriguez confirmed, irritated by the assassin's tone.

"Why am I required?"

"Because you're the best at that business."

"Right. But you're not asking me to take a contract, are you?"

"No. We need you to stop him. He can't be allowed to carry out his plan."

"Which is?"

Rodriguez nodded at the other men. The shortest, wearing a pale blue shirt and a retro tie, leaned forward.

"He's going to try to execute a dignitary. A very important figure. If he's successful, it would be disastrous."

"Do you have any information on when and where?"

"Negative. But we can guess."

"So guess."

"We believe he'll make his attempt in ten days. Here, in Mexico City."

El Rey's eyes narrowed. "So why drag me off the side of the mountain? This seems like a routine security task. Am I missing something?"

Rodriguez dropped the pen he was toying with on the table. "We need you to find him before he can carry out the hit."

"Who's the target?"

"The Chinese paramount leader. The *de facto* ruler of China."

El Rey blinked twice. "And why would an assassin come to Mexico to kill him?"

"Because he'll be vulnerable here – much more so than in China."

"What's he going to be doing here? The paramount leader?"

"He's supposed to sign an agreement with the president to transition our oil industry into Chinese hands – or rather, have them partner with us to get it out of the ground and refined. It would be a terminal blow to the agreement if an assassination attempt took place while he was here. Worse yet, if it succeeded."

"Can I have some water?" *El Rey* asked.

Rodriguez leaned over and murmured to one of the men, who rose and exited the room.

El Rey and Rodriguez stared at each other in silence for a few moments. Rodriguez finally spoke.

"That's it? You're told that the number one man in China is the target of an assassination plot by one of the world's most dangerous assassins, and all you can muster is a request for something to drink?"

El Rey shrugged. "I'm parched."

The door opened and the man returned carrying several plastic water bottles, which he set on the table. *El Rey* grabbed one, twisted the top off, and downed it. He set the empty container back on the table and regarded Rodriguez with dead black eyes.

"I specialize in killing people. Not in security assignments."

"I understand that. But it takes a thief to catch one. And you're our pet assassin, so it was decided to put you to some use. We need you to stop the German before he can carry out his plan. That's the assignment."

"I'm the wrong man for that job."

"Perhaps. But you're our best shot. And the clock is ticking. You've done these types of sanctions before. You're a specialist. So you know how one would think – what he would look for in the precautions, how he's likely to respond to events, how he would plan on carrying it out. We need that expertise. And I hate to remind you, but you owe us. Remember our deal..."

"How can I forget?"

"Good. Then it's agreed. I'll get you everything we have on Rauschenbach by tomorrow morning. And I'm making an office available for you..."

"Absolutely not. I'll take care of my own arrangements. I'm not going to work out of this building. That's not my style."

Rodriguez frowned. "I don't care what your style is. You'll work out of here if I say you will."

El Rey smiled. "If you want me to be effective, you won't push your luck, *Señor* Rodriguez. And a word of warning – men have died for speaking to me more politely. I understand I need to cooperate with you in order to get my shots. But there's a limit to how much I'll tolerate. You don't want to discover the limits of my patience."

Rodriguez glared at him, but *El Rey* saw the telltale bob of his Adam's apple as he dry swallowed.

"There's another condition, and this one you're really not going to like. But it's not negotiable," Rodriguez said, eyeing him with hesitation.

"Everything's negotiable."

"Not this."

CHAPTER 8

Cruz pushed his way through the entry of the latest condo the *Federales* had leased for him and sniffed at the air. A seductive smell drifted from the small kitchen, and as the door swung shut behind him he heard the sound of pans clanking against the stovetop – Dinah's presence announcing itself in the muted clamoring of the dinnerware.

"Sweetheart? I'm home," he announced over the culinary din, setting his briefcase down.

"Mmmm. Good. I need another pair of hands in here to help," Dinah called, sounding her usual cheerful self. How she managed to remain upbeat after working all day in the school was beyond him – but he was always glad she did.

"My hands have been itching to help you all day, my love," he assured her. "Let me slip into something more comfortable and I'll be right there."

Dinah glanced over her shoulder as he passed the kitchen and threw him a harried smile. Cruz made a mental note not to dally in the bedroom changing out of his uniform. He knew that look, and it meant he could earn some points by being a good domestic partner.

Three minutes later he was back, wearing jeans and a rugby shirt, and approached her as she stood at the stove.

"Mmm. You smell good. How did I get so lucky?" he cooed in her ear.

"Somebody upstairs must like you. Now, can you help me with the onions? I need them chopped while I whip this into shape," she responded, twisting to kiss him on the mouth.

"Absolutely. Chopping, whipping...I'm all over it," he assured her, and reached to the butcher block for one of the knives. "How was your day?"

"The usual chaos. Misbehaving kids, too many reports to complete in too little time, backstabbing colleagues...nothing ever seems to change," Dinah said.

"Sounds like my job."

"Yours is probably less dangerous. And they let you wear that handsome uniform, and give you a nametag. I get none of that," Dinah pouted as she stirred spices into the pan with the chicken she was sautéing.

Cruz's cell phone rang just as he was about to begin slicing. He cursed and put down the knife, then fished the phone out of his pants pocket.

"Yes?" he answered.

"*Capitan* Cruz. Sorry to call you after hours. This is Eduardo Godoy," a smooth voice crooned.

"What can I do for you?" Cruz asked warily. Godoy was his superior – an entirely useless political appointee who was nonetheless as dangerous as a snake.

"I need you to come to my office tomorrow morning, first thing. Let's say...nine o'clock?" Godoy said.

Cruz paused. "Fine. What will be the topic of discussion, if you don't mind?" he asked, wary of being blindsided. Whenever Godoy wanted to see him, it was usually bad, and involved Cruz getting the pork put to him in one way or another.

"We have a delicate situation I need you to handle. I'm not comfortable speaking about it over the phone. Just be here at nine, please," Godoy snapped.

"Yes. Of course. It's just that if I knew what this was about, I could come prepared..."

"All I need is you – nothing else. I'll see you in the morning," Godoy said, and then the line went dead.

He stared at the phone. *Now what?* As far as he knew he hadn't crossed any lines, and he had been spectacularly successful with a number of delicate anti-cartel operations over the last few months. Godoy had no reason to reprimand him that he could think of. Which didn't mean anything. In the real world, many of the top brass were nothing more than mouthpieces for special interests – and the cartels were some of the richest and most powerful special interests in Mexico. Being a multi-billion dollar criminal syndicate apparently bought a lot of political clout, even as public rhetoric condemned them.

"Honey? Who was that?" Dinah asked.

"Oh. Nothing. Just somebody from work."

"Is everything all right?"

"Fine. They were just setting up a meeting. Nothing more." He tried a smile, but Cruz's tone betrayed his uneasiness.

"They're calling you at home, at dinner time?" Dinah wasn't buying it.

"It's my boss. Godoy. He's not really good with things like common courtesy."

"I got that. Are you going to chop those onions, or do I have to?" she asked, dropping the subject.

Cruz nodded and returned to his duties, his eyes beginning to water within seconds of the first few slices. Dinah glanced at him, and in spite of herself, giggled at the sight of her husband, tears welling in his eyes like someone had wrecked his new car. Cruz's easy laugh reflected that he thought he was the luckiest man in the world to have wound up with Dinah. Attractive, funny, smart, and in love with him. And willing to put up with a life that would have been a deal-killer for most – moving every few weeks, no sense of permanence, the constant danger that went with his career an unspoken irritant, like a glass sliver just under the skin.

"Are we drinking wine or beer tonight?" he asked, wiping his face with the back of his arm.

"Whatever you want, *mi amor*. We've got both in the refrigerator." She reached across him and lifted the white plastic cutting board and then scraped the chopped onions into the sizzling pan, along with tomatoes and peppers.

"Do you have a preference?"

"I'm going to stick to mineral water. I've got a big day tomorrow." She lifted the pan off the gas flame and adjusted the height, then set it back down. "Go on into the dining room. I hate to see a grown man cry."

"Thanks. How long until it's ready?"

"Maybe ten minutes."

He swung the refrigerator open and peered into the interior, then retrieved a Negra Modelo. But even as he moved to the counter to open it, his mind was already on other matters. Like why his boss, who typically avoided him, wanted to see him first thing.

To say that it was irregular was an understatement.

He padded into the small living room and sat on the couch, then groped around behind him and retrieved the television remote. The flat panel flickered to life and the day's news rolled across the screen, mostly bad – a litany of corruption, senseless violence, tragedy, and heartbreak, punctuated by soccer scores and earnest politicians insisting that they were working hard to bring change.

The same story as last night. And the night before.

With one notable exception: The slaughter at the cartel house was the lead story and was reprised at the end, with an update that unconfirmed sources had leaked – *El Gato* had been apprehended and was in custody. Cruz swore under his breath, but he wasn't surprised. The news was bound to get out eventually. He'd hoped for another day or two of breathing room before having to deal with the inevitable press circus that a high profile arrest would bring, but the toothpaste was out of the tube now.

"All right, honey, dinner is served," Dinah called from the kitchen, and then swept into the dining room and placed two plates on the table with a flourish. Cruz gazed at her with adoration and turned off the TV, taking a final pull on his beer before standing.

Whatever was going on with Godoy, he wasn't going to let it bother him any more tonight. He'd know what it was all about tomorrow. No point in speculating.

"It smells wonderful. Let me grab another beer and I'll be right in."

Dinah watched as he strode past the dining room into the kitchen, and felt a warmth course through her. This was the man she loved, whom she had married, and he had proven himself to be a good and honorable mate. She felt fortunate that circumstances had conspired to thrust them together, and as she sat down and dropped her napkin into her lap, she felt a wave of gratitude wash over her. Two souls had found each other, and persevered through some difficult times. That was more than many got during their lives, she knew, and her mind flitted to the thoughts she'd been having increasingly of late – thoughts of a dog, a house, and a family, of a normal life where they could stay in one place and not have to worry about being safe. Right now, a dream, she knew; but hopefully not forever.

"Do you ever get tired of this, Romero? Moving constantly, the job, the pressure...the danger?" she asked, waiting for him to sit before taking a taste of her meal.

"Of course. I'm hoping that this will only last a few more years, and then maybe I can get a job as a security consultant with one of the big firms here, or in Monterrey or Guadalajara..."

They'd had this discussion increasingly of late, Dinah subtly lobbying for him to think about a future. A future without the job in it. A safe future together. Some days it seemed attainable. And then others, like this, when he was getting calls at night, it was a million years away.

Both sat, making appreciative noises, lost in their thoughts: Cruz dwelling on the next day's meeting in spite of his best intentions, Dinah on how to get her husband to pursue a safer line of work. When they were done with dinner, she curled up in his arms on the couch as they watched one of the inevitable talent shows that seemed to dominate the airwaves. She snuggled against him and the tension fell away, and they were finally both able to relax, secure in the moment, their troubles fleeting as long as they had each other.

CHAPTER 9

"The director will see you now." The receptionist sized Cruz up in his civilian attire with an expression he was sure she reserved for vagrants. "You know the way to his office, yes?"

Cruz stood, having been kept waiting for fifteen minutes past his appointment time — an expected part of the ritual whenever he was summoned before his superior, to underscore who was in charge. Cruz didn't take it personally, but the receptionist's attitude annoyed him. He bit back any of ten terse responses and merely nodded and strode down the hall to Godoy's door, which was closed, forcing him to knock.

"Yes. Come in," Godoy called out, and Cruz pulled the door open. "Ah, *Capitan* Cruz. Come in. Have a seat, won't you?"

Cruz did as instructed, and waited for Godoy to broach the topic of the meeting. He eyed the man's urbane, too-slick countenance that had all the warmth of a granite statue, and remarked to himself for the hundredth time that men like his boss had to have come from some factory where they removed all semblance of humanity before shunting them off the end of the assembly line.

"Congratulations are in order for the apprehension of *El Gato*, I think," Godoy started, as if uncertain whether the capture of one of the most wanted men in Mexico City warranted praise. "It's a pity that we lost so many officers getting him," he continued, a faint reprimand in his tone.

"I agree. I spent most of yesterday calling and meeting with the spouses of the dead men. It's a shame that these cartel thugs are so well armed, and think nothing of taking the lives of honest police." Cruz's rebuke was subtle, but it registered on the arrogant peacock; he could tell by the flash of anger in Godoy's eyes.

"Yes, well, what's done is done. The important thing is you got your man. Has he talked yet?"

"No. And he's unlikely to, I know from experience. The cartel bosses at this level rarely say anything. They know better."

"Hmm. And what are you planning to do with him? You still have him detained downstairs, correct?"

"Yes. But the district attorney is getting anxious. He'd like him moved to a proper facility to await trial. We're not really set up for long term stays, as you know."

"That's one of the matters I wanted to mention. I got a call from him yesterday afternoon. He wants *El Gato* out of here before the end of the day. I assured him that would be no problem," Godoy said.

Cruz decided to play nice. "No problem here, either."

"Good. Again, job well done," Godoy said with a wave of his hand.

"Thank you. It was a team effort."

Godoy rocked in his overstuffed executive chair, and Cruz wondered how long it would take the man to get to the real reason he had summoned him. He didn't have long to wait.

"I have some other news, which you may not be excited about. I'm going to take you off active duty with the task force."

Cruz's eyes widened. "What! Why? We're finally making real progress..."

"Don't worry. It's just temporary."

"Temporary...," Cruz echoed.

"Yes. We have another matter that takes precedence. Something I need you to manage. I have it straight from the president's office – you're to handle this issue personally, and I will provide whatever support you need."

"What issue?"

"Ah. Just so. We received information from CISEN yesterday about a threat we need to get in front of. An assassination attempt."

"Assassination," Cruz repeated, his mind churning furiously.

"Yes. As you might have seen in the news, Mexico is getting ready to sign a historic accord with the Chinese, ushering in a new age of mutual cooperation. It's something that we've been working on for a year. The Chinese leader will be here in eight days to ratify the agreement in a ceremony with the president. We got word that an assassin is targeting the Chinese leader, and that an attempt on his life will take place while he's in Mexico. A German – Werner Rauschenbach – is going to try to kill him.

Your job is to stop that from taking place." Godoy went on to explain about the German.

Cruz didn't say anything for a few moments. "Why me? Isn't this more the territory of the security force that guards the president?"

"In theory, yes, but you made quite a reputation for yourself with the capture of our own super-assassin, *El Rey*. The president is very impressed with your performance, and your name was mentioned as the perfect candidate to head up a team. So you're a victim of your own success, I'm afraid."

Cruz knew better to fight this if the president was involved. That was a battle he couldn't win.

"Fine. What resources do I have access to, and who do I talk to in order to get all the information you have?" he asked.

"You'll be coordinating with CISEN." Godoy held up a manicured hand at the expression of distaste on Cruz's face. "It will be your show, but the information came through them, so they'll stay in the mix. No way around it." He glanced at his watch. "Commandeer whatever staff or resources you require. There are no limits, within reason, on this. Oh, and one other thing."

Cruz waited for what he was sure would be another piece of bad news.

"CISEN has graciously agreed to provide a liaison for your team, as well as an expert in these kinds of things. I think we're fortunate they are providing the expert, but it will cause some friction, so I want to head that off now."

Cruz rubbed his face with one hand, feeling ten years older than when he'd walked into the room. Godoy had that effect on him – he was like a dwarf star that sucked any positive energy out of the surroundings.

"You'll have to put aside any animosity you have, in the interests of the country. I know that won't be easy, but you're a professional, and I expect you to behave professionally," Godoy warned.

Cruz's gut did a somersault at the preamble. Whatever this was, it wasn't good. "And...what specialist does CISEN propose I work with on keeping the Chinese leader safe?" he asked, afraid to hear the answer.

Godoy leaned back, as though he was afraid Cruz might try to strike him. His eyes flashed with a decidedly satisfied look – a look that Cruz knew meant serious discomfort for him. Godoy hesitated, as though savoring the words he was about to speak, and then picked up his coffee cup and took a long sip before dropping his bomb with a smirk.

"*El Rey.*"

❧❦

Cruz stared open-mouthed at the bureaucrat, and had to force his breathing back to normal before responding.

"Has everyone lost their minds? *El Rey?* Working with me? Absolutely not. That's not an option," he spat, furious at the suggestion.

"He was a professional assassin. He knows the ins and outs of how this sort of an attempt will be carried out. And he works for us now," Godoy said reasonably.

"He *is* a killer. Completely without conscience. A murdering psychopath responsible for the deaths of countless police, politicians, innocents..."

"All that is behind us. As you know, he's a free man with a presidential pardon. And he's committed to stopping this assassin. And he's part of your team, whether you approve or not."

"No. I won't do it. If you want my participation, that's not negotiable."

"*Capitan.* I understand you feel strongly about this, and you have some history with him, so I'm not surprised," Godoy began.

"He killed my wife's father, for starters, as well as some of my best men."

"I'm not apologizing or excusing anything he did. But again, that is the past, and he's now a CISEN asset, to be used for the nation's good. I need you to put aside your dislike for him and work together. We don't have the luxury of time to soothe everyone's feelings on the matter. A hit man is coming for the Chinese — for all we know, he's already within our borders — and he cannot be allowed to succeed. We have one of the foremost assassins in the world working for us, and we will use him to full effect. That makes perfect sense."

"To you, maybe. He didn't kill a bunch of your friends. And he didn't murder your wife's father..."

"Believe me, I've fantasized about how much it would cost to get him to do so...," Godoy joked, and then seeing the expression on Cruz's face, cut it short. "*Capitan*, this is very simple. The president wants you running this task force. You don't get to say no to that. And CISEN insists on using *El Rey*, so you don't get to decline that generous offer, either. This is an extremely delicate and important assignment, which is why we're drawing on the very best we have. Between you and *El Rey*, we all believe this is our most promising chance at stopping Rauschenbach and saving the accord. So let me put this as plainly as possible. You will work with *El Rey*, or you won't have a job with the *Federales* any longer. Your career will be over, and any expectations you might have of a pension will turn out to be sorely mistaken. Refusal to do this will result in your dismissal, without benefits, and I'll be unable to offer any kind of positive reference for you." Godoy's voice had a tinge of steel in it, and then his expression softened. "Which would be a shame, because we really need you now more than ever before. And nobody wants to deny you what you've earned. But the stakes are too high to screw around. We need you on board, and we'll use whatever we have to in order to ensure you are."

"So you're blackmailing me, threatening to withhold a retirement I've already earned," Cruz stated flatly.

"I'm trying to convince you to play ball, Cruz. Trying to get you to see reason, and earn the new president's undying gratitude. And offering you a chance to save your country. This accord is critical to Mexico's prosperity moving forward. It cannot be allowed to be derailed. Too much is riding on it."

"You're no better than an extortionist," Cruz spat, furious at the turn the discussion had taken.

"Welcome to the real world, *Capitan*. When you get to a certain point in government, you have to make decisions – hard decisions – that are distasteful, but required for the common good. Making plain what you have to gain – or lose – based on your response to this assignment is one of the unpleasant realities I have to grapple with today; and it gives me no pleasure, I assure you. But I do it because I have no choice. So understand that if you refuse, I'll have no alternative other than to take the action I described. It's not an idle threat. And it would be a shame to have a twenty-year career go down the tubes over one decision. Think this through. You work with this killer for a few days, and then you're done. Like taking a dose of unpleasant medicine. Don't throw an entire career away over one ugly episode. You're bigger than that. And we wouldn't be asking if it wasn't critical."

Cruz shook his head and gave him a venomous glare. "You aren't asking. You're holding a loaded gun to my head and dictating terms."

"Out of necessity. Believe me, I wouldn't do it if it wasn't imperative that you cooperate."

"So the ends justify the means?"

Godoy snorted. "Always. Are you really that naïve?"

Cruz had to bite back an angry retort. It wouldn't do any good to lose his cool. He was already too close to the edge. He wouldn't give his arrogant superior the pleasure. And a part of him believed that Godoy would rather he not go for the deal than take it, for all his protestations to the contrary.

"Yes. I guess I am. I thought we were the good guys. Good guys don't blackmail each other to get their way. I suppose that's a moral nicety that you never learned – obviously didn't, by the tone of this conversation. Be that as it may, it sounds like you've got a real situation on your hands. I'll think about this and get back to you later today with my decision. Is there anything else?"

Godoy scowled. "I need your answer now."

Cruz shrugged. "No, you *want* my answer now. You need me to say yes. Which I may. Or may not. But you won't know until later, like I said. I need to think this through. Especially since I may be a civilian very soon, which would mean that your needs and wants wouldn't matter to me at all at that point. You've made abundantly clear the lengths you're prepared to go. So now you'll wait for my decision. Or you can always claim I said no, which I'll rebut as a lie – and then you'll be forced to explain to the president why you didn't give what you're calling 'your best hope' a chance to think through your demands. Your choice; but I wouldn't want to have to do that – especially if the Chinese leader winds up eating a bullet on Mexican soil because of your impatience." Cruz stood. "Your problem is that you misjudged me, Godoy. You think I'm afraid of a future without a safety net. Guess what? I'm not. I've stared death in the face too many times to care about any of it. Give the president my regards. I'll be in touch."

And with that, Cruz walked out, leaving a stunned Godoy watching as the door to his office closed, his sure-fire ultimatum having backfired on him in as big a way as possible.

CHAPTER 10

The exterior of El Cordon didn't offer a warm welcome to lure in reluctant customers – slightly peeling orange paint slapped over a façade that had seen better days in a district on the edge of downtown that was sliding inexorably into squalor. Cruz pushed through the saloon-style doors into the darkened wooden interior and approached the bar. At ten in the morning there was nobody else in the establishment other than an aging man behind the counter with a pock-marked, mustachioed face that time hadn't been kind to. Cruz glanced around, as if not trusting his initial take, and then took a seat. A crooning voice lamented love's folly over a strident melody pulsing from the overhead speakers, the song a favorite with the honest working men who frequented watering holes like it. Usually the clientele arrived in the late afternoon or evening, but the bartender wasn't there to judge, and studied Cruz with a neutral expression.

"What'll it be, *Jefe*?" he rasped at Cruz with a sandpaper baritone.

"Tequila. El Jimador. And a Modelo to wash it down."

The man nodded as though Cruz had just offered him the winning lottery numbers for that evening's jackpot and turned to retrieve a tall bottle filled with smoky fluid. He expertly palmed a shot glass and set it down in front of Cruz – a double tall one for seriously committed drinking. Seconds later the glass was filled and an icy cold can of beer appeared next to it, and the bartender retired back to the far end of the bar, the tequila bottle returned to its place in front of a smudged mirror with its brethren.

The burn of the tequila made Cruz's eyes water as it seared its way down his throat, the beer affording cooling relief after the liquid fire. The glow of warmth radiated from his stomach outward to his limbs, and his fury at Godoy's ultimatum slowly abated. He took another long pull on his beer and then nodded at the bartender, who obligingly returned and topped off the empty shot glass again without comment.

The second slug of tequila went down easier than the first, and Cruz closed his eyes after another swallow of beer. After over twenty years of loyal service to the *Federales*, of sacrificing everything, of giving them his very life, to be treated so shabbily was like a physical blow. And to demand, no, to *order* him to work with a sociopath, a serial killer who had been responsible for countless deaths, including his own men – men he'd had to bury while their grieving mates and children cried in anguish only feet from him – that insult couldn't stand. He wouldn't do it. It was impossible. Godoy and the whole power structure could go screw themselves. To try to blackmail him out of his pension was just the lowest betrayal he could imagine, although it didn't surprise him that the ruthless bastard had gone there without hesitation. Godoy was a shit, to whom nothing was sacred. Of course, he would be crying the loudest if he were ever forced to confront the sort of danger Cruz did on a daily basis, but that gave him slim comfort. Like it or not, Godoy held Cruz's financial future in his hands, and could destroy it with a few phone calls.

The anger bubbled to the surface again, battling for supremacy, and he considered his options. Unlike in some countries, he couldn't go to the media and tell the story of his pension being stolen – it would be censored with a single call from Godoy. Nobody would touch it; and frankly, it wasn't really news. People were forced to do ugly things every day by uncaring, malevolent superiors – they worked in dangerous conditions, breathed toxic dust on construction sites, toiled for pennies, sold their bodies and souls for a few tortillas and a scrap of bread. That was reality.

He could contact the companies that had expressed interest in hiring him for security consulting work, but he knew that if the government was vindictive it could exert enough pressure to nip that in the bud. And if Cruz walked now, when the nation was facing a crisis...the administration would be vindictive, he could be sure.

Perhaps even of graver concern was the issue of personal safety. Cruz had made many enemies over his career, and some of the most dangerous and violent psychopaths in Mexico wanted him dead. The list of cartels that would cheerfully cut his heart out and stick his head on a pike was too long to contemplate. There was a reason that he had to move every five or six weeks. If he quit, that would be over, effective immediately, and he would be on his own. Which would mean going into hiding without the resources of the *Federales* to protect him.

He could manage it, but Dinah...the risk to her would be too great. She would need to quit working with children – something she loved – and they would need to disappear, for years. The money wouldn't be a problem, but the disruption to their lives...

The bartender glanced at him with an eyebrow cocked as he busied himself cleaning some glasses, and Cruz held up a finger and then pointed at his beer. When the bartender delivered another Modelo, he reached for the tequila glass and then hesitated, eyeing Cruz.

"*Uno mas?*" he asked. One more?

Cruz shook his head and gave the glass a baleful look.

"No, *muchas gracias. Listo...*," he replied, requesting the check. He was done. If he had another double shot of tequila, it would turn into the whole bottle, and he couldn't afford to be incapacitated. He needed to think – to think through his next moves.

He sat, listening to a seemingly endless procession of singers bemoaning the unfairness of fickle love, and over time, hit a plateau where he no longer felt angry, but rather resigned and very, very old – far beyond his forty-something years. He took his time with the beer, nursing it, and when two men entered, laughing noisily, it served as his cue to leave. He dropped a few peso notes onto the scarred wooden surface of the bar and pushed back, finished with his internal debate. It could have gone either way, but ultimately the thought of Dinah dictated his actions. He couldn't just fall into a bottle and shut out the rest of the world. He would need to join his fellow struggling humans and suck up the ugliness, and choke down his pride and morality in favor of cynical pragmatism.

There was really no other choice. Godoy had painted him into a corner where no matter what he did, he was screwed. As unpleasant as it was, the option of working with the assassin was the lesser of the evils he'd been presented with.

But he wouldn't give Godoy the pleasure of knowing it until the end of the day.

Sunlight hit him full in the face when he stepped out onto the sidewalk, and he squinted, his eyes adjusting from the comfortable gloom inside the cantina. He would go home and take a nap, sleep off the residual effects of the alcohol, and then call Godoy just before business hours were over. It was childish, he knew, but that was fine. He would take even the smallest vestige of autonomy and self-respect at this point.

He flipped out his cell phone as he fished for his sunglasses and dialed his administrative assistant.

"*Capitan* Cruz's office."

"Celia, this is Cruz."

"Oh, good. I have about fifteen messages for you. When will you be back in?"

He thought about it. "I'm going to be out of touch the rest of the day. Reschedule any meetings, and tell any callers that you haven't heard from me."

"Yes, sir..." The young woman sounded unsure.

"I have a few errands I need to attend to, and I don't want to be disturbed. The world can wait a day," Cruz said, and then wondered if he was slurring. He decided he didn't much care.

"Of course, sir. Will there be anything else?"

"No. But remember: You haven't talked to me."

"I understand. One thing, though. We just got word that *El Gato* is going to be transferred this afternoon. Some judge ordered it."

"Damn. Have you seen the paperwork?"

"Yes. It's all there."

Cruz sighed. "Fine. Then it's out of my hands. We've done what we can. Now it's up to the system to deal with him."

An uncomfortable silence hung on the line. No point in unloading on Celia. It was time to get off the call.

"I'll be in early *mañana*. Hold down the fort today," he said, then disconnected.

He watched pedestrians move along the sidewalk as he got his bearings, then squared his shoulders and turned, moving away from the bar towards a row of taxis waiting for the early lunch rush to begin. He flagged one down, and a man separated himself from a group loitering by a tree and approached unhurriedly, dropping his cigarette butt into the gutter as he gestured to the first car.

Cruz gave him the address of his apartment and sank into the back seat, hating himself for what he knew he was going to do. He shut his eyes and tried not to think, but it was pointless, and as the cab darted through traffic, horn honking periodically in belligerent complaint, he cursed Godoy and the entire power structure of unthinking bureaucrats and petty tyrants that had placed him in this impossible position.

He wanted to decline the assignment about as badly as he'd ever wanted anything in his life, but he knew there was only one possible response.

Because, like it or not, his country needed him.

And as always, he couldn't refuse the call.

CHAPTER 11

The hills west of Montemorelos, in Nuevo León, were cool in the afternoon. A breeze tickled the tops of the thick trees around the spacious villa, well off the main highway, down a three-mile private drive that was heavily guarded by gunmen. An iron gate featuring two dancing stallions blocked the way, and three men with assault rifles occupied the gatehouse. The bouncing beat of music emanated from a small radio next to their sophisticated communications gear – the technology surprising in a rural area, but not to anyone who knew the property well.

One of the dozen ranches owned by Manuel Heraldo Alvadez, the current leader of the Los Zetas cartel, easily the most violent and powerful criminal syndicate in Latin America, it was remote and vast, ensuring the reclusive owner's privacy. Alvadez moved around constantly, and the actual title to the property was held by a network of shell corporations, impenetrable and anonymous to the myriad law enforcement agencies that had targeted him. The enigmatic leader had taken power from the old leader, Sanchez Triunfo, in a bloody series of clashes that had left hundreds butchered in its wake, but the younger Alvadez was now the undisputed top dog after Triunfo had fled the country, weary of the escalating violence that had claimed most of his family.

Four ponies trotted in a large wood-fenced area to the side of the main house, which was majestic in a time-worn hacienda way, ravaged by the sun and elements but still standing proudly, a testament to the care that had gone into its construction almost a century earlier. A dozen men with leathery brown skin stood at strategic positions around the buildings, their Kalashnikovs and AR-15s held with comfortable familiarity – each of them an ex-marine who had gone into private practice for ten times the money with the cartel, and all veterans of countless armed skirmishes and massacres.

A heavy-set man in his late-thirties, wearing jeans, pointy-toed ostrich-skin boots with hammered silver toe caps and a red western-style shirt, waved his white cowboy hat at the man in the corral, who returned the signal with a nod before returning to the horses. The man set the hat back on his head and turned to the three men standing attentively by his side, all of whom were similarly attired. Alvadez cleared his throat, the dust kicked up by the hooves cloying, and spoke softly, an unmistakable undertone of menace in his voice.

"I don't care who he is. He must pay for my nephew's death, as well as the amount he's cost us with his most recent raids. I want it known that to go up against us is to invite destruction," he hissed.

"*Si, Jefe*. But he's untouchable. The head of the D.F. anti-cartel taskforce. We've been trying to learn his whereabouts for months, with no success. He's like the invisible man," one of the entourage – Alvadez's most trusted inner circle – complained.

Alvadez spat onto the dirt by his feet and glared at the speaker – Jorge, a captain who had been with him for six years. The subject of their discussion had engineered a raid where he had lost over a dozen men, as well as one of his sister's sons, a young man he'd been grooming for a leadership position in the cartel.

"There's always someone who knows. And it's always a matter of money. I don't care what it costs – I want him. This is personal, do I make myself clear? So put the word out however you need to. Pick a number for the reward that will sway even the most loyal."

All the men grinned at the idea. Los Zetas' annual revenue was in the tens of billions of dollars, and money was like water for Alvadez. Gold-capped teeth flashed in the sun at their leader's suggestion.

"There's also, of course, the danger that going after him invites even greater retribution. He's the number one man in Mexico when it comes to law enforcement and the cartels. The outcry will be...well, I don't need to tell you what the reaction will be," Jorge persisted.

One of the ponies let loose a whinny and broke into a canter and Alvadez smiled at the sight of such a perfect form, so innocent and unspoiled, the result of centuries of careful breeding.

"Since the election we've been getting pounded. I thought we had a deal, but apparently not, and it's getting worse, not better. We've tried diplomacy. Now we need to go for the throat. This man has made himself a visible target of our wrath, and in his latest foray his men killed one of my family. I don't care what it takes. I want him dead. Is there some part of that you find ambiguous or confusing?"

The three men's faces blanched. Their leader's tone had taken a dangerous turn, and they knew from experience that his anger could manifest in a dramatic and violent fashion. Nobody wanted to be on the receiving end of a tantrum. The fields around the hacienda were littered with the buried corpses of personnel who had disappointed in one way or another.

And then, like storm clouds parting before the sun, he grinned as he watched the trainer work with the horses, directing them this way and that. With his smile, the tension diffused, and the men observed the equestrian display with approval.

"Now what else do we have to talk about?"

"As you're aware, in addition to the regrettable death of your nephew, we lost a fair amount of know-how in the latest explosion. But we estimate that our meth volume will only dip for a few months, at most. We're diverting some of the Malaysian product in order to meet demand so nobody steps in while we're short," Jorge reported.

"Very good. And how's the push into Central America going?"

"Well. We own Guatemala now, and the same with Honduras and Nicaragua, except for pockets where Sinaloa still has loyalists. But we've taken an 'exterminate on sight' policy with the local gangs that don't play ball with us, so we'll prevail. You can see the effect in the murder rates for all the countries – Costa Rica, Honduras, Nicaragua, Panama..."

"The goal was to have us in firm control of all Central America within a year, and it looks like that will happen. And why? Because I spared no expense, and have been laser-like in my objectives. But in spite of all this, you can't find one lousy federal policeman? This...Cruz continues to elude you?" The menace was back without warning.

"It will be our top priority, *Jefe*," Jorge assured him, and his two companions nodded solemnly, neither one wanting to attract attention by speaking out of turn.

"Do that. I want results, not excuses. And now we have one more item for the morning, no? The family of the informant we believe gave this Cruz the information about the Mexico City lab? Where are they?" Alvadez growled.

"In the garage, *Jefe*."

The drug lord stalked from the corral to a stand-alone building large enough to house four vehicles, and threw open one of the doors. Inside were four men wearing black uniforms with the Los Zetas crest emblazoned on the left chest and holding M4 assault rifles. One of the men put his rifle down upon seeing his boss enter and picked up a roll of duct tape. He caught Alvadez's eye and motioned with his head at three women, their hands bound behind them, kneeling on the floor, which had been covered with a heavy plastic sheet. Alvadez moved to each and glared at them, then stepped back and addressed the captives.

"You know why you're here? Because your boy Javier decided to roll on me and sell me out to the *Federales*. All right. Start the video," he instructed, and a fifth man flicked on the record button of a handheld video camera. Alvadez and his group stepped out of range of the lens and stood against the wall behind the camera man, watching the masked and uniformed man with the tape curse at the captives and then move to each, slapping a piece of duct tape across their mouths.

"You see what happens, you lying weasels? You think you can screw us over like we're your bitch? Guess again. This is what happens, *puta*," the masked man snarled at the camera, and then picked up a two-by-four from the ground. Tears streamed down the women's faces as he approached them, and then he slammed the first one in the back of the head, knocking her face forward onto the floor. He quickly did the same to the other two, and then tossed the beam aside and retrieved a rusty machete.

The decapitations were captured on film, each blow and hack memorialized, and after a few minutes there was nothing left but the cleanup. The camera was switched off, the video to be distributed via the web, and Alvadez stepped forward and spit on the corpses before turning, careful to avoid the pooling blood, and moved back towards the daylight streaming under the door. He swung it open and stepped outside, waiting a few seconds until his eyes adjusted to the sun, and then gestured to his men to follow him to the house.

"Now, what's for lunch? Deisy said she was going to prepare a surprise." Deisy, the head of the kitchen staff, was a short woman of Mayan ancestry and a culinary wizard. "Come, all of you. Join me. There will be time enough to discuss the rest of our business over a decent meal."

Alvadez took a final appreciative look at his ponies, then turned and moved to the front porch, trailed by his subordinates, who exchanged dour looks.

Nobody had reacted to the executions – that was par for the course, and didn't warrant comment – but the directive to go after Cruz was a different issue. Taking on the *Federales* in a frontal manner was tantamount to declaring open warfare on the Mexican government, and none of them was so foolish as to believe that there wouldn't be a terrible price to pay for that. But nobody wanted to cross Alvadez, either, so they were resigned to what they would have to do – prepare for yet another long, bloody campaign once Cruz was dead. It was inevitable, but Alvadez was the boss, and questioning his wisdom was a recipe for an early grave.

The men trudged towards the house, the sound of clomping pony hooves following them, each lost in his thoughts, wondering how they were going to get the information their leader wanted; and then how they would reach a man who was as untouchable as any in Mexico.

CHAPTER 12

Cruz started awake with a jolt, momentarily disoriented, then remembered where he was, and why. Home, in bed, a long *siesta* having purged most of the effects of the tequila. He glanced at his watch and groaned. Almost four o'clock. He rolled over and tried to think of a reason to put off calling Godoy, and couldn't think of one.

Cruz waited another few minutes, then swung his legs from beneath the sheets and set his feet on the cool travertine floor. After a brief trip to the bathroom, he punched his cell phone to life and selected Godoy's number. The receptionist connected him almost immediately, and then, after answering, Godoy told him to hang on, and put him on hold. For five minutes.

Typical.

When he came back on the line, Cruz told him that he would agree to head up the Iron Eagle task force, and he could almost hear the smirk of triumph in Godoy's voice.

"I need you to jump right into this, *Capitan*. It's the highest priority, as I indicated. I'll make a call and see if I can get CISEN to have you meet with their people today."

"It's too late today. I'll need time to assemble a team on my end and brief them before I'm ready for that," Cruz protested.

"Much as I appreciate your logistical concerns, I'm afraid I need to insist. I'll call you back as soon as I have confirmation. The clock is ticking, *Capitan*. No time for dallying," Godoy said, and Cruz wondered whether he was just trying to get even with him for making him wait most of the day for an answer. The line clicked and went dead, and Cruz was left staring at his phone. Godoy had hung up on him.

Ten minutes later the receptionist was on the line, instructing him that he needed to be at CISEN headquarters by six p.m.. With rush hour traffic being what it was, he would be lucky to make it. He called his office and told them to have his car and driver ready in five minutes, and then pulled a uniform out of the closet and hurriedly dressed. Cruz was buttoning his shirt when he heard the front door open.

Dinah appeared in the doorway a moment later, surprised. "You're home! What, did they legalize drug running and money laundering today? Are you out of work?" she teased.

"I wish. No, I needed to change into uniform before I go to a big meeting this evening. I'm sorry, *mi amor*, but I expect it to last a while. I'm not sure what time I'll be home," he apologized as he belted his holstered Glock in place. "I've got to run. I'm already behind, and it's not the kind of meeting I can be late for..."

"So...I'm on my own tonight for dinner?" Dinah asked, stepping aside.

"I'll call you as soon as it's over. I'm hoping maybe I can get back by nine."

She kissed him on the cheek as he brushed past. "No problem. Go keep the world safe. I suppose having a husband who's overworked is better than having to worry about him running off with his secretary."

"Right. Who's got the time?" he agreed, and then was moving towards the foyer. "Like I said, I'll call. I'm sorry...," he called out.

"Go on. Get out of here. Shoo."

Cruz closed the front door softly behind him, the beginnings of a smile warming his usually-serious expression. Dinah was one in a million, and he was always amazed that, with a life like his, visited with more hardship and heartbreak than most would ever dream of, something as wonderful as their relationship had landed in his lap at the most unexpected time.

He would have to tread carefully with his current predicament, though. *El Rey* had butchered her father, and no matter what duty Cruz had been forced into honoring, she would never forgive the assassin. That would make Cruz's working with him, even at gunpoint, a slap in the face for her.

As he walked down the hall, he turned over in his mind how he would explain the operation to Dinah in a way that would be palatable. It occurred to him to just not tell her about *El Rey*'s involvement, but he discarded the idea. Whenever he tried to be stealthy, it wound up blowing up on him. Dinah seemed to be able to tell without effort when he was only sharing partial truths, and he knew himself well enough to know he'd never be able to keep something that big from her.

He waited for the elevator and adjusted his pistol, reassured by its comforting bulk. The next few hours were going to be as ugly as any he'd ever spent, but he would get through them somehow, no matter how unpleasant the task. Cruz was pragmatic, and he'd gotten his marching orders – and whatever his feelings, he was a creature of the law, and had to respect the very same law he was sworn to uphold. *El Rey* was now forgiven for any wrongdoing by the system, the sins of the past pardoned by the highest authority in the land. Cruz might not like it, but it was official, and he needed to remember that even if he didn't agree with it.

The elevator arrived, and he entered and jabbed the button for the parking garage level beneath the lobby.

It was a lousy situation all around. Nobody was going to be happy about it – he could just imagine how his staff would react to the news that they were going to have to work with the most notorious assassin in the country's history. Yet another reason to keep the circle of those who knew about it as small as possible. If the press got any wind of what was afoot with the Chinese it would be disastrous, but if somehow it leaked out that the *Federales* were working with *El Rey*...

There could be no way of explaining that, no rationalization that would make sense. It would destroy the nation's credibility, as well as that of his office. The outrage would be almost as devastating as if the assassination attempt was successful.

For a fleeting second he wished he'd kept drinking instead of sleeping it off.

Then the doors opened and Cruz strode to his waiting car – another perk of being Mexico's most visible cop. Whatever his misgivings, he now had a job to do, and he would have to lead his team with assurance. But there was no part of him that was looking forward to the coming meeting, and as he slipped into the back seat of the sedan, he had a sinking feeling in his gut.

He'd been saddled with yet another impossible assignment, where the odds of success were slim, and blame for failure would fall squarely on him. He glanced at the back of his driver's head and groaned, then caught himself and choked it off.

"Where to, *Capitan*?" the driver asked, eyeing him in the mirror.

He hesitated for a moment, and then cleared his throat.

"CISEN. And use the siren."

CHAPTER 13

El Perro Bravo was quiet at just after five, the evening drinking crowd having not yet trickled in. From the outside, the bar looked like a trendy watering hole, all black leather and chrome and mirrors. The bartender was a small man in a highly starched white shirt and black vinyl apron, thinning hair trimmed close to his head, like his carefully groomed goatee. Lips permanently pursed in judgment, he was busily polishing the gleaming bar top with a rag as muted lounge music drifted from hidden speakers. In three hours the place would be standing room only, filled with young professionals with money to spend and time to kill, looking for that one special connection that would satisfy their desires for the night; but now, during rush hour, it was dead.

The stylish doors pushed open and a medium-sized man in his thirties with conservatively cut black hair and a mustache entered and looked around the dimly lit interior. The bartender eyed his understated rugby shirt and tan slacks without interest and returned to his chore, leaving the newcomer to find a place to sit and order something whenever he was ready.

He chose a booth in a far corner, facing the door, checking his watch as he sat down, and after tossing the jacket he'd been carrying on the seat next to him, pulled a smartphone from his pocket and checked his e-mail messages, peering at the tiny screen intently, seemingly unaware of the bartender. After a few minutes, another man entered – this one older, tall and thin, his movements measured, wearing a black leather jacket and jeans, the dome of his shaved head shining from the beams of the overhead can lights, the shadows accenting his cadaverous features.

The new arrival's eyes scanned the bar and then settled on the only other patron, still fiddling with his phone. He took long, fluid strides across the black and white checkered floor and took a seat across from the younger man before glancing at the bartender, who stopped what he was doing and came around the long bar to their table.

"What'll it be, gentlemen?"

The older man looked at the bottles standing sentry in back of the bar. "Chivas. Neat."

The younger man put his phone on the table top and regarded the bartender. "Do you have Bohemia?" he asked.

"Yes. Regular or dark?"

"Regular, please."

The two men didn't speak until the drinks had been brought and paid for, and the bartender had moved out of earshot.

"What do you have for us?" the older man began in a surprisingly soft voice.

The younger man took a pull on his beer. "I put out the word to everyone I know, and I think I got a bite on the location you were asking about."

The older man nodded, then took an appreciative sip of his drink. "Good. Were you able to get any details other than a location?"

"Only after a long night buying my source tequila shots and staying out till three in the morning."

"Sounds like rough duty."

"You don't know the half of it. I feel like I was dragged behind a garbage truck for a few miles."

"I'm sure it was terrible. Now what about the information?"

"It was harder to get than I imagined. Nobody else even had a hint of anything helpful. That's almost unheard of. It should be worth more. A lot more."

The older man sighed, weary of the game. "How much more?" He bit off each syllable.

The younger man reclined and took another drink of beer. It was promising that the older man hadn't just gotten up and left, confirming his instinct that the information was valuable.

"I was thinking double."

The older man's eyes narrowed to slits. "In every relationship, there comes a point where one of the two parties involved realizes that he's not getting adequate value from the other to continue."

"Which wouldn't be the case here, as this is the most hotly sought info I can recall, and a bargain at four times the price. Besides which, if anything happens once I give it to you, I'll be under substantial scrutiny, as will everyone else who had access. That additional risk needs to be compensated for. It's not unfair."

The older man sat back and contemplated killing the younger one, right there, and then calmly walking out of the bar. He could do it. It wouldn't be the first time.

The younger man seemed to understand the internal struggle. "Don't take this the wrong way, but I have a pistol pointed at you under the table," he announced in a flat voice.

The older man offered up a wan smile that never reached his eyes. "That's not really in the spirit of friendship, is it?"

"No. But I don't want to wind up another Los Zetas casualty. Just in case you were so offended by my explanation that you were considering terminating our relationship. Not that I think you would. Purely precautionary."

"If I wanted you dead, you'd be dead," the older man replied easily. "You can put your gun away. It's unnecessary."

The younger man nodded and eased his weapon back under the jacket next to him. "So where do we go from here? Are you prepared to meet my price, or do we enjoy our drinks and agree that this isn't a good exchange?" he asked.

The older man removed a bulging yellow envelope from his jacket and slid it across the table, watching the bartender to ensure he wasn't paying any attention.

"This is the amount we agreed to. I don't have any more with me. If the information vets, I'll get you another envelope with the balance within twenty-four hours. But I won't wait. You know I'm good for it. Now it's your turn."

The younger man hefted the envelope and then pulled a scrap of paper out of his pocket and passed it to the older one, who unfolded it and read the few details with interest.

"What about security precautions?"

"Two men in the lobby at all times. Armed."

"That's it?"

"A driver. But from what I understand, they vary the pick-up times, so there are no set patterns. All very clandestine and hush-hush."

"Any chance of turning the driver?"

"Zero. His daughter was killed in a cartel gun battle. Collateral damage at a plaza in Michoacán. It's personal for him."

"Ah. Well, then, no point in dreaming about what might have been." The older man finished his Chivas and slid out of the booth. "I'll be in touch with the rest of the money. I think if I were you, I'd consider a long vacation at the beach. Soon. You probably don't want to be around. You have any time due?"

"I haven't had a break in two years."

"Then it's your big chance. I'll arrange another meet so you can get paid." He turned to go.

"No hard feelings?" the younger man asked, the hint of concern in his voice betraying his anxiety.

"It's just business. Don't sweat it."

He watched as the older man strode to the door and swung it open, then stepped out into the waning light and was gone.

CHAPTER 14

The sedan pulled up to the security gate and, after the driver showed his credentials, was waved through. It rolled to a stop at the building entrance, the rear door opened, and Cruz stepped out into the dusk and marched up the stairs into CISEN's headquarters. Once inside, an armed guard escorted him to one of the meeting rooms, and he sat cooling his heels for a few minutes before footsteps approached from down the long hall.

Rodriguez entered, followed by three other men. He recognized the last man; his hair was longer, but the studied blank expression was as familiar as his dead black eyes.

El Rey. The assassin, whom he'd last seen at the arraignment.

The newcomers took seats around the large conference room table and Rodriguez nodded to Cruz.

"Thank you for coming on such short notice, *Capitan* Cruz. These men are my associates, working the Iron Eagle case. And I believe you've already met...Carlos." Rodriguez motioned to *El Rey.*

"Carlos? Is that what you're calling him?" Cruz spat, struggling to maintain his composure now that the assassin was seated across from him. This, the man who had been responsible for so much misery, who had killed his men with abject ruthlessness, and almost killed the president. For a second his vision blurred and he literally saw red, a crimson haze from his blood pressure spiking before he fought his emotions back under control.

"Romero was taken," El Rey said with a shrug, goading Cruz by using his first name.

Cruz resisted the urge to jump across the table and strangle the killer. Instead, he forced a humorless smile. "That would have been confusing," he acceded.

El Rey turned to face Rodriguez. "For the record, I don't think this is going to work. It's a spectacularly bad idea, actually."

Cruz nodded. "On this, we agree."

Rodriguez looked at his men and then returned *El Rey*'s glare. "Everyone's familiar with your objections. But we don't have any choice, so we have to make the best of a difficult situation," he said.

"Why is that, again? Perhaps I'm just slow today, but explain to me again why a lowlife serial killer is a necessary part of this operation. I know he got a pardon, but why am I being saddled with him? Did I miss where he's got any background in investigations?" Cruz said.

"That's not your point, it's mine. My, er, skills, aren't tracking and finding assassins, gentlemen. As I've said before," *El Rey* said.

Rodriguez shook his head in frustration. "Can we please stop this? We're wasting time we don't have. I understand neither of you wants to be in the same room as the other – you've both made that abundantly clear. And I've made it clear to you that you have no choice in the matter, so rather than wasting your energy protesting the unchangeable, I suggest you start focusing on catching the German before he can carry out this assassination."

Cruz started to speak again, but Rodriguez cut him off.

"With all due respect, *Capitan*, get over your righteous indignation. I'm not asking you two to go shoe shopping together. Your assignment is to work with each other to find the German. The clock is ticking. 'Carlos' here is part of the team, representing CISEN, and that's the end of the matter. I'm familiar with your sentiments, and they've been recorded for posterity. But now we have a job to do, and I'd suggest you get with the program. Am I making myself clear?"

Cruz scowled. "Perfectly. That's why I'm here," he said.

"Very well. The first order of business is to get you a home base from which you can run the operation. You can't do so easily from *Federales* headquarters, so I'd like to propose that you do so from here. I can make a suite of offices available to you..."

"Absolutely not. CISEN is too high-profile. I see nothing wrong with headquarters, except for our friend *El*...Carlos. And that's just too bad. Headquarters is where I work," Cruz said forcefully.

"If you think I'm going to start commuting to *Federales* headquarters, you're out of your mind," *El Rey* agreed.

One of the men leaned towards Rodriguez and whispered a few words. A murmured conversation ensued while Cruz and *El Rey* stared death at each other. Rodriguez straightened and resumed speaking.

"May I suggest a compromise? We have certain facilities at our disposal. Offsite locations where you can work without issue. One is a block of offices downtown. I can arrange to have as many as you need ready by tomorrow."

Cruz eyed him distrustfully. "There will be a lot of specialized equipment. And security concerns."

"Make a list of what you need and I'll arrange for it. I'll also have a team in place to guard it twenty-four hours a day. It will be accessible round the clock. At your exclusive disposal," Rodriguez assured him.

"Figure on enough room for two dozen men, minimum, with at least three or four private offices and a large common area for analysts," Cruz said.

"And state-of-the-art computers and communications gear, I would presume," Rodriguez said.

"Yes. Do you have some note paper? I can give you preliminary requirements right now."

Rodriguez snapped his fingers and the man nearest the door wordlessly rose, returning after a few moments with a stack of legal pads and pens. He placed them in the center of the table and Cruz took one, then began making precise bullet points of his necessities. *El Rey* watched him without comment, and then took a pull on the water bottle he'd brought.

"So what's your first move? Other than making a shopping list?" he asked in his soft voice. Cruz glanced up at him and continued writing.

Rodriguez cleared his throat. "In addition to Carlos, we're also assigning a liaison. Claudio Ibarra, here, will work with you closely. You may rely on him for anything you need."

Claudio, a paunchy middle-aged man wearing a rumpled brown suit, a film of sweat clinging to his forehead, nodded at Cruz and *El Rey*. "Pleased to meet you," he said without enthusiasm.

"All the latest information we've been able to glean is in these. The data is current as of one hour ago." Rodriguez slid folders to *El Rey*, Cruz, and Claudio. The only one who opened it and studied the contents was Claudio. *El Rey* peered at the folder without interest.

"Do we know if he's made it into Mexico yet?" *El Rey* asked.

"Regrettably, we don't. That will be part of what your team will handle – watch for anything suspicious at the borders. You'll have complete authority over immigration, local and federal police, any interfacing with Interpol...whatever you need," Rodriguez assured him.

"That never really did you any good when you were hunting me," *El Rey* observed. "Why would you think it would make any difference now?"

Rodriguez frowned. "That's exactly why you're part of this group. We need your expertise. You have considerable depth in areas where we might be lacking. The expectation is that you'll be looking in places that would be second-nature for a professional, but that we might overlook."

"I know. We covered all that. Somehow I'm supposed to second-guess a hitter from the other side of the planet and stop him, with exactly zero experience ever doing that before. My position is pretty clear on this. You're deluded," *El Rey* said matter-of-factly.

"All right. Here's the list," Cruz interrupted, pushing the pad to Rodriguez, who picked it up and studied it while Cruz turned his attention to the file contents.

"We'll have it set up by tomorrow, six a.m.," Rodriguez assured him.

"Fine. But you haven't got anything more recent for a photo of the German? You're telling me that for over a decade, the man hasn't had his picture taken?" Cruz snapped.

"I gave you what we have. We're pulling out all the stops, but we have to be careful about what we ask for in Germany. There's a strong likelihood he's plugged in over there, and will hear something the moment we really start probing."

"That's all well and good, but I'm not sure that I really care if he knows we're after him or not. We have to assume he's expecting to be tracked."

El Rey shook his head. "I disagree. If he gets a warning, he'll be even more careful than usual, and I don't have to tell anyone in this room that a motivated assassin can elude even the most carefully crafted security. I've proved that enough times. You'll need every edge you can get."

Cruz studied him with seeming disinterest. "You didn't elude me the last time, did you?"

"Was that the time that I successfully detonated the helicopter on the president's head, or the time I penetrated the G-20 and placed a bomb that would have turned it into a slaughterhouse?" *El Rey* shot back.

"I guess you probably get them confused when you've failed that often," Cruz sneered, tossing the pen onto the table with a clatter.

"Gentlemen. May I remind you that we don't have the luxury of the mutual admiration society? I need you to work together."

"Where are these offices? I want to swing by and inspect them tonight, after this meeting," Cruz said, changing the subject. Sparring with the assassin wouldn't get them closer to their objective, and Cruz knew it was childish to taunt him. Besides which, the bastard exuded exactly zero emotion, so his efforts probably weren't working.

"Claudio will accompany you there once we're done," Rodriguez said.

El Rey stood after glancing through the file and checking the time. "Which we are. There's nothing that sitting around here any longer is going to accomplish," he declared in a mild tone. "And I'm getting hungry."

Rodriguez pushed back his chair and also stood. "As discussed, you will cooperate with *Capitan* Cruz for the duration of this operation. How you do so is up to the two of you, but I'd strongly suggest that you coordinate your schedules and commit to making this work." Rodriguez turned his attention to Cruz. "*Capitan*, in that file is the cell phone number for our friend here, as well as my private cell number. If you have any problems, call me. I expect you to hit the ground running tomorrow."

"Rodriguez, with all due respect, that's going to be hard, given the paucity of information you've given me. We have nothing. I repeat. Nothing. A tip – really, nothing more than a rumor. I'm not sure what you're expecting, but I'm not a magician. Nothing ever happens fast, and in one of these cases, when we do make progress it's inevitably because of patient, methodical police work, not wild hunches by ex-killers. I'll play along with this because I've been ordered to, but don't expect much. You've provided me almost nothing to go on, and it'll be a miracle if we can catch this man before he acts," Cruz groused.

"Well, there's a winning attitude that should pump you full of enthusiasm," *El Rey* said to the CISEN staff. "Looks like I'll have to do this by myself."

Rodriguez ignored *El Rey*. "I understand what you're saying, but we need a miracle here. That's why we've teamed you together. This unorthodox approach is our best shot. The German has successfully evaded the best security in the world for years. I have no doubt that he'll put ours to the test if we don't try something out of the box."

"This is about as unusual as it gets, I'll grant you that," Cruz conceded, and then moved around the table.

"Carlos, would you like to accompany the *Capitan* to look over the offices?" Claudio asked as the meeting broke up, addressing *El Rey*.

He shrugged. "Not really. I'll leave the paper clip counting to the methodical assassin hunter, if you don't mind. I'm going to get something to eat."

Cruz threw him a black look, but he ignored it.

"We'll open for business at nine tomorrow morning. Please be there at ten so I can coordinate my efforts with whatever you have to offer," Cruz said in a tone that indicated very clearly that he didn't think *El Rey* could provide anything of value.

"Fine. Call me and confirm the address when you've confirmed you'll take that space," *El Rey* said, and then pushed his way through the door and was gone.

Rodriguez and Cruz exchanged glances, and Rodriguez extended his hand to shake. Cruz took it reluctantly.

"Nobody said this was going to be easy. I hope you two can work out your differences and make it work."

Cruz stared down the corridor at where the assassin had disappeared from view.

"Me too."

CHAPTER 15

When Cruz finally made it back to the condo it was already ten o'clock, and he could hear the drone of the television from the living room. He closed the door gently behind him and twisted the deadbolt, then walked towards the clamor of a studio audience applauding the latest contestant in a singing contest. Dinah was lying on the couch in sweats and a T-shirt, one leg swinging off the edge. She looked up when he stepped into the room, and a warm smile broke across her face.

"*Hola, amor*! You're back! There's a plate of food in the refrigerator with your name on it. Enchiladas. Just pop them in the microwave for two minutes," Dinah said, rising to greet him.

"Perfect. Let me get out of my monkey suit and I'll be right back," he said, kissing her lightly on the cheek.

Cruz emerged from the bedroom a few minutes later wearing his favorite jeans and a sweatshirt. The aroma of enchiladas filled the air, and Dinah placed the warmed-up meal on the table in front of him, along with a cold beer. Cruz looked at her gratefully and dug in, the rich sauce reviving him as he shoveled heaping forkfuls into his mouth. She sat across from him, watching him eat, and sipped her soda, waiting for him to finish. He made short work of it, and soon was patting his stomach appreciatively.

"You're the best cook in the world, my love."

"Is that the only reason you married me?" she teased.

"That, and other obvious reasons. Which I'm looking forward to exploring later..."

She lifted his plate and slid past him into the kitchen, then turned to study his face. He looked fatigued and worried. Tense.

"Why the long hours? What's going on? Is it something you'd like to talk about?" she asked.

Cruz closed his eyes. Here it was – the moment of truth. He'd agonized about how to break the news to her on the way home, but hadn't come up with anything that he was happy with. Still, he couldn't lie to her. Maybe not tell her the complete truth, but he couldn't flat out lie, much as that had appeal just then.

"It's a special assignment. I've been painted into a corner, and I've had to accept a mission that's going to have me working around the clock for the next eight days."

"Good lord. Will you be safe? What is it?"

"It's classified. I can't really say much, other than that it involves an assassination attempt." Perhaps that would be sufficient to satisfy her curiosity. He hoped it would be.

"Assassination? I thought...I thought your problems with *El Rey* were over. Did he resurface?" she asked with alarm. For months after she'd been blackmailed into helping the assassin she'd had recurring nightmares, and the fallout from her revelations about it had almost resulted in her and Cruz breaking up.

"No, it's a different killer. But as dangerous, if not more so."

"At least it's not him. That's a relief. He's a menace."

"He was, but he's out of the game. This is a new threat, but equally deadly."

She did a double take. "How do you know he's out of the game? You seem so sure. I thought he was still at large...escaped from prison. Did something change?"

"I..." Cruz debated his next words carefully. "It's classified. I'm sorry, Dinah."

Her eyes narrowed. "This is the monster who killed my father with a sword we're talking about, remember? Who forced me to turn on you? He destroyed my life, and nearly destroyed our relationship. And the best you can manage is to say it's *classified*?" Dinah was getting angry, which was extremely rare, but when it happened, not to be trifled with. "That's not good enough, Romero. On anything else it might be. But not this."

"I can't discuss it, *mi amor*. You'll have to just accept that..."

"No. Not on this. Tell me what happened." Dinah's voice was dangerously quiet. He'd never heard her like that before. A host of possible responses ran through his head, but none seemed adequate.

He sighed and plopped down on the couch. "You have to swear to never repeat this to anyone. Ever. It would be grounds for arrest – for treason. I'm not making this up," he warned.

"Treason?" she repeated, not comprehending the sudden change in Cruz's mood. "Treason in what way?"

"Treason in the way that they would throw you in prison and throw away the key. And me as well. I'm not joking. It's that serious. You have to promise me, and mean it, or I can't tell you another word." Cruz stared deep into her large brown eyes, trying to decide whether she fully grasped what he was saying.

"Fine. I'll never tell a soul. I swear. Satisfied?" she demanded, still agitated, and struggling to maintain control.

He nodded. "It all started with his prison break..."

Five minutes later he was finished, and the look of shock on her face was worse than anything he'd expected.

"So all of his crimes have been forgiven? His record expunged? For Christ's sake, he tried to kill the president, not once, but twice. He murdered those men right in front of the cathedral..." Her voice trailed off as she fought for understanding, but failed to find it. "And his punishment was to have his slate wiped clean? What about justice for the countless he killed? What about my father? How can anyone just wave their hand and let this animal walk?" Her eyes had widened as she asked questions that he couldn't answer. The truth was there were no good answers.

"It's done. There's nothing I could do. I was told by...by some of the highest authorities in the administration. It's already taken place, and it's final."

"And you allowed this? You let them do this?" The hurt and betrayal were palpable, each word like a slap across his face.

"I had no choice in the matter. I fought it, protested it, even threatened to quit my job – but none of it did any good. It came down from the very top – a presidential pardon."

"The same president he nearly killed? Pardoned him?" Dinah was sputtering now and turning red, flushed from fury and agitation. Her mouth worked, but she was at a loss for words. Cruz sympathized. He remembered the day he'd been told that *El Rey* was a free man, immune from prosecution.

"I know, *mi amor*. It makes no sense. The whole thing is just so wrong...but there's nothing I can do about it. The pardon has been granted and in the eyes of the law he's now as innocent as you or I. It's not fair, it's not right, but it is what it is." Cruz shrugged.

"How long have you known about this?" she asked quietly. Too quietly. Cruz chose his words with the care of a surgeon excising a brain tumor.

"Long enough to know that he's out of the game and no longer a threat."

"That's not an answer."

"It's the only one I can give. Call it a few months. I don't know, exactly."

She stood and began pacing – another very bad warning sign of a pending meltdown. He'd never seen her this upset before. Sad, yes. Devastated when her father had been murdered, yes. Fearful and remorseful when her forced betrayal of him had been discovered? Yes. But never with this much...*rage*. That was the word. She looked like she was going to explode from anger. Her hands were clenched tightly into fists, she was trembling ever so slightly, and she was regarding Cruz like he'd raped her.

"So for months you've known about this, and every night, come home to me, chatted with me like everything was fine, made love with me...all the time living with the biggest lie I could imagine," she stated flatly.

"It's not like that, Dinah. Please. Be reasonable. It's classified. I'm the only person other than the president's staff who knows. And with all due respect, the last time you had access to classified material–"

"How dare you. How fucking dare you bring that up and throw it in my face. I was blackmailed by the same shitrat you pardoned!" Chances of a full-blown melt down had just doubled. When Dinah swore, which was almost never, the situation had reached critical. Like a nuclear reactor, this would be about the time that the klaxons went off and the normally calm technicians began running panicked from the plant. Cruz understood the instinct. Part of him wished he could do the same.

But he couldn't. This was his wife. The love of his life. Who right now looked like she wanted to strangle him with her bare hands.

"It's not me. I didn't pardon him. I would just as soon have put a bullet in him, and I told you, I fought this tooth and nail. But my influence doesn't extend to the decisions of the new president. Don't make this about me. It's been hard enough..."

"Then he's out there. Right now. Walking the streets, a free man, rich, young, with absolutely nothing to worry about. While my father is forever dead. As are your men. Everyone butchered by him, permanently robbed of another moment of life, their children growing up without fathers...and you remain a part of this, this...*abortion* you call a system? How can you do it, Cruz? How *could* you?" Now she was calling him by his last name. No Romero or *amor*.

"I considered quitting, but it wouldn't have changed anything, and there's still tremendous danger out there for me. For us. Every cartel miscreant in the country wants me dead. In case you haven't noticed, that's why we have to move every six weeks. That's why we have the armed guards downstairs, why my car is armored and I'm not allowed to drive it, why we can't meet with your friends anymore, why you had to be transferred to a different school and use a new last name...we need that kind of protection, and we won't get it if I quit. So I've done what I had to do. Which hasn't been easy. Especially now." Cruz regretted the last words even as he said them, and desperately wished he could pull them back into his mouth. His only hope was that Dinah was so enraged she wouldn't notice.

It wasn't his lucky night.

"Especially *now*? Why *now*? What's happened that it's even harder *now*?" she asked with glacial calm. Probably the single most alarming trend yet.

"What I meant was, now that I've told you," Cruz explained, hoping his dishonesty wouldn't be obvious.

"No, you didn't. You're lying to me. I always know when you are. So one more time. What happened? Why is it even more difficult *now*?" Dinah would have been a brilliant prosecuting attorney. She was relentless and had an impeccable nose for the truth.

He rose from the couch and approached her, but she backed away, refusing to be mollified, holding his gaze with a look of fury, hurt, and...something else. Revulsion. A part of him died when he saw it, but it was unmistakable – and, he supposed, understandable. But how to proceed from here? He couldn't tell her the truth. Not when she was like this.

"So help me, if you don't tell me what's going on, I will flip out. I mean it. Don't test me on this." Her voice had an edge, as well as a tinge of hysteria. She was barely holding it together, the revelation of the assassin's escape from justice eating at her even as she cast around for an object to hate – Cruz being the obvious, closest target, in spite of his protestations.

Had he grown so inured to constant compromise, living in a no-man's land of moral ambiguity, that his own outrage had been blunted to this degree? Her reaction brought back all of his emotions when he'd heard that the assassin would walk, a free man, untouchable. He'd had the same response, but had buried it, choosing to be pragmatic rather than righteous. Had that been cowardice or prudence? he wondered, watching Dinah pace. Had he just seen too much, made too many pacts with the devil, lived in a brutal purgatory of sin and corruption so long that he'd lost any moral barometer he'd ever had?

Something snapped inside of him. He was done with the subterfuge. If she wanted the truth, she would have to deal with it, just as he had been forced to. She would get what she wanted, even though the reality of their situation might destroy anything they had.

"Honey, why don't you come over here and sit down. I'll get you a glass of wine. You're going to need it," Cruz offered, gesturing to the couch.

"Don't *honey* me. Just spit it out. What the hell is going on here? What could possibly be worse than my father's killer walking away scot-free?"

"Fine. Then I'm going to have one. And please, try to remember that I haven't done anything bad or wrong. I didn't decide to let the assassin loose. I didn't pardon him. None of what I'm taking the hits for from you was anything I had control over."

"That's not true. You could have put a bullet in his skull when you captured him," she said contemptuously.

"Dinah. That's not the job. I'm not the judge and executioner. I'm supposed to catch them, not catch and then kill them," he said, padding to the kitchen in search of a glass.

"Maybe you should change the job description."

"Don't think it hasn't occurred to me." Cruz opened the refrigerator and extracted a bottle of white wine, uncorked it using his teeth, and poured his glass half full before returning to the living room, where Dinah was waiting, glaring at him like he'd just killed her puppy. "I really wish you'd sit down. You're making me a little crazy with the nervous energy."

"Deal with it. Now tell me what else is happening."

Cruz exhaled with a groan and contemplated where to begin. "There's going to be an assassination attempt in eight days," he started.

"Another one? How many times are they going to try to kill the president in any given year? Doesn't he have his own security team to protect him?" Dinah demanded.

"Yes, he does, but it's not going to be against him. It's another dignitary. But it's almost as bad."

"That's where you've been all evening?"

"Yes. In a planning session. But you're really not going to like the rest of this. First off, I'll probably have to spend most of the next eight days in the office. Every minute will count in foiling this plot."

She digested that. "So I'm not going to see you for a while, is that it?"

"Sort of. As part of the assignment, I've been ordered to work with CISEN on stopping the assassin."

"CISEN. I thought you hated them."

"I do. And never more than today. They've assigned me a specialist I have to work with on this operation." He paused, waiting for it to register. "It's *El Rey*. He works for CISEN now."

"What! Are you all insane? The man is an animal – a vicious killer. He'd just as soon cut your throat as shake your hand. What are you thinking? You can't do it."

"I told them I wouldn't. And they said I had to. It came from the president's office. I still refused, and they threatened to fire me."

"Fine. Quit. Take your pension and go do something else. One of those security things you were talking about. You don't need this, or them. Tell them to screw themselves." Dinah's tone was final.

"I did. And they told me that I'd lose all the retirement I've accrued, as well as the security that's keeping us alive. And they'd probably find some reason to prosecute me, or at least make my life hell."

"So be it. I have some money from my father. We'll go someplace where we can live simply, open up a shop or a little restaurant on a beach somewhere, and they can rot in hell."

He shook his head. "It's not that simple, *mi amor*."

"It is to me. You can't do this."

"I don't have any choice. I told them I would." There. The bomb had been dropped.

"Change your mind. It's too much to ask. Walk away from it. I'll stand by you no matter what happens. But don't do this. I'm begging you. Don't."

"I have to. They've got me in an impossible position. I can't lose everything I've worked for my entire life. I just can't."

"What about me, Romero? What about losing your wife? Has it occurred to you that that could happen? Do you think I'm just going to stand by, barefoot in the kitchen, while you work side by side with the man who killed my father? Because I won't. So deal with that impossible position. Figure out what's more important to you – your job, or me. Because this is a relationship ender. There are few things I'd leave you over, but this is one of them," she seethed, and then whirled and stormed to the bedroom.

"Dinah. Come on. Please. Take some time to cool down, to think things through."

"Plan on sleeping on the couch. Get drunk on the wine. Do whatever the hell you want, but don't approach me for any reason but to tell me that you'll quit. I don't want to hear anything else."

"Dinah…"

The bedroom door slammed, sounding like a gunshot in the small space, and Cruz was left staring down the hall, wondering what had just happened, and whether Dinah could possibly mean what she'd said in anger and haste.

His instinct was to give her some time to cool down, to think. A day, maybe two, and she'd have perspective. Right now she was just lashing out and making impossible demands. It was purely emotional, he knew. She'd soften with some time to think.

At least, that was his hope.

He downed the glass of wine in three gulps, then rose and went to refrigerator for another one. The astringent Chablis burned on the way down, especially after the afternoon's tequila, but he didn't care. The only way he was going to get any sleep was if he was out of it. Hopefully he'd drift off after another bottle. And hopefully Dinah would reconsider her ultimatum. She had to.

Cruz pulled the cork and carried the new bottle to the living room, then sat on the couch and shut off the lights and muted the TV. A long pull emptied a quarter of the wine, and he frowned at the taste — he really should spend more on the stuff they drank, he thought bitterly.

He looked at the glass sitting on the table and dismissed it. More efficient just to drain the bottle directly. Eliminate the middleman. Cut to the chase.

A muffled thud came from the bedroom, where Dinah was making her displeasure unmistakable, even though he wasn't in there.

It was going to be a very long night.

CHAPTER 16

Werner Rauschenbach's home on the Spanish coast near Moraira was spotlessly clean, furnished in a Germanic no-nonsense fashion, everything utilitarian and in its place. Rauschenbach didn't place a lot of value on art or expensive clutter, and his home reflected that philosophy to an almost Spartan degree. That wasn't to say that he didn't enjoy the finer things in life – he allowed himself a few luxuries, like the sixty-inch LCD screen television mounted on the living room wall and the twelve-hundred dollar espresso machine. But he couldn't see the point of pouring money into signature couches or designer tables – the entire exercise seemed pointless to him, the pastime of the spoiled and weak.

The other reason that he chose to forego creature comforts was because of his vocation – he could never be sure that he wouldn't have to run at a moment's notice, leaving everything behind. As his career had progressed, that seemed less likely, but he could never know with a hundred percent certainty that this day wouldn't be the one when any of a dozen nations' law enforcement agencies came through the door with guns and cuffs.

From the outside, the cottage resembled countless rustic vacation homes owned by prosperous Europeans with a taste for warmer weather and a more relaxed pace, but closer inspection would have revealed state-of-the-art security equipment, belying the benign exterior. Rauschenbach had hired a group from Finland, among the best in the world at what they did, to outfit the house, and they had been methodical and comprehensive in their approach. Motion detectors, hidden surveillance cameras, pressure sensors, reinforced steel doors, and bulletproof glass windows had been only the first stage in their makeover.

Half the basement had been converted into a high-security vault that rivaled any of the banks in the area, and this was where the assassin was now sitting, going over the satellite imagery of his target location. The Mexicans were lackadaisical in many ways, but the security for the event where he would kill the Chinese leader would be world class, with not only the nation's finest keeping it secure but also a substantial force of Chinese bodyguards, who were not known for sloppiness. It would be a difficult hit, to be sure; but the money would be sufficient for him to retire, when added to the already substantial pile of cash he'd accumulated over his career as Europe's foremost contract killer.

His eyes were beginning to burn from hours of poring over blueprints, satellite images, and maps, and he leaned back in his Aeron chair and stretched his arms over his head, his mind reflexively making notes even as he tried to relax. He had nine days to get into the country and confirm his choice of approaches – a heartbeat in mission timing terms, but sufficient for a specialist of his skill.

His next hurdle would be entering Mexico undetected. He'd researched it extensively, and the easiest way to get in was through the United States – entry was a mere formality, and in the Baja region, you could just drive across without any checks. The problem of course being that getting into the U.S. was considerably harder. He'd ran a number of scenarios, and it seemed that the most reliable plan would be to slip across from Guatemala or enter by sea. He had seriously considered an ocean approach, although it would take several days on board a cargo ship to make it into one of the ports – either Manzanillo or Veracruz. He could rendezvous with a tramp steamer that plied the trade between South America and Mexico and make it aboard in international waters via either a high-speed boat out of Belize or Honduras. But the time factor was too undependable, so after looking at all his options, he had decided to fly into Santiago, Chile, via Madrid, and then travel north to Guatemala City, where he had already gotten in touch with a group that could get him across the border with no complications.

The Los Zetas cartel had expanded its operations into Africa and Europe, and he knew them, if not intimately. The good news was that they were seasoned smugglers and controlled much of Guatemala, so once he was in their care the trip north would be much faster and less fraught with complications than a sea voyage into one of the Mexican ports.

His neck was stiff, and he rolled his head to loosen the muscles, then decided to call it a night. His flight was the next morning, and he would need time to get to Valencia, where he would catch the first commuter flight to Madrid, and from there to Chile. His bag was already packed, with the bare minimum he'd decided he could carry – a few days' worth of clothes, twenty-five thousand dollars in hundred-dollar bills, and two sets of false papers. He would be able to withdraw money from one of his Mexican bank accounts, set up when he'd agreed to take the job two weeks prior, and he'd already arranged to have a hundred thousand dollars of operational funds wired to them, waiting for his arrival, using a blind corporate account.

Getting a weapon onto the planes was a taller order, but one that he had solved with a little ingenuity, using a ruse he'd perfected over time. He stood and stretched again, then walked over to a black seven-foot-long hard tube-case. He methodically removed one end, a cap that he then bounced in his hand several times, and placed it on his work table and moved to his weapons cache. He opened a metal cabinet. Inside were a dozen guns of every imaginable variety: revolvers, semi-automatic pistols, sniper rifles, assault rifles, submachine guns. And the weapon he'd chosen for Mexico – a custom-made .338 caliber Arctic Warfare AWM rifle that he'd paid a small fortune for and which had been heavily modified, consisting of little more than a barrel, a single-shot chamber altered to accommodate longer cartridges, a tubular shoulder stock, a high-powered scope, and a hand-made silencer. He reached out and lifted the ebony matte-finished gun from its resting place and studied it for a few moments, then moved to his workbench and dismantled it into its component parts, the feel of the cool steel reassuring in his practiced hands.

Once it was nothing more than seemingly random pieces of metal, he moved to another corner of the room and returned with four fishing rods. He carefully unscrewed the butt on the first one and slid the barrel into it, the neoprene-coated interior acting as a snug sleeve inside the thin lead sheath he'd painstakingly crafted to line the cores of the rod handles. He reassembled it and placed the section on the table, then removed five CNC LN-105 .338 caliber very low drag bullets and placed them next to it. The remainder of the rifle fit into the handles of the other three rods along with the rounds. When he was done he moved to the wall, where he lifted a welding mask from a peg and pulled it over his head.

Twenty minutes later he was finished. The rifle had been sealed into the rod stocks, which were covered in cork for a more convincing cosmetic grip, and featured reel seats that were now undetectable as being segmented for the weapon's storage. He inspected his work with satisfaction. While it was entirely possible that he would be able to source a weapon in Mexico, this eliminated the need – and his custom-made gun of choice for this assignment would be accurate at ranges most couldn't even imagine. Of course, there was always the chance that once he was on site and had physically evaluated the location he'd chosen for the execution he would opt for some other approach than a gun, but it never hurt to have your own tools in the field.

Unlike his usual contracts, where he would have a special-purpose one-time-use weapon he would buy in-country and then discard once the job was done, on this one he was going into an area of the world where he'd never worked before, so his resource base was limited. For anywhere in Europe or the former Soviet Union he could make two phone calls and have a weapon waiting for him, but not in Mexico, and this was far too high profile a sanction to trust to an unknown.

The reel case was purely for theater, and he would discard it along with the four reels once he was in Mexico City. It would take an hour of painstaking work with a metal file to dismantle the rods and extract the rifle, but he wasn't worried. The delicate part of the operation was passing through airport security – although he knew that the fishing gear would pass with flying colors and receive only a cursory, obligatory inspection.

He wiped a bead of sweat off his forehead and slid the case strap over his shoulder, and then stooped to pick up the reel box before moving out of the vault room, taking care to shut the door and spin the combination lock. He'd never had a break-in at his home, and it was unlikely that he would while he was gone on his fishing holiday to Central America, but he was naturally cautious – underscored by the papers and photos he'd put in his pockets, to be burned upstairs before he left. He had memorized what he needed to know, and there would be no trace of his intent when he departed for the airport in Valencia at five the next morning.

His tickets had been bought online using credit cards linked to three shell corporations, and he'd carefully chosen the carriers and the routes to avoid in-depth scrutiny of his passport. The one he was traveling on was in the name of Edgar Simms, native of Canada. Nobody ever suspected the Canadians, he'd found.

He hummed the Canadian national anthem as he mounted the stairs, a small smile playing across his face. He would have a nice glass or two of an excellent Rioja he'd been saving for a special occasion, and then get his customary six hours of sleep before embarking on his trip. His preparations were complete, and now he could unwind over dinner and a good red.

Upstairs, he did a quick check online and noted that the first half of the sanction funds had been deposited into his Austrian account – a formality, to be sure, but an important one nevertheless. He'd had no doubt it would be there, but it was nice to see all the zeros, and the sight brought another smile to his lips.

It would be eight days, and then he would be retiring a comfortable, if not rich, man, who could indulge his pursuits in peace somewhere he could disappear into the woodwork. Perhaps Australia, or maybe Vietnam. He was in no hurry to choose. There would be plenty of time for that once his last job was finished.

CHAPTER 17

The CISEN-supplied offices were nondescript, a three-story building in a commercial area that would raise no eyebrows. After spending a fitful night of scattered sleep on the couch, Cruz rose early and was behind his new desk in his headquarters for the next eight days, already making calls at seven-thirty. He had carefully considered whom from the *Federales* he wanted to work with, and had a short list of fewer than a dozen men who were able, talented, and entirely dependable. He called each at home and gave them the new address, swearing them to secrecy and ordering them to hand off whatever they were actively working on to others on the task force, and report to the new offices by ten.

The lingering after-effects of the wine had his head pounding, and he dry swallowed three aspirin as he dialed the last of his picks for the team – Lieutenant Fernando Briones. The younger man answered on the third ring, and was as surprised as any of the others when Cruz gave him a series of precise instructions, ordering him to stop by the headquarters offices before coming, to set up a direct link from the new digs to the *Federales'* servers.

"What's the new assignment, *Capitan*? And why work from a remote location?" Briones asked, the sound of the television droning in the background.

"I'll tell you everything when you come in. Just get the link taken care of and clear the boards. We're going to be working round the clock until further notice."

"Not even a hint, sir? Nothing you want me to bring?"

"No. Just yourself. It's going to be long hours, that's all I can tell you."

"No problem, sir. I'll be out the door in a few minutes," Briones assured him.

Cruz disconnected and reclined in his executive chair, staring into space. He had thought long and hard about bringing Briones into this, but on balance had decided to include him. He had as much experience from the *El Rey* attempts as Cruz did, and sometimes his perspective was valuable. Looking at the dearth of information they had to work with, they would need all the insight they could get. He just hoped that Briones could put his history with *El Rey* behind him. It was a chance Cruz had to take, although he had misgivings at just how much Briones could compartmentalize. After all, he'd taken one of the assassin's bullets – Cruz knew from harsh experience how difficult it was to forget something like that.

He rose and moved to a small table in the corner of his new office and poured himself another cup of steaming coffee from the pot he'd brewed upon arriving. He had to give CISEN credit – everything he'd asked for was there: equipment, supplies, and a subtle security presence in the lobby consisting of four hard-looking men, their concealed pistols bulging through their dark, loosely tailored suits. Cruz supposed if you had an unlimited budget like the intelligence agency did and literally no restrictions on how you spent it, you could afford the best. He contrasted the computers at his headquarters with the new systems sitting in the common area and decided there was no comparison – his task force gear was coming up on three years old and showed it, whereas these systems were cutting edge technology.

His thoughts turned to Dinah and the fight they'd had the previous night. He could appreciate her perspective, but things weren't as black and white as she had made them out to be. She wasn't seeing the big picture, and was so focused on her hatred for *El Rey* that it was coloring everything else. But he had faith that she would cool down, given some time. He knew her pretty well by now – she wasn't volatile and had a level head on her shoulders. She would come around, he was sure. She would think it through, consider the safety issue, the retirement benefits, and arrive at the same conclusion he had. It was a lousy situation, but there weren't a lot of alternatives, and when push came to shove, she'd support him.

Which reminded him that he couldn't put off the call he'd been dreading any longer. Procrastination would take you only so far, he thought, as he slid his cell phone from his pocket and dialed a local number.

When the assassin answered, it was with that eerie calm voice that Cruz was already learning to hate. "Yes?"

"We're getting set up. The offices are ready," Cruz said.

There was no response, the faint hiss of a cell line the only noise.

"I was thinking that you would want to come in and go over the intelligence as it arrives."

"Intelligence. I see. What have you gotten so far?"

"Nothing besides what was in the file, yet. But the team will be assembling by ten."

"That's nice. Maybe order breakfast. As for me, there's nothing I can do without more information."

"You can study the location of the accord signing and meet your fellow team mates."

More silence.

"*Capitan*, I don't have any team mates. I have an assignment I don't want, with a group of inept cops who couldn't find their asses with both hands. I'd just as soon skip the prayer meeting. Call me when you have something more substantial."

"Fine by me, but that wasn't how CISEN thought it was going to go. Have you informed them you won't be participating? I didn't get the impression that was an option, although I'm overjoyed to hear that we won't be rewarded with your presence..."

The assassin waited a few beats. "If I see you, I see you."

"Here's the address." Cruz spat out the building number and street, then hung up.

It was pretty obvious to him that he wasn't going to be getting a Christmas card from *El Rey*. That was fine. There was no love lost on either end. He sipped his coffee and considered the morning's agenda. Meet with everyone, give them marching orders, and start coordinating with immigration and the security teams that were going to be responsible for the delegation's protection. If they were lucky, the German would be picked up at one of the ports of entry – his first order of the day would be to get the name and photo onto watch lists at every airport and border crossing point in Mexico, although he wasn't optimistic. The cartels moved hundreds of tons of drugs, cash, and guns across the borders without detection every week, and there were just too many crossing points to manage effectively.

He flopped back down in his chair and jiggled the new wireless mouse, activating the computer monitor, and tried not to sink into a pit of despair before the hunt had even started. It was hard, because as he knew from trying to stop *El Rey*, the search for a single, skilled professional was incredibly resource and labor intensive, with a slim chance of success. If the odds had been better, then his last two run-ins with *El Rey* wouldn't have turned out the way they had. As it was, both had been successes from the assassin's standpoint – he had reached his target both times, even if circumstances had colluded to save the president's life.

The ugly truth was that a determined pro could almost always outflank even the most dedicated and conscientious security. It was simply impossible to safeguard against every eventuality. That was the dirty secret of security teams the world over, reinforced by assassination attempts against even the most protected men on the planet – Kennedy, Reagan, Sadat. A killer with enough motivation was every team's worst nightmare, and for good reason, as Mexico had seen on both of *El Rey*'s attempts. Now, for the third time, Cruz was faced with the grim duty of trying to keep the unthinkable from happening, against impossible odds, with almost no time and precious little information.

Other than that, it was shaping up to be a good day.

CHAPTER 18

Over the next hour Cruz's handpicked men arrived, and he greeted each newcomer and gave him a quick rundown on why they were there, promising to provide a more detailed briefing at ten o'clock. Each had worked with Cruz for years and were seasoned veterans of the drug wars, having run countless operations, most of which had been successful. Their countenances were grim at the news that they would be working on an assassin hunt – all had been involved in the attempts to bring down *El Rey*, and they remembered how those had played out. The assassin's eventual capture had been as much luck as anything, and everyone knew it, in spite of the media's portrayal of a crack team that had performed flawlessly.

Cruz glanced at his watch at ten, the group waiting expectantly in the common area, and decided to delay the meeting for a few more minutes to give Briones a chance to arrive. He, of all of them, had been instrumental in the prior operations, and Cruz knew that he could have encountered some unexpected delays at headquarters while setting up the link. In the meantime, he issued terse instructions to the technicians wiring up the communications center and networking the computers together – a team from CISEN that went about their business in silence, working efficiently.

Their CISEN liaison, Claudio, appeared five minutes later, looking like he'd just fallen out of bed, followed closely by Briones, who appeared harried.

"Who are the goons in the lobby? They aren't ours, are they?" he asked as he set down his soft black nylon briefcase.

"No. Courtesy of CISEN, our generous benefactor in this operation. Although I think I'd like two of our own to augment them. I'll need extremely tight-lipped, dependable men. Can you see to it?" Cruz asked.

"Of course."

"Round the clock shifts, eight hours apiece, two men per shift."

"I'll attend to it immediately."

"No, after the meeting. You won't want to miss it."

"What's this all about, sir?"

"You'll find out shortly." Cruz looked at the gathered officers, some sipping coffee, some munching on breakfast rolls that had been thoughtfully provided. "All right. Let's get this over with. Everybody into the conference room."

Once the gathering was seated, he stood at the head of the table and gave them a fifteen-minute presentation, including everything he had been provided by CISEN. When he was done, the room exploded in discussion. Cruz waited until the initial flurry had died down and motioned for quiet.

"Before we wind this down, are there any questions? I don't want any confusion. We'll be working very long hours. Lieutenant Briones will be the number two man if I can't be reached. You have complete authority to commandeer any resources you think you require, from any agency. If you encounter any resistance, let me deal with it. But we can't afford bureaucratic delays, so don't screw around or try to massage anyone's ruffled feathers. They either cooperate, or I'll get involved, and if necessary, run the issue all the way to the top. We've been given carte blanche by the president to do whatever's necessary to stop this, so there is no higher authority," Cruz told the room, catching each man's eyes as he spoke.

"How are you thinking we should proceed with the border checkpoints? They're notoriously lax, even if we raise the alert level to emergency status," Briones asked.

"That's one of the problems we have. It's not practical to staff each point with additional *Federales*, so we'll have to rely on whatever is currently in place. Besides which, the chances that we get lucky and catch him as he enters the country are slim to none. But we have to try," Cruz said. "I want the German's information circulated to immigration within the hour, and anyone even slightly resembling him questioned more intensely. Guillermo, what's deployment of the identification cameras like?"

Guillermo, one of the older officers in the room, shifted uncomfortably. "It's a joke. Only a few of them are active, and the system is plagued with problems."

"I thought the system was supposed to be active a year ago?"

"It was. Welcome to Mexico. It's been a never-ending stream of issues. Equipment theft, problems with connectivity, software issues. Long story short, it's not operational."

"How are we supposed to have a chance of catching him at the border if we can't access the data in anything resembling a timely fashion?" Claudio blurted. Everyone stared at him, and then Cruz spoke softly.

"We'll just have to do it the old-fashioned way, which is grossly inefficient and further reduces our odds. But we'll work with what we have." Cruz paused, then cleared his throat. "One final thing. We'll have a specialist working with us, courtesy of CISEN, and that may present some difficulty for a few of you. I'm going to ask that you put your personal feelings aside and focus on your duty, not your emotions. Trust me when I tell you that this was extremely unpopular with me, but it's a done deal, and isn't to be questioned. And it could turn out to be an advantage for us – at least that's what the experts have decided."

The men exchanged puzzled glances, and then a dark-complexioned man in his forties with a face like a losing prize fighter raised his hand. "Who, sir? Who is this mystery man we're going to have problems dealing with?"

Cruz sighed. "You know him by his professional name. *El Rey.*"

Half the group was too shocked to speak, and the others uttered stunned exclamations.

Briones went pale, shaking his head. "Is this...is this some sort of a joke, sir? *El Rey* working with us? How? Didn't he escape from prison?"

"It's a long story, but the essence of it is that he now works for CISEN, and received a full pardon for his crimes." Loud voices protested the announcement, and several of the men cursed, visibly outraged at the news.

"He works for CISEN? The man who tried to kill the president...how many times?" Guillermo barked.

Cruz allowed the men to vent for thirty seconds, and then spoke in his calmest voice. "Look. I don't like this any more than you do. But it's done. The authority comes from the president, who has the ability to do what he deems best for the country. And apparently having *El Rey* working for our intelligence agency is what he thinks is best," he said, looking at Claudio, who squirmed as the other men turned their attention to him – the only CISEN representative in the room.

"I had nothing to do with any of this. It was decided over my head. It's above my pay grade. But what *Capitan* Cruz says is true. This has everyone's blessing, and the thinking is that it takes one to find one. Remember that in addition to all his sins, he's also the best assassin anyone has ever seen. That can't be discounted."

"As much as I hate to say it, after having the night to think about it, CISEN's right. We don't have a lot to go on, so we need any edge we can get. So I'm going to ask all of you to park your objections and do your jobs. If you can't, speak up and I'll find a replacement for you – you can go back to headquarters and resume your duties, and I won't hold it against you. But I'll be disappointed, because I personally chose each of you. You're the best we've got. Having said that, I'll understand perfectly if you won't do it," Cruz said.

The men grumbled, but Cruz could sense that he'd won the round. Nobody quit, which was positive, even if not much of a victory.

As the meeting broke up, Briones approached Cruz, a look of confused concern on his face.

"Do you really believe this is best, sir?" he asked quietly, obviously struggling to keep his tone even.

"I have my orders, Lieutenant. I wasn't given a lot of options."

"You can always choose to decline the job, sir."

Cruz studied him before speaking, choosing his words carefully. "Who better to lead this group, Briones? Who has more experience chasing assassins than we do? Nobody. If I walk away from this, it would not only be a slap directly in the president's face, but it would decrease the odds of success in an already awful situation. How could I live with myself if the Chinese leader was slain on Mexican soil because I let my misgivings interfere with my duty?"

Briones sensed there was more to the story than his boss was letting on, but decided not to press. He trusted Cruz with his life, and if Cruz didn't feel like sharing anything more, it was his prerogative. Briones would follow his lead.

"Then I can hardly refuse to work on this with you, can I, sir?" Briones conceded.

"I mean it when I say that if you don't think you can bury your history with the man, you should back out. I won't hold it against you."

"I understand. That won't be necessary. The past is the past. And it actually sounds like we'll need all the help we can get."

"You got that right," Cruz said, then gestured for Briones to accompany him to his office.

The common area had already become a working situation room as they passed through it, and the men were settling into their workstations, some already on the phone, murmuring instructions and demands. As they approached Cruz's office, the entry door swung open and a figure dressed in head-to-toe black stepped in, looking around at the gathered officers before spotting Cruz and Briones, abruptly stopped in their tracks. The newcomer ignored the evil glares from the assembled men and moved towards Cruz, his gait fluid like that of a large jungle cat. Cruz touched Briones' arm and they continued to his office, where Cruz motioned for Briones to sit at the small corner table ringed by four chairs. The lieutenant took a seat, his eyes never leaving the black-clad figure.

El Rey stopped at the doorway and threw a small off-hand salute to Cruz. "So, I'm here. What do you have?" he asked, ignoring Briones.

"Thanks so much for joining us. Pity you missed the orientation meeting where I described our operation and data in detail," Cruz said sarcastically, his tone scathing.

If *El Rey* registered it, he gave no indication. "I'm here now."

Cruz decided that this wasn't the hill he was willing to die on, and motioned to the table. The assassin nodded and moved to one of the vacant seats, only then looking directly at Briones, his killer's eyes taking him in without expression as he eased himself into the chair. If looks could kill, *El Rey* would have been dead on the floor, but he seemed unfazed by Briones' seething glare.

Cruz sized up the situation and knew that this was the most difficult moment – he would need to get Briones past it for the man to be any use. He sat down behind his desk and waved a hand at the two men.

"Lieutenant Briones, this is...Carlos. You've met before, but it was in different circumstances. Not the best, I'll grant you."

"*Carlos*. How fitting. Someone has a great sense of humor," Briones said tonelessly.

"I moonlight as a comic. Now can we get to it?" *El Rey* said, impatience tingeing his words.

"You don't remember me, do you?" Briones asked, nearly whispering.

El Rey regarded him. "Of course I do. I never forget a face. You're lucky to be alive. Most who crossed my path aren't."

"Last time I saw you, you were wearing a nun's habit and bleeding out on my windshield," Briones spat.

"A greeting card moment, I'm sure." *El Rey* turned to Cruz. "For the last time. What have you got for me that was so important I needed to come in?"

Cruz took him through the various contingencies he had put into place, and *El Rey* listened silently until he was finished.

"You won't catch him at the border. That's a waste of time and energy," *El Rey* said.

"Perhaps, but we have to do it all the same," Cruz conceded.

"What, do you have some other suggestion? Something we've missed?" Briones snorted.

El Rey eyed Cruz. "*Capitan*, are you going to be able to keep your attack dog leashed, or is this going to be a recurring problem?" He leaned towards Briones across the table. "You need to let it go, or this isn't going to work. And you might get me angry. You don't want to get me angry."

"Are you threatening me?" Briones hissed, his upper body tensing.

"I'm giving you advice."

"Gentlemen, please. I know this is difficult. For all of us. But Lieutenant, stand down. That's an order. Remember our earlier conversation – if you can't do this, say the word and I'll replace you," Cruz interrupted.

Briones exerted a visible effort to restrain himself and shifted in his seat, the tension draining out of him. "That won't be necessary. I'm a professional."

"*Capitan*, this is all very touching, but you're wasting my time," *El Rey* said.

Cruz forgave the insolence and decided then and there that he wouldn't allow the assassin to get a rise out of him. That was simply playing into his game, and he wouldn't take the bait. "We were discussing the borders."

"Yes. Put simply, he'll get in without any effort, and you'll never know it. He's a pro. Borders never posed any problem for me. He'll have multiple identities, and be able to change his look at will. Some cotton in his mouth, a beard or moustache, any of a dozen drugs that will temporarily alter his complexion, skin dye... Even assuming that he comes through an airport or a border crossing, your amateur immigration people wouldn't know what they were looking at. That's a fool's errand. Just accept that he'll make to Mexico City, if he hasn't already."

"I'm not disagreeing, but we have to start somewhere," Cruz replied evenly.

"Not there."

"If not, then where, *Carlos*?" Briones asked, pronouncing his name like an insult.

"I want to know everything about the Chinese leader's itinerary. How he's arriving, how he's going to be transported, where he's going to sign the document, where he's going to be staying, if he stays at all. I'll need not only his agenda but a full rundown on every security precaution being taken. We start at the end – the point where the German will kill the target. Then we work backwards from there. Figure out how he's going to do it, or is likely to do it, and then we have a chance. But mount a manhunt and you're just spinning your wheels," *El Rey* stated flatly.

"In your opinion," Briones countered.

"Lieutenant. One person in this room has carried out more executions than you've had birthdays. The others are cops who got lucky one time. Do you want to stop this assassin, or do you want to posture like some sort of juvenile peacock? I don't really care, either way." *El Rey* stood. "When can you have that information?" he asked Cruz.

"I've already requested it all. We should have it within a few hours."

"Very good. Call me once you have everything, and make me a copy so I can study it. And I want to look over the location where the signing is to take place."

"I think the idea was that we work as a team on this," Cruz said.

"Teams fail more often than they succeed."

Cruz shook his head. "Maybe so, but we're going to do this my way."

"Get me the data, then we'll talk," *El Rey* said, and then moved to the door and opened it without another word.

Cruz and Briones watched incredulously as the assassin sauntered across the situation room floor and through the exit.

"Are you serious about working with him? I've never seen a more arrogant, dismissive prick in my life...," Briones began.

"Yes, Lieutenant, he's all of those things. But he has a point. Both times we hunted him, it was individual action and intuition that stopped him and ultimately resulted in his capture. Not a team. So while he's abrasive, he's also probably right. Which underscores why he's here. Not to win friends. To be right."

Briones considered Cruz's muttered observation. "I still don't like it."

"Neither of us do. But if we're going to be successful, we'll need to be flexible. And right now, Carlos is our best option."

"He's an annoying shit, in addition to all his other faults."

Cruz nodded. "Yes. He is. He is indeed."

Briones was seething, but he wore his best poker face as he rose. The stink of *El Rey*'s aura was like a toxic cloud in the room, and his passing left a subtle pollution of the soul that made Briones want to take a long shower to purge himself of the blight. He understood that Cruz believed this was the best way to progress, but it had been all he could do to resist drawing his gun and blowing the assassin's head off. The scar from where the killer's bullet had seared into his shoulder pulsed and burned as though it were a living thing with a mind of its own, and the memory of the other slug slamming into his chest, stopped only by the bulletproof vest, was as vivid as though it had been yesterday. Cruz could pontificate about duty and the mission all he wanted, but at his core, Briones only knew that the assassin had escaped justice and was flaunting that as if daring him to do anything about it. Briones moved to leave, but as he did, a vision of himself pulling the trigger of his weapon and watching *El Rey*'s filthy head explode clouded everything, and it was all he could do to get out of the office and to the bathroom before he threw himself into a stall and vomited his fury into the uncaring bowl.

CHAPTER 19

Five hours later, Cruz had gotten the itinerary and all the detail on the signing ceremony, and had forwarded it to *El Rey* at a blind account CISEN had created for his use. Thirty minutes later, Cruz's phone chirped at him.

"I got it. I want to head over to look over the physical location. I know it well – if you recall, it was the site of my red herring bomb gambit," *El Rey* said.

"Yes, I remember. Then you're already familiar with the possible approaches."

"Never assume anything. Things change, and there might be different avenues that he could exploit. I won't know until I spend some time there. Probably today until it gets dark, then all of tomorrow."

"What time are you going to be there?"

"I'm headed out right now. I'm notifying you as a courtesy, in the spirit of cooperation with CISEN. Frankly, you'll be unlikely to spot anything I wouldn't, so it's purely a formality."

"I still want to come. I'll meet you at the main entrance in...forty minutes."

"Don't bring an entourage, and for God's sake don't wear your uniform – it's a dead giveaway. For all we know he's already here, watching every move at the facility. I would be."

"Just you and I, then."

The assassin grumbled, obviously annoyed, then acquiesced. "If you say so."

Cruz dropped the phone back into his shirt pocket and re-entered the meeting he'd ducked out of and excused himself before going back to his office to change to civilian clothes. He'd brought a light duffle with pants and several shirts in case he needed to go incognito. He hurriedly changed, pulled his black windbreaker over his shoulder holster, and then moved to the bathroom to check his appearance before leaving. He hadn't slept well, and the hangover from the cheap wine was lingering, and he looked it. Checking his watch, he quickly calculated that his car could have him at the site within twenty minutes.

The ride to the Congress building took longer than he'd expected due to a traffic accident, and he was five minutes late when he sprinted up the steps to the massive array of steel and glass doors. Congress wasn't in session, so the area only had a few guards loitering around, *Federales*, but not the best-in-show by any means. Tourists climbed the long flight of wide stairs to have their pictures taken in front of the building, but Cruz didn't see *El Rey* anywhere.

When his phone sounded, he nearly jumped. He stabbed it on and held it to his ear. "Where are you?"

"Behind you."

Cruz slowly turned around, and watched as one of the doors opened and *El Rey* stepped out, waving at someone inside.

"How did you get in there?" Cruz demanded, *sotto voce*.

"I offered to help one of the maintenance workers with a box he was struggling with. It doesn't matter. We can assume that the interior of the building will be swept – but we should still insist that the guards get beefed up, effective immediately, and any maintenance or custodial staff be checked on a daily basis to ensure there are no new employees. I would have the area blocked off from now till the signing, and put draconian security measures in place. It would be child's play at this point to penetrate the building. Remember what I did at the cathedral. I posed as a maintenance worker at least a week before the event and stashed a grenade. Security never starts early enough, and that's one weakness we can avoid."

"A valid point." Cruz made a quick call and relayed instructions to Briones, who assured him that he would contact the appropriate agencies to coordinate it. When he was finished, he squinted at *El Rey*.

"What else?"

"From memory, there are literally dozens of vantage points from which a sniper could shoot anyone on a podium on these steps. Over there, there, there, and there. Just to name a few. And the German is a seasoned long-range sniper, so it opens up hundreds of places. Which means you'll have to widen the security perimeter to at least one kilometer on this side. Maybe more, just to be safe."

"What? One kilometer? Do you have any idea how many thousands of people live and work in that large an area?"

"Probably a lot. But you can make the job simpler by being selective and only sequestering the buildings where you would have a direct line of sight. It's still a huge area, but you can simplify your life by having the signing take place inside, and keeping the target off these steps. Then you'd only need to worry about the south side, near those doors, where he would enter the building."

"Fair enough. I'll alert the president's staff."

El Rey had frozen, transfixed by something, and Cruz followed his stare into the distance.

"The metro station will need to be treated as a risk area. Personally, I would cordon off the entire Congress building grounds effective immediately and make it a high security area until the event is over. The more of the vicinity that's off-limits, the lower the likelihood of a threat. You'll also need to be on the alert for everything from contact poison on any surface the Chinese leader comes into contact with, to a gas attack, to an assault on the motorcade. Oh, and a helicopter from the airport to the Congress would be preferable to surface transportation. Otherwise the route is going to be a nightmare. What is it, about two and a half kilometers from the airport? Every inch of which could pose a threat."

"All of this is threat reduction, not catching him," Cruz observed, making a note with his Blackberry.

El Rey continued, ignoring the complaint. "The biggest problem with a chopper would be a surface-to-air missile strike, or some kind of sabotage of the craft, like a hidden explosive charge, or hidden damage to the rotors or engine. I know what I'm talking about – let's just say I speak from experience."

"You...when...?"

"It's not important. But have all the maintenance staff checked and rechecked, and have the chopper gone over by explosives experts and mechanics looking for anything suspicious. And have the phone company block all cell phone use in this area until he's on his plane back home."

"Are you joking? That will impact millions of people."

"So will having the Chinese leader shot on Mexican soil. Or did I get that part wrong?"

Cruz took a few steps away from the assassin and stood, pensive, studying the buildings across the highway, each one concealing a potential deadly threat. Even now the German could be watching, undetected, putting the finishing touches on a plan they were powerless to stop unless they had an unprecedented stroke of luck – something that rarely happened, he knew.

"I'll also want to get a blueprint of the sewer system. I remember the last time I looked at this location that the sewers were a potential point of entry. I briefly considered a gas attack using the sewer system as a red herring, but then opted for the explosive device in the plant your men found."

"My men didn't find that – it was the security forces. They aren't complete incompetents, you know," Cruz corrected.

"Yeah. I know. Look at how effective they were at stopping me."

Both men stood studying the area, minds lost on the imponderables involved in averting the crisis.

"You've had a chance to look this over. How would you do it?" Cruz asked.

"Every assassin will have his preferred technique. One of my strengths was that I wasn't married to any particular one. I'd just as soon use a knife as a gun; a bomb as gas or poison. But our man is a shooter. Most of his attributed kills are with a sniper rifle – a shot, usually to the head. There's probably some ego involved there. He likes the challenge, the difficulty of the impossible shot."

"Then that's a weakness we may be able to exploit."

"Perhaps. But he's also used an RPG to blow up a car, as well as a pistol, at least twice, and has strangled, stabbed, and used explosives. So while he may prefer a rifle, he's flexible enough to alter his approach if circumstances dictate it. My hunch is that he'll try for a rifle shot, though, at first blush. It's just instinct, but if I was going to bet on it, that would be his method."

"If you're right then that would narrow things down, I would think."

"Yes, to only the buildings within a thousand meters or so. Which as you pointed out is a huge number. I wouldn't get celebratory quite yet."

"I know. But it's better than nothing."

"True. Right now we have two advantages. First, we know what he's planning – at least in a large sense. Second, he doesn't know we know. But you can expect that he will sooner or later – he'll have contacts either at Interpol or with the German police, and possibly also with the BND. He'll get word that he's been flagged, and then the real cat and mouse game will begin."

Cruz shook his head, fatigue from the prior night slamming into him as the enormity of the job ahead loomed large before him. It was worse than a needle in a haystack or being struck by lightning. At least you could increase your chance of a lightning strike.

"Do you really think we can find him?" Cruz asked softly, as much to himself as to his unlikely new associate.

"I think I can. The question is whether there's enough time, and whether you can keep your clumsy pack of wolves from worsening your odds. This will require delicacy – looking at the man's dossier, he's about as good as it gets."

Cruz frowned and rubbed his chin, where a light dusting of stubble had already begun forming.

"How about compared to you?" he asked.

The assassin stood silently for several moments, and then strode off, tossing his response over his shoulder.

"Nobody's that good."

CHAPTER 20

It was eight-thirty by the time Cruz had finished walking the grounds with *El Rey*, and he had his driver stop at a *torta* restaurant on the way home, pulling to the curb twenty yards from the busy café, a line of hungry commuters spilling onto the sidewalk, waiting to pick up their dinner. Most took it to go, wrapped in white paper, each sandwich the size of a small football. Cruz stood patiently amidst the throng – everything from laborers to pickpockets to businessmen on their way home from a long day in the office – and felt the last of his energy drain from him. It had been another long one, and tomorrow would be even worse, as the countdown to the event ticked away and the pressure mounted.

When he got to the counter he ordered his sandwich, and then, after a momentary consideration, ordered one for Dinah, too. She hadn't answered the phone the two times he had called, but that didn't necessarily mean anything – she was probably still angry; but she, like he, was a sucker for a good *torta*, and the gesture would hopefully win him points. His stomach growled audibly as he stood, patiently waiting for the cooks to finish their culinary ministrations, the rich aroma of cooking meat enveloping him as he salivated like a dog.

A portly older man in an indifferently cut gray business suit sidled up next to him and nodded a greeting, one of the courteous-yet-standoffish ways that residents of densely populated areas conveyed politeness without inviting conversation. That was just as well to Cruz, and he returned the nod. His mind was a million miles away, going over threat vectors, perimeter weaknesses, and the logistics of keeping the target alive for his stay.

Fortunately, the Chinese leader was scheduled to fly in, go straight to the Congress for the signing ceremony, then fly out, with a meeting and dinner already scheduled to take place in Washington with the U.S. President. He would arrive in the morning, and with any luck at all, leave, alive, a few hours later – just a quick stop on a diplomatic junket that would take him to twelve countries in a week.

El Rey, as much as Cruz hated to admit it, was as sharp as they came. He'd analyzed the surroundings with a professional eye and found countless weak spots that could be exploited by the German. Cruz had phoned in instructions to the security detail about changing the signing ceremony location to the interior of the Congress building, and was awaiting a formal approval. It was lunacy, given what they now knew, to have it take place as planned outside on the steps. His only problem was that the new president was an attention sponge, and would likely put up a fight to keep the photo opportunity outdoors, where he could be framed with the Congressional mural in the background, shaking hands with the Chinese leader and making a speech about new vistas and progress for tomorrow.

Cruz sincerely hoped that it wouldn't turn into a battle. He had enough on his hands without that. Although, when all was said and done, he served at the pleasure of the king, and if the president was adamant about holding the ceremony on the steps, there was little he could do except remind him about the *El Rey* assassination attempt and how close he'd come to being executed. Hopefully that would still be fresh in his mind. With the Iron Eagle on the loose, conducting the ceremony outside would be akin to suicide.

A three-hundred-pound woman with mahogany skin waddled to her customary position behind the counter with a plastic bag and called his number, and he pushed through the crowd to claim his meal. Out on curb, he peered into the bag with satisfaction, then strode to his waiting vehicle, where the driver leapt out and opened his door. Cruz felt a twinge of embarrassment at having a federal policeman in full regalia chauffeuring him, as he always did when he was in public places, and then dismissed the sentiment, choosing instead to focus on some of his very real problems.

El Rey was an enigma, but Cruz had to concede that perhaps CISEN had made a good call bringing him into the case. Cruz had developed a grudging respect for his approach as he had run through his mental list and issued tersely worded suggestions for Cruz to convey to the appropriate parties. No, truthfully, they had been *instructions*, not suggestions. Matter-of-fact and completely dispassionate, but orders nonetheless. The young man was definitely among the most arrogant Cruz had ever met, but it was more than that – his sense of assurance, the conviction that he was completely right, wasn't puffery. He was, in fact, right, about everything they'd discussed. He radiated a quiet confidence that was unnerving, and Cruz had found himself, by the end of their promenade, glad *El Rey* was on his side.

Not that Cruz was any slouch himself. But event security wasn't his forte – the truth was that if he hadn't gotten involved in the original assassination attempt in Cabo, he wouldn't have been dragged into the next one, and now this train wreck. That was how bureaucracies worked – you became an acknowledged expert in something even if the totality of your contribution was simply showing up enough times. Like it or not, Cruz had become the *El Rey* expert, and since his capture, obviously had been bumped up the hierarchy to the *de facto* resident assassination authority in general. A position he felt completely unqualified for – he was a career cop who specialized in the drug cartels that were tearing the nation apart, not a super-sleuth who could stop contract killers cold. But no matter. He had the title now, whether he liked it or not, which had resulted in him being blackmailed into running this show. Any protestations that he was unqualified to do so would just be met with smiles, the clueless wonks who made the decisions mistaking his legitimate protests for humility.

As they wove their way through the still-dense traffic, Cruz's thoughts turned to Dinah and the fight that his revelation had precipitated. She was usually logical, but he could understand what a shock *El Rey*'s re-emergence in their life was, and he knew it would take some time for her to adjust and realize that he really had no choice. Much as he might have wanted to give the power structure the middle finger and walk away from it all, it wasn't practical. Perhaps in the old days, ten years younger, he might have thrown caution to the wind and refused the assignment; but now, as he aged, he had developed what might have passed for budding wisdom.

That all of it was unfair was a given. And while the threat of withholding his pension had crossed important lines that might have stoked his moral outrage, it hadn't completely surprised him. He was a leaf on a stream, and when the men who ran the country wanted something from him, they would use whatever means they needed to in order to force him into compliance. It was a valuable lesson he would remember and use in the future – assuming he was successful. If he wasn't, he wouldn't need any bargaining chips. He would be the man who had allowed the unthinkable to happen on his watch. A man with a suddenly terminated career.

He dug his phone out one last time and called home, but just got ringing that went to voice mail. Same as all day. He next called Dinah's cell, but met the same response. He punched the call off and shook his head. This was worse than he thought. She'd never gone completely dark on him before. Maybe he'd underestimated how upset she was. He tried to put himself into her shoes – father killed by *El Rey*, blackmailed and forced to betray Cruz by *El Rey*, watching everything she valued almost destroyed by *El Rey*...

The security gate of the condo's underground parking entrance slid open, the motor straining to shift the iron barrier, and Cruz rehearsed what he was going to say to her. A plea for consideration. An assurance that it would all be over in a few more days. Perhaps even a promise to quit the force after it was finished and pursue the corporate security work she'd been pressing him about. All he knew was that he loved Dinah and didn't want her to be distressed, and the job had now strained their relationship beyond what it could reasonably bear. She'd been understanding of so much – having to live a transient lifestyle, moving constantly. Bodyguards. Most wouldn't have been willing to make the sacrifices she had. But it looked like she'd finally reached her limit.

He wasn't looking forward to the conversation to come.

The car rolled to a stop in front of the elevator. The driver waited until it arrived and Cruz stepped in before pulling off to the assigned parking space, where the night shift driver would take over in case Cruz needed to go somewhere in an emergency. That would be one of the two guards on permanent rotation in the lobby – a fixture of his living situation.

When the elevator slowed and stopped at his floor, he stepped into the hall and moved slowly to the condo, dreading what was to come. Some days he felt about a hundred years old, and this was one of them.

"Honey? I'm sorry I'm so late. I brought dinner," he called as he pushed open the front door. Silence greeted him, and the condo was dark. He flipped the lights on and walked to the kitchen, then set the bag with the sandwiches in it on the counter and listened for any signs of life. Again, nothing.

Cruz strode to the bedroom and peered inside, and his breath caught in his throat. A note lay on the dresser, folded neatly, as was Dinah's way. He approached it with trepidation, then picked it up like it was a poisonous snake and moved to the bedside lamp and flicked it into life. The writing was precise, the message short.

My darling husband,

I love you more than you will ever know, so this is the hardest letter I will ever write. I know you have your reasons for agreeing to work with that murderer, but I can't go along with it. You know how much misery he has brought to my family and the unforgivable things he's done, and I can't bring myself to wish anything but death upon him. For you to choose to cooperate with this travesty is a betrayal of everything we have, and I can't look at you knowing you would choose that over us – the relationship we've built. So I'm leaving. Maybe I will feel differently in time, maybe not, but for now, I can't go on. Just as with infidelity, there are some things that are too big to ignore. This is a deal breaker. I'm sorry, my love, but it is, and I can't be with a man who would do this to me. I wish you well, and hope you'll be safe and cautious. No good can come of this. Don't bother me at work – I don't want to hear from you. Please respect my wishes.

Your wife, Dinah.

Cruz numbly re-read the missive, unable to believe his eyes, and then his whole form seemed to collapse in on itself, as though the pressure of the unbearable atmosphere had crushed him like an empty beer can. He felt for the edge of the bed with a trembling hand, his eyes unfocused, searching his cognitive resources for where he had made a mistake understanding the meaning of the words. Dinah, gone? Left him? Impossible. He had gotten something wrong, misread some key indicator, misinterpreted some important bit of information.

The mattress pushed against the backs of his knees and he sat down numbly on the bedspread, which was neatly tucked in, probably one of Dinah's last acts in leaving a tidy vacuum in which Cruz would spend an eternity without her. He wasn't sure how long he sat, gazing into space with the thousand-yard stare of a chain gang prisoner, but eventually he was back in the moment and forced himself up. He approached the wide dresser and pulled open the top drawer of Dinah's side, and didn't need to look down to confirm what its weight already had. Empty: her clothes gone, only the faint smell of her perfume lingering in the wooden rectangle.

He turned and moved to the closet and swung the doors open, and saw what he expected – her luggage missing, her side of the space empty. He stared at the empty clothes rod, the barren shelves, and the enormity of the situation hit home.

She was gone.

Dinah was gone.

Like an automaton, Cruz selected a speed dial number on his phone and pressed *send*. Two rings, and a deep male voice answered.

"Yes, sir. Is there a problem?"

"You tell me. Did you see Dinah today? My wife?" Cruz asked one of the men on duty downstairs in the lobby.

"No, sir. But I only came on duty at eight tonight. Why? Is something wrong?"

Cruz ignored the question. "Who was working the day shift?"

"Diego Vasquez and his partner. Do you want me to try to reach him?"

"Yes, please. My wife may have left...on vacation. I'd just like to confirm that someone saw her."

"Very good, sir. I'll call and then get back in touch with you."

Cruz disconnected, and then sat down again, staring at the closet's maw, the emptiness like a shrine to his failure as a husband and a man.

He knew what the call would say.

When it came a few minutes later, it was as he thought.

"Sir, she took several suitcases down to her car and then left. There was no foul play. Do you...is there something we should do? Something we need to know?"

Cruz thought about it for a moment, then sighed. "No, that's fine. I just wanted to verify that she got out of here okay. That's all."

When he hung up, he tossed the phone onto the bed and lay back, everything redolent of Dinah – the pillows, the sheets, the air itself. Twenty minutes later he was fast asleep, snoring gently, fully clothed, his body having finally succumbed to its requirement for rest.

CHAPTER 21

Guatemala City was blanketed in smog as the flight from Chile dropped on the final descent, buffeted by updrafts from the mountains surrounding the metropolis. The tired Boeing 737 was on its last legs, running routes between South and Central America after being retired from a U.S. airline, and the seat that Werner Rauschenbach occupied was at least forty years old if it was a day, the cushion and springs having long ago given up any pretense of offering comfort.

A particularly violent gust shook the plane and it lurched to one side, and then the jet dropped a few hundred feet in seconds, the sensation much like that of a roller-coaster, but missing the assurance of a safe conclusion to the ride. The cracked ventilation nozzle overhead whistled a malodorous stream of stagnant air at his pate, serving no purpose other than to annoy him during the final half hour on the long trip from Santiago. He reached up and twisted the air off, and then peered out the window at the dark gray bank of clouds below. It wouldn't be long now, and then this leg of his journey would be over and he would be traversing the third-world Guatemalan countryside on his way to the coast, where he would embark on an ocean voyage that would have him rendezvousing with a Mexican fishing trawler that night, five miles offshore, which would ferry him into Mexico without having to deal with niggling details like customs or immigration.

Another bump and a loud grinding hum vibrated from the wings as the flaps activated in preparation for landing. They dropped into the overcast and the plane was knocked around like a lottery ball before they broke through and he could make out the city dead ahead in the early morning light. When the wheels struck the runway and the engines screamed as the plane fought to slow before it ran out of space, Rauschenbach closed his eyes and exhaled evenly, thankful that the long hours on planes from Spain were finally over.

The fishing rod gambit had worked like a charm, and his precious cargo was safe in the belly of the jet, none the worse for the transatlantic journey. If all went well, he would be in Mexico City the following evening, at the latest. It would all depend on the efficiency of the group he'd arranged to smuggle him into the country. The Los Zetas cartel had established a considerable network in Africa, with a drug pipeline to most of the major regions in the Russian Federation and Europe, and it had been merely a matter of spreading a boatload of cash around to find the right conduits to arrange for his safe passage once in Guatemala. The cartel had almost complete control of whole sections of the country, and it routinely moved drugs, arms, slaves, and illegal immigrants from the beleaguered Central American nation into Mexico, so if anyone could get him in without triggering alarms, Los Zetas could.

The plane taxied to the terminal and the safety lights winked off, and Rauschenbach waited patiently as the tired travelers queued up to disembark, the atmosphere redolent of the peculiar dank odor of wet dog and slightly burnt wool that was a constant on long flights. The couple in front of him started moving slowly down the aisle to the exit, and he hoisted his carry-on and dutifully followed them, for all appearances a fatigued businessman.

Immigration and customs were cursory, and within twenty minutes he had retrieved his fishing rod and reel cases and had made his way to the taxi stands, where he gave the driver of a tired Nissan station wagon an address on the outskirts of the city. The morning traffic was light, it still being well before business hours in the commercial district, and in no time they pulled to the curb near a dilapidated restaurant featuring a hand-painted image of a dancing goat playing pan pipes on a precariously mounted sign over a grimy picture window. The German flipped a few notes of the local currency to the appreciative driver and then watched as the cab rattled down the cobblestoned street, mud and oil coagulating along the filthy gutters like toxic plaque.

Inside, a hard-looking man in his fifties looked up from his position by the cash register when Rauschenbach entered with his bags and took a table in the corner. He was the only patron, and the proprietor seemed unenthusiastic about his good fortune in having attracted a customer. He approached carrying a stained laminated menu and handed it to the German, and then asked in a rapid-fire burst of Spanish whether he wanted coffee and was going to be ordering breakfast. Rauschenbach answered that, yes, he was indeed going to be taking his morning meal there, and then used the series of code words that had been agreed upon several days before. The man's eyes widened, then he nodded and gestured for his guest to follow him to the back of the shabby establishment. They passed a kitchen that more resembled a science experiment than a place to cook food, and Rauschenbach was glad he hadn't chosen to avail himself of whatever passed for breakfast there.

In the rear of the building, his guide knocked on a dark wooden door, and after a few moments it swung open and a younger man, perhaps in his late twenties, stood staring at the new arrival, a pair of opaque sunglasses shielding his eyes in spite of the dim light.

"You ready to get going?" the young man asked, looking him over.

"Yes. But I'll want to get something to eat. If you don't mind, I'd just as soon pick up a roll and some coffee somewhere to go," Rauschenbach said. "No offense."

"None taken. I don't eat here either. You have the money?"

"As agreed. You want it now?"

"Yes. Give it to him." He motioned to the older man, and Rauschenbach pulled a wad of American currency bound with a rubber band from his back pocket and handed it over. The man counted it quickly, and then nodded.

"All right. You're in business. Now let's get out of here – we're already running late," the younger man said, then offered to help carry the German's bags. Rauschenbach handed him the reel case and trailed him out the back door to where a battered baby-blue Ford Ranger pickup truck waited in the alley. The man placed the reels into the cargo bed and Rauschenbach did the same with the rod case, preferring to keep his carry-on bag with him in the cab. The proprietor watched from the doorway, absently scratching his belly, and then pulled the rusting steel slab closed and bolted it.

A cloud of dark smoke belched from beneath the truck's bed, and then the engine settled into a rough idle as the young man put the truck in gear. Neither man was feeling chatty, so they bounced down the street in silence before turning onto a larger artery and making for the road that led north, out of the city.

The hundred miles to the coast took six hours to navigate, and it was after lunch time when they arrived at the ocean side town of Champerico, roughly twenty-five miles south of the Mexican border, whose chief attractions as far as the German could tell were a mosquito-infested lake and a black sand beach. They drove down the dismal main street, past buzzing motor scooters and un-muffled cars, until they hit the waterfront, such as it was – a sad string of thatched-roof open air restaurants and some of the most squalid looking hotels Rauschenbach had seen outside of Africa. The truck eased to a stop in front of one of the most unlikely structures, whose weathered sign proclaimed it to be the Hotel/Restaurant Submarino, and the young man, who hadn't spoken six words since they'd left Guatemala City, pointed to the building.

"Take a room there, wait until night, and at ten, as the restaurant is closing, be outside. Someone will pick you up and take you to the boat. You'll go up the coast and meet the Mexican ship in open water, and before you know it you'll be back onshore, this time in Mexico."

Rauschenbach nodded, then climbed out of the cab and retrieved his rod case and reels before making his way into the ramshackle lobby. He rang the countertop bell and paid for a room as the truck pulled away, belching oily exhaust as it retraced its route out of town, the driver eager to get back to the city before dark. The clerk was an ancient woman with a face that spoke of a lifetime of drudgery, and she took his money without interest before pushing a worn brass key across the wooden counter as she croaked out a room number, a single stubby finger pointed at the ceiling.

He trudged up two flights of creaky stairs, toting his luggage without any offer of help from the cheerful staff, and when he opened the room door he left it wide for a few minutes so the pungent odor of disinfectant and mildew could blow off. After a dubious look around the small quarters he set his luggage on the bed and weighed his need to get some food into his stomach against the non-existent hotel security. He eventually decided to take his carry-on with him, and after locking the corroding deadbolt, descended to the ground floor and walked thirty yards down the beach to the nearest restaurant, from where he would be able to keep an eye on his room while he ate.

The fish was fresh and delicious, and after a relaxed meal, watching the surf roll gently onto the beach, children running, screaming along the sand, peals of laughter marking their delighted passage as an indifferent flock of gulls wheeled languorously over the water, he ordered a second bottle of the excellent local beer and considered his upcoming job. Once in Mexico City he would need to buy some specialized equipment he hadn't felt comfortable trying to transport from Spain, and he wanted to verify that his preliminary choice of locations for the assassination was viable. The job had been contracted on relatively short notice – much shorter than he would have preferred – but he was confident that if the Chinese leader could be killed, he would do so. It was all a question of timing and method, nothing more. No matter how exalted or insulated a target might be, there was always a way.

Satiated and tired, he returned to his room and set his phone alarm to wake him at nine forty-five. He would skip dinner and make up for the sleep he had lost traveling, then be ready for whatever was thrown at him that night. The bed was only slightly better than sleeping on the hood of a car, but at least it was quiet, and the breeze from the ocean cooled the air that wafted through the barred open window of his room. He was asleep in minutes, and slept soundly until the screeching of the alarm jarred him awake.

The night was inky black, any stars obscured by a coastal marine layer, and he had to pay close attention to keep from tumbling down the unlit stairs as he carried his bags to the road. When he rounded the building's corner, he came face to face with a figure in a green hoodie, smoking a cigarette. The man looked him up and down, flicked the butt into a nearby puddle of black liquid, and turned towards the ocean.

"Come on," the man said gruffly, and Rauschenbach accompanied him down the beach.

Soon they were at a pier that jutted into the darkness, and they traversed three quarters of the length before the man abruptly stopped and pointed to the railing.

"There."

They moved to the pier's edge. Rauschenbach glanced over and saw the faint outline of an open skiff bobbling in the water, a single outboard motor mounted on the stern, and a figure dressed in dark clothing sitting in the bow. His guide took the rod case and the reels from him and dropped each over the rail to the man below, who caught them and stowed them in the boat. Rauschenbach swung himself over the side, climbed down a corroding steel ladder, and was in the boat in moments, his carry-on bag jammed under the bench seat. The motor cranked to life as the man on the pier untied the line and tossed it into the bow, and within seconds they were easing into the night, a date with a fishing trawler imminent.

"How long will it take to get to the rendezvous point?" Rauschenbach asked once they were underway.

"Three, maybe four hours. The seas will get bigger once we veer away from the shore, so we'll have to go slow once we get closer. The final ten kilometers will take the longest — it's supposed to be ugly out there tonight. Bad luck for you. Hope you don't get seasick easily."

"I don't. How rough?"

"Two-meter seas with white water, but it should die down by the time we hook up. But you never know with the ocean. Sometimes she don't read the weather report," the seaman cackled.

Rauschenbach turned and watched the bow as it sliced through the waves, already substantial even this close to the beach, and hunkered down for a difficult few hours, eyes squinting against the salt spray, his back already sore from the slamming of the hull against the sea's frothy surface as they pounded their way north.

CHAPTER 22

Cruz studied his reflection in the bathroom mirror with a sort of numb detachment as he went about his morning ablutions, the condo silent other than the sound of water splashing in the sink and his slippers shuffling against the bathroom floor. Finished with his joyless ritual, he rinsed and dried his face with a freshly cleaned towel that reinforced his aloneness. She had done the laundry before leaving – was that cause for hope? Did it mean anything more than that she had tossed some items into the stacked washer/dryer before he'd gotten home and dropped his bombshell, and had put the laundered items back into their proper place before abandoning him? Or was it a sign – that she cared enough about him to want him to be taken care of, and that this entire episode might be about her getting her point across in an unmistakable way?

His musings wound around one another, each idea giving birth to ten more flashes of thought, the notions intertwining like a serpentine Gordion knot. He checked the time and realized that he'd spent more of his morning than usual getting ready – moving about in a haze, his mind elsewhere.

The distinctive sound of his cell phone warbled from the bedroom, and he practically tripped over his own feet in his haste to reach it. He held it to his ear, only to hear Briones' voice.

"Good morning, sir. I hope I'm not calling too early?"

"No...no, of course not. What is it – is something wrong?"

"Not at all. I was just calling because I'm leaving my place, and I wanted to see if you felt like going to the site with me and showing me around? So that we're all on the same page?" Briones suggested.

Cruz had told him that he was going to the Congress building the next day to review the layout with the assassin, and he realized that Briones probably felt excluded. He kicked himself for not including him and nodded as he spoke.

"Of course. I'm sorry. So much was going on yesterday...I'd value your input on the location."

"If you like, I can pick you up. I can be at your place in twenty minutes or so."

Cruz suddenly realized that he would enjoy the company. Anything to get his mind off the current situation. Briones was reaching out to him. There was zero reason not to take advantage of the offer.

"That would be great. I'll be down on the street waiting for you," Cruz said, then hung up.

❧

Down the block, the disconnecting cell line flipped a green light to red on an elaborate panel in the rear of a van, and a swarthy man with a faint white scar running along his right jawline from a knife gash, a souvenir from his frivolous youth, pulled off a pair of headphones and tossed them onto the console, then fished a phone from his shirt pocket and placed a call.

"Change of plans. Abort on the garage." The rest of the conversation took place in a hushed whisper, and by the time he disconnected, the beginnings of a grin were creasing his face – an ugly sight even under the best of circumstances.

❧

Cruz eyed the text message that had just come in as he rode down to the lobby level on the elevator, and swore under his breath as the building's reinforced concrete skeleton killed the cell signal, blocking his ability to respond until he was in the lobby. He had sent a request to his assistant at headquarters to run a computer search on hotels for any trace of Dinah, using both her real name as well as her newly adopted, government-issued alias. She was requesting a written confirmation from him, even if just a message, so that she could use it to force the relevant department to comply.

When the elevator reached the ground floor, he gripped his briefcase and dropped the phone back into the breast pocket of his uniform before brushing imaginary dandruff from his left shoulder with his now free hand.

Regardless of what was going on in his personal life, he needed to put on a brave front and be professional – there was a lot at stake in this operation, and he couldn't afford to be scattered, his mind on his domestic worries.

The door slid to the side with a whoosh, and Cruz stepped into the lobby, the day shift of his security team having arrived a few minutes earlier, the smell of their freshly brewed coffee flooding the area as they watched the front entrance and joked with the lobby attendant. Both men's demeanors instantly changed when they registered Cruz's presence, and their relaxed postures stiffened as they realized that their boss was there – they normally didn't see him, his comings and goings limited to the underground parking area.

He looked the men over, their submachine guns hanging from uniformed shoulders, and made a mental note to instruct them to come to work in plainclothes. They were about as subtle as a fireworks display, and even the most oblivious tenants had to be wondering why the *Federales* were holding an armed vigil in their building.

"As you were, officers," Cruz said, responding to their worried glances. "I'm being picked up this morning by a colleague. Condo's empty."

"Yes, sir," the older one barked, a twenty-something squat man who resembled nothing so much as a bulldog wearing a badge. His partner looked indecisive, as though wondering whether it was necessary or desirable for him to voice assent as well, and Cruz waved them off with an absent hand as he ran the morning's tasks through his head. He would spend an hour, maybe two, at most, with Briones at the Congress, and then he had to get back to the office to pore over whatever intelligence had come in overnight. Cruz had total respect for his team and didn't doubt their thoroughness, but his experience demanded that he study the data himself – nobody would do as comprehensive a job as he would, and he couldn't afford to discover two days from now that a report had gotten overlooked that would have led them to the German.

The bulldog rushed from the reception console to the front door and made a display of opening it for Cruz, who nodded his thanks, his mind worrying over what he would do if the hotel search resulted in a hit. Dinah had expressly forbidden his bothering her at her work, and he would honor her wishes, but she hadn't specifically said anything about wherever she was staying.

He stepped through the door onto the sidewalk and was reaching for his cell again when his peripheral vision detected something unusual – movement, hurried, from between two cars twenty yards down the sidewalk, the suddenness unlike the rest of the sparse pedestrian traffic going about its morning business in the largely residential downtown block. His eyes instinctively moved to the commotion, some primitive portion of his brain signaling danger to his body even before his conscious mind had time to process it, and a split second later he was reaching for his pistol and ducking to the side, trying for whatever cover he could find as two menacing-looking men raised the ugly snouts of their compact micro Uzis as they rushed him.

Time compressed and his sensory awareness narrowed as he freed the Glock 21 from his hip holster with one hand while he tossed his briefcase aside and then threw himself behind the rear fender of a nearby Chevrolet Lumina. He was chambering a round in the powerful .45 caliber handgun when the stuttering bark of the micro Uzis shattered the quiet, and concrete divots tore out of the sidewalk near his left leg.

Screams echoed off the building façades as passers-by ducked for safety in doorways and behind cars, and then Cruz's handgun began its lethal coughing, and slug after slug slammed into the lead gunman, knocking him off his feet and sending him hurtling back into his companion. Cruz dropped flat against the ground and fired at the second assailant's legs from under the car, the third shot shattering his ankle in a spray of bone and blood. The attacker fell forward, still gripping his gun, and Cruz shot him in the torso as his body hit the concrete.

The distinctive grouping of a load of double-ought buckshot puckered the fender above Cruz's back, and he instantly rolled, firing as he did. A tall, thin man wearing a long overcoat, presumably to cloak the pump-action pistol-stock shotgun he was pointing at Cruz, stumbled backwards as a round caught him in the middle of the chest, a red blossom spreading on his white dress shirt as his eyes glassed over and he tumbled onto his back. The shotgun skittered harmlessly away as he lay still, and then time resumed its ordinary flow as Cruz's tunnel-vision broadened and his awareness returned to normal.

He slowly stood from behind the bullet-riddled Lumina and scanned the street, wary of another attack. The two *Federales* from the condo burst through the entrance, guns at the ready, a few seconds too late, their eyes wide at the carnage – the gunmen lying in pools of thick blood, bullet holes peppering the nearby cars. Cruz had counted his shots and knew he had another four rounds in the Glock, but he still felt vulnerable, his pulse hammering in his ears as his eyes roamed over his surroundings.

Satisfied that the immediate danger was over, he strode purposefully to the surviving gunman, who was moaning, clutching his wounded stomach, his skin blanched from shock and pain. When Cruz got to him he stood over the man's prone form, pistol trained on his head.

"Who sent you?" he demanded, his tone silky but deadly.

"Fuck you," the gunman snarled through clenched teeth.

"Fuck *me*? Right now your bowels are leaking shit into your abdominal cavity, mixing with your blood, which is seeping onto the street. The pain will get worse in a few minutes, and by the looks of it, you'll lose your foot unless you get cared for quickly. They tell me that there are few more painful ways to die than a gut wound, but it can take a while. Tell me who you are, and I'll ensure an ambulance is here in minutes. If not, well, you know how bureaucracies are. The inefficiency can be a killer. Things that should take a few moments can take hours."

The attacker considered Cruz, then shook his head. "They'll kill me if I talk."

"I think you're unclear on how this works. You're dead unless you get to a hospital quickly. But it'll be an excruciating death, I can assure you. Do you really want to trade a possible death in the future for a certain, agonizing one right now?" Cruz knew he had to get the man talking or he was going to lose him to shock. And it was only a matter of a few short minutes before he lost consciousness from blood loss.

"I...I can't."

Cruz shook his head and scowled. "Then say hello to the devil for me. You'll be seeing him shortly."

Cruz stepped away, and scraped a trace of the man's blood from the sole of his shoe. Then he appeared to reconsider. "Last chance. Who sent you? This is over. You failed. If you don't die here, and I don't put you into protective custody, you'll be dead within a day of hitting the jailhouse floor. Especially if a rumor circulates saying you cooperated with us. So choose. You want death today, death at the end of a shank in a few weeks if you survive today, or death in old age? It's your choice. Make it."

The man just shook his head, then winced, his face contorted by the agony of the stomach wound.

"Have it your way." Cruz spit at his feet and holstered his weapon, then turned at the sound of tires screeching to a stop in the street next to him. He ducked as he whipped his pistol back out and pirouetted to face the new threat.

Briones leapt from the dark blue Dodge Charger and ran towards him. "What the hell happened?" he asked, his weapon drawn.

Cruz exhaled noisily in relief and slid his Glock back into place, then pointed at the three downed assailants.

"Hit team. Three of them; or if there were more, the others turned tail when they saw their buddies eat it."

"But how...?"

"Good question. That one's alive, but he refuses to talk. Got him in the leg and the stomach. The other ones, dead as mackerels."

Briones regarded the wounded man dispassionately. "That's got to hurt."

"I offered him help, but he seems to feel that he'd be better off dying today. Make sure that everyone takes their time processing the scene, and that the ambulance takes the long way. I don't want it leaving with him until there's an armed escort, in case his friends decide to try to break him out or silence him. I understand that could take a while, but it's only prudent."

The downed man was listening to the instructions, and at the last statement, groaned. "All right. Just get me to a hospital," he begged, his resolve cracking.

"After you tell me who sent you. Better speak up. Once I leave, you're out of luck."

Cruz approached closer so as not to miss what he was going to say. He needn't have bothered. The gunman raised his head and licked pink spittle from his lips, then grimaced as he dropped it back against the hard concrete and reached a tentative hand to his side to trace a simple design in his own blood.

Briones and Cruz stood frozen in place as he finished. His final reserve of strength spent, he closed his eyes and croaked two words.

"You're dead."

Cruz and Briones stepped away, the killer's symbol unmistakable.

He had scratched a single letter in the coagulating crimson fluid, which had remained like a rusty brand before losing its form and becoming just more of his life draining into the gutter.

A lone character, in and of itself innocuous, but in this context, blood-chilling.

Z.

The universal symbol for the most violent and deadly criminal syndicate in Mexico.

Los Zetas.

CHAPTER 23

Dinah spit toothpaste into the shower drain and then set the toothbrush on the ledge as she rinsed the shampoo from her hair, the warm surge of water making her scalp tingle from its needle-like pressure. She closed her eyes and luxuriated as the stream washed away her worries along with the apricot-scented body rinse that the hotel provided its guests. Steam filled the glass-enclosed marble stall as Dinah fiddled with the shower handle, then twisted it off with a resigned sigh. First day on her own, and she had a lot to do, a lot to think about – she couldn't hide in the bathroom forever, much as the idea appealed to her.

She stepped onto the cushy bath mat and toweled herself dry, serenaded by the whirring hum of a tiny exhaust fan sucking the moist air out into the city sky, then moved to the sink to begin her morning ritual. Fortunately, it was quick – Dinah had never been a big makeup fan, and was as low-maintenance as anyone she knew. She pulled a brush through her thick black hair and inspected herself, then nodded with satisfaction. She didn't look nearly as lost and confused as she felt – the reflection staring back at her was of a confident woman in her prime, not the insecure schoolgirl she felt like today.

Her first errand would be to find a less expensive hotel than the one she'd chosen on a whim. While it was one of the nicer in Mexico City, that luxury came at a steep price, and it was unsustainable for more than a couple of nights. She'd been so anxious to get out of the condo while Cruz was still at work that she hadn't really thought through what she would do from there, but she'd kicked the can down the road long enough, and today was the first day of her newfound freedom – a thought that terrified her more than anything. She loved her husband, and even with all the complications of his job, their life together was one she treasured and which fulfilled her.

So why had she reacted so dramatically to his announcement? It had been visceral, and no matter how hard she had tried to talk herself down, every time she thought about Cruz working with that...that evil scum, she went a little crazy. Even though she'd thought enough time had passed that she could react logically and dispassionately, the truth was that her thoughts were flooded with the bloody images of her father, bisected with the Japanese sword in his apartment, and then of the assassin forcing her to spy on Cruz and betray him. She still remembered the hurt in his eyes when he'd confronted her with her deeds, and between the savage killing of her dad and the assassin's cold-blooded manipulation of her...

Enough, she chided herself, and then exited the bathroom to dress. At least she didn't have to worry about work today – she'd taken a few days off, so if Cruz was tempted to not honor her request to leave her in peace, he wouldn't find her at the school where she taught second grade. She wanted – no, she needed – the time to herself so she could get clear on how to proceed. She was old enough to know that offering ultimatums that left no wiggle room for the other party was a recipe for disappointment. Everything in life was about compromise, and in her more lucid moments, she realized that she hadn't left Cruz anywhere to go. She'd boxed him in and ignored his reasons for taking the assignment, which had felt good at the time, but now seemed rash and counter-productive.

Her father had always been so good at counseling her, listening patiently to her concerns and objections, and then always reminding her that she needed to get clear on what she wanted out of any situation. "What's your objective?" was his favorite question when she was conflicted, and it had always forced her to focus on the end-result rather than her feelings as she went through the process.

So what's your objective with this stunt, Dinah? Her inner voice would have to stand in for her father now that *El Rey* had ended his life in a flash of brutality. The thought flooded her with rage, and she felt herself losing her grip on the reasonable, calm perspective she'd been coaxing into bloom that morning.

Just shut up. Not everything has to be deconstructed. Sometimes your gut was right.

Perhaps, she argued with herself. And sometimes your gut was just rationalizing your bad decisions, or anticipating them.

She slipped her jeans on and pulled a light sweater over her head – the weather was cool, typical for spring in the city. At least it wasn't raining. Dinah glanced at the room service tray with the half-eaten toast, the remnants of her *huevos rancheros*, and a pot of excellent coffee, and felt the urge to procrastinate return.

Another cup before she got going wouldn't hurt, and it would help get her fully awake. There was no harm. And she'd certainly paid enough for it. A liter of coffee at the hotel was eight times the price of a liter of gasoline, and all they had to do was run boiling water through some grounds.

A knock at the door startled her out of her funk, and she considered ignoring it before thinking better of it. She moved to the door and leaned into it.

"Who is it?" she asked.

"Housekeeping," answered a female voice, muffled by the door.

Dinah squinted, peering through the peephole, and saw a short, middle-aged woman with her hair pulled back in a severe bun, wearing a dark blue apron over her uniform. The woman looked bored out of her mind, and had the air of defeat that a life of harsh blows cultivated. Dinah felt a stab of guilt – here she was, feeling sorry for herself, dining like royalty and preening like a movie star at a private spa, when the less fortunate were having to clean up after her, day after mind-numbing day, with nothing on the horizon but an endless future of the same.

"I'm not...oh, never mind. Just a second. I'm just leaving," Dinah called, then edged to the bed and sat down before fumbling to put on her running shoes. She cinched the laces tight, taking care to double-tie each knot, then stood and collected her things – her purse, the light jacket she had worn out of the condo, her cell phone. Her wad of emergency cash was still in the room safe, and she momentarily considered pulling it out, then discarded the idea. It was safer in there than on the streets of Mexico City – one of the most dangerous cities in the northern hemisphere. She checked the time and calculated that she had three more hours before she had to check out or pay for another night, so she didn't have to rush herself with finding something more affordable – assuming that she didn't decide to return to the condo and compromise.

After scanning the room one last time, she picked up the tray with her meal on it and approached the door, then set it on the chest of drawers by the entry.

When she unlocked the deadbolt, she was surprised to see that there was a man in a suit standing just behind the maid, and then everything happened fast and became a pain-hazed blur. Her legs lost their ability to support her and every nerve ending simultaneously exploded with agony as the demure service woman pressed a stun gun against her throat and zapped her. Synapses misfired as the jolt knocked her off balance, and she collapsed backwards towards the bed as the maid and the man moved into the room before closing the door softly behind them.

A band of pain tightened around her chest like a vise as wave after wave of electric shock pummeled her. The tray with her breakfast on it crashed to the floor as the pair struggled with her, and then the last thing she registered before everything went black was the man, a leer twisting his features, leaning over her with a syringe in his hand while the woman looked on, expressionless.

CHAPTER 24

The office was filled with activity when Cruz and Briones finally made it in, and after catching the sidelong glances from the gathered officers both men knew that word had already circulated about the botched attempt on Cruz's life. That wasn't surprising – the *Federales*, like all law enforcement agencies, were a tight-knit group, and when something as shocking as an execution attempt against the ranking member of the elite anti-cartel task force took place, the news would spread like wildfire.

Cruz was in no mood for lengthy explanations, but he needed to get everyone's minds back on the job, so he stood near his office door and called for everyone's attention. The common area grew still, all eyes on him, and when one of the phones rang, an officer snatched it up, and after listening for a few seconds, told the caller in a hushed voice that he would get back to him.

"By now it's obvious that everyone's heard about the morning's events. Let's address it so we can move on. Three cartel members tried to ambush me outside my building today. Two are dead for their efforts, and the third probably won't make it – and if by some miracle he does, he'll be walking on sticks for the rest of his life. I've called for additional security for these offices, which is now in place, so there's nothing to worry about. But it seems that I angered someone important, and they wanted to express their displeasure in an unmistakable way. I don't want to overdramatize this or have it divert attention from our work, so that's all I'm going to say about it. An investigation is ongoing," Cruz said, hoping that would end the matter.

One of the men in the back raised his hand and spoke. "Any idea which cartel?"

Cruz had expected it, and had decided to hedge after swearing Briones to secrecy. "We're not sure, but it has all the earmarks of Los Zetas.

Specialized automatic weapons, ex-military personnel, the works. They were good. Just not good enough. That's confidential, by the way, for your ears only. I don't want any discussion outside of this room. Are there any other questions?"

"Are you okay?"

"Yes, of course. It takes more than a few punks with pea shooters to take me down."

Cruz studied the assembled men with an expression that didn't invite further inquiry, and after a few moments of silence, he wrapped it up.

"That's it for the drama. Everyone get back to work. We're running out of time."

The men broke into murmured conversation as they returned to their tasks, and Cruz spun and moved towards his office, then looked over his shoulder at Briones.

"Come in, sit down, and close the door," he ordered, then strode to his desk and sat behind it. He slid open a drawer as Briones took a seat and withdrew a box of bullets, then ejected the magazine from his Glock and reloaded it.

"I need a new condo. It's pretty obvious that location is blown. Please arrange for it. By tonight, if possible – send the crew in and have them pack everything. There's some cash in my nightstand and some personal papers in the desk. I'll want a signed inventory from whoever's in charge. If a new place can't be arranged by tonight, I'll need a hotel room and security," Cruz rattled off with precise, practiced efficiency.

"I'll get right on it," Briones assured him.

"I also want regular reports on the condition of the shooter, and whether he'll make it. It's possible we can get more out of him."

Briones nodded, nothing to add.

"Get a full listing of all suspected Los Zetas we know about in D.F., as well as any rumored associates. I want to know who directed this. We need to respond."

"I'll put a team on it at headquarters."

"Launch a full investigation into the affairs of every person who knew the condo's location. That's a very small group of people. Maybe we'll get lucky and there will be some trace of unusual financial activity – big cash deposits or some lavish purchases. I doubt it, but you never know."

"Yes, sir. It had to be someone in the inner circle. Your living arrangements are as close to a state secret as we have."

"Somebody sold me out. I hate to believe it, but that's the only thing that makes sense. That means nobody can know about the new place, except for you, me, the person in charge of leasing it, and God. And I'm pretty sure I don't want Him to have the exact address if it isn't absolutely necessary."

"Consider it done, sir."

Cruz hesitated, and seemed to fight an internal battle before continuing. He issued instructions for another five minutes, as Briones scribbled frantic notes. When Cruz had covered everything he could think of, he again cautioned the younger man about confidentiality before he dismissed him. Briones assured him that he understood, then exited the office and went to his workstation to begin making calls.

Cruz held his right hand out and studied it. A slight tremor, almost imperceptible, the by-product of the massive adrenaline rush from the morning's excitement. He'd had worse.

He rose and strode to the coffee machine to prepare a new pot, taking his time with the task, a sort of therapy, a ritual that calmed his nerves. Once done, he returned to his seat and placed his cell phone on the desk in front of him, and then, nodding to himself, pressed a speed dial key and lifted it to his ear. The line rang, then forwarded to voice mail. Dinah still wasn't answering. He glanced at his watch and realized that she would be in class now, and probably had the phone off. Cruz pressed another key and waited.

When the secretary answered, Cruz was polite but firm.

"Yes, good morning. I need to speak to Dinah Lobredor. She teaches second grade. This is Captain Romero Cruz of the *Federales*. It's an emergency."

The woman seemed flustered, but quickly recovered. "Of course. Let me take a look at the class schedules. I'm going to have to put you on hold for a few minutes. Stay on the line, please."

Saccharine pop music, a female singer who sounded like a cat in heat, played in his ear, and Cruz found himself growing impatient as one minute stretched into five. He was about to call back and read the woman the riot act when the music stopped and a male voice came on the line.

"*Capitan* Cruz? This is the principal, Eduardo Navarez. You're trying to reach *Señora* Lobredor?"

"That's correct. It's a matter of considerable urgency."

"I'm afraid she isn't in today."

"What? What do you mean, she's not in? Did something happen?" Cruz asked, now agitated, his heart rate climbing as butterflies danced a tarantella in his stomach.

"Not that I know of. Says here that she requested and received two sick days. There's a temp instructing her class. Perhaps you should try her at home? I presume you have the number..."

"When did she do this?" Cruz snapped, then reined in the worry in his voice. No point in alarming the man.

"Yesterday, early. We haven't heard from her, but expect her to be back tomorrow."

"I see. Thank you for your efforts. We have her home number."

"Let me know if there's anything else you require, *Capitan* Cruz."

"Of course."

Cruz couldn't disconnect fast enough. Damn Dinah for her stubborn streak. He should have anticipated that she wouldn't go in, but still, it had caught him off guard. He needed to start thinking more clearly. If this was any indication of how he was processing, both he and the Chinese leader were as good as dead. He'd gotten extremely lucky this morning with the Los Zetas hit team, but he couldn't rely on good fortune indefinitely. He needed to be smarter and faster, not just luckier. And he hadn't seen Dinah's move coming, although in hindsight it made sense.

Shit.

The hotel search.

He'd been so involved with the shooting and the ensuing pandemonium he had completely forgotten to get back to his assistant with the written authorization. He quickly jotted out a note on his computer and e-mailed it to her on the secure server, then fumed at his carelessness. He'd lost another three hours – time that could have been used to find Dinah.

Annoyed at himself, he called Dinah's cell phone one more time and left a message. Maybe she was still not taking his calls, but she would listen to her voice mail. He knew her that well.

"Sweetheart. It's me. You need to call me as soon as you get this message. There was an attempt on me this morning. Three gunmen. I'm okay, but I need to talk to you immediately. This isn't some ruse to get you to contact me. I'm serious. Call me the second you get this message. I...I love you, and I'm sorry about the other night. Please, *amor*. Call."

He disconnected with a sense of futility. He needed to talk to her now, not whenever she got around to checking her messages. The attack had changed everything. She would have to be in protective custody at all times until he could deal with the threat. Her decision to go off on her own had probably made perfect sense to her at the time, but it could wind up being disastrous.

A chime sounded and he looked up, an expression of abject hopelessness flashing across his face before he got his emotions back under rigid control.

The coffee was ready.

CHAPTER 25

Just after lunchtime, the hotel search came back with a hit. Dinah had checked into a large hotel in Mexico City, only fifteen minutes from his new offices. Gazing at the computer screen, he punched in the number and spoke with the reception desk, but when they put him through to Dinah's room there was no answer. He tried again, but got the same response. Frustrated, he made a decision and stabbed in a two-digit extension and waited. Briones picked up on the fourth ring.

"I need to you take a ride with me."

"Yes, sir. When? I'm kind of in the middle of—"

"Now. You're driving." Cruz's tone left no room for question. Briones was in his office within three minutes, having sidelined his tasks.

"Where are we going, sir?"

"Camino Real Polanco hotel."

Once in the car, Cruz sat stone-faced for a few blocks, then turned to Briones. "Dinah...we had an argument the other night when I told her about this new assignment. She didn't respond...positively...to the idea that I'd be working with the man who killed her father. We...it didn't end well. She decided that she needed to get some distance on it. Some perspective. For a few days."

Briones nodded, sagacious, preferring not to comment. Both men knew what Cruz was trying to say, while saving at least a modicum of face.

"But she doesn't understand the risks to herself." Cruz seemed to deflate with the last words. "And now, with the attack..."

"Who else knows where she's staying?" Briones finally asked, twisting the steering wheel and cutting off a taxi, who pounded impotently on his horn.

"Nobody."

"Then there's no problem. You can't have a leak if nobody knows anything," Briones said simply.

"True, but we have to assume that there was surveillance on the building. And we have no idea for how long. If they were watching it when she stormed...when she left, she could have been followed."

"Agreed." There was nothing more productive to say. Cruz was right. Neither man wanted to consider the possibilities too closely. No point in speculating – they would be at the hotel soon enough.

When they pulled into the drive of the iconic Ricardo Legorreta-designed landmark, gaudy pink and purple and yellow hues coloring the stunning architectural elements with a boldness that was timeless even five decades after it was built, they entered a different world from the crowded, bustling one out on the street. A valet hustled to open Briones' door as a bellman swung Cruz's wide, and within moments they were both striding purposefully across the massive, opulent lobby to the expansive reception area, easily fifty feet wide and crafted from contemporary exotic wood.

"Yes, sir. May I help you?" a young man in a uniform far more elaborate than Cruz's asked, a trace of disapproval on his face. The Camino Real wasn't accustomed to armed *Federales* in the lobby. It was an edifice that reeked of wealth and gentrified exclusivity, and the intrusion by law enforcement wasn't appreciated.

"Room 321. Call. Now."

Something in Cruz's tone sobered the receptionist, and he mutely lifted a telephone handset to his ear and keyed in the room number. He stood, waiting, then hung up.

"I'm sorry, sir. There's no answer. Would you like to leave a message for the guest?" he asked in his smarmiest tone.

"Get someone who can open the room. We're going up," Cruz ordered, a look of glacial indifference to the receptionist's attitude the only warning he was going to offer.

Cruz's tone arrested any protest the young man was going to make; instead, he lifted the phone and placed another call, then turned away from them as he had a hushed discussion. When he turned back, he gave his most winning professional fake smile and hung up with a noisy decisiveness.

"One moment, sir. Someone will be with you shortly."

"You have two minutes to get someone who can open the room, and then we're going to go up and shoot the lock off," Cruz informed him, trying not to mimic the man's grin, which took a sudden vacation as he registered Cruz's words.

"I'm sure that won't be necessary...," the young man started.

"Two minutes."

The receptionist lifted the phone again and had another whispered discussion.

Cruz was just about ready to make good on his threat when an imposing figure in a dark gray suit approached him with a neutral smile on his face. Cruz absently wondered where they taught these wonks such phony expressions, then decided it didn't matter when the man launched into his act.

"Gentlemen. My name is Antonio Arabiera. I'm the manager here. How may I be of assistance today?"

"Unless you can open the door of room 321, you can get someone to meet us there. We're going up and we need to get in. This is an emergency," Cruz said.

"I...this is most irregular. Our guests have an expectation of privacy. Unless you have a warrant..."

Cruz took a step towards the man, invading his space, and put a hand on his shoulder, then guided him away from the counter to spare him embarrassment.

"This is an emergency situation. Either you open the door now, or I will make your life miserable, do you read me? That's my wife in there, and she's in danger. Now be a nice man and call housekeeping or whoever and have them meet us up there, or you'll wish you'd never been born, and the rest of your guests will get an experience they'll be talking about on the internet for years," Cruz murmured, for all appearances having a friendly discussion of matters requiring discretion.

Arabiera wasn't the manager because he was stupid, and he wasted no time in finding a key card that would open every room in the building.

"I'll accompany you gentlemen. This way," he said with a hand gesture, then began walking across the lobby to the entry to the room wing. Cruz and Briones followed, Briones trying to contain the smile forming on his lips as their boots tromped along the oversized marble slab floor.

When they reached the room, Cruz knocked on the door, his sense of unease growing as they waited for a response. After thirty seconds, he knocked again, this time longer, his knuckles reddening.

Nothing.

"Open it," Cruz commanded, and Arabiera acquiesced. He slipped the keycard into the slot and then pushed the door open, beckoning to the two officers to have at it.

Cruz led the way, Briones in tow, Arabiera waiting outside, glancing around nervously lest any of his guests spot the intrusion.

Fifteen seconds later, Cruz and Briones were back.

"Seal off the room. Don't touch anything. I'll have a crime scene squad here within half an hour," Cruz ordered, his heart thrashing like a caged animal fighting for escape. The breakfast tray on the floor and the luggage still in the closet told the whole story. He didn't need to see anything else. He turned to Briones.

"Get them here, now. And put out an APB on her. Circulate the description. It's a long shot, but we might find someone who saw something," Cruz said woodenly, on automatic pilot as his mind churned, a million miles away. Cruz flashed back to the last time he'd dealt with a kidnapping – the last time he had ever seen his wife and daughter alive. A vision he'd stuffed into the nether reaches of his memory forced itself to the forefront – his baby daughter and wife's heads in a box, and his screaming blind rage at the cosmos as he slammed his fists into his desk, over and over and over, until his staff had to forcibly restrain him for his own safety, two fractures ballooning his left hand.

It had been a dark time; the kind of period that drove men mad, or to drink, in a feeble attempt to erase the unthinkable for a blissfully empty few hours of oblivion. The thought that he would lose the only other woman he had ever loved in the same way almost paralyzed him. It was the realization that only he stood between Dinah and the unspeakable that stopped him as he teetered on the edge of the abyss, the dark looking back into his soul, taking his measure, staining him indelibly, as it always did.

Cruz paced as Briones made his calls, thoughts whirling, apportioning blame and promising revenge in the same moment, a tiny voice inside screaming in protest as he struggled to maintain an outward calm. They had her. *You know how this ends. You've seen it before. Your family paid the price, but it wasn't enough. You had to keep baiting the bear, swatting it on the nose, daring it, goading it to action. Your career, your drive to be so different, so special, so superior, has killed everything you ever held dear, and it still wasn't enough. Never enough.*

And now they had Dinah.

His hand dropped automatically to his Glock, seeking reassurance in the familiar shape, its bulk comforting, not least because it had spit death at those who tried to harm him only hours before, equalizing, killing with brutal efficiency, its purpose unambiguous, clean and clear. As his fingers found the grip and stroked it as tenderly as a lover, he was consumed with only one thought.

They will pay for this, mi amor. Whatever they do or have done, they will pay tenfold. I am justice, and I will prevail. And in doing so I will extract a terrible price.

Whatever happens, they will pay.

CHAPTER 26

El Rey stood impatiently in the lobby of the office building, studying the now dozen heavily armed *Federales* in a state of high alert, as he waited for his identification card to be validated by an anonymous computer somewhere upstairs. On his prior visit, security had been relaxed, with a quick, cursory check and a wave through. Now the officers were behaving as though the building was filled with gold bars and he was a thief.

Eventually the computer gave the okay, and the guard handed him back his ID and gestured to the elevator. He pulled the lanyard that dangled from the card over his head and waited for the doors to open, the hair on the back of his neck prickling from the room full of eyes staring at him. When the elevator arrived he pushed a button and then exhaled a small sigh of relief when it ascended, carrying him away from the trigger-happy monkeys in the lobby.

When he arrived at the command center floor he stepped into a kind of controlled mayhem, the energy of the place completely different than it had been before. Dark glares greeted his arrival, but he'd expected the reception, so they didn't faze him. What surprised him was how grim everyone was.

He walked across the common workspace towards Cruz's office but was intercepted by Briones before he'd made it halfway there. The lieutenant blocked his way.

"What are you doing here?"

"I'm working with this task force, remember? You know, the expert sent by CISEN? Your best hope in the world of catching the assassin before he drills your Chinese dignitary? Ringing any bells?"

"What do you want?"

El Rey noticed the tension just beneath the skin of the lieutenant's face. Something was wrong. "To see your glorious leader. Now get out of my way."

"He's occupied right now. Busy. You can tell me whatever you have for him."

"I don't think so. I want to talk to the big man, not his lap dog."

Briones bristled, then choked down his anger. The assassin was just trying to goad him into an explosion. It was a game, and he wasn't going to play it – he wouldn't give the murderous prick the satisfaction. A smirk twisted his lips.

"Have you recovered from the collision? I heard you suffered brain damage or something. Couldn't happen to a nicer guy."

"Speaking of brain damage, what are you doing to catch the German, besides wasting my time when I've come to see your boss?" *El Rey* asked.

"None of your business. But as I told you, he's busy, so I'm handling all of his duties until he can free up."

"Not good enough. New get out of my way, or I'll move you."

Briones stepped back and regarded the assassin. "What is it with you? Much as I'd love for you to try, after what's happened today, I'm surprised you'd even show your face here. In case you haven't picked up on it, the mood towards cartel killers isn't at its most forgiving right now."

El Rey paused, eyes narrowing. "What happened today? You lost me."

"Ah, I keep forgetting. You're not in the loop. This morning, three cartel gunmen tried to kill the captain. They failed, but it looks like they grabbed his wife, too. So he's a little preoccupied, you could say. Much as I'm sure you believe everyone lives and breathes to serve your needs, it's not the case. He's got his hands full today, so for the last time, what the hell are you doing here and what do you want?"

El Rey nodded. "Hmm. No wonder. So that's why all the additional security. I had no idea. Do you know what cartel, just out of curiosity?"

"What's it to you which one of your scumbag employers tried to knock him off? Why – you want to offer to do the job for them and collect a bonus?" Briones spoke as though explaining photosynthesis to a five-year-old.

"No, you dolt. It's because I still have extensive contacts, even though I'm out of the game. And I'm curious which group would raise the stakes to the level that they would try to take Cruz out. That would bring a lot of heat for no good purpose. Seems counter-productive, is all. They're in the business of making money, so this is a little out of character."

"Well, Mister Curious, it's the worst of the bunch. Los Zetas. And it's unclear as to why they would be suddenly gunning for him, although I would guess that he's at the top of every cartel's kill list because of his position."

"I'm not so sure that's true. He would just be replaced by someone else, so it wouldn't solve anything."

"You're wrong. It was them, and their intentions were obvious. Hard to mistake three armed hit men trying to gun you down."

"And you say they have his wife?"

Briones realized his error – he'd talked too much. It was time to do some damage control. "That's none of your affair. It has nothing to do with catching the German."

"Are you really so dim that you believe that the leader of our little group having been attacked and his wife kidnapped isn't going to affect the effort to find Rauschenbach? Or are you telling me that you think he's going to remain unaffected? That the hunt for the assassin will get a hundred percent of his attention?"

Briones regarded *El Rey* with curiosity, in spite of his hatred. "What's it to you, anyway? I didn't get the impression that you cared whether we got him or not."

"I care because this is my assignment, and it was made clear to me that I was to do everything I could to stop Rauschenbach. If your part of the effort is distracted by personal problems, that will affect everyone, including me. Frankly, I'd just as soon not have to work with any of you – you're about as effective as homeopathy, but apparently CISEN wants to play nice and include you, so I'm stuck in a position I'm not thrilled with."

"Why don't you just quit? Do us all a favor."

"I wish I could."

"What does that mean?"

El Rey peered over Briones' shoulder at Cruz's door. "Nothing. I need to talk to your boss. When will he be available? And please spare me the bit about talking to you. I need to discuss some issues about the site, and he was there with me yesterday. You probably haven't even been there yet, am I right? So talking to you would be about as useful as talking to a rock."

Briones hesitated, then put aside his enmity and nodded. "Wait here. I'll go interrupt him and see when he'll be available."

El Rey watched as Briones hurried to Cruz's office and disappeared inside, only to return again two minutes later.

"He's on a conference call that will probably go on for quite a while. I'll see that he gets in touch when he's done. Figure an hour or two."

"Great. So the situation is already interfering."

"Like I said. He'll call when he has a free moment."

El Rey shrugged and turned, then paused and looked back at Briones. "Just out of curiosity, who's the ranking Los Zetas honcho in D.F. these days? Used to be *El Jaguar*, if memory serves. That still the case?"

"Sounds right."

El Rey glanced over his shoulder at the men watching the encounter from behind him.

"Tell your boss I'll be waiting for his call. I'm headed out to the site for another look around. I had a few ideas of how to further tighten things up."

Briones didn't answer. The assassin sauntered back to the elevator, and a few moments later the steel cube swallowed him up and some of the tension in the room dissipated. The distinctive ring of Briones' line sounded from the common room's work area, and before long the encounter with the assassin was out of his mind as he dealt with a flurry of calls while Cruz coordinated with the team that was investigating Dinah's disappearance.

CHAPTER 27

Rauschenbach dropped his luggage on the bed and surveyed with relief the room at the upscale apartment hotel he'd checked into for three nights. The trip had been grueling, and he wanted nothing so much as to take a long hot shower to wash away the fish stink – the trawler had been right on time, but it was at least fifty years old, every one of which had been spent as a working fishing boat, which meant that every surface was saturated with the residue of the sea. When he had finally climbed off just before dawn and been spirited ashore in the creaky old scow's tender, he felt like he'd spent the night in the hold with the cargo of dead shrimp.

The port had been quiet and his passage unnoticed, but when he found his appointed rendezvous spot for a ride inland to the airport, things had gone awry – the vehicle hadn't been there. He had waited for an hour, watching the sun come up, but once day had broken he had felt exposed and decided not to wait. There were any number of possible explanations for the car not making it, from a breakdown to an accident, but it was doing him no good to wait in vain.

There hadn't been much in the way of transportation in the tiny berg of Puerto Madero, so he was left to fend for himself with the local bus that ran to and from Tapachula, a medium-sized city whose international airport was only six miles from the port.

He'd found a passable family restaurant that was just opening for the working crowd, and wedged himself into a booth, his gear next to him. Watching the dining room fill, he'd had a friendly conversation with the waitress, who had told him where to catch the bus over his third cup of coffee and assured him that they ran every hour or two.

The ride had been everything he'd expected, and it had been with considerable relief that he'd arrived at the small airport and made his way to the passenger terminal, where he was informed by an uninterested ticket vendor that the next flight to Mexico City left in three hours. He paid his fare, noting the machine-gun armed soldiers loitering in groups around the building, and after a hurried washing-up in the men's room, had settled in to wait in the departure lounge, which would have made any bus station in Europe seem lavish by comparison.

The flight had taken a little over an hour, and when he had arrived in Mexico City he had spent some time in the airport internet café looking for suitable accommodations. He wasn't worried about his identification – it was indistinguishable from the genuine article, even under close scrutiny. Nobody at the airport security checkpoint in Tapachula had given him a second look, and his passport had been barely glanced at by the ticket agent. He had worried that the lack of an entry stamp would be a problem, but needn't have – nobody seemed to care.

The apartment hotel he had found was perfect for his needs – anonymous, large, in a decent area of town – not inexpensive, but not five star by any means. The sort of place thousands of businessmen stayed in all over the world when their companies assigned them to spend a week somewhere, poring over a sales office's books or meeting with prospects. Rauschenbach fit the image of his fellow lodgers – shopworn road warriors with ever-diminishing prospects – and was as forgettable as any of them.

He walked to the window and parted the drapes and found himself looking out over miles of shabby buildings, traffic snarling through the clogged streets four stories below him, laundry hanging on lines, corner markets advertising cheap beer and artery-hardening snacks. He exhaled with a sense of accomplishment – he was here, in Mexico City, the difficult part of entering the country laughably easy, in retrospect. His choice of crossing via Guatemala had been a good one – the border zone was patrolled in a haphazard fashion, and once inside Mexico there was virtually no security other than army patrols whose purpose seemed as much to intimidate the local population as to stop smuggling or prevent human trafficking.

He unpacked his bag and hung up his clothes, and then secreted his valuables in the room safe before stripping down and taking a long shower. Once finished, he caught sight of himself in the partially fogged mirror and smiled at his hair, now dyed gray and trimmed close to his head. He looked completely different than he had even a few days before starting his junket, when his hair had been longer and chestnut colored, with only hints of gray at the temples.

Rauschenbach was an expert at changing his appearance, so this latest incarnation was routine for him. A few small tweaks would add ten years to his age, and a perennial three-day growth of beard would further disguise the inherent fitness evident in his face. He knew from experience that nobody suspected older men of anything, their usefulness and vitality dried up, so he would be virtually invisible as the downtrodden, fifty-something widower he appeared to be.

He tossed the clothes he had worn on the boat into a plastic bag, to be disposed of somewhere other than the hotel, and resolved to run his first productive errand of the dwindling day – to buy several sets of clothes, so that he would further blend in with the local population. These were small things, but he was meticulous, and it was the small things that could trip one up. He had an entire laundry list of items he would need to get, but first things first: clothes, a good meal, and then some sleep. There would be plenty of time tomorrow to scope out the target and arrange for a meeting with his contact. For now, he wanted to get a sense of the place, soak in the local ambience, and familiarize himself with the pace so he wouldn't stand out.

Being a human chameleon was as much a mental adjustment as it was being adept at changing his appearance, and when he took a sanction that required him to be in a foreign country for any length of time, going the extra distance to immerse himself in the local culture was a necessary step. He wasn't worried about the language issue – his Spanish was fluent from living in Spain – but he was concerned about the accent, which would place him as not from Mexico. Probably not a huge issue, but the more time he spent listening to the locals chat, the more he could modify the giveaways so he would be undetectable.

When he exited the lobby, offering a polite smile to the reception clerk as he passed the counter, he was immediately struck by the sheer multitude of teeming humanity on the sidewalks, business hours having ended and the population now making its way home from work. The melodious cacophony of horns provided a contretemps to the blaring music from storefronts desperate to attract the attention of potential shoppers. At first it seemed chaotic to him, an incessant din of unbearable noise pollution, but as he settled into the pedestrian flow and ambled down the medium-sized thoroughfare it all began to make a certain kind of sense. Every city had its own beat, its own tempo, and Mexico City was no different. He had never been there before, and so had no idea what to expect, but what he found was similar to Madrid or Rome, albeit dirtier.

That was good. People would be in a hurry in a busy big city, less likely to notice things that didn't immediately concern or affect them. It would make his job easier if the gestalt of the place was bustling, which it was.

He paused by a trash can and deposited his clothes bag, confident that it would be retrieved within minutes by an enterprising homeless person who didn't mind the fishy smell, and then meandered for block after block until he came to a clothing store featuring decent quality men's casual wear.

Fifteen minutes later he was back on the street, three new pairs of pants and four shirts the richer, and he continued his walk, taking a circuitous route back to his hotel. The district he was in was working class, residences mixed with commercial buildings, with no apparent zoning or restrictions that he could tell. The tops of many of the buildings were unfinished, rebar sticking out at odd angles from the remnants of structural beams, the workers having never bothered to cut them off. Bright colors seemed to be mandatory, and many façades were painted a psychedelic rainbow of neon hues, with no evidence that anyone had given any thought to the neighboring schemes, resulting in a somewhat desperate carnival atmosphere.

One commonality were the bars that adorned every window within two stories of street level – a reminder that in addition to being one of the world's most populated cities, it was also one of the more crime-ridden. Razor wire and broken glass topped every wall, and most of the buildings had the look of fortresses that had been secured against even the most inventive and industrious intruders.

Two blocks from the hotel, he came across a cell phone store and purchased a Nokia with a local number that he could charge with a pre-paid card containing a hundred minutes. The transaction was efficient, and the clerk dutifully marked down the information from his passport – a requirement that had been created to quash the rash of kidnappings that plagued the city, where ransom calls were routinely made from cell phones with no owner information.

He returned to the hotel lobby and got several restaurant tips from the clerk, and then set out again, darkness now shrouding the city, mitigated by a riot of glaring lights from the storefronts and the endless procession of headlights on the busy street.

Four blocks away, he found the first recommendation – a massive hall already filled with hungry locals seated at rustic wooden tables, laughing and chatting over beer and local delicacies. After a look at the menu he took a seat, his journey over, and the real work of preparing to assassinate one of the most prominent men in the world about to begin.

CHAPTER 28

Cruz's night was spent tossing and turning on a couch that had been brought to his office in the early evening. There wouldn't be a new condo until tomorrow, so he had chosen to stay at the office, where a skeleton crew was working the night shift and the bathrooms were equipped with a shower he could use. An officer arrived at eight p.m. with a suitcase and a Styrofoam carton containing enchiladas, rice, and beans, and he'd eaten a glum meal before hiding away in his office, the blinds on the window overlooking the common area drawn, working on the computer until he became tired enough to snatch a few hours of rest.

At some point in the wee hours he actually drifted off, and his dreams were ugly and violent: Dinah's head arriving in a box during an office birthday party for him, gunmen shooting at him in the shower, and his daughter, Cassandra, dead for so many years, crying out for help, begging for her daddy to rescue her as a dark figure prepared to do the unthinkable; then her childish frame morphing into Dinah as he watched, powerless to do anything, frozen inside the dream, and yet outside, as an observer.

When he started awake, disoriented, not knowing where he was, he was bathed in sweat, his pulse pounding a tattoo in his ears as he fumbled with the blanket he'd found in one of the office cabinets. It took him a few moments to get his bearings, and then he groaned, a mournful sound, and peered at his watch in the dark. Four a.m., his mouth coated with a sour, bilious film from the meal and the two Tecate beers the officer had thoughtfully brought with dinner. He closed his eyes again and tried to get comfortable, but the rest of the short night was spent in fits and starts, each bout of slumber punctuated by ugly images that wouldn't relent.

He was back at his desk at seven, wearing the same dark blue slacks with a new uniform jersey, his six a.m. shower having been followed by a lukewarm meal ordered from a local café and picked up by one of the security team, and was going over the morning intelligence dispatches when his cell phone rang. He looked down at the flickering screen and saw a number he didn't recognize. When he answered, he already half knew what the call was about.

"*Capitan* Cruz. Do not say anything. We have your wife. She hasn't been harmed, but that can change whenever we decide that you aren't cooperating."

"You're a dead man."

"You don't listen very well, do you? I said not to talk. I'll keep this short and sweet, for now. If you do as we say, your wife will live. If not, you'll get pieces of her sent to you in the mail. Is this call being recorded?"

"No. What do you want?"

"You. But in the shorter term, we want you to stop any further actions against our group. You know who we are, yes?"

"I know."

"Then you know we will carry out any threat we make. We want you to stand down from this ill-considered campaign you have launched against us. You can make that happen. If you have to move against one of our locations, you must give us notice so we can take appropriate action. There will be no exceptions."

"I can't do that."

"Then your beautiful young wife will die, after we've amused ourselves with her for a while."

Cruz had to stall for time. That was the first rule of dealing with any blackmailer or kidnapper. Buy time. "No. Wait. I can sideline anything we have on the boards, demand more evidence, choose not to move yet. But I want my wife back."

"That's not an option at this point, *Capitan*. Perhaps once you've proven that you understand the rules, and your task force has been effectively neutralized, you'll get what you want. But for now, we own you, and you must do exactly what we say."

Cruz hesitated. He couldn't give in too fast – they would be suspicious if he just rolled over. "I don't have the power you think I have."

"You're lying. You run the task force. Nothing big happens in D.F. without your express approval. Don't try to bullshit me. You don't want your beauty's face carved up, do you? Shall I send you some fingers or her nose to get your attention? I thought you were smarter than that."

"You tried to kill me. It's me you want, not my wife."

"True, but after some consideration, we decided that you could be more useful to us alive. So it's your lucky day, really. But not for your wife if you screw with us. If you want to find her hung off a freeway overpass, just try me."

Another long pause.

"You won't hurt her if I cooperate?"

"That's what I said."

He cleared his throat and then lowered his voice to a whisper. "Then I have no choice."

"We have eyes and ears everywhere, so don't get cute. We'll know within minutes if you try to double-cross us."

"I can't stop the search for Dinah. That would look suspicious, and it's not how things work."

"Don't worry about that. We aren't worried. Like I said, we have ears everywhere. Let the whole thing play out. It's not your concern. Just do as I instructed, and kill anything that will endanger our operations."

"I want to hear Dinah's voice. How do I know you haven't killed her?"

"I was wondering how long it would take you to get to that. Here."

Cruz heard a rustling as the phone changed hands, and then he heard the most beautiful sound possible.

"Romero. I'm so sorry I—"

Dinah's voice sounded scared, and then she was cut off and there was more rustling, and Cruz heard a sharp crack – a slap.

"There. You know what you have to do. Don't blow it."

The line went dead before Cruz could respond.

The good news was that Dinah was alive. And the cartel had established contact, its demands simple. He could buy himself breathing room by simply standing down on any pending raids. But a more troubling aspect to the call had been the clear inference that they had people on the inside feeding them information. That meant the task force was compromised, and he would have to be extremely careful trying to locate Dinah. And the assurance with which the caller had dismissed the kidnapping investigation efforts currently underway, meant only one thing – somehow, they also had a pipeline into that group as well. It was separate from Cruz's task force, so they had penetrated multiple levels of the *Federales* – not completely surprising, but disconcerting nonetheless.

He had been expecting the call, and knew from the hundreds of kidnappings that headquarters dealt with every year that it would be impossible to trace it. Whatever phone they had used would be a burner they would immediately dispose of, registered to a maid in Toluca who would claim that she had lost it a week ago and had been too busy to report it. The cartels bought dozens of phones per day from people who needed the hundred dollars they would pay for a cell that had cost twenty, and there was no way to disprove a claim of loss. It was one of the loopholes in the system that everyone knew about but couldn't stop.

But the fact that Los Zetas had sufficiently co-opted officers in his own team to subvert any effort to find Dinah made things much, much harder. It meant that he couldn't mount his own effort, and would have to rely on the investigation group – which he had just been told had no chance of saving her.

That wasn't an option. He had to find his wife. Even if he had to do it completely on his own, he would. The alternative wasn't pretty. He knew how these butchers worked – they would string him along, raping and beating her periodically, and then when they felt his usefulness was done, they would contrive a meeting where she was to be handed over, and then kill them both. There was no other way he could see it ending.

He had to save her before any of that happened.

Even if he died trying.

There was no other way.

CHAPTER 29

When Briones entered the command center at seven-fifty, Cruz let him get settled and deal with his stack of inbound reports and messages before calling him into his office and pouring him a cup of coffee. Briones looked as though he'd gotten about as much sleep as Cruz, which didn't bode well – this investigation would be a marathon, not a sprint, and it wouldn't do to have everyone exhausted by the time the big day arrived.

Cruz told him about the call and the conclusions he'd come to, and Briones was visibly shaken and furious.

"The penalty for selling out your colleagues should be death. Especially if the information leads to disastrous consequences, like yesterday. It's a straightforward transaction – they're being paid to furnish data that results in you or your loved ones being killed. I say an eye for eye," Briones seethed.

"I appreciate the sentiment, and I don't disagree, but none of that will help right now. I can't trust anyone. That was made abundantly clear, and was actually smart of them. If I'm isolated, then I'll be less effective. They know their psychology."

"So what are you going to do? We obviously can't just sit around and twiddle our thumbs while an investigation that we both know is going to go nowhere meanders with no results, sir."

"I haven't figured that out yet. But I wanted to enlist your support. You're the only one I completely trust. The others...I mean, I trust them, but not with Dinah's life. We have a leak. Multiple leaks. And I can't take the chance that one of the men out there isn't part of the problem. There's someone on the cartel task force that's feeding them info – although I question how high up they are. If they were part of the top tier, we wouldn't have had any success with operations like the meth lab sting. They would have been warned and gotten everything out of there before we had a chance to take it down."

"It could be someone who is in the command chain, but not privy to the operational decision making..."

"Exactly. But I can't be a hundred percent sure...and I can't afford to dilute this team's focus on stopping the German. That's still got to be the priority for them. But I need to come up with something better than just sitting around waiting for the next phone call..."

"The only good news in any of this is that we don't have anything active planned against Los Zetas right now. So it won't be doing much to play along and claim that you've intervened against any raids. You'll have the benefit of appearing to be doing exactly what they've demanded, without actually cooperating."

"I suppose that's a bright spot. But I can't say it's much of one."

They sipped thoughtfully on their coffee, and then Cruz turned to business. "What progress have we made on Rauschenbach? Do we have anything?"

Briones took him through the long list of preventive measures that had been put in place, and updated him on the data collection process. The results weren't reassuring.

"Then we don't have anything more than we did when we were alerted to this."

"I'm afraid not, sir. Nothing has come back from immigration, either. He hasn't entered the country yet, at least not in any traceable way."

Cruz leaned back in his chair and stared at the ceiling, then out the window at the city's sprawl. "Oh, he's here. It's only a gut feeling, but he's in the country by now. There's no way that a professional would leave things to the last minute. And our captive assassination expert, *El Rey*, agrees. When we were out at the site, he made it abundantly clear that it would take significant planning to pull this off. I believe him."

Briones looked troubled for a moment, then cleared his throat, his expression turning sheepish. "I'm sorry, sir. I completely forgot. Yesterday, he came by and wanted to see you. You were on the call with headquarters dealing with...with Dinah's kidnapping, so I didn't want to interrupt. I told him that he could talk to me, but he wasn't interested. Said he needed to talk to you because you had been to the site with him. With everything that happened, it just...I'm sorry. It slipped my mind."

Cruz waved his hand. "That's understandable. Frankly, I'm not sure I would have been much good yesterday. But did he give you any hint what he wanted?"

"No. He just repeated his contempt for our approach and said he would talk to you, and nobody else. He's really a complete prick."

"Yes, he is that. But he's also very good at what he does."

"Which is kill people for money."

"Yes. Or at least that used to be his vocation. Before he turned over his new leaf."

"Do you believe any of that for even a second?"

"It doesn't matter what I believe. But for the record, yes; I sense that he's out of the game. He's made enough money to last ten lifetimes, and this has afforded him a chance to start fresh without having to look over his shoulder every day. So yes, I think he's done with the cartels and the killing. I can see it in his eyes."

"Maybe, but he's still a killer. And he's still part of that world, even if he's switched the sides he's working for. Now he's just CISEN's killer," Briones spat.

Cruz's hand stopped with his coffee mug halfway to his lips, his eyes with a faraway look in them, and then he slowly put it back onto the table top and steepled his fingers. Briones was working himself up into another indignant froth, but then hesitated when he saw the expression on his Cruz's face.

"How did you leave it with him? With *El Rey*?"

"I...well, I suppose I told him that you would get back in touch with him once you had a free moment..."

"And that was the totality of what you discussed? There was nothing else?"

Briones suddenly found a spot on his boot of considerable interest. "He wanted to know why you were too busy to see him."

"And?"

"I told him about the attempt on your life."

"Nothing else?"

Briones looked away. "The kidnapping might have come up."

"*Might* have?"

"Now that I think about it, I'm sure I mentioned it, because he was concerned that all of this would render you ineffective – that it would distract you from finding the German. He's very critical, and felt your mind wouldn't be fully engaged..."

Cruz rose and began pacing. "Looks like he was right about that. But I wonder..."

"What? You wonder what, sir?"

Cruz slowed and then paused in front of the window, peering out at the surrounding buildings as if seeing them for the first time. "Nothing... Lieutenant, if you don't mind, I need to make a few calls. Let's plan on resuming this discussion in an hour." Cruz sounded suddenly distant.

Briones stood and finished his drink, then placed the cup by the machine. "Of course, sir. In an hour. Are you...going to call *El Rey?*"

"Among others. Now, not a word to anyone. Remember that everything we've discussed has to stay in this room."

"I understand. It's between you and me, sir. I get it."

"Very good. Please close the door behind you."

Briones did as instructed, and then walked slowly to his desk. He knew his superior well enough to know that something was brewing. But he wasn't thinking clearly if it would in any way involve the assassin. The irony being that *El Rey*'s big concern was exactly that – that Cruz would be so preoccupied with his missing wife that it would color his judgment.

Whatever he was considering, Cruz had Briones' sympathy. That he was functioning at all in light of the kidnapping was a kind of small miracle and a tribute to the captain's fortitude. Briones knew and liked Dinah, and her being stolen from Cruz in that manner by the cartel, especially in light of what had happened with his family years before, the horror that had become a cautionary legend for its viciousness and cruelty...

It was too horrible to contemplate.

CHAPTER 30

The lobby guards were only slightly less unfriendly than they had been the prior day, and treated *El Rey* as though they had never seen him before in spite of the fact that he recognized at least four of them from his other visits. The entire elaborate ritual was drawn out again until the terminal cleared him with a beep and he was directed to the elevators.

When he entered the foyer of the command center, there were more men there than earlier, so apparently staff had been added to keep up with the data streaming in. His gaze swept the room with interest, then he proceeded to Cruz's office, where his progress was blocked a few feet from the door by Briones.

"Look. I want to apologize. *Capitan* Cruz didn't get the message until this morning."

"What does that mean? You didn't pass it on?"

"It was hectic yesterday."

"I'll take that as a 'No, I didn't.'"

"It's been a tough twenty-four hours. Everyone's on edge. We're all doing the best we can," Briones countered, his tone becoming defensive at the assassin's imperious attitude.

"Right. But my concern has always been that's just not good enough. This merely confirms it."

Briones decided not to escalate. "He's waiting for you. Follow me."

"I want to speak with him alone."

"You will. But I'll be there as well."

El Rey eyed him with his dead look and shrugged. "Whatever. Are you done wasting my time now, or do you want to posture some more? It's very impressive."

Briones pivoted and led him to the door, then knocked twice.

"Enter," Cruz's voice called.

When *El Rey* was seated in front of Cruz's desk, Briones standing unobtrusively in the far corner behind him, Cruz and the assassin locked eyes.

"You wanted to see me?" Cruz began.

"Yes. I've gone over the information you sent and I spotted some more problem areas. I also think it would behoove you to start thinking offensively in terms of the weak spots. If you don't, unless we catch a break, this assassin is going to get a shot at the target."

"I presume you have suggestions?"

El Rey pulled two folded pieces of ivory stationary from his pocket and slid them across the desk to Cruz, who picked them up and read them slowly, pausing to glance over the top of the documents at *El Rey* periodically.

"I see you've been busy. This all looks good. I'll circulate it and get the various teams acting on them. Lieutenant, would you please take these and have someone type them up and e-mail them to me?" Cruz motioned with the papers, and Briones approached the desk. He clearly wasn't happy to be dismissed from the discussion, but didn't have much choice.

"Of course, sir. Now?"

"Yes, Lieutenant. Now. Don't worry. I think I'll be safe for a few minutes alone with our guest."

Briones clumped out, and *El Rey* watched Cruz watching him for a few moments before Cruz finally spoke.

"You've no doubt heard about my recent...challenges."

"Your lap dog told me yesterday."

No 'I'm sorry' or sympathy from him. Fine. None was expected. Cruz nodded. "It's a difficult situation. I can't do anything officially for a host of reasons..."

"Namely, your organization is compromised," *El Rey* stated flatly.

Cruz's eyebrows arched. "I didn't say that."

"You didn't have to. How else would they have been able to find you, and then your wife? That was the sequence, wasn't it? Someone had to have told them. Trust me – these guys are not the sharpest. You figure that out once you've dealt with them enough. They have a certain animal cunning, and the natural instincts of any good predators, but few of them are that smart. So there's no way they planned a hit on you, presuming your living location was protected and also secret, and abducted your wife, without inside information. Simple. Which means that you don't know who you can trust."

Cruz regarded him with newfound respect. "In a nutshell, yes."

"Why are you telling me this? What does it have to do with this operation?" The assassin's stare was emotionless, cold, his expression a blank.

"You mentioned that you've dealt with them."

"I've done work for all the major cartels. What of it?"

"This was carried out by Los Zetas."

"Bad news. And...?"

"I don't know quite how to say this, so I'll just come out with it. I would appreciate your help in finding my wife." There. It was in the open now. Cruz sat back, equally expressionless as the assassin, two seasoned professionals playing poker with one another, neither willing to concede any advantage or display any weakness.

El Rey shifted his eyes to the window. "I'm not in that business anymore."

"I understand that. But you must still have contacts."

The assassin shook his head. "Why should I help you?"

"Because you can. And because you never know when you'll need the head of the anti-cartel task force as an ally. Someone who would owe you a favor. You're working with CISEN. I'd imagine that's not entirely voluntary – there's got to be a story to it. However that may be, I'm one of the most powerful law enforcement officials in the country. Ask yourself whether that could come in handy at some point."

"The president pardoned me. It doesn't get much more powerful than that."

"True. But tell me: Does he owe you a favor, then?"

"You could say that."

"Then why are you working for CISEN?"

"It's complicated."

"Yes, it always is."

El Rey paused a few beats. "What did you have in mind?"

"I need to find Victor Torres. *El Jaguar.*"

"I suspected as much."

"What do you mean?"

"I asked your boy about it yesterday."

"Why?"

"I figured it couldn't hurt to nose around. As you say, I still have an infrastructure – a network of contacts that have access to information that you, as a police officer, wouldn't."

"But that doesn't explain the why..."

"Because I knew that eventually you would come to me."

Cruz didn't say anything for a moment. He stood and gestured at his coffee machine. "Can I get you some coffee?"

"No. I don't drink it."

"Very well. But I'm curious. I didn't even know I was going to approach you until a few hours ago. How did you..."

"Then you aren't firing on all cylinders. It makes perfect sense. I have a background with the cartels. I'm working with you on this project, whether I want to or not. And you're desperate. It's your wife. I've met her, you know."

"Yes, I do know. The less said about that, the better."

"I did what I had to do. Just as you're doing what you have to do now. It's the way of the world."

Cruz poured himself a half cup of coffee, then turned back towards the seated assassin. "She's an innocent."

"They all are, aren't they? But that never helps them. The innocents get hurt just as do the guilty ones. Again, it's the way of the world."

"Very philosophical. But I need your help."

"I know."

"What do I have to do to get you to cooperate?"

"Offering up a big favor is good. But it would help if there was more."

"I could force you to do it, you know. You have a price on your head. Few know where you are, but that could change overnight."

El Rey's eyes narrowed to slits. "Don't go down that road. You've done well up until now. You don't ever want to threaten me." The cold menace in his voice was as palpable as though he were holding a gun to Cruz's head.

"Fine. Now you're in a position of power. What do you want? Name it. As long as it's within my ability, I'll do it. This is my wife we're talking about."

"Good. You understand the value of my services. Here is my condition. You will owe me a favor, all right, but there will come a time when I need to collect it, and you won't want to honor your agreement. Right now, you'll agree to anything, but once I perform, and you get your wife back, you'll start telling yourself that my contribution wasn't that big, and that you would have probably gotten her back without it. You'll invent reasons to deny me my favor when I need it the most. My condition is simple. If I get your wife back, or provide information that gets her back, you will not deny me. If you do, she will die. That's it. That's my condition."

"Once I give my word, I would never renege on it."

"Perhaps. But this is my way of making this personal for you. Because if I wind up needing your help, and you screw me for any reason, I want you to be completely clear on what will happen. You might as well pull the trigger yourself at that point."

Cruz nodded. "I understand. Only I can't do anything overtly illegal. I can bend rules. Supply you with information. But I can't be involved in anything that would harm someone like the president. I can't help you kill someone on my team."

"Then hopefully it won't come to that. But there can be no conditions. You either agree, or you don't. If you don't, we go on talking about the German, and that ends my involvement. If you agree, you owe me that favor, and I'll help you get your wife back, hopefully unharmed."

The choice between two evils put Cruz in an impossible position. Although at heart, it wasn't. Not really. He had to save Dinah, and if bargaining with the devil was what it took, then he would do so. He had already lost too much. It was an ugly world, and sometimes it called for gutterball tactics.

"Fine. I agree."

El Rey offered a wan smile. "I knew you would."

"Very well. You're a genius. So what now?"

El Rey turned and looked at Cruz's table, the coffee machine sitting proudly to one side, and spotted an array of bottles. "I could use some water."

Cruz stepped back to the table and grabbed a plastic bottle, then moved to *El Rey* and handed it to him.

"I was thinking more in terms of what the next step would be in our agreement."

El Rey twisted the top and took a long, appreciative pull on the water before setting it down in front of him and fixing Cruz with a chilling stare.

"I already know where *El Jaguar* can be found."

CHAPTER 31

"What? How?" Cruz sputtered, clearly flummoxed by *El Rey*'s revelation.

"I did some checking yesterday. Spent most of my evening on it. I know exactly where he'll be in about" – he looked at his watch – "six hours, more or less."

Cruz's mind raced at the news. It could change everything.

"But you have an ethical dilemma to face. I could tell you where, and you could send in the storm troopers, and hope that he didn't die fighting, and then further hope that he would tell you what he knew about your wife's whereabouts – which I think given your track record, you would agree is a long shot. Or, I could *not* tell you, handle the questioning myself, and show up tomorrow morning, or even late tonight, with your wife's location."

A subtle smirk tugged at his lips.

"Welcome to your first moral quandary. Do you do this by the book, the legal way, or do I handle it...effectively? Which we both know won't be anything close to legal."

"Hypothetically, what would 'effectively' entail?"

"You don't want to know. Or maybe you can imagine. Pretend you don't have the job you do, and that you would do anything required to get the information you needed, regardless of the consequences."

"I...maybe you're right. I don't want to know."

"But you do need to make the decision. What's it going to be?"

"What are the odds he knows anything?" Cruz asked, stalling for time.

"The ranking boss here? What do you think?"

"Stupid question, I guess. But here's a better one. Why would you do this? Why not just give me the address?"

El Rey rubbed a hand across his lower face, tiring of the exchange. "Because you'll blow it. And then when she shows up in pieces, you'll be useless. So any favor you owe me will be uncollectable. Worthless. So decide. I'm running short of patience."

Cruz paced, his mind searching for a way out. "I don't want to know the details. You think you can get what we need?" he asked, defeat in his voice. And more. Hunger. Eagerness. For results. For *El Rey* to go do what he did better than anyone else. A thing that Cruz would have hunted him to the ends of the earth for if it hadn't been to save Dinah.

Funny how the moral certitude folded when you had skin in the game, he thought. His convictions suddenly took a back seat to expediency. And now he and the most dangerous assassin in Latin America, if not the world, were discussing logistics, exactly the same way any of the cartel bosses had discussed them with him before a high-profile execution.

"I wouldn't have offered if I couldn't," *El Rey* said simply.

Cruz's compulsive walking came to a halt a few paces from the assassin's chair. "Do whatever you need to do."

"You're sure?"

"As sure as I've been about anything in my life."

El Rey stood, and tossed his empty water bottle into the trash. "Then we have a deal. Leave your phone on. And try not to sleep too deeply."

Cruz watched as *El Rey* exited his office and moved across the floor with that oddly balletic stride of his – not a hint of wasted motion, easy and effortless – and then sat heavily in his seat, pondering what he had just put into motion. He had unleashed a force of nature to do what he couldn't, and in doing so had violated every oath he'd taken, as well as the principles he held dear. He despised the assassin for what he was; and yet now, when he was at risk of losing Dinah, he didn't hesitate to turn him loose, and damn the consequences.

How could he hold his head up? Look at himself in the mirror? In trying to save her, had he lost himself?

Briones' return terminated his wallow in doubt.

"I sent you the document. I hate to say it, but he makes a lot of sense in it, and definitely caught a number of holes in the security planning that could have been disastrous if the German is on his game."

"And we have to assume that he is. I don't get the impression that he's a man who does things in half measures."

"Nor does our captive assassin."

Briones waited for Cruz to tell him whatever he would need to know.

163

Cruz made a few notes on the yellow legal pad on his desk and then regarded Briones with a strained expression.

"He's going to help find Dinah. Says he should have some information by tomorrow, at the latest. Possibly as early as tonight," Cruz said without preamble.

Briones started in surprise. "Well, that's great! I'll be damned. Do you mind me asking how, sir?"

"It's probably best if you don't know the details. But the reason I'm telling you is so that you can be ready when we get the word."

"I'll assemble an assault team. Only the best men."

Cruz shook his head. "No. We don't know who we can trust. That's been the problem all along. If we start preparing for an incursion, it's possible that word will leak, and then Dinah..."

He didn't have to finish the thought.

"Then how do you want to handle it?"

"We need to be flexible. Our new friend will call when he has the information, and we'll decide then what we'll do. It'll probably depend on what we're walking into. But for now, this has to be confined to you and me. Nobody else."

Briones nodded. "I understand. What about ordnance?"

Cruz scribbled a terse missive on a piece of his stationery and signed it with a flourish. "Here. This will enable you to get whatever you need. I'd say a couple of ARX 160s with night vision scopes, a couple of UMP 9s, extra magazines, body armor, and night vision gear for both of us. And two silenced Berettas. We'll have to go in hard, so we'll need all the firepower we can carry. I want to be ready for anything."

"Are you sure you don't want me to involve a few of my most loyal officers?"

"I'd say make up a short list of five that you trust with your life, but don't call anyone until I give the go-ahead. This might have to happen fast, and I want all the options I can get. Maybe it's just the two of us, maybe it's more. But for now, it's only us." Cruz studied him. "Are you up for this?"

"Absolutely, sir. If he can deliver the goods it's a major break. I'm honored you would choose me," Briones said with quiet fervor.

"You might not be so thrilled once the bullets start flying."

"Sir, I mean it when I say that I'll make you proud."

"I'll settle for not getting shot, and getting my wife out intact."

"Yes, sir. I'll go down to headquarters and hit the armory, then be back in a few hours. Is there anything else?" Briones asked, suddenly anxious to get going.

"No. Wait. Yes. There is. Thank you. This is way above the call of duty."

"I'm absolutely sure you would do the same for me, sir," Briones said, and then spun and left, leaving Cruz to his thoughts.

A soft groan escaped Cruz's lips after the door had closed, and for a moment, his resolve wavered as he watched Briones crossing the command center floor on the way to the elevators. The lieutenant was all about honor, loyalty, and pride, and had proved his mettle more than most of the other officers on the force. He was reassuringly steadfast, and his trust in Cruz was absolute. But was that trust misplaced?

Briones might have been sure, but was Cruz? Would he have done the same thing if it had been Briones being held instead of Dinah? Made a bargain with the closest thing to Satan he'd ever encountered?

He mentally shook himself. After all the rhetoric, all the sentiment faded, his career had cost him everything. He had fought the good fight, and his reward had been a dead wife and daughter, and a command chain that was willing to take everything away from him that he'd earned in order to get its selfish needs met. Cruz might not have been sure of many things, but one was crystal clear to him: He wasn't going to lose Dinah to the same monster that had claimed his family. Unlike that time, the assassin had presented a unique option, and as much as he felt like he had embarked on a road from which there was no turning back, he was equally sure that he had to do everything in his power to save his wife's life.

When all was said and done, and the flags stopped waving and the speeches were over, that's all that mattered, and all he cared about.

Getting Dinah back alive.

CHAPTER 32

The estate on the exclusive Paseo de la Reforma boulevard, host to the most expensive homes in Mexico City, was quiet, the dinner hour having come and gone and the privileged residents having settled in for the evening, some watching television or reading, others preparing for sleep. A massive villa with a pseudo-Roman façade stood proudly on the huge corner lot, jacaranda trees offering up their purple blooms to the gentle breeze, and its lights twinkled in the darkness behind the eight-foot high walls topped with decorative ironwork.

Traffic still rolled past, but it was sporadic now, most of the residential area having tucked in for the night. Behind the walls, seven armed guards patrolled the perimeter, another three stood inside, and *El Rey* watched from his hidden vantage point as a cloud of smoke rose from the closest of the men – a smoker, taking a break, chatting with one of the others to kill time and make the dull duty more bearable.

Crime in the area was not unheard of, but it was rare, especially since so many of the residents had full-time security. Bodyguards were a necessary status symbol for the nation's rich and famous, and the neighborhood boasted plenty of both – actresses, captains of industry, politicians; all called the twelve-kilometer-long boulevard home, and most had seasoned ex-police or military to safeguard them. This was rarefied air in a city known for its violence and lawlessness, an oasis from the harsh reality outside its confines. Police patrolled the area assiduously, and the response time was said to be the fastest of anywhere in Mexico.

It didn't surprise *El Rey* that the man who was currently at the top of the city's most wanted list was staying in the most lavish section of town. The media made a great show of how committed the government was to cleaning up organized crime and ridding the nation of the death grip exercised by the cartels, but the truth was that their leaders had lived for years without being caught, their hundred billion dollars in annual revenue buying a certain selective blindness from law enforcement — after all, nobody was paid what they were worth, and that was especially true with the police, who might average four hundred dollars a month in pay. Throw a few grand the way of a commanding officer every so often, and it was hardly surprising that they were unable to apprehend their benefactors.

It was all a game, he knew, just as it was everywhere in the world. The smugly superior U.S. played by the same rules — it just took more money to buy immunity from prosecution. But human nature being what it was, those with the gold got to make the rules, and as always, they tended to operate by a different set than the rank and file. His nemesis and former employer, *Don* Aranas, the head of the Sinaloa cartel, whose ten-million-dollar bounty for his head was still the hushed topic of cartel gunman dreams, couldn't be caught, even though his romantic dalliances included a wife who spent much of her time in San Diego, a beloved firecracker of a pop singing star who was a pin-up sensation and the object of countless male fantasies throughout Latin America, and a shockingly gorgeous television star who defined the new breed of Mexican glamour queen in spite of her tender youth. Even with these well-known associations, the police hadn't been able to find him for two decades, and yet he managed to operate the most lucrative drug smuggling business in the world from his numerous hideouts in Mexico.

The power of the cartels was staggering, the income from their operations an inevitable part of the economy, as hotels, markets, casinos, gas station franchises...anything that could be used to launder the tsunami of greenbacks from the U.S. was purchased by anonymous corporations and operated by front men.

And those that laundered for the cartels, whose battles in Mexico killed over ten thousand a year, including many women and children, shared the cartels' miraculous ability to dodge the laws that everyone else had to obey. When a mega-banking conglomerate was revealed to have been acting as the laundering bank of choice, right down to where cartel soldiers were bringing in their cash deposits in specially designed containers that would just fit through a teller window, it did a deal with the American Justice Department, agreeing to a fine of $1.8 billion dollars — equivalent to roughly five weeks of its operating profit.

None of the executives or managers who had been assisting the most bloodthirsty, ruthless criminal gangs in history to launder their money were indicted. The toothless American law enforcement apparatus declared that if the mega-bank was actually charged under the law and the profits from the partnership in the illegal scheme clawed back, it would endanger the world economy. Likewise, the executives couldn't be prosecuted for their roles because it would jeopardize the stability of the bank. Some of them had to forego a small portion of their bonuses as punishment, while kids caught with a few ounces of marijuana went to jail, and anyone suspected of being involved with trafficking at a lower level forfeited all their assets, the assumption being that everything was the fruit of illegal gains.

None of the mainstream media outlets covered the outrage, of course, just as none of the Mexican media dared highlight the mockery of justice that was the daily cartel norm. The citizenry of the United States continued on its merry way, dutifully paying its taxes and sending its children to die in undeclared wars, while its law enforcement agency made sweetheart deals with murderers and criminals.

At least Mexicans understood that their government was hopelessly corrupt, and that any claims to the contrary were lies. *El Rey* had been raised in an environment where the double standard that money bought was celebrated by his mentor, who gleefully butchered whole families while remaining impossible to prosecute. The evidence that life wasn't fair, nor ever would be, was an accepted part of his existence. You did what you had to do to get by, and hoped that you wouldn't get squashed when the elephants were dancing their cash-fueled fandango. It had never occurred to him to speculate that things could be any different; it was naïve and simple-minded to do so. Money bought insulation, and the greatest crime in any country was to be weak and poor. It had been that way forever: under the Spanish, the French, and then Mexico's own rulers, just as it had been true in Europe for as long as there had been recorded history, as well as it had been in the rest of the world.

He glanced at his watch, the oversized luminescent hands of the Panerai Luminor glowing in the gloom, and resigned himself to a long night. *El Jaguar* wasn't showing any signs of getting down early, and *El Rey* was at the mercy of the cartel boss's nocturnal habits, which at present involved two stunningly beautiful exotic dancers from one of the most expensive clubs in Mexico City, a bottle of tequila, and a whole lot of cocaine, from what he could see through the small binoculars he'd brought. *El Jaguar* apparently liked to party. Not surprising, given the business he was in. *El Rey* just hoped that he would wear himself out sooner rather than later. What he was planning would be better carried out under cover of night, and while there were many hours to go before the first light of dawn streaked the orange-tinged sky, time could get away from him quickly, complicating things.

He watched as the drug lord whipped off his dress shirt and twirled it around his head, howling like a wolf to an unheard melody as his young companions cheered him on, fortified with alcohol and Peruvian coke. One thing was obvious to the assassin, as he watched the kingpin's paunch jiggle: The cartel boys knew how to blow off steam.

Enjoy it, my friend, he thought as he smiled with a humorless grin.

It will be your last night on the planet.

CHAPTER 33

El Jaguar stirred, the combination of alcohol and drugs having disturbed his sleep cycle, and one eye flittered open as he registered a sound: a tearing, like fabric, only louder. He was just coming to when a strip of duct tape smacked across his mouth, and then every nerve in his body radiated pain as a blow struck him just below his right ear. By the time he had regained control, his hands were bound behind his back and he was lying face up on his king-sized mattress.

"Shhh. Don't struggle," a soft voice whispered, and then, when he ignored the instruction, another starburst of agony shot through his body from another strike, this one at the junction where his neck met his chest. Everything went numb after a few seconds, and then as his nerves resumed transmitting, pain washed over him in waves as he struggled to breathe, tears streaming down his face.

"That first pressure point is called *Dokko*. The second, *Hichu*. Both are extremely effective, I think you'll agree. Should I continue with my little demonstration, or are you going to behave?" the voice asked reasonably.

El Jaguar nodded meekly.

"If I take the tape off your mouth, will you agree to stay quiet? Not that it will do any good for you to scream. This room is so well insulated it's almost soundproof – a big plus to dampen the traffic noise, but not very bright if one considers the other implications. That door is really something, by the way. What is it – steel with a foam core? You could stave off an army with that thing." A dark hand motioned at the bedroom door twenty-five feet away.

El Jaguar nodded again, and *El Rey* tore off the tape, ignoring the muffled cry of pain when he did so.

"You're fucking so dead. I'm looking at a dead man," *El Jaguar* hissed.

"Well, no, not really. But you're close. What you're actually looking at is death. My specialty is relieving people of their obligation to continue breathing. It's an exhausting affair, all the blood circulating, air entering the lungs, lymphatic system flushing toxins, organs filtering…"

The crime boss's eyes narrowed, and for the first time his fury was replaced with something else. Awareness. And fear. He felt a tickle of the unexpected sensation in his stomach, and struggled to swallow.

"Who are you, and what do you want?"

"Ah, much better. A man who asks good questions. My nom de plume, which you might have heard of, is *El Rey* – The King of Swords. And what I want is information. Actually, a very simple piece of information. Trivial in the scheme of things. A trifle," *El Rey* whispered, as if telling the cartel man a secret.

"*El Rey? The El Rey?* Fine. Whatever you're being paid, I'll double it. In fact, I'll triple it for you to go back and kill whoever your client is."

"That's a very attractive offer. What if I told you that your life cost a million dollars? That is the price tag for eliminating you?"

"Then you just made an extra two million. Now untie me," he snarled.

"If I'd known it was this easy to get rich quick, I would have changed my business plan a long time ago."

"Stop screwing around. Let me go. I have enough cash here to pay you the whole thing. Now."

"See, that's the problem. I don't completely trust you. I'm a man of my word; but, well, with all due respect, under the present circumstances, I could see you exaggerating or misstating. A sad state of affairs that the world is so distrusting, but there it is."

El Jaguar was starting to feel trepidation again. The discussion wasn't going the way it should have. "How do you want to do this?"

"You tell me where to find the money, I count it and take two million, and then you go back to sleep and I disappear."

"How do I know you're not going to rob me and kill me?"

"You don't. But do you really think that I came here to rob you? Not very smart, are you?" *El Rey* asked, almost to himself.

El Jaguar flushed with anger. "Nobody talks to me like that and lives."

"I believe you. Now are you going to tell me where the money is, or should I put the tape back on, rape you for a half hour, and then we'll resume the discussion? I'm sure the rumors about your adventure will raise your standing considerably with your men. Are you feeling experimental?"

"You...fine. In the closet – there's a panel on one side. Slide it forward. Behind it is a safe. There's about five million in it."

"I figured you might have a little walking around money. Very prudent." *El Rey* walked over to the closet and had the safe exposed in seconds. "What's the combination?"

El Jaguar told him, and within another few moments the assassin had the safe open. He whistled softly.

"Wow. Crime really does pay." He reached past the neatly bundled stacks of hundred dollar bills, and withdrew a pistol – a custom .45 made by JPL Precision, with a lightened slide, ion bond coating, Bomar sights, and a black oxide grip treatment. "This is beautiful. A work of art," he said, hefting it, then checking the magazine before chambering a round. "You must love this gun."

El Jaguar didn't say anything. Something was badly wrong, he could sense it. "You have the money. And my gun. Now let me go and our business will be concluded. There will be no consequences."

El Rey stepped away from the open safe, the pliant soles of his boots soundless on the Italian marble floor, and approached his captive again, slipping the gun into his waistband.

"Not completely. I still need a piece of information. Where are you holding the woman? The wife of the task force captain?" *El Rey* asked, as nonchalantly as if he was asking for cream in his coffee.

The drug lord's blood froze. "What the hell are you talking about? What is this? You have the money–"

"Yes, and your gun. We agreed on that. Now I need the information I came for. Where is she?"

"No. I can't." The fear in his eyes was real.

"What do you think will happen if you don't?"

"I'd be a dead man – and they'll get my family, too."

"You aren't paying attention. You're a dead man if you don't tell me."

El Jaguar glared at him defiantly. "I'm not afraid to die."

El Rey nodded. "I believe you. I see it in your eyes. You've known much death, and you know how easily life ends – how little drama there is. But there are worse things. Much worse."

"I can't tell you. I won't. I don't know."

"Now you're insulting me. The top dog for the Zs here doesn't know where the kidnapped wife is? Please." *El Rey* sighed, a sad sound, part impatience and part resignation. "I guess we'll do this the hard way, then." He reached for the roll of tape he had placed on the night table, tore off another piece, and placed it over El *Jaguar*'s mouth as he screamed for help and tried to pull away, and then drew a switchblade from his pocket and flicked it open. The drug maven's eyes widened as the evil blade gleamed in the dim moonlight from the street-facing window, and the assassin turned it slowly, as if inspecting it.

"Here's what I'm going to do. I'll start with your balls, then work up. By the time I make it to your neck, you'll have told me everything I want to know. You'd kill your mother for relief. I believe you aren't afraid to die. But I wonder if you'll be afraid to spend the last few moments of your life being slowly dismembered? I can control the bleeding and keep you alive for hours. It'll seem like an eternity to you, but I have a lot of practice at this, so I know what it will take to keep you breathing. Maybe I'll leave you alive, without your manhood, so that every waking moment of your miserable life is spent in horror. We'll see how I feel once I've gotten done with the first bit."

El Jaguar's eyes darted side to side in panic, and *El Rey* sliced his pajama bottoms open with a single swipe.

"I spent hours sharpening this today. While I was waiting for you to finish with the girls. I hate a dull knife. It's...imprecise. Sloppy. Now last chance – where is she?"

Ten minutes later, *El Rey* was sure he had been told the truth.

After an expertly placed cut, *El Jaguar* painlessly exsanguinated on his bed, his brutal life departing his body as the assassin stuffed half the safe's cash into his backpack, leaving the rest with the door open. Whoever found the corpse would probably take the cash and come up with some pretense to delay discovery while they made off with the money, further buying time.

He glanced at the bed again, having taken no pleasure in his work, and then with an eye on his watch, slid open the second-story window and pulled himself into the night.

CHAPTER 34

The stuttering neon lights on the stylized sign depicting a prancing red horse outside *El Caballo Rojo* flickered on and off like an arrhythmic heartbeat as battered cars growled past on the dark street, leaving a pall of exhaust in their wake. A few haggard working girls loitered on the sidewalk, flashing their wares at potential customers with a world-weariness far beyond their tender years. The bar was one of countless watering holes where men went to drink. There were no other attractions – no live music, no dancing, no mingling or rubbing shoulders with eligible singles. It was a mission-specific saloon where hard working laborers went to drown their sorrows and numb the pain from body blows that a harsh and all-too-brief existence delivered at every turn.

Inside, the rustic tile floor was stained from countless spilled beers, vomit, and blood from the inevitable fights that broke out once the evening had degenerated into a blurry haze for the inebriated patrons. Two stocky bartenders stood like sentries behind the long wooden slab fielding screamed drink orders from the harried cocktail waitresses whose outfits left little to the imagination and even less to modesty. The walls were all rough-hewn planks and adobe brick, with an occasional cow skull or rusting horseshoe adorning the spaces between faded black and white photographs of corrals, horses, and *vaqueros*, the iconic Mexican cowboys from the turn of a forgotten century. Even though smoking had been outlawed for several years, every surface area seeped fossilized nicotine from decades of men sucking smoke into ravaged lungs and fouling the unfiltered air.

Rauschenbach shook his head *no* as he pushed his way into the darkened interior, declining the desperate company one of the cadaverous prostitutes offered, his eyes roaming over the crowd until he spotted his contact sitting in the shadows, wearing the agreed-upon red button-up cowboy shirt, drinking beer from a long-necked, rust-colored bottle.

He made his way past the hard-scrabble crowd, pulled another stool from beneath the small table, and sat down across from the hulking man, taking in his buzz cut and sallow complexion, his skin the jaundiced tone of a junkie or someone suffering from chronic liver disease. A waitress came over and he pointed to his new friend's beer, and she nodded and offered a perfunctory smile, the fading beauty of a prime now past still lingeringly attractive in the shabby surroundings. Neither man spoke until she returned and deposited another bottle in front of the German, then cocked a carefully plucked eyebrow at his companion, who shook his head. She teetered off on too-high heels and Rauschenbach took a short pull on his beer.

"I have a few items I need within the next few days," the hit man started, seeing no point in wasting time with small talk. "I could probably have them ordered locally, but I was told you could handle this. Acquire them in the U.S. and ship them down."

"What have you got?"

Rauschenbach pulled a matchbook from his windbreaker and tossed it across the table. The man read the neat script jotted on the inside without comment, then nodded and put the matches in his shirt pocket.

"I can do that. Anything else?"

"Papers. Local driver's license, work permit. I can e-mail you photos."

"Not a problem."

"And I could use a pistol. Something recent, in good condition, preferably with no history – or alternatively, with the serial number removed."

"SIG, Glock, or Beretta? I have all three."

"Which model SIG Sauer?"

"P226. Hardly ever fired by a little old lady on Sundays. .40 caliber, so better stopping power, unless you want 9mm. I've got those too."

"P226's a nice weapon. But I prefer the 9mm."

"I've got a beauty. A P226 X-5 9mm with a nineteen-round clip. Like new."

Rauschenbach appeared to think for a moment. "How much for the gun and a box of ammo? Hollow points?"

The man took a long swig of beer. Guns were illegal in Mexico, and possession without a very-difficult-to-obtain permit was a felony except for certain hunting shotguns and small caliber rifles.

He named a figure in dollars, and Rauschenbach didn't blink.

"Seems pricy. What is that, about three times what it cost you in the U.S.?"

"Then fly to the U.S., buy one, and try to get it into Mexico."

Rauschenbach named a lower figure, half of what the man had asked. Both took sips of their brews and regarded each other, like prizefighters between rounds. The jukebox kicked to life and a rollicking accordion blared from the crackling speakers, soon joined by a tuba and what sounded suspiciously like a bus boy dropping a tray of used silverware in time to some beat only the musicians could discern. A wailing tenor piped in, singing about loneliness on the trail and the rough life of the cowboy, and a few of the more lively celebrants screamed along in what they imagined singing might sound like.

The man threw out another number, two-thirds of the asking price, and Rauschenbach nodded. He wasn't cost-sensitive, but haggling was mandatory, and he would arouse considerably more suspicion if he simply agreed to the first figure.

"Terms?" the German asked.

"Half up front. Half upon delivery in three days. Four, max. I'll e-mail you for a meet when I have everything in hand."

"Fine. How do you want to do this?"

"Finish your beer, then go to the restroom and count out the money. I'll be there in a minute, and I'll knock on the stall door. You hand it off, and that's it. But don't short me. I'll check it once I'm in my car."

"Got it. Bathroom, no shorting, one minute. Nice place you picked, by the way," Rauschenbach said, eyeing the crowd. Two men at the bar were posturing drunkenly, scrawny chests puffed out, glaring belligerently at each other – a fight waiting to start. The other patrons seemed bored by the brewing altercation, and Rauschenbach got the feeling that there were more than a few tussles on any given night. One of the bartenders caught his eye, his hair a greasy oil slick combed straight back off his forehead, a broken nose and a scar on his cheek badges of honor. Rauschenbach shook his head, and the bartender shrugged and returned to the television he was watching – yet another in a long string of soccer matches that seemed an inevitable part of Mexican life.

"Everybody minds their business here. Nobody wants any more trouble than they already have."

"It's got that going for it," Rauschenbach agreed, and then the fight broke out amidst breaking glass and a few rowdy cheers. The other bartender swung from around the bar with an axe handle clenched in his hand, and both men stopped when they saw him approach – neither wanted his night to end with a trip to the emergency room, a fractured skull or a broken hand their memento from their visit. Both separated, and then one made his way to the door as the bartender glared at his back. The scuffle was over before it started, and the bar returned to normal even as a cleaning woman hurried to sweep up the broken beer bottles.

Rauschenbach flagged down the waitress and tipped her ten pesos, then wove through the drinkers towards the bathroom, which lived up to every expectation he'd had from the lounge area. The two stalls reeked of urine and boasted cursory, infrequent cleaning, and neither had a seat. A large roll of toilet paper was mounted on the wall near the entry, where visitors took a few lengths when entering and hoped they guessed right. Rauschenbach stepped into the stall and pushed the creaky door closed and secured it, then peeled off a small wad of hundred dollar bills and folded them.

When the knock came he flushed the toilet, then opened the door and edged past his new friend, slipping him the money as he mumbled a hasty "*Lo siento*," and then he was out of the nauseating pit and making his way to the exit, the pungent stink of the toilet seeming to trail him like a noxious fog.

Outside, he moved past the hookers and loitering criminal types and flagged down a cab – an always-dangerous risk in the city at night, where gypsy cabs were used for kidnapping – and gave the driver the address of a restaurant a block from his hotel. If the driver had any thoughts about trying to assault the German, they quickly died when he appraised him in the rearview mirror.

Rauschenbach reclined on the cracking vinyl seat and watched as the tawdry parade drifted past his window, the taxi taking its time winding through traffic, which was heavier as they turned onto a main artery.

One important errand out of the way, he thought with satisfaction.

Tomorrow he would get some photos taken and the papers would be handled, and then he would be more than halfway home. He'd spent considerable time scoping out all the possible strike points that day, and he had a good idea of where he would have the highest odds of success. And the best part was that it would be completely unexpected. Even the most aggressive security details, which he knew the Chinese would be, wouldn't see his gambit coming. It was too much of a long shot. Literally.

Which would work in his favor.

The only way he was going to pull it off, given what he'd already seen in preliminary security precautions, was to plan something nobody would expect.

Which was why he got paid the big bucks.

He specialized in the impossible, and celebrated the unexpected.

In a week he would be in position, waiting, ready to end a man's life, whom he had nothing against and who had never done anything to harm him. But that man had offended someone, threatened some plan, and the client had been willing to pay a nosebleed price to eliminate him on Mexican soil.

The lights of Mexico City sped by as the cabbie increased speed, and Rauschenbach took another draw of reasonably clean air through the cracked window, the constant pall of pollution that hung over the city smelling like pure alpine air after the misery in the bathroom. He wouldn't miss D.F. a bit, and was looking forward to pulling the trigger and then getting out of there and back to his villa, where he could live out the rest of his life in comfort and style, thanks to one spectacular final payday.

CHAPTER 35

The blaring ringing of his cell jarred Cruz awake from his dozing on the couch, the lights off in his office, the blinds drawn. He'd chosen to spend another night there rather than dealing with getting situated in a new apartment. And truthfully, he didn't want to see any reminders of his life with Dinah – anything from the old place would be just that. The less emotion that clouded his fatigued judgment, the better.

He stared at the phone like it was radioactive, then noted the time as he picked it up and held it to his ear. Three-twenty a.m..

El Rey's voice crooned in his ear. "She's being held in a warehouse on the outskirts of town. Six man armed cartel team."

"Where?"

He gave Cruz the address, who scratched it on his legal pad and then rubbed sleep out of his eyes.

"We should hit it as soon as possible. Within the next hour or two, best case. Once *El Jaguar* is discovered, all hell will break loose and they'll probably kill her in the chaos. There will only be one chance at this."

Cruz didn't ask what had happened with the Los Zetas captain. "Do you think that two of us can take them?"

"Who, you and pussy boy? Old man, come on. When was the last time you ran a few miles, much less were in peak fighting form?"

"You'd be surprised. I took down three gunmen yesterday. The way I see it, that makes me my best option."

El Rey grunted noncommittally. "What have you got for weapons?" he asked.

Cruz rattled off his choices from memory.

"That should do. I'll meet you a block from the location, at a closed market on the corner named *La Esquina*. The warehouse is in a *barrio* with mixed residential and industrial. Not a very big building, but fairly well fortified," the assassin said.

"Meet me there? Where are you?"

"Near the market. I figured a little reconnaissance couldn't hurt before your goon squad showed up with all the subtlety of a tank."

"That's...unexpected. And appreciated."

"Let's not get all weepy about this. My best chance of being able to take advantage of the favor you owe me is if you're still alive, which you won't be unless I help you. With all due respect, you and your pit bull are no match for six Los Zetas ex-marines, no matter what you think. But this is the kind of thing I do in my sleep. So I'll throw you a bone and save your bacon."

"You seem awfully confident."

"Because it'll be over before they know what hit them."

Cruz saw nothing to be gained by arguing. If *El Rey* wanted to go in with them, his help would be invaluable. For all his arrogance, he was absolutely correct about his abilities. Six cartel gunmen against one *El Rey*, as well as Briones and Cruz, was a better-than-even match.

"I can be there in an hour."

"Fine. I'll want one of the ARX 160s and one of the silenced Berettas, with a few spare clips. And find a combat knife. KA-BAR if you have one. But sharp. Whatever it is, it's got to be sharp. Hopefully the ARX is sound-suppressed, too."

"It's suppressed. Anything else?"

"Try not to attract attention when you arrive. Keep it low-key. It's dead here, but they might have spotters in one of the surrounding homes. Don't bring a police vehicle – something unmarked would be best. A beater would be even better. This isn't the greatest area."

"I know it well enough. We've run operations there before, a few years ago."

"Great. I'll see you in an hour."

The line went dead in Cruz's hand and he stared at the phone for a few seconds, mind processing the deluge of information, and then he called Briones. The younger man's voice was thick with sleep when he answered, but he roused quickly when Cruz told him that they were a go.

"I can be there in half an hour to pick you up."

"Perfect. That should be more than enough time."

"Have you given any thought to calling in some of the men, sir?"

"Yes, but I've decided that won't be necessary. It'll just be the three of us."

"Three?"

"*El Rey*...Carlos... will be participating in this operation."

Briones was speechless for a moment. "But...I mean, why on earth...?"

"Maybe he's bored. Maybe he's trying to earn some good faith from us. Who the hell knows? What's important is that he's lethal as a cobra and has done this sort of thing more times than we could count. And right now, he's our best shot at getting Dinah out alive."

"I...all right, but I want it on the record that I don't like it. I don't trust him. I don't know what he's up to, but you can bet that whatever it is, it's only good for *El Rey*, and nobody else. He's not on our side. He's on his own side, and we have no idea what that is."

"I don't disagree. But he's the only choice right now. And he's already there."

"At the site?!"

"Correct. So better get your butt in gear. I'll be waiting for you downstairs," Cruz said. Briones had a point – the assassin served no master but himself. Cruz didn't know what deal he had made with CISEN, but it had to have been at gunpoint.

And there was the question of the promise. Dangling out there, a liability with no bounds, Cruz's considerable power now in the hands of the most lethal man in Mexico. Cruz had no doubt that he would have to do something unconscionable sooner or later to wipe the slate clean; but at that moment, Dinah's well-being was his paramount concern. Everything else was noise.

The assassin had performed, he would give him that. He'd found the Los Zetas boss in a matter of hours, and had somehow extracted information that could save his wife's life. The how's of it didn't matter, as far as Cruz was concerned. He had no doubt that whatever mess *El Rey* had left of the drug lord, the cartel would clean it up and nobody would ever hear about it. The last thing they'd want was any hint that they were vulnerable; so the body, assuming that the assassin had left much of one, would be spirited away and dumped in an unmarked grave somewhere, and a new Mexico City chief quietly appointed.

Which led him to his next concern – if they were successful rescuing Dinah, questions would have to be answered. How had they discovered her location? How had they rescued her? Who had participated in the raid?

He resolved to put them aside until they'd actually saved her. He would have to still be alive by morning for any of it to be an issue. Besides which, he wasn't especially worried about his career after being blackmailed by Godoy. Perhaps this was all a sign that his time in public service was drawing to a close, and after the German was stopped – or not – he would hang up his badge and turn to other things.

As he pulled on his belt and checked his Glock, his shoulders slumped. He had given the best part of his life to fighting an unwinnable war against adversaries that were interchangeable, and who were more motivated and better funded than the police. For all his efforts, how had the landscape changed over the last decade? Sixty, seventy thousand people dead, Mexico reduced to a war zone, and for what? The cartels were more powerful and richer than at any point in their history, their wealth an entrenched part of the economy, and they now owned more mainstream businesses than ever before.

It was a senseless fight that he was losing. So many innocents killed, and nothing changed, regardless of which politicians were in office or what brave initiatives were floated. He was a cog in an ugly, futile machine that was more for appearances than anything.

He checked the Glock's magazine and pocketed a spare, then replaced it in the quick-release hip holster.

Whatever obligation he owed the assassin, he would repay.

Whatever the cost.

He would get Dinah back, alive.

That was all that mattered.

CHAPTER 36

Gravel crunched under the oversized tires as Briones guided the Dodge down the dirt road, the cinderblock buildings on either side covered with graffiti and filth and the tarpaper shacks fashioned from discarded lumber and filched materials lending an aura of disrepair to the area. These were the hovels of the working poor, with no social net to catch them when they stumbled – their everyday existence as harsh as any third world population's, with non-existent sanitation and pest infestation battling disease and crime as the primary scourges of the grim shanty town. Running water had only made it to the unfortunate residents within the last decade, with most electricity bootlegged from the few overhead power lines running to the industrial buildings. Sewage was a continual problem, as the rough septic tanks the more industrious neighbors had installed cracked from the region's constant earthquakes and the wastewater seeped into the ground. Still, it was an improvement over the open trench latrines that soured the air; and little by little, progress was being made.

Cruz pointed to the dark market and Briones pulled the car to the side of the road, near two rusting mid-eighties Chrysler sedans that had seen their best years fade behind them in clouds of oily, partially combusted smoke. Both men got out once the engine died, and Briones' nose wrinkled involuntarily at the fetid stink of raw human waste.

When El Rey materialized soundlessly behind them, both men jumped, their nerves already on edge.

"What the...don't do that," Cruz blurted, hand on his Glock.

"Sorry. Occupational hazard. Where are the weapons?" *El Rey* asked, not bothering to acknowledge Briones, who silently walked to the trunk and popped the lid. Inside, an arsenal sat ready. *El Rey* appraised the trove and then reached in and grabbed a silenced Beretta, then one of the rifles and a knife. Last, he fished out a set of night vision goggles, then pulled them over his head and switched them on.

"Hey. That only leaves us with one set of NV gear," Briones complained, but *El Rey* cut him off.

"You have a weapon with a night-vision scope. Use that."

"But—"

Cruz intervened, uninterested in yet another unwinnable squabble between the two. "I think Carlos here would be better served with them than without," he said, then turned to the assassin. "So what's the plan?"

El Rey knelt by the car and hastily drew a rectangle in the dirt, then drew another inside. "It's a walled lot, with a single building, probably no more than three hundred square meters. There are four guards outside and, from what I can tell, two inside. The four outside are carrying shotguns or AKs, and the interior guards are probably similarly equipped. There's no security gear, so that will make this easier. The grab was apparently a last-minute decision, so they're keeping her in one of their low-traffic places. *El Jaguar* was clear on the number of men and the lack of security equipment, though."

"Wait. You found *El Jaguar*?" Briones blurted.

El Rey grunted assent.

"Well, where is he?"

"Enjoying his eternal reward," *El Rey* said dryly.

Cruz and Briones exchanged a look.

"Here's what we're going to do. I'll go in here, on the back side. *Capitan* Cruz, you take the high ground there, in that abandoned two-story building across the way from the warehouse. Use the night vision-scoped rifle to pick off anyone I don't get, but only fire if I'm hit. I'd rather not wake the whole neighborhood if we don't need to. And you, Lieutenant, when the captain gives you the signal, come through the front gate; but again, don't shoot unless you see me in trouble. We should be able to do this silently, with any luck at all."

"What, you mean you plan to try to take out all six yourself, without alerting anyone?" Briones scoffed.

"It's not like I haven't done it before. This is your best play. Just be a nice boy and do as you're told. Don't shoot, and stay out of my way. Unless you want the captain's wife to pay for your blunders with her life," *El Rey* finished.

"Lieutenant, I think we have to do this his way," Cruz warned, seeing Briones bristle. He eyed the assassin. "I hope you know what you're doing."

"Give me five minutes to get into position, and then I'm going in. Remember. *Do. Not. Shoot.* If either of you gets trigger-happy, this blows up and your wife dies." *El Rey* paused and glared at Briones. "I presume you both have cell phones. *Capitan,* call the lieutenant when I go in so he knows it's begun. You, turn your phone to vibrate so you don't alert the guards."

He spun, and was just about to trot into the darkness when Cruz grabbed his arm.

"Good luck."

"Don't worry. I won't need it."

And then he was gone.

Briones turned to Cruz, shaking his head. "I don't like this. He's up to something. He's excluded both of us...it feels wrong," he protested.

"He did, but I think it's because if he told us to wait in the car, we wouldn't have. So he gave us tasks to keep us occupied."

"I really think we need to reconsider–"

"Lieutenant. So far, he's located the key Los Zetas player in Mexico City and extracted the whereabouts of my wife in about as much time as it would have taken us to submit a report requesting permission to begin surveillance on him. I think we play this his way."

"That's another thing. Aren't you concerned about how he handled *El Jaguar*? I mean, he obviously killed him, and probably tortured him."

"I think that if you're going to kidnap family members, it changes the rules. Besides, is the world such a bad place without *El Jaguar* polluting it? How many lives will be saved because he's dead? No, I have mixed feelings about this. I wish I could say I was shocked, but I'm actually just glad he's on our side."

"When did we become vigilantes?" Briones asked.

Cruz understood his moral outrage, but knew him well enough to understand that it was more for show than anything. Years of working on the anti-cartel task force hardened you, he knew from personal experience.

"We're not vigilantes. We're mounting a mission using assets from another government agency. One that operates with considerably different latitude than we do. Fortunately, for Dinah's sake. Let's not get all self-righteous on this. Remember our objective. And remember what happened to my wife and daughter. If I'd had someone like him back then, maybe they'd still be alive."

Briones had no response.

"I'll take full responsibility for this operation, Lieutenant. All I ask is that you put your feelings aside and pull on the same oar with me."

Briones appeared to think about it for a few moments, and then nodded. "Okay, sir. I'm in. Let's get into position. By my watch, we've got about three and a half minutes before all hell breaks loose."

Cruz watched as Briones flipped on his night vision goggles and then jogged down the dirt road towards the compound. He was still uneasy about his lieutenant, and uttered a silent prayer that he wouldn't let his obvious dislike for the assassin spill over and make him do something stupid. Cruz hefted the rifle and then sprinted for the abandoned structure, a flutter of anxiety building in his stomach as his boots clomped against the loose dirt of the sad road to nowhere.

CHAPTER 37

The warehouse yard was dark and the area still except for the sound of murmured conversation from the rear, where two guards were lounging by the back wall, lying to each other about their most recent sexual exploits. The younger of the two, a little tank of a man with long, greasy hair and a goatee, was laughing quietly at the rollicking story his companion was telling.

"Anyway, I'm standing there with my pants off, and she sees my gun. So then the freaky bitch—"

He was interrupted by a scrape from the wall thirty meters away — metal on concrete.

Both men stiffened at the sound, and then the storyteller hoisted his shotgun and pumped the slide, chambering a round before making a hand gesture for the other to stay put. The younger man needed no encouragement, and remained standing by the rear wall, his back against it, his Kalashnikov assault rifle dangling loosely by his side.

"It's probably a dog or something," he whispered to his older companion, who made another hand gesture to be quiet, and then crept forward into the gloom.

A few seconds went by, and then a loop of rusting wire slid from the top of the wall and around the younger man's throat, surprising him. As the impromptu garrote tightened around his neck, his eyes bugged out and he reflexively dropped his weapon, both hands clutching at the snare strangling him while he danced an involuntary jig. Pressure from above almost lifted him off his feet as the wire sliced into his skin, and then blood seeped from around the wound before spraying onto the wall when the carotid severed.

The entire macabre scene played out in fifteen seconds in complete silence, other than the thud of the AK47 hitting the weeds and the muted stamping of the gunman's feet as he performed his death dance.

When the older man returned from his fruitless exploration, he hissed a whisper at his younger partner, whose shadowed figure was leaning against the wall in the dark.

"I didn't see anything. You're right, it's some animal or—"

A form covered in head-to-toe black dropped to his right; he barely registered the glint of steel before a stinging slice lacerated his trachea. His free hand groped for the gash as blood first bubbled and then gushed from the wound, and then the world spun as tiny pinpoints of light shimmered through the enveloping darkness and he slumped forward with a choking moan. *El Rey* stepped aside, catching his shotgun before it hit the ground while avoiding the bloody torrent that spurted from the guard's neck.

Two of the six guards down in only a few seconds, and *El Rey* hadn't broken a sweat. He returned the blade to his belt sheath and peered at the front of the compound, where he knew the other pair of guards were patrolling, oblivious that their number had just been reduced by half.

The assassin crept forward, the night vision goggles illuminating the dark in fluorescent green, and then spotted the first of his targets, the guard's assault rifle hanging from a shoulder strap as he relieved himself against the crumbling perimeter wall.

Gerardo traced his name on the deteriorating mortar with his splattering stream, the liter of water he'd drunk having finally worked its way through his kidneys and demanding release. The night duty wasn't so bad, he thought, except when it rained, and their hard-ass shift leader made them stand in the drizzle, as though anyone would be moving against an empty warehouse in a downpour. After a few more seconds his flow slowed to a trickle and he sighed in satisfaction, then zipped up after a few vigorous shakes.

The spike of searing pain in his upper spine was as sudden as lightning, and the force of the blow knocked the wind out of him. He fought for a gasping last breath, but his nervous system had abruptly stopped obeying his brain's commands and his lungs remained empty, and then he was falling, his bulk leaden, his legs no longer supporting his weight, knees not so much buckling as his whole body collapsing at the speed of gravity, like a controlled building demolition.

El Rey knelt and wiped the KA-BAR's bloody blade on the man's shirt, pausing to watch his eyes glaze, and then swept the other side of the yard with the night vision goggles, searching for the remaining guard. He was just about to stand and inch along the wall when a gruff voice called to him out of the darkness on his left.

"Hey, Gerardo, you got a smoke—"

The first subsonic 9mm Parabellum copper-jacketed round from the Beretta M9's silenced barrel caught the speaker in the jaw, tearing half his face off as the soft lead hollow point mushroomed into an ugly blossom of destruction. A split second later its twin dotted a neat hole directly between the guard's eyes, and the deformed slug careened through his cerebrum like a willful pachinko ball, instantly terminating his life.

El Rey rose from his kneeling crouch and moved swiftly to the dead newcomer. What was left of his head was twisted at an unnatural angle on the hard-packed dirt, and after a quick once-over, the assassin decided that even with the blood splatter he would serve the immediate purpose.

A few seconds later, he had the night-vision goggles off and the man's loose jacket on, the Beretta just fitting in one of the pockets. He laid the goggles to one side and then returned to the other corpse and relieved it of its black baseball cap, which thankfully didn't have much blood on it, though it stank of sour sweat and grimy hair. He pulled on the hat and then fished in the dead man's overcoat, stopping when he found a pack of Marlboros and a plastic butane lighter. He glanced over his shoulder at the two warehouse windows in the near distance, seeping dim amber light, and then straightened and walked to the building entrance.

The two seated interior guards registered the front door swinging open, and then a growling voice followed a cloud of cigarette smoke through it. They relaxed as they saw the familiar jacket of one of their crew, and never had time to register their oversight.

"Shit, it's colder than hell out there—"

The Beretta popped through the jacket's fabric, and the first guard took two rounds to the chest. His partner was swinging an assault rifle up as the next series of four shots stitched a frying-pan-sized pattern of bloody wounds in his upper abdomen. The rifle crashed to the concrete floor as the man tumbled back in the chair and dropped in a heap on the ground. *El Rey* approached the two prone forms, and seeing that the first gunman was still breathing, toed his weapon out of reach before confirming that the other one was dead.

"Where's the girl?" he asked, and the man's eyes flicked to the left. *El Rey*'s gaze followed his to the interior office door.

"Anyone in there?"

The man shook his head, then coughed blood, the chest wounds burbling as he struggled for breath.

The assassin covered the ground quickly and threw the door open before ducking around the jamb and sweeping the darkened room with his pistol. Light streamed through the doorway into the room, and he could just make out a figure seated in a chair in the far corner. There, biting against a rag that was stuffed in her mouth and held in place with silver tape, was Dinah.

He felt around for a light switch and was rewarded by an overhead bulb sputtering to life. Dinah looked dazed, and then her eyes widened in panic when she recognized him, his gun clenched in his hand, blood smeared across his coat.

"Relax. I'm here to get you out of here," he soothed as he approached her and felt for the edge of the tape. "This is going to hurt, but don't make a sound. Are you okay?"

She was nodding a yes when he ripped the tape off and she whined in pain, the adhesive leaving a red welt, tears welling in her eyes from the sting. He pulled the filthy rag out of her mouth and she coughed, then spit to the side. He slid the blade of the KA-BAR from the sheath and for a second the terror returned, and then he was talking again, softly, rhythmically, coaxing her to calm.

"This will only take a second. I need to cut the bindings. Can you walk?" he asked, then placed a hand on one arm as he bent down with the knife. "Hold still. I don't want to cut you."

"I...I can walk," she whispered as he sawed through the rope, and then her hands were free and she was clenching and unclenching her fingers, trying to get circulation to return. He knelt and repeated the process with her ankles, the line falling away as he sliced, and then he stood and studied her. One side of her face was discolored by an angry bruise, and the eye on that side was swollen half shut.

"I'm getting you out of here, do you understand? Your captors are dead. Your husband is waiting outside. It's over. You're free," he assured her, and for a moment the look in her eyes was of incomprehension, and then, slowly, disbelief.

"What? You...my husband...how...?"

"Long story. Come on. Stand up. I'll help you." She was suffering from shock, and probably dehydration, judging from her stupor. "Did they drug you?"

"N...no. No drugs."

"Okay, then. Come on. Up." He slipped his arm under hers and lifted her to her feet, and then inched towards the doorway. She took one hesitant step, and then another, and then they were walking, slowly, out of the makeshift cell and towards the front door. Dinah's eyes took in the two bodies and then she shut them, tears rolling down her face, and began sobbing as they moved, all the fear and anxiety and hurt from her ordeal purged in a swell of relief.

When they stepped through the entryway, he guided her through the night and towards the front gate, the darkness enfolding them both in its anonymous arms. A clatter sounded from in front of them, and they looked up as the gate swung open with a creak, Briones pushing it forward on rusting hinges.

They were halfway to him when *El Rey* slowed. Briones continued approaching, and the assassin's mind whirled as he watched the lieutenant raise his submachine gun and point it at them. Time compressed into slow motion as he aimed the weapon at *El Rey*, and then it was too late – he'd pulled the trigger.

They heard a thump behind them and *El Rey* swung around, jerking his Beretta free as he glimpsed the body of the surviving bodyguard sprawled near the door, a pistol gripped in his lifeless hand, his brains spattered on the warehouse wall behind him. Dinah stood alone for a second, taking in Briones, gun still raised, and the assassin, who was slowly spinning back to face him, and then she stumbled and *El Rey* reached out and caught her.

Briones flipped the goggles out of his line of sight as he held the UMP 9 steady with his other hand. The two men exchanged a look, and Briones lowered the weapon, the moment past.

"Missed that one, huh?" Briones asked with a smirk, and then Cruz was standing at the gate as Dinah, energized, stumbled unsteadily towards him. He dropped his rifle and threw his arms around her and hugged her close, laughing with relief as she cried. Then his eyes drifted towards the assassin, standing framed by the light from the warehouse door, facing Briones, as if the two men were about to fight a duel in a hellish last stand of their own devising.

"Let's secure all our weapons, so there's no trace we were here," *El Rey* said, and turned to where he'd left his night vision goggles. "I left my rifle in the back, on the other side of the wall," he said, and before they could respond he was gone as soundlessly as he had appeared, the only evidence of his presence the six dead men scattered around the compound.

CHAPTER 38

"I thought your boy there was going to plug me, for a second," *El Rey* said, his voice slightly distorted by the cell phone.

"He would never do that. He promised me...," Cruz replied, Dinah's head on his shoulder as they stood by Briones' cruiser.

"Hell of a way to find out."

"Where are you?"

"Don't worry about me. Get your wife somewhere safe and take care of your business. I'll touch base tomorrow once I've gotten some rest."

Cruz hugged Dinah's form closer. "I...I don't know how I can ever thank you..."

"I'll think of something – remember, we have a deal. Now make sure all the weapons are accounted for. I left the guns and the night vision gear leaning against the market wall, around the corner from where you're parked. You might want to clean them and return them to inventory. As far as I can tell, looks like another regrettable cartel battle took place between two warring factions. That's the way I'd frame it," *El Rey* said, and then the line clicked, and Cruz was holding dead air.

Briones came huffing from the gate and popped the remote trunk release with the stab of a button. Cruz told him about the other weapons, and he retrieved them, returning with the guns a few moments later.

In the near distance, they heard a whoosh, and then flames licked from the warehouse compound's walls. Apparently *El Rey* had decided to eradicate the physical evidence – a smart move, and one that reminded Cruz again of how the assassin had made his fortune.

Nobody spoke as Cruz and Dinah slid into the back seat. Briones started the engine and then pulled down the dirt road, lights extinguished. He didn't illuminate them until he was a hundred yards away, swinging onto the pavement of the larger street that would lead them back to the city proper.

"Where to, boss?" he asked as he gave the big sedan gas.

"Didn't you say that we've got a new condo leased and waiting?"

Briones nodded. "I did indeed."

Dinah looked up from where she was leaning against him. "I want to take a long shower, get some new clothes, and sleep for a few days," she declared.

Cruz nodded. He hadn't commented on the bruise or the damage to her face. There would be time enough to talk about it when she was ready.

"Are you sure you don't want to see a doctor?"

"I want a bath and bed."

Cruz looked at the back of Briones' head. "You heard the lady. Take us to our new digs."

∾◅

It was six a.m. by the time they made it to the new flat. Dinah gratefully inspected the bedroom and bathroom and declared them acceptable, and then closed the door so she could bathe. Cruz sat at the dining room table, a generic contemporary affair much like the ones in the last four condos, and thought over the night's events as he watched the first stabs of a new dawn pierce the sky, all shimmering orange and red and streaks of violet and fuchsia. The ever-lingering pall of smog did make for spectacular sunrises and sunsets, even if it was toxic, he thought appreciatively, then rose and opened the refrigerator, which had been thoughtfully stocked with staples, including a six-pack of Modelo beer.

He popped one open, took his seat again, and downed half the can in a gulp. He burped, then took another pull, then rubbed a tired hand over his face. They – no, *El Rey* – had accomplished the impossible, without a single casualty, leaving no trace of their passage to tip anyone off. Perhaps if law enforcement worked like that, there would be less of an appetite for lawlessness. Far more cartel members were killed by each other than had ever been killed by the police, and arrest was viewed as a deserved break from the ugly realities of the street. Maybe if criminals knew there was a bullet waiting for them, or the sharp blade of a silent knife...

His thoughts drifted to the assassin's performance, and then to his suggestion that Cruz leave well enough alone and not report their role in the night's adventure. He had a point. It would be Cruz's group that ultimately investigated a cartel-related execution scene, and nobody would really expect them to arrive at any conclusion besides the obvious – that the cartel business was a rough game in which disputes were settled with a bullet. So six miscreants had been butchered. Better sixty, or six hundred. The world was certainly no poorer for it.

The cold beer soothed his parched throat as he reasoned through how he would explain Dinah's sudden reappearance. Then he realized that the explanation didn't have to be logical. The cartel had set her free. Why? Maybe they got scared from the heat being brought by the investigation. Or maybe it wasn't cartel-related at all. Perhaps it had been a gang of kidnappers that had chosen a convenient target of opportunity, and when the word had hit the street that the full weight of the *Federales* was going to land on whoever had kidnapped her, they couldn't get rid of her fast enough. Random and inexplicable events took place all the time. Sometimes, they worked in the good guys' favor – a welcome relief from the norm.

When the smoke cleared, it would be his word against...*nobody's*. It was the perfect scenario. No one would connect the massacre at the warehouse with Dinah – there was no reason to. And once the blaze had worked its magic, there wouldn't be much to sift through. The assassin had covered all the bases, and all that remained was for them to keep their mouths shut.

He had no doubt that Briones would go along with whatever story he told – his loyalty to Cruz was absolute. The bad guys had lost a round, and an innocent had been saved.

Some days were good ones.

Today was one of them, he thought, watching the sky lighten, the light show over as the sun rose over the hills.

Sometimes you had to take the wins where you found them and leave the heavy thinking to someone else.

Perhaps this was one of those times.

Cruz heard the door open behind him and smelled Dinah before her arms curled around his neck. He finished his beer with a final swallow and set it down on the table and rose, then turned to hold her in a loving embrace. He kissed her face, taking care to avoid the worst of the bruising,

195

and then she pulled away and took his hand before wordlessly leading him to the bedroom, her eyes moist – whether from sadness or relief, he couldn't be sure.

They would discuss what had happened to her in captivity when she felt strong enough to tell him what had happened. For now, she was back where she belonged, and that was enough.

For now, it was everything.

CHAPTER 39

Rauschenbach hung his left arm out the open window of the rented sedan and enjoyed the feel of the sun on his skin as he motored south from Mexico City and into the wilds of the mountains that were part of El Tepozteco National Park. He had turned off the highway half an hour earlier and was now on a dirt road that was rapidly becoming more of a game trail than anything intended for cars. When he reached a promising cluster of trees, he pulled the vehicle off the path and rolled twenty yards into the thicket, where it would be out of view from anyone passing on the track – unlikely in the rural area at this early hour on a weekday.

He shut off the engine and stepped round to the back, opened the trunk, and extracted a guitar case. With a final look at the car, he set out into the wilds, following the trace of a route that deer had recently used, judging by some droppings he spotted. Rauschenbach was an accomplished tracker, a skill he'd developed as part of his professional disciplines, and it didn't look like any humans had been in the area recently – there were no footprints or mountain bike tire tracks, and it had drizzled two nights ago, so if anyone had passed since then, they would have left evidence.

Eventually he came to a large clearing. He set the guitar case down, lifted a pair of binoculars to his eyes, and methodically scanned his surroundings for any signs of life. After a few minutes of study, he placed them on top of the case, which was concealed in the tall grass by the edge of the tree line. He then stood and began taking large, measured steps across the field.

Thirty minutes later he stopped pacing and found himself a dozen yards from a pine tree – one of the few that grew in the otherwise open field. He withdrew a disposable diaper from his jacket pocket, unfolded it, and secured it to the tree trunk first with the adhesive strips and next with a length of cord. Stepping back, he studied his handiwork, then extracted a red Sharpie from his jacket and drew a red circle the size of an apple on the white surface, taking care to color it in. With a final glance at his project, he turned and retraced his steps to the guitar case a mile away.

A lazy breeze rustled the tree tops as he opened the lid and assembled the rifle, taking care to ensure that the parts were impeccably clean as he joined them together. When he was finished, the scope and silencer locked securely in place, he withdrew three of the five precious bullets from his pants pocket and set them on the case, and then lay down, balancing the rifle on a photographer's tripod he had purchased the prior day.

He scouted around the clearing with the high-powered Schmidt & Bender PM II 10×42/Military MK II 10×42 scope until he found the diaper pad. Once sure of his bearings, he unscrewed the custom-made bolt and slid the first bullet into place, then screwed the bolt back into firing position and cocked it. The scope had been dialed for a range of twelve hundred meters, but he wanted to ensure that it would be effective at fifteen hundred – the longest shot he had ever made for a sanction. Most other weapons couldn't deliver accuracy at that range, but the combination of the barrel, the silencer, and the ammo gave this weapon reasonable accuracy at fifteen hundred meters and beyond – assuming a host of other variables were also in his favor, such as elevation, temperature, humidity, and wind velocity.

He next reached into the case and extracted three devices his contact had sourced for him: a handheld ballistics computer; a Minox meter that measured air density, barometric pressure, temperature, and wind speed; and a laser range finder. He first confirmed the distance to the target, at fifteen hundred and twenty meters. Next, he took a measurement on the Minox, and studied the readout with interest before powering the computer on and entering the data.

Mexico City was seventy-five hundred feet above sea level, which would improve accuracy because there was less atmosphere. In the mornings, by ten a.m., it had been averaging just under seventy degrees, which also improved accuracy, as measured as an expected ballistic coefficiency number. The higher the number, the more accurate the round. This weapon at that altitude and temperature, assuming no wind, would be extremely high, in the range of 1.0 or higher, whereas a normal cartridge might have an expected coefficient in the .265 range at sea level. Expressed another way, those rounds fired through that barrel and silencer would be almost four times more accurate than a typical bullet, which was critical at ranges over seven hundred meters. He entered a coefficient assumption of .95, just to be conservative.

Finally, Mexico City was humid, averaging seventy-five percent or higher humidity that time of year, which would further improve accuracy – because contrary to seeming logic, water had less density than dry air, so higher humidity was actually optimal for shooting. At the end of the day, the biggest random variable would be wind. If under ten miles per hour, he could adjust for it and expect adequate results. More than ten and the kill shot wasn't impossible, but the likelihood of shift would increase – the possibility that the bullet wouldn't hit exactly where he had aimed it.

He peered through the scope again and centered the hand-drawn red dot in the crosshairs, now ten times larger than life due to the scope's 10X magnification, and then exhaled smoothly and gently squeezed the trigger. The rifle stock slammed into his shoulder with a kick, which he expected – he had clocked over fifty rounds with the weapon in Spain to acclimate himself. After a brief moment he steadied it again and peered down-range at the target. A hole had appeared seven inches to the right of the red mark's center, and three below it.

He did a quick mental calculation and then adjusted the screws on the top and side of the scope, then repeated the process of chambering another and went through his careful aiming ritual before firing again. This time, the hole appeared an inch to the right of dead center, but at the correct elevation. He made one final adjustment and fired the last round, and the bullet hit in the center of the target a second and a half after he pulled the trigger. The sound of the silenced rifle, about as loud as a muffled firecracker, would take roughly four seconds to reach the target, and the round a second and a half at that distance – the muzzle velocity with the silencer being nine hundred and twenty-five meters per second, and the speed of sound being three hundred and forty-two.

Rauschenbach took the same care breaking down the weapon as he had taken assembling it and then returned it to the false bottom in the guitar case. He closed it, picked up the three shell casings, and then carried it to the target a mile away.

By the time he made it back to the car, another hour and a half had passed, and he was getting hungry. He stowed the guitar case on the rear seat and started the engine, then backed out of the bushes and returned down the trail, bouncing along contentedly with the air of a man whose time had been productively spent.

His mind drifted to the job and the level of difficulty he'd bitten off when he'd agreed to go forward with it. He had already circled the target site numerous times, and arrived at the conclusion that his best odds lay elsewhere. And that elsewhere would require the ability to hit a man's head with a high degree of reliability at up to sixteen hundred meters – a distance of over a mile.

Nobody would expect it, for good reason. Absent a high degree of training, perfect shooting conditions, a specialized weapon and ammo, consummate skill, and nerves of steel, it wouldn't work. Few shooters in the world would be able to pull it off – a handful of snipers in Afghanistan and Iraq, perhaps two other hit men he'd ever heard of, and a smattering of competitive target shooters. And him.

Which was why he was the right man for the job.

The road eventually turned from dirt to gravel and then to asphalt, and before much longer he was back on the highway weaving his way north through slower traffic, back to Mexico City, another essential element in his preparations concluded.

The hardest part, other than the actual money shot, still lay ahead: figuring out how he could penetrate the location on execution day. Security had already been ratcheted up, which made sense to him now that he knew that his involvement had been leaked. A source at Interpol had sent him an e-mail from a blind account warning him that the Mexicans were on alert.

That was fine.

It changed nothing. He assumed that they had his old photo from his days with the East Berlin police – but he hadn't resembled his old likeness for years, thanks to a talented plastic surgeon in Budapest who'd later died in a car accident. It was amazing what a slightly different nose, an altered chin, and a little eye work could accomplish – his own mother wouldn't have recognized him now, even without his disguises. No, he wasn't worried at all, either about being discovered or the level of difficulty involved in the hit. He routinely performed impossible feats. That was his claim to notoriety. This sanction would be no different. He had absolutely no doubt that he would find a way in, and soon have the Chinese leader's distinctive profile in the crosshairs. Now it was just a matter of logistics. He knew how he was going to do it, and where.

All that remained was for him to figure out how he'd get in and out, and stay alive in the process.

Piece of cake.

CHAPTER 40

Cruz sat staring at his computer screen, aware of the rapid passage of time. The day of the signing was drawing steadily closer without any progress on his end. Three days had whizzed by since Dinah had been saved, and as he had expected, nobody had linked the charred remains salvaged from the warehouse embers with her abduction. When he had announced two days ago that Dinah had reappeared, safe and sound, the reaction from the group responsible for the investigation into her disappearance had been muted. They always had more work than they could handle, given the constant kidnappings in Mexico City, so an assignment taken off the board would be regarded as a relief rather than a cause for concern.

He printed out the presentation he had been working on and then rose, stopping at the printer to gather the pages before placing them into his briefcase and exiting his office. Briones was on the phone, his voice calm, but he was glowering – an increasingly regular occurrence. The pressure was mounting on everyone involved in pursuing the German, who had so far been undetectable, as predicted by *El Rey*, who had put in only a few appearances to check on the status and huddle with Cruz about more security safeguards.

Perhaps the most surprising aspect of this case so far was how easy *El Rey* had been to work with since their nocturnal foray. He'd been low-key, relaxed, and, while concerned as the signing date had ground inexorably nearer, mostly civil – even with Briones, with whom there had been some sort of unspoken truce. He was still arrogant and abrasive, and displayed as much empathy as a cobra, but he seemed to be making an effort to explain things that to him were self-evident, and had stopped peppering his comments with diatribes about the incompetence of the security force, the *Federales*, and everyone else.

Cruz gave Briones a curt wave and then took the elevator down to the lower level, where his car was waiting, armed *Federales* standing guard by both the elevator and the parking garage entry. Since the attempt on Cruz, the security teams had stepped up their game and were on constant high alert – no doubt due in part to the scathing report Cruz had issued about events surrounding his near-miss.

Dinah had taken a leave of absence from school and was spending her days in their new home, recovering. The purple discoloration on her face had faded to ochre, but she didn't want to be seen in public, and he didn't blame her. The doctor who had come the day after her rescue had advised her to ice it and to rest in bed, and she'd taken his instructions to heart. Thankfully, she didn't want to discuss Cruz's assignment or his working with *El Rey* – not that she seemed any more positively disposed towards the assassin since he'd saved her life, but rather because she knew it was a *fait accompli*. Now a precarious cessation of hostility was in effect, and life had returned to a tranquil pace, with no discussion of what had transpired while she'd been held captive, or about their future long-term plans.

Cruz gazed through the car window as the driver beat a path to headquarters, his mind preoccupied by the innumerable details of the search so far, none of which amounted to much. The security force had deployed countless advance personnel; the president had agreed to hold the signing indoors rather than on the Congress steps; the Chinese had approved a helicopter to transport their leader from the airport; and the most comprehensive precautions in Mexico's history had been put into place, every subcontractor entering the meeting hall having been investigated and the maintenance and security staff thoroughly vetted, and a new system requiring all entrants to pass through a metal detector having been deployed.

They were doing everything they could, and yet he had the sense of spinning his wheels, which was reinforced each time he met with *El Rey*. They would listen patiently to the reports, consider all the available data, and then exchange a worried look. Neither believed for a second that any of it would be adequate to stop a committed killer, and the best they could hope for was to deter him – the German wouldn't pursue the hit if he didn't have a clean way to escape. He was doing this for money, not ideology, so he would want to live to spend it. The punt strategy they'd arrived at was to make it almost impossible for anyone to take a shot at the target, and if they managed to, completely impossible to do so and not get caught.

It wasn't perfect, but it was the best they had.

When the car coasted to a stop inside the headquarters parking structure, Cruz groaned as he climbed from the back seat, and made a mental note to stop doing that. It was becoming habitual, more a clue as to his state of mind than a sign of any particular physical discomfort.

In Godoy's office he found the pomp strangely reassuring, the consistency mildly grounding for him. The receptionist was typically snotty, Godoy's assistant an ass, as always, and Godoy, once he'd forced Cruz to sit doing nothing for fifteen minutes in his antechambers, as artificial and condescending as ever.

"*Capitan* Cruz. Very nice to see you again. I've taken the liberty of asking our colleague at CISEN to join us so that we're on the same page," Godoy said, scrawling something of no doubt huge importance on a sheaf of stationery – his grocery list, or perhaps he'd taken up poetry.

"My pleasure," Cruz responded in obligatory fashion, his tone making clear the lie.

Godoy made an elaborate display out of checking the time on his gleaming, patently expensive watch. "Our associate should be here any moment. In the meantime, may I just say how relieved I am that your wife was returned safely, and that the attack on you was unsuccessful. What are we to do with these predators? It's shocking, the levels of barbarity they'll stoop to..."

"Thank you. I'd say they got the worse end of that deal, though."

"True, too true. Are your current accommodations suitable?" Godoy asked, equally uninterested as Cruz in the discussion so far.

"Fine. I spend so much time at the temporary offices now, it hardly matters where I call home."

"Yes, well, fortunately not for much longer. Ah, that must be our man!" Godoy practically trilled when his intercom buzzed.

Rodriguez strode into the room, a palpable presence, impeccably coiffed and dressed, as usual, and acknowledged Cruz with a nod before taking the other seat in front of Godoy's massive desk. "*Capitan*. Godoy."

"Rodriguez. Thanks for coming – I know how busy you must be. Very well. Let's begin. I asked *Capitan* Cruz here today to fill us in on progress on the Rauschenbach matter," Godoy announced with an unctuous air of authority.

"Hmm. Right," Cruz muttered. "The good news is that we've made real headway in tightening up the security, so it's better than ever. The bad news is that we're no closer to finding the assassin than we were when we started – as Assistant Director Rodriguez no doubt is aware, from the reports his liaison sends him on a daily basis."

"How can that be? You're burning money like kerosene, and you've commandeered half the available personnel in D.F., yet you're telling me you have nothing to show for it?" Godoy blustered, practically sputtering.

Cruz wondered if there was a hidden camera taping the meeting, or if the pompous ass really couldn't help grandstanding even when there was no point. Probably the latter, he concluded.

"I wasn't aware that we were on a budget," Cruz remarked drily.

"Well, it's always a concern."

"If you aren't satisfied with the way I'm running things, I'd be more than happy to step down. Perhaps you could run the task force...," Cruz suggested.

"No, no. Of course I'm satisfied. It's just that everyone's frustrated that there's been no real progress..."

"Exactly as I warned there wouldn't be. This is worse than a needle in a haystack. It's like trying to locate a drop of water in a river. We have nothing to go on...except, well, a lead that came in this afternoon, but even that's a long shot..."

"What is it?" Godoy demanded.

"We got a tip from an informant who was arrested for armed robbery and possession of narcotics. A lead we're following up on. I don't want to say anything more until we've developed it. As you know, these types of investigations will turn up countless red herrings and false starts. Every crook in Mexico is trying to barter his supposedly valuable information in exchange for leniency." A particularly loathsome little weasel had intimated that his acquaintance, a low-level cartel-associated gun smuggler and general miscreant, had fulfilled an order that could have been for their target – but it was speculative at that point. Cruz didn't want to announce anything only to have it turn out to be vapor.

"Mmm. Rodriguez, do you have anything to add?" Godoy asked.

"Not really. *Capitan* Cruz is right that I'm getting daily updates. So unless there's something more...," Rodriguez said, preparing to rise, obviously annoyed at having had his time wasted so that Godoy could have an audience.

"We're only a few days out from the event. It's time to alert the Chinese and give them a data dump. They need to be in the loop," Cruz stated flatly.

"Ah, well, *Capitan*, I appreciate your concern, but that's being handled at a different level. At a *diplomatic level*." Godoy pronounced each syllable with care, as though with careful elocution he could stave off objections.

"What does that mean?" Cruz demanded.

"It means that it's above your pay grade, *Capitan*. Just focus on apprehending the German, and we'll handle the international diplomacy side of things," Godoy dismissed.

"That's not good enough. You placed me in charge of this. My reputation and career are on the line. Withholding information from the Chinese...if word ever got out, we'd have a major incident. And if the unthinkable happens, and it turns out we knew for weeks that there was a legitimate threat, and didn't tell them...," Cruz protested.

"With all due respect, we assigned you to this in order to catch the assassin, not to consult with the Mexican government on how to handle its diplomatic affairs. It's not your concern. And if you would do your job, we wouldn't have to worry about it," Godoy snapped.

Cruz recoiled like he'd been slapped, then his eyes narrowed and he adopted an eerily calm tone.

"You gave me nothing to work on other than a rumor. I've been putting in twenty-hour days, and so has all my staff. If you have any suggestions as to what I'm missing, I'm all ears. In fact, I think that my offer to allow you to take this over is even more attractive, now. Given my obviously inadequate performance to date, right?"

Godoy couldn't put it in reverse fast enough. "Now, now. That didn't come out right. I simply meant that we're all frustrated that the German is still at large, in spite of everyone's best efforts. I didn't mean to imply that you weren't doing everything possible."

Rodriguez stood. "I'll leave it to the two of you to sort this out. I have work to do. Gentlemen," he announced, and then before Godoy could protest he stalked to the door and left.

Cruz couldn't contain a small smile at Godoy's discomfort. Taking his cue from Rodriguez, he rose, and handed Godoy the report he had printed. "Everything we know is contained in these pages. We're coordinating with the security team on an hourly basis, and think we've made significant progress on preventive measures. But this has always been a long shot, given the dearth of information we've gotten. So while we can certainly hope that something breaks in our favor, right now I'd say that we won't be able to stop the assassin from trying to kill the Chinese leader, unless he can't figure out a clean escape plan. So that's what we're focusing on, even as we follow up all the other leads."

"It's possible that he's seen the elaborate measures we've taken, and decided not to attempt it, isn't it?" Godoy asked hopefully, floating a theory that had increased in popularity within the president's inner circle. His desire to have the optimistic notion reinforced was almost pathetic, and for a second Cruz almost felt sorry for him.

"Anything's possible. But I'm not betting on it, and neither should you," Cruz said, and spun on his heel, glad to be out of the oppressive atmosphere – a combination of expensive leather, sour cologne, and flop sweat. If the powers that be really had talked themselves into the idea that the German would quit because the hit had become more difficult, they were delusional.

Which was nothing new, he supposed, as he rewarded the receptionist with a sneer when he blew past her. It gave him a childish sense of pleasure to be nasty to the imperious woman in return for her arrogant treatment of him whenever he was summoned, but he immediately felt bad about it once he was out of the suite.

She was just mirroring her boss's attitude. Like a dog began resembling its master after a while, she had begun taking after Godoy.

Which, in the scheme of things, was punishment enough.

CHAPTER 41

Dusk was fading into night as the daily rush hour clogged the streets, horns honking as drivers cut one another off to gain a few feet of fruitless advantage on the overpass near the green two-story building that housed a hardware store below and two residential units above. The neighborhood was seedy, even by Mexico City standards. The two plainclothes police detectives that had been recruited by Cruz's task force had seen everything in their combined thirty-seven years of duty, and while this wasn't a district most would be advised to be strolling in after dark, at least it didn't boast multiple murders every night, like some of the surrounding areas.

Joel Ortiz and Ruben Lariel had been called in because they knew the streets better than any, and had protected their identities over the years, so they wouldn't be spotted by someone who knew them while they investigated the lead that had come from the snitch who had told the task force about his friend's recent transaction involving a gun and some papers for a foreigner. The transaction itself was almost routine; but most of the underworld business involved locals, or cartel-related new arrivals from Guatemala, El Salvador, and Colombia. His friend had gotten the impression that this one had been from Europe – something about the accent, he'd said, while drinking heavily the other night with the informant, who had later been involved in a regrettable incident in which he'd been mistaken for a robber by the police.

Ruben eased off the gas of his twenty-year-old Pontiac and parked illegally at the filthy curb a few dozen yards from the suspect's building – the home of one Virgilio Pontescu, who was not unknown to the authorities for his involvement in gun-running, forgery, blackmail, assault, and slavery. But other than an arrest as a teenager, he'd managed to evade spending serious time in jail, and he paid off the right people to be allowed to operate his little cottage industry without making waves. He had recently been linked to Los Zetas; but again, rumors were as thick as the rain that pelted the city during monsoon season, and even if he was, whispered talk on the street was a far cry from proof – and there were far more doing far worse than Virgilio, who wasn't given to overt violence, at least that anyone had been willing to swear to in court.

Joel regarded his partner with a blank stare, and then rolled down the window and lit a cigarette – an annoying habit that infuriated Ruben, but to which he'd grown accustomed during the last decade they'd operated as a team. It had been some time since they'd been out on the streets, having traded their field shoes for desks a few years earlier, but in their day they had been the best, and their track record as investigative detectives was as impressive and lengthy as their tactics were unorthodox.

"How do you want to do this?" Ruben asked, shutting off the roughly idling engine and waving away some stray smoke.

"We watch for a while, and hopefully he shows up. Then we take him before he can get inside."

"What if he's already in there?"

"Do you see any lights on?" Joel countered, eyeing the dark façade.

"No, but maybe he's taking a *siesta*."

"Or maybe he's not there. We watch and wait."

Ruben grumbled a little and then settled in, having developed powerful muscles for sitting in one place for long periods of time on countless stakeouts.

Three hours later, the lights went off in the store below, and the proprietor exited through the front door, locked it, and then pulled down a steel security barrier to keep thieves from breaking the glass display windows. A shambling junky holding a hushed conversation with imaginary demons moved past the front of the shop ten minutes later, but other than that, the sidewalk was quiet, a downtrodden stray dog nosing piles of trash their only companion on the cul-de-sac.

Eventually, Ruben looked at his watch. "It's almost midnight. Why don't we check to see if he answers his door?"

"Don't think so. No lights."

"That's okay. Maybe he left it open and we can take a quick look around while we're waiting...," he suggested, and Joel grinned.

"You want to take it, or should I?"

"Go back to sleep. I'll be right back," Ruben said, and opened the glove compartment and removed a leather bag with the tools of his trade in it.

Watching Ruben jimmy the front door was a thing of beauty, even as a few brave pedestrians hurried by. To all appearances he was fumbling with his keys – the trick being that he was picking the lock with practiced dexterity that would have made a magician gape. After twenty seconds of fiddling, he was in.

Joel eyed the street in the cracked side mirror, wary of being snuck up on while engrossed in Ruben's artful craft. Two minutes later his cell phone vibrated, and he groped in his shirt pocket for it and stabbed it to life. "What?" he growled.

"It's not good. Virgilio wasn't taking a nap. Judging by the smell, he's been dead for two days, maybe more."

"Shit. From what?"

"My guess is that the pen stabbed through his right eye is the cause of death. But I'm no coroner," Ruben rasped.

"I better call the crew."

"Yeah. This is a dead end."

"Very funny. Don't ever lose that childlike naïveté."

Joel disconnected and dialed the task force and broke the news, and his contact told him that they would handle forensics – to just get out of there and leave it to them. Joel didn't need to be told twice, and when Ruben returned, the engine was already running.

"What do you think? Is this all a coincidence, that this guy they're looking for was maybe doing a deal with Virgilio, and next thing Virg turns up smoked?" he asked rhetorically.

"Sure. Probably unrelated. People die every day."

"Might have been an accident."

"Yeah. He was signing a check and stabbed himself in the eye."

"Or committed suicide."

"Seems reasonable to me. You see anything suspicious?"

"You mean besides the corpse with a Bic jammed through his frontal lobe?"

"Yeah. Besides that."

"He had lovely curtains. Might have been, what do they call that now, metro-sexy?"

"Metro-sexual."

"What you said."

"I don't think that's suspicious."

"Speak for yourself."

Ruben pulled away and rolled down the street, his exhaust proclaiming his blissful lack of concern for mundanities like tune-ups or preventive maintenance, and then the old wreck turned the corner and was gone, leaving the mangy, miserable dog, still foraging hopefully, as the only witness to their departure.

CHAPTER 42

The mood in the room was bleak as Cruz announced that their only lead had turned up skewered with a writing implement. One wag ventured a morbid joke about pens being mightier than swords, but the laughter was forced.

"Gentlemen, I know we've all been putting in a hundred and twenty percent, but we're getting down to the clinch now, and we can't let up. We got this lead by following up on every detail, no matter how seemingly random, so we need to stay focused and not lose steam. He's out there somewhere, and we need to keep turning over rocks until we find him."

Briones raised his hand. "Why don't we release his photo to the press? Plaster it all over the TV and the newspapers? It can't help but stir the pot. Offer a reward. It's worth a shot."

Cruz couldn't tell him that he'd floated that very idea past Godoy that morning, and it had been shot down. CISEN and the president's team were obviously playing a game with the Chinese, where they didn't want to alarm them. That was the only reason for not distributing it on every street corner.

"I ran that up the flagpole. Still waiting for a response. Good suggestion, though," Cruz said.

"How about circulating the photo to every cop in D.F.? That would be a good start. Maybe we'll get lucky?" Briones suggested.

El Rey was sitting quietly in a corner at the back of the room, studying his fingernails, and when he heard the suggestion, he looked up. "Has that ever worked? You did that with me. Did it help?"

Briones flushed at being called out in front of his peers, but Cruz interrupted.

"It's a good idea and a necessary step."

"Well, I suppose it can't hurt, but those photos are ancient history, and the likelihood that he still looks even vaguely like them are slim to none.

Take my word on this. You don't become the highest paid assassin in Europe by not taking simple precautions like changing your appearance regularly. That's kind of Hit Man 101, if you get my drift. I think you need to stop relying on this man behaving like a moron and start preparing for reality. Unless you get a miracle, you're not going to find him in time," *El Rey* said, then returned to his examination of his cuticles.

"Well, then what do you suggest?" Briones countered. The officers on either side of him nodded with raised eyebrows, and one threw his pencil down on the table in disgust.

"Circulate the photo to the media. Why? Because it'll put him on notice that the risk just increased. At this point, psychology is all you have. Your best bet is to make his chances so poor that he gives up, and being all over the TV, even if he no longer looks anything like the photo, will have an effect on him. Assassins are a paranoid bunch. They have to be, to survive for any length of time in this business. Seeing an image of yourself is never good news, especially if it's out in the open. That signals that the stakes were just raised and the odds of a clean getaway went down."

Cruz held up a hand as the room exploded in conversation, the men talking over each other, and gave it twenty seconds to settle.

"Noted. As I said before, it's in the works. What else?"

"Everyone in this room should go to the site and walk it, and then walk the neighborhood around it, and study the layout. If an idea comes up, no matter how outlandish, bring it up. If you see anything that seems off, bring it up. If someone looks at you crosswise, bring it up. Preparation is your best defense right now. Because you're not going to catch him in time. I agree with you on that point."

More muttering and angry exclamations sounded from men who had poured their souls into the investigation. *El Rey* seemed impervious to it all, not an iota of concern disturbing his matinée idol-smooth features.

The meeting continued for another twenty minutes and then broke up in disarray, the reality of the situation settling in. Cruz gestured to *El Rey* as he moved towards the door.

"Can I see you in my office for a moment?" he asked, more a demand than a request.

El Rey nodded, once, and then waited for Cruz to lead the way.

When they were both seated at the meeting table, Cruz leaned forward, both palms on the smooth wood-look vinyl surface. "They're not going to release the photo to the media."

"I kind of figured that. And there's only one reason not to. They haven't told the Chinese, have they?"

"I don't think they have. I was told it was above my level of *need to know*."

"That's rich. They want you to stop this, but they're holding out on you. So they're hedging their bets – they don't want to alert the media and have a photo out there, even if it's on some invented charge, because if he's successful they don't want any proof that they knew about this in advance and didn't say anything. And they've set you up to take the fall if that happens. You're a better man than I to be able to put up with this shit," *El Rey* said.

"Believe me, this wasn't my first choice of responsibilities. The cartels were keeping me more than busy."

"Then why? Why take this on? It's career suicide. You're smarter than that," the assassin observed.

"Not that smart, obviously," Cruz deflected, a trace of bitterness in his tone. "I could ask the same question. What does CISEN hold over your head that has you working with them? You're young, rich, smart...and yet you're here, with me, on the crappiest duty I can imagine."

"Are you hoping to get lucky with me?"

Cruz waited a beat. "You made a joke."

"I have a richly evolved sense of humor," *El Rey* said, deadpan.

"I never got that before."

"I take back everything I said about you being smart."

Cruz shook his head as if to clear it. "We have two more days. That's forty-eight hours to stop him."

"You won't. I already told you. Best you can do is have a hell of a punt strategy and disincentivize him. Make it his worst nightmare going in. I know from personal experience that the worse my exit from a sanction looked, the less likely I was to do the job. I'd rather return the money. Let some other guy die trying. I wanted sanctions I could live through. Everyone does. Remember that this isn't personal for him. It's a gig, nothing more."

"What do you think they're paying him?"

"Good question. Millions. This will have to be his last hurrah. After this, he'll want to get off the board, so it has to be enough to last the rest of his life. I'd guess three to five million, minimum."

"Who would pay that to knock off the Chinese leader, on Mexican soil? And why here?"

El Rey's face could have been chiseled from marble. "Now you're asking the right questions. Follow the money and you'll learn enough to be dangerous."

"What does that mean?"

"It means that someone really wants to send a message to the Chinese. Don't come into our sandbox. So figure out who has the most to lose by this deal getting signed, and there's your motive. But my intuition says that's a dangerous line of inquiry."

"Dangerous, how?"

"Think about it. There are a lot of moving parts to this. The Mexicans playing cagey with information they should have shared a week ago. A foreign hit man and a dramatic execution. Economically disastrous consequences, not only for the country, but specifically for the new ruling party. Those are deep waters. I'd just as soon stay on shore."

They stared at each other, the assassin's eyes unreadable.

"You never answered my question," Cruz said after a pause.

"What was it again?"

"Why are you here?"

"Are you getting all existentialist on me?"

"See? You keep deflecting the question."

"Huh. Almost like I don't want to answer it."

"Come on. Your secret's safe. We've been through a lot."

"How is she, anyway?" *El Rey* asked, his tone softening. "Your wife."

"As well as can be expected. And don't think I'm not noticing that you're changing the subject again."

"You're a razor-sharp mind."

"So what's the story?"

El Rey hesitated, and then told Cruz about how CISEN had blackmailed him – injecting him with a neurotoxin that would kill him without a shot of antidote every six months for at least a year and a half. And then forcing him to become a CISEN asset in order to get the remaining two injections.

"That's unbelievable. How can they do that?" Cruz was actually shocked, an unfamiliar emotion for him.

"Because they can, and will, do whatever they want. What it comes down to is that they have the power. So we do as they say. Believe me, I feel screwed. They made me a deal, I did the job, and they reneged. But that's how the world works. It always has." He stood. "Tomorrow, let's plan on walking through the sewer system. I want to see every place he could use to gain entry to the Congress, no matter how unlikely. I also want to review all the plans for anti-rocket defenses, and every other counter-measure we haven't discussed yet. Call me. You know the number."

Cruz watched him leave, and thought about the story he'd been told. The guaranteed death if he didn't receive at least the two antidote shots over the eighteen months following the initial shot. And the lingering, unspoken doubt that they would actually allow him to live through it all anyway. Because if they did, and *El Rey* held a grudge...

For the first time in days, Cruz didn't feel like he had it all that bad. Some had it worse.

He didn't think it was possible, but a tiny part of him actually felt sorry for the most dangerous killer in Mexican history.

He pressed a button on the coffee machine and listened to the hypnotic sound of water percolating, then rose and made his way back to his desk.

What an odd journey this had been so far.

Cruz was momentarily overcome by an impulse so powerful it felt like a physical need, and he reached for his phone and dialed a number. When Dinah answered, she was surprised to hear his voice.

"Why are you calling? What's wrong, *mi amor*?" she asked, concern obvious in her strained tone.

"Nothing's wrong. I just wanted to say...I just wanted to tell you I love you."

Silence greeted the declaration for a pregnant moment.

"Why, Romero, I love you too," she said in a tiny voice, a quaver in her words. "Are you sure you're okay?"

A pause, a momentary hesitation filled with an ocean of things unsaid.

"I am now. I just wanted to hear your voice."

"I love you, my big strong warrior."

He swallowed hard, and then sighed.

"That's all I needed to hear."

CHAPTER 43

The street that ran in front of the Federal Police headquarters was teeming with traffic at rush hour, as were most in Mexico City, as the population embarked on its evening slog from the downtown business areas to the suburbs along the outskirts of town. As the day shift wound down, hundreds of officers moved down the wide steps of the entry to the sidewalk, some to catch a bite to eat, most to catch one of the packed buses that swarmed in and out of the endless procession of vehicles, pulling to grinding stops to on-load commuters.

Officer Porfirio Lopez waved goodbye to the three *Federales* he was chatting with and split off to grab a taco at one of the curb vendors, where throngs of passers-by stopped and consumed the soft corn-wrapped meats while passing cars honked their progress. It wasn't dinner, more a snack – he got hungry by six, and this would tide him over until he got home and hooked up with his friends at the local cantina, which had a two-for-one special on Thursdays on their succulent pork *carnitas*; an irresistible deal.

As he stood munching the *arrachera* steak taco, he felt a sense of...something odd, but he couldn't put his finger on it. Maybe too much coffee – he'd drunk at least seven cups that day, which was close to a record for him. The food quieted his stomach, and when he was done, he tossed the paper wrapper into a trash can and strode to the bus stop, where hundreds of workers waited for their ride home with the dogged determination of spawning salmon.

A paperboy moved through the crowd, holding the evening issue of *La Prensa* aloft, a lurid photograph of four people found dead in a poor barrio on the front page, the victims of feral dog attacks that had polarized the city. The wild dogs lived in caves near the park where the victims had been found, dead of blood loss from multiple bites. The prevailing theory was that roving packs looked for opportunistic targets and then killed the unsuspecting for food. Such was the outcry that the police had gone in and rounded up dozens of dogs, whose incarceration was now a cause célèbre and had created considerable consternation for the mayor and other public officials, whose plan was to euthanize them without question.

He bought a paper and read with marginal interest until his bus arrived with a hiss of air brakes, and he shouldered through the clamoring crush to get aboard before it rolled away. He dropped his few pesos into the fare box and took the small receipt offered – proof of payment in the event of an impromptu inspection by the transit police, and a handy way for the drivers to be held responsible for all the money they had taken in on their route. The drivers were each issued a roll of tickets, and when their shifts were done, the number missing was counted, which established how much every driver owed in fares. The inspections were regular, making collection of the tickets by the riders mandatory to avoid heaping fines.

The bus rocked to and fro as it negotiated the uneven asphalt, the press of tired humanity staring dully into space, carefully avoiding all but momentary eye contact in the way that regular commuters usually did. Nobody wanted to have to strike up a conversation after a long work day, and the entire packed conveyance had the air of a slaughterhouse, the resigned bovines waiting patiently in line for their turn at the sledgehammer.

Officer Lopez gripped the overhead bar and tried to read his paper, folded in quarters so as to take up as little space as possible, but the near constant starting and stopping interrupted him with the regularity of a ship on the high seas plowing through oncoming swells. Bored on the hour-long commute, he snuck a look at a young woman eight feet away, who studiously ignored him, the twinkle of her wedding band all the warning he needed. Returning to the news, he read the latest list of murders with indifference – every day more were found, victims of crime, rage, random violence, or drug trafficking. It was an unending procession of misery to which he'd grown inured as part of his job, and he liked to joke that with human nature being what it was, he'd never be out of work.

The ride was tolerable in the spring, except when it was raining, when it became a misery, as hundreds of wet fellow travelers, many of whom wanted for indoor plumbing, packed onto the buses, their hygienic challenges painfully obvious. Then in summer, the heat of August and September again made it especially unpleasant – the buses rarely had air conditioning, and the opened windows were woefully inadequate. Now, however, it wasn't so bad, and he'd learned to try to get as close to the younger women as possible, who usually huddled together, their heady perfume almost as much of an attraction as the possibility occasionally flashed from mahogany eyes.

Porfirio was twenty-nine, and had been with the *Federales* for eight years, having snagged the plum position with the help of an uncle who was on the force. *Federales* were the cream of the law enforcement crop, paid better than their lowly civil police counterparts and bribed with more generosity because of the vastly greater power they wielded. The best duty, that of highway patrol, was reserved for the fortunate few. None of that lofty branch of officers rode the bus, preferring to motor to work in their new SUVs, impossible acquisitions on their pay but unquestioned by the system. The graft involved in stopping drivers for indiscretions of speed or registration was an accepted part of the job, although publicly decried by administration after administration. He was hoping that maybe in another few years a slot in the hotly contested mobile force would open up, and then he too could trade the bus for the opulent Lincoln Navigator he'd had his eye on forever.

Lost in the daydream about how his life would change for the better, he almost missed his stop, on the outskirts of the metropolitan area only a few blocks from one of the more infamous slums, where the unfortunate and downtrodden spent lives of brutal hardship. He stepped down onto the cracked sidewalk with several dozen other commuters and then trudged the three long blocks to his home – a two-story apartment building with eighteen single-room flats, each with a flyspeck bathroom and a dangerously unventilated propane stove serving as kitchen. He could afford better, but saw no reason to squander his money – he was single, was rarely home except to sleep, and was saving for whenever he met a girl he got serious about. His marriage had ended in divorce, thankfully with no children, after seven years of bitterness and recriminations as he failed to bring home sufficient bacon to appease his young bride, and he had been footloose for two years, in no hurry to try that again anytime soon.

His boots crunched on the gravel as the sidewalk gave way to dirt and rocks, and he failed to register the shadow that darkened his building's doorway as he unlocked the rickety front door – his landlord was a cheap bastard who never did any maintenance, and cockroach spray and air freshener were staples in all the dwellings. As he swung the door open he felt pressure on his upper back, and then a voice hissed in his ear.

"I have a gun, and I'll blow a hole the size of a softball in you unless you do exactly as I say."

He froze, and then felt a hand pull his service revolver from his belt. "Are you insane? Robbing a federal policeman? Do you really want this on you?" Porfirio asked incredulously. "Do you know what this is going to do?"

"Let's go to your apartment. Don't talk anymore. Now. Move."

"I don't have anything of value–"

The assailant swatted the back of Porfirio's head with his service piece, just hard enough to get his attention. "I said shut up. That's your only warning."

They trudged down the gloomy hall until they came to the second to last door, and then Porfirio stopped.

"I need to reach into my pocket for the key," he explained, growing angrier by the second at the balls of the thief. Robbing a federal police officer was suicide – the neighborhood would be crawling with cops who wouldn't rest until the perp was found. Of course, part of his annoyance was at the grief he would take from his peers at having been blindsided, and there was the money...he had a quarter of all his savings in the little room, in cash, stashed in the freezer, where he accumulated the bribes he was lucky enough to get, preferring his apartment hiding place to having to explain in any sort of departmental investigation where the money he'd deposited in the bank had come from.

"Slowly." The voice sounded odd – something about the accent, although it was barely detectable. Porfirio did a double take, and then retrieved his key ring from his pocket and opened the door, thinking he must have been mistaken – why would a common thug have the refined accent of a Castilian native from Spain?

His assailant pushed him into the room and closed the door softly behind him.

"I told you, I don't have anything of value," Porfirio started, hoping that would dissuade the robber, and then he was cut off by another smack on the back of his head, this time harder.

"I'm not interested in your money," the man said, and then Porfirio heard a rustle just before a lance of white hot pain stabbed through his back and his heart stopped pumping.

Rauschenbach stepped aside as the dying officer fell face forward, the handle of the twelve-inch flathead screwdriver he'd sharpened to a stiletto point sticking from between his shoulders, and eyed the twitching body with cold indifference as all the young man's hopes and dreams died with him. Once Porfirio's corpse was still, the German's eyes roved over the room, stopping at the closet.

It took him ten minutes to ransack the room and find the money. He methodically destroyed the place before he removed the dead man's watch and wallet along with the few other obvious valuables, and then packed them into the empty nylon carry-all he'd brought, folded under his jacket on the long bus ride.

With any luck the cop wouldn't be missed for a couple of days; and then, when found, the murder would look like a robbery gone wrong. At best they'd find the prints of the hardware store clerk who had rung up the screwdriver purchase smudged on the yellow plastic handle, and that would send any investigation into a tailspin, buying him time. By the point that anyone realized that the robbery had been about something more than a few thousand dollars' worth of pesos stored in a frozen coffee can, he'd be winging his way out of the country.

Rauschenbach took a final look at the dead man and hoisted the bag over his shoulder with a gloved hand. He moved to the door, listening intently for half a minute, and then eased it open and slid out into the empty hall, a phantom, the single low-wattage incandescent bulb that dangled precariously from the ceiling providing the scantest of illumination as he made his way down the dismal corridor to the front exit.

CHAPTER 44

A distorted voice blared flight information over the loudspeaker as a small crowd waited patiently for loved ones to exit the terminal. Inside, arriving passengers moved from the gates against the flow of departing travelers, who thronged the seating area while waiting to board.

El Rey, Cruz, and Briones were in Terminal Two of the Benito Juarez International Airport, walking the hall, eyes poring over the security precautions with approval – a routine part of air travel safety and stricter than at almost any other installation in Mexico. Everyone had to go through metal detectors, with no exceptions, and even the trio, two in uniform, had to be signed in by the ranking federal police officer so that they could keep their side arms.

El Rey squinted out the windows on the eastern side of the terminal at the hangars in the near distance and the broad expanse of tarmac between the terminal and the government planes grouped there. A military helicopter sat squarely in the middle of the restricted area set aside for arriving dignitary aircraft, as well as the Mexican President's Boeing 757 whenever he was traveling internationally.

"Tell me again about the security here," he said, estimating the distance from the VIP area to the terminal.

"It was decided that the Chinese would land here instead of Santa Lucia, which was discarded even though it's only twenty miles away," Briones started, referring to the military base north of Mexico City. "The Chinese dismissed it out-of-hand because of the danger of a surface-to-air missile strike on the chopper ride into the city. Even if there was a helicopter convoy, it posed too great a threat."

"I agree. Too many areas a chopper could be picked off." *El Rey* nodded as he continued surveying the runways and maintenance hangars.

"The Chinese will arrive around nine a.m. and stay aboard the plane until a chopper arrives to transport the leader to the Congress building. Patrols will be constant on the access roads and the perimeter road, and there will be hundreds of police and military troops in the neighborhood to the south. Which isn't considered to be a huge risk due to how low the buildings are, as well as virtually no line of sight to the aircraft once it's in final position."

"I'll still want to go through the neighborhood," *El Rey* said.

"The army will have snipers on the rooftops of the nearest structure. They'll also be occupying the entire line of buildings that front onto the road that runs along the south side, which will be closed that morning until the Chinese have taken off again."

"Fine. What about this terminal?"

"We'll have snipers distributed on the roof, as well as the roofs of the nearby hangars, and we'll search the hangars early that morning, and then sentries will watch the area until the Chinese leave. It'll be buttoned up tight."

"Tell me about the helicopter."

"Your advice about the maintenance concerns were taken to heart, and they'll have a crew of mechanics and observers going over every inch of the chopper that morning to ensure no tampering has occurred. It's a fully armored beast that can withstand any sort of rifle fire. Anything short of a direct hit by a surface-to-air missile won't affect it."

"What about the flight path of the chopper to the Congress hall?" Cruz asked.

"It will be decided five minutes before takeoff. One of six routes that will skirt the populated sections of town, to the extent they can. So anyone planning to try to shoot it down, or at it, en route, will have to be psychic."

"What about the buildings across the runway?" *El Rey* asked.

"That, over there, is Terminal One. One of the largest passenger terminals on the continent. And the hangars over there" – Briones pointed at a distant row of buildings, and everyone had to struggle to make them out through the haze of pollution – "will get the same treatment as the nearer ones; although both they, and the terminal, are too far away to pose a threat. Still, they'll have a few snipers on the roof, just in case."

El Rey surveyed the surroundings and shook his head. "What are we missing? I can feel it in my bones. There has to be a weakness in all this we aren't seeing. He's a shooter, so he'll likely use a gun to pull this off."

"Agreed, but not here. Look around you. How would he get a rifle in here? The security is designed to prevent exactly that, and it'll be stepped up to an insane level for twenty-four hours prior. There are easier ways to do this than to try to crack the most fortified area in town," Cruz said.

"Yes, but this would be the most unexpected. If I was going to try to take the Chinese leader out, there would really be only two choices: here, or when he's in front of the Congress, once the chopper lands. Those are his two most vulnerable spots. The only times he'll be exposed outdoors. So that makes it pretty easy," the assassin said. "That's where the hit will take place. They're sweeping the hall for bombs, they have radiation detectors going in, and the place will be literally crawling with security. Even the sewers will be patrolled – talk about crap duty. So that leaves the two weak points."

"And they've taken precautions against a gas attack as well. I've never heard of anything remotely like this in terms of precautions, for anything," Briones reported.

El Rey continued staring out at the planes taking off and landing, the runways operating at ninety-seven percent capacity at the busiest hub in Latin America. A huge jet gathered speed as it shot down the runway and then lifted slowly into the sky. A few seconds later another appeared at the opposite end of the runway, hovering over the city, and then touched down, wheels smoking as they hit the ground.

"I'm telling you, we're missing something," he grumbled under his breath, and Cruz touched his arm.

"Come on. Let's go up to the roof so you can evaluate it from up there."

The three men walked slowly along the massive hall that housed the jetways towards the lobby area, where airport personnel would meet them to escort them to the roof. Nobody gave a second glance to the custodian off to the side emptying out one of the trash bins into his cart. If they had, they would have seen nothing unusual – an older man, skin burnished a coffee hue, going about his thankless job.

Rauschenbach watched the two *Federales* and the younger man out of the corner of his eye and then returned to his study of the terminal. He'd had no problems making it into the departure lounge with his forged ID and paperwork, but he'd also instantly seen that it would be all but impossible to sneak a weapon in. He had considered machining something that would fit into a cart's steel frame, but the security guards were going over the rolling trolleys carefully. Even if he had a metal shop and could build one in the two days left before the hit, getting it into the facility would be practically impossible – and then he would have to be able to disassemble it, extract the rifle, and find a way onto the roof that didn't have a dozen cops guarding it – not to mention the inevitable snipers that would be stationed there the morning of the Chinese dignitary's arrival.

He hummed to himself, his soiled uniform rendering him all but invisible, and reconciled himself to leaving, his goal of finding a way in – and perhaps more importantly, out – having eluded him. He would have to study the airport blueprints that night more carefully and see if there was anything he'd overlooked. There was always a way, he told himself, and decided that he would go over to the far terminal to look around in case he came up with a breakthrough idea. Then, after lunch, he would spend the day in the neighborhoods around the Congress doing the same thing – searching for that which had escaped him: a spot that would be vulnerable, that he could get into without being caught, from where he could shoot the target and then escape before anyone knew what was happening.

He nodded courteously to an armed policeman walking slowly along the terminal floor, talking to a well-dressed woman holding a clipboard and pointing, and then pushed his cart towards the maintenance area, where he would leave it and slip out, then work his way to Terminal One.

The Mexicans were definitely taking the threat seriously, but he had expected that. That went with the territory. But there was no way he was going to give back the half of the four million dollars he'd already received to do the job. One way or another, he would find the weak link and capitalize on it.

❧

That evening he made his decision, and went to meet one of the contacts provided by the Los Zetas cartel members who had gotten him into the country. The man, Pedro, an ex-marine, smiled and nodded when the German told him what he wanted.

"That should be easy enough to get. Figure tomorrow. I can arrange for one to disappear from one of the nearby military bases. But you could just buy one in the United States, and it would be way cheaper. There's no reason you couldn't have it here within a couple of days, maybe three on the outside."

"I have my reasons. Just name the price."

After a few more minutes of negotiating they reached an agreement, and Rauschenbach shook the man's hand, sliding a wad of cash to him with the other. "I'll see you *mañana*," he said.

"For that kind of money, count on it." Pedro shook his head in wonder as he left the rendezvous. That was the easiest cash he would ever make. Sometimes people were crazy, he mused, as he disappeared into a metro station near the Congress building.

Thank God.

Crazy was good for business.

CHAPTER 45

The lights of Cuernavaca sparkled in the distance as Rauschenbach drove the stolen Mitsubishi Gallant south from Mexico City, his nerves dead calm in spite of the fact that tomorrow morning he would be executing the Chinese ultimate leader. He peered over at the guitar case next to him and then took a peek at the pack lying on the rear seat. Pedro had come through with flying colors, so he was as ready as he would ever be for his night's work.

It was late, nearing one-thirty a.m., when he pulled through the airport gate into the private plane area and approached the main hangar, a long building with a row of roll-up doors where the smaller prop planes were stored, he knew from his research the prior day. When the facility had been open, he'd approached the two maintenance men and asked about the cost of a hangar and a service program, and after twenty minutes of talk, walked away with everything he needed to know.

He stopped near the door at the far end from the entry drive and got out, stretching as he scanned the area for any hint of the security guard who would walk by every two hours to make sure nothing alarming had happened. After verifying that the man was nowhere to be seen, he walked over to the stall he wanted and stooped down, calmly sliding a pick and a strip of metal he'd created from a soda can inside the lock and feeling for the tumblers. He had it open in thirty seconds, and found himself face to face with a Cessna 150L prop plane from the mid-seventies he'd spied – a relatively primitive beast he could fly with his eyes closed. A quick inspection of the interior told him that the plane was perfect for his purposes, if a little cramped.

By his estimate he had thirty minutes before the guard would make it back, at the worst – more like forty-five, but he didn't feel like cutting it too close. He hurriedly unpacked his items from the car and carried them to the plane, and then retrieved a toolkit he had bought that afternoon and set about his final preparatory task – removing one of the plane's doors. He had the hinges unbolted in ten minutes, and once the door was stowed in the hangar's depths, he had nothing left to do but start the engine, warm it up, and take off.

The noise of the motor revving sounded like a hurricane in his ears, the roar amplified by the hangar and the lack of the door. He eyed the gauges, confirming that he had sufficient fuel for what he intended, and then he inched the plane forward, increasing the RPMs as he pulled out onto the runway and strapped himself in.

It was a perfect night – not too cold, partially cloudy, perhaps a fifteen-knot wind from the west. He increased the revs and the little plane began a lazy roll forward. Then he pushed the throttle to the firewall, adjusted the flaps, and soon he was climbing into the night sky at a rate of roughly six hundred feet per minute.

The engine settled into a comfortable drone as he ascended through the eight-thousand and then the ten-thousand-foot level, and he hoped his luck would hold and he could get the plane to its maximum operating ceiling of fourteen thousand feet. The wind from the door opening buffeted him and tore at his heavy jacket with the violence of a hurricane, and as the temperature dropped he was glad he'd had the foresight to wear gloves.

The radio crackled as he scanned the frequencies, and then he picked up the expected warnings directed at him as he approached Mexico City. He would be well clear of the commercial airlines on approach or takeoff on the course he had plotted, which was essential to his plan – it wouldn't do to be clipped by a 737 as he edged past the perimeter of the city.

The plane would be reported as stolen almost immediately by Cuernavaca ground security, and the assumption would be that it was a drug smuggler trying to secure transportation for a small shipment at no cost. By the time anyone had figured out that there might be another explanation, it would all be over but the shouting, and he would be long gone. He eyed the altimeter and made a few adjustments – the plane was straining at a little over thirteen thousand feet, and didn't seem like it wanted to go much higher. When he hit thirteen thousand three hundred, he engaged the Stec 50 autopilot with altitude hold and slowed the speed to seventy miles per hour – twenty or so above the plane's stall speed, and well short of its cruise speed.

After another few minutes, the lights of the international airport were plainly visible off to the left, and he made his final preparations. He entered a course on the autopilot that would take it on a northeasterly direction, and then estimated the fuel – an eighth of a tank, so it would probably run out over the mountains northeast of Pachuca and crash somewhere in that uninhabited area.

He reached beside him and hoisted the parachute he had gotten from the Los Zetas contact – a medium-performance Ram-air parachute that would slow his drop to just over twenty feet per second and had good glide characteristics. He donned the seven-point strap harness, cinching it to ensure it was secure, and then strapped the rifle across his chest with a nylon quick release clip he'd created specifically for it. He'd wrapped the weapon in neoprene so it wouldn't be picked up on the tower radar, which he knew would be adjusted to tune out smaller objects like birds – and a bird was what he would look like to the radar as he dropped from the plane.

When he could see the airport a few miles to the southwest, he lowered himself onto the wheel strut, the wind tearing at him with incredible force, and then hurled himself into space, releasing the chute only four seconds after beginning his drop so as to have maximum maneuverability room.

The parachute slammed the harness into his torso as it deployed, and then he was in control, directing his glide to put him north of the airport and well out of the path of its traffic, which was a hazard at any time of night or day.

Ten minutes later he was on the roof of Terminal One, which as expected was empty at that late hour. There would undoubtedly be snipers moving into position in the early morning, but by then he would be hidden, in position inside one of the ventilation ducts he could just make out in the dark. He had dropped north of the airport, gliding in from over the city, so the likelihood of being detected was minimal at three a.m. – nobody would be watching for a nocturnal parachute ingression.

Rauschenbach quickly rolled the chute up, stuffed it back into the pack, and toted it to the duct. He extracted a small portable toolkit and set about removing the outer grid. Six minutes later he was done, and he moved to the next duct and removed those bolts as well, and then the next three in the line. His chore completed, he dropped the pack into the shaft and then eased himself in, and soon was lying face down on the cold steel surface. He pulled the grid closed so that if there was a cursory inspection, the missing bolts would appear to be the result of typically shoddy maintenance, same as the rest of the shafts in the area.

He fished a small camping headlamp from his shirt pocket, pulled it onto his head, and flicked it on. The pitch black shaft, approximately five feet wide by four high, brightened. He carefully set the rifle down, the camera tripod next to it, and maneuvered so that he was facing away from the opening. Rauschenbach knew from studying the blueprint he'd found online where the shaft ultimately led, but he wanted to prepare for a quick exit after the assassination – now a little under six hours away.

Forty-five minutes later he was back. He first retrieved the parachute and pushed it down the chute, and then returned for the rifle. If anyone bothered opening the grid in the morning they would see an air duct; and even if they bothered with an exploration, they wouldn't be coming as far as he would be lying in wait, biding his time. The only wrinkle would be if they stationed a sniper right by his position, but that was luck of the draw. If they did, he would deal with it once it was light out. Now that he was in position, he had options, and could shoot from any number of locations.

The hard part was over. He turned off the lamp and returned it to the breast pocket of his dark blue shirt, and then slipped the baseball cap he'd pilfered over his head and settled in for the long wait till dawn.

CHAPTER 46

Cruz had agreed to meet *El Rey* and Briones early at the Congress building to go over last-minute checks and to see whether there was anything that caught the assassin's expert eye as being a hole in the security. At seven, all three were standing in front of the huge edifice, soldiers and *Federales* everywhere, the air overhead shredded by the blades of helicopters holding snipers, their rifles stabilized with gyro-harnesses. A kind of controlled pandemonium reigned: army vehicles formed a crude gray perimeter, wooden roadblocks painted bright yellow lay ready to be set in place, and hundreds of armed police marched from their deployment location to the surrounding neighborhoods, supported by a contingent of menacing-looking marines with black knit balaclavas pulled over their faces.

Briones and Cruz were both in uniform, and *El Rey* had a *Federales* badge and credentials on a lanyard around his neck. His eyes were in constant motion, roving over the building silhouettes, his operational instinct clamoring a warning – the German was here, in the city somewhere, and he would make an attempt on the Chinese leader's life this morning. He was as sure of it as an arthritic grandmother knew when rain was coming, and the certitude had him restless, nerves close to the surface and hyper-aware.

The anxiety was contagious, and soon both Cruz and Briones were also unsettled as they moved from position to position, checking with the security teams, their Chinese counterparts already in place, having flown in on an earlier jet dedicated to their transport, their glacial eyes sharing the roaming vigilance of their Mexican colleagues.

After spending an hour reviewing the precautions, they decided to move to the airport to check on things there – it would take a half an hour in rush hour to make it using surface streets, so they would have thirty minutes to nose around and see if they could detect anything amiss. Cruz bought a couple of newspapers for them at a café and two coffees for himself and Briones, while the lieutenant went to fetch the cruiser from the nearby lot, the assassin having declined anything, as was his custom.

When Briones pulled to the curb, emergency lights flashing, Cruz climbed into the front seat and *El Rey* took the back. A traffic cop waved them through the already congested intersection, rubberneckers everywhere wondering at the awe-inspiring display of firepower in the nation's capital. Cruz handed one of the papers to *El Rey* and then took an appreciative sip of his steaming beverage as he studied the front page.

"Huh. Can't recall ever seeing that before," Briones commented, catching the headline out of the corner of his eye.

"What's that?" Cruz asked.

"Someone stealing a plane and then crashing it. Weird."

"The ink must still be wet. Says it only happened a few hours ago," Cruz commented. "Computers have enabled the papers to change the cover story right up till the first run comes off the presses. Brave new world."

El Rey read the short article, obviously written in haste, and then flipped the page, where a celebrity TV show host was gushing about her new baby and the tribulations of living with her multi-millionaire soccer player husband. A group of protesters had already gathered across the street from the Congress, and placards announced a host of uncoordinated complaints, railing against everything from the new accord the Chinese leader would be signing to steadily rising gas prices to the loss of Mexican jobs. The chanting hadn't started yet, the protest leaders enjoying their coffee like everyone else before the cameras started whirring, and Cruz was struck by the pre-determined formality of the scene – protestors protesting, police officers policing, killers angling for a shot, politicians grandstanding through it all.

By the time they reached the airport, the perimeter road had been closed off, and Briones was able to park right in front of the terminal, his glower daring the local police at the curb to say anything about it. The officers on duty looked away – they had no dog in that fight.

The three entered the huge hall and moved to the security checkpoint, their progress tracked by dozens of armed federal police carrying assault rifles. Cruz made a cell call to advise the ranking *Federales* officer that his party was coming through and request that he meet them at the scanners to facilitate their passage. The officer was there in a few minutes, and they repeated their walkthrough, studying the runways where military vehicles and federal police assault vans were now parked in strategic locations, in anticipation of the Chinese plane's arrival.

"Quite a show, eh?" Cruz said to nobody in particular, taking in the hundred or so armed men in clusters down on the tarmac, heavy fifty-caliber machine guns on the vehicle turrets manned by attentive soldiers, every one a combat veteran from the cartel wars that had been raging out of control for a dozen years. These were seasoned combatants used to taking fire and returning it, and Cruz found their presence reassuring, even if part of him knew that their presence was mostly for effect.

Their host, Captain Gabriel Guzman, looked equally fit to his retinue, and was only a few years younger than Cruz. He walked them through the steps he'd taken, politely answering their questions between fielding near-constant inquiries over his crackling radio. Cruz and Briones listened attentively, but the assassin seemed distant, lost in his thoughts as he searched in vain for a clue as to how the German intended to pull it off.

Forty minutes later, a charge of electrifying energy ran through the men as a Boeing 747 with the People's Republic of China emblem on the tail dropped out of the sky and set down with the unlikely grace of an obese swan, its bloated torso defying physics with its ungainly flight. All eyes tracked it as it slowed at the far end of the runway, barely visible through the shimmer of polluted air, and then turned its bulbous nose slowly in their direction and taxied back towards them.

"Does anyone have binoculars?" *El Rey* asked, and Captain Guzman muttered into his radio. A few moments later a younger *Federal* came jogging up with a pair of spyglasses and looked quizzically at the group. The assassin motioned for him to hand them over, and then, without comment, he began studying everything within sight, taking his time, pausing now and again at a vehicle or structure. He could make out three snipers on the hangar roofs across the VIP area — one at each corner, facing the spot where the plane would come to rest, and one in the center.

He turned to Cruz. "I want to get up on the roof. How many shooters do you have up there?" he asked, shifting his focus to Guzman.

"Five at this terminal. Two more facing the staging area, and three facing the frontage road."

"Let's get up there," Cruz said, and the four men made for the elevator to the upper level, where a guarded stairwell led to the roof.

"How's it been going?" Briones asked, making small talk as they moved across the floor.

"Hectic, as you can see. They can't just close down the terminal, so with the passenger traffic it's been juggling a lot of balls. And the plane scare last night didn't help."

"Why did that affect you?"

"It flew by us, just a few miles east, so I got woken up in the dead of night. My fault for telling my subordinate to call me if anything unusual happened. Stupid bastard wound up crashing up by Pachuca. Got what he deserved."

El Rey followed the conversation without comment, and then stopped, just for a brief second, something nagging at his awareness. Then it flitted away, a ghost dancing at the periphery of his consciousness, too insubstantial to solidify.

"What's eating you? You look like someone just walked across your grave," Cruz asked him, taking in his agitation.

"I don't know. Maybe I'm just looking for meaning where there isn't any. Something about the plane scare... it's probably nothing."

When they opened the rooftop door they were immediately struck by the stench of jet exhaust, which had bled an amber stain across the skyline. Supposedly the smog was far better than a decade earlier, but it was hard to tell that morning, and everyone's eyes began watering within five minutes of being outside. *El Rey* took a few steps away from the group, his attention pulled to something on one of the nearby equipment enclosures – movement. A large black bird – a crow – was grooming itself, but seemed to sense the assassin's scrutiny and abruptly stopped before fixing him with a beady eye. A chill ran up the assassin's spine, and then the bird flapped into the air, away from the men and their airport, leaving them to their mundane duties.

He returned to Cruz's side and they did a circuitous tour, nodding at the snipers, who were slowly panning their rifles, watching for any signs of a

234

threat through their scopes. Briones nudged *El Rey* and motioned to the binoculars, the impulse to join them in their vigil too strong to resist. The Chinese jumbo jet had coasted to a stop in the designated area and made a half turn so that the doors would be facing away from the city – a common-sense measure that put the plane's bulk between the nearby buildings and the spot where the helicopter would land. Everything seemed to be under control, the security impenetrable.

Perhaps they would get lucky, and the German had decided to skip his date with destiny.

Cruz looked at his watch. Twenty more minutes, and the helicopter would be there.

CHAPTER 47

Rauschenbach squinted through the ventilation grill louvers at the plane in the distance. Only a few minutes to go now. Hundreds of hours of effort and planning would all culminate with a man he'd never met dying a mile away so that he could retire four million dollars richer. What a strange and wonderful world it was.

He'd watched the snipers take up their positions after a hurried reconnaissance of the roof, and fortunately the closest was at least fifty yards away. That solved a lot of problems for him, because he could shift the grill open a few inches, which would afford him just enough room to slip the rifle barrel out and sight the scope through the gap. Once the jet had drawn to a stop, he'd pinged it with the laser range finder, which read fifteen hundred and ninety-six meters – farther than he'd hoped, but not by much, and still doable. The variable now was the crosswind. It had been impossible to get an accurate reading on the velocity from inside the shaft, so he had to guess – he figured it at seven miles per hour, but couldn't reliably judge what it was out in the middle of the field, on the runways.

Wind had always been a risk, but he'd seen no other viable alternatives. The damned Mexicans had put measures in place unlike anything he'd ever seen. He now had a grudging admiration for their acumen – several other options he'd considered had been cut off as he'd watched the preparations, so they had at least one person who knew what he was doing.

His digital watch made an almost inaudible beep and he became more alert. The door to the plane would open at any moment, the stairs would roll forward, and then the great man would step out into the Mexican sun and move down to the tarmac, where he would be greeted by the mayor and a row of suited dignitaries, and then be whisked off to the helicopter and up, out of the German's reach. His chance would come either at the top of the stairs, or once the target was standing, being greeted by the government wonks.

The moment he had been waiting for arrived. The door swung wide, and a few seconds later the mobile steps that were waiting nearby lumbered forward and pressed against the fuselage in an almost lascivious manner, west meeting east, the thrusting stairs unmistakably phallic to his eye.

A winsome young woman looked out from the plane doorway and then moved onto the platform, followed by a coterie of hard-looking security men in matching navy blue suits, their jackets bulging with weapons, ear buds discreetly in place, eyes no doubt scanning automatically from behind the darkened lenses of their sunglasses. They were small even in the high-powered scope's lens, but he felt increasingly confident as one, then two, and then finally two more stepped onto the landing, turned outward to face any attack, their job to give their lives to shield their charge from harm.

Not this time, boys. It's not your lucky day.

A portly functionary moved onto the platform and then slowly down the stairs, followed by six more bodyguards, who stationed themselves at the base of the steps, facing the waiting Mexicans like life-sized pawns in an elaborate chess game. Four more members of the Chinese delegation then exited the plane and descended, and Rauschenbach's pulse slowed as he focused upon modulating his breathing, every iota of his awareness now concentrated on the image in the scope. The procession seemed to go on forever, and then the Chinese leader's distinctive profile emerged from the gloom, a politician's smile plastered on his face with all the warmth of rigor mortis, ferret-like eyes darting to and fro. For a fleeting moment it was hard for Rauschenbach to believe that the largely unremarkable doughy-soft features, the man's butter-faced expression tinged with distaste, were those of the second most powerful man in the world.

The Chinese leader stood just outside the doorway, frozen in a photo-op moment, waving at a non-existent crowd for the cameras, and Rauschenbach began exhaling his carefully metered final breath, his finger caressing the trigger with a familiarity born of intimacy; and then his zen-like calm was shattered when an Aero Mexico jet's engines roared as it began its takeoff run, momentarily blurring across the scope's field of vision and disrupting his concentration.

"Shit," he cursed; and the first opportunity was lost as the Chinese leader edged forward and descended the steps, his bodyguards having taken up position in front and immediately behind him, a slow-moving Asian conga line inching down the stairs as the bemused Mexicans waited in a kind of suspended animation.

Rauschenbach gathered himself and returned to trailing the crosshairs on the target's head, following the leader's movements until he arrived at the base of the steps. There he paused, but only briefly – not long enough for the slug to cover the distance. That was the tricky part about a long-range shot: You needed the target to be stationary for at least several long seconds, or by the time the bullet reached him, he could have moved.

He watched as the Chinese leader stepped forward to greet his Mexican hosts, and then stood stock still as the mayor made a few ceremonious statements of fellowship and greeting – the second moment the German had been waiting for. Every fiber of his being seemed to synthesize down to the scope, and his pulse beat in his ears as he exhaled his lungs' accumulated air and pulled the trigger.

෬∾ೕ

The Chinese leader was irritable, but trying not to show it – the trip across the Pacific had been bumpy, and he'd lost a night of sleep as they'd continually changed altitude, trying to find comfortable air. Thankfully, he only needed to sign the document and nod agreement, and then he would be out of this stinking city, the air a travesty, the smell of toxicity as plain as if he was standing in front of a mass grave.

Not that China was any better, but he didn't have to go out in the soup, and his residence and the party headquarters where he conducted his business were filtered and purified and climate-controlled. Now, standing under the sun's glare, a blanket of amber filth stretching as far as the horizon, it was getting to him after the long flight and the drying effect of the jet's processed atmosphere. His eyes burned as he stood grinning at the group assembled on the tarmac, doing his obligatory courtesy wave to demonstrate how warm and inviting the misunderstood Chinese pseudo-communists really were, and he had already begun counting the seconds until he could get back in the plane and take off as he took the first red-carpeted step leading to his waiting hosts.

Once he was on terra firma he forced himself to listen attentively as the rotund Mexican idiot in the poorly cut suit badly mangled a greeting in Cantonese – the mayor, one of his entourage whispered in his ear. The waiting helicopter's slowly rotating blades beckoned to him like a love-struck virgin as he endured the boob's prattling, smiling the entire while as his eyes itched in rejection of the polluted sky.

❧

Rauschenbach watched through the scope a nano-second after the gun bucked into his shoulder, and then his quivering smile of triumph froze as the little Asian man's expression changed, just a little, as if he sensed the approach of the bullet.

❧

The Lapua Magnum round whirled in deadly rotation as it streaked across the runway, its end point the center of the Chinese leader's temple; and then an imperceptible shift occurred as it crossed runway number two – a gust of wind coaxing it westward, a rogue eddy toying with it like a kind of cosmic joke. And yet still it raced towards its destiny, ultimately missing the Chinese leader's cranium by a few scant millimeters, thrown off trajectory by the shifting vagary of the mercurial breeze, and punched into the tarmac thirty yards behind him, unnoticed. The noise from the helicopter as well as the landing and taxiing aircraft all around the delegation masked the sound of its impact, the telltale whining snick of a ricochet lost on everyone as the Mexico City mayor assured the leader that they were now brothers in peace and prosperity.

❧

"Un-fucking-believable," Rauschenbach muttered, even as his fingers gripped the back of the rifle chamber to unscrew it and eject the spent round and slip another into place. He knew from practice that it would take exactly seven seconds. Attempting to reload it any faster only caused it to take longer, as though the rifle resented his rushing and battled him accordingly. There was no point in trying to hurry it. The target would either still be standing there, or he wouldn't, by the time the rifle was ready again.

෪ඏ

El Rey grabbed Cruz's arm and screamed in alarm as he stared through the binoculars at the far terminal in the distance.

"A shot. I just saw a flash on the Terminal One roof. Get the Chinese leader out of here, and radio the sharpshooters over there. He's on the roof. The last ventilation housing before the hotel."

Cruz was so shocked to hear the otherwise quiet assassin raise his voice that he stood for a second, frozen. Then he leapt into action, turning to watch the delegation even as he raised his radio to his lips to sound a warning. Visions of the leader's skull exploding in an eruption of bloody effluvia played through his head as he put out an all points alert, and yet nothing happened. The mayor continued to drone on in a stage voice, struggling to make himself heard over the helicopter's din, but other than a small nod of the Chinese leader's head, the ceremony continued relentlessly forward.

"Come on. We need to get over there, now!" *El Rey* grabbed Briones' arm as Cruz issued terse commands, and then the three of them were running for the roof door.

"You! Up on the far roof, on the other terminal. Last ventilation structure on the right. There's a shooter," Cruz yelled at the nearest sniper, who looked at him like he was mad before turning his weapon and sighting at the building a mile across the air field.

"Get out of my way. Now," he bellowed, as three more *Federales* armed with rifles burst through the door. The startled men leapt aside as the trio ran for the exit like madmen and then disappeared down the steps in a flurry of furious activity, Cruz's voice barking commands into the radio even as he ran down the stairwell like the devil himself was coming for his soul.

෪ඏ

Rauschenbach seated the bolt home with a final twist and cocked it before peering into the scope again, half expecting the opportunity to have passed, four million daydreams sailing away for distant shores with nothing to be done about it. But fate had smiled upon him, and the little man's oddly shaped head, resembling a genetically warped gourd, hovered in the crosshairs as though he was posing for a portrait.

The German sensed what had happened on the last shot, and corrected for it by pointing the rifle just a hair off center, and repeated his exhalation, this time accompanied by a silent prayer to a deity he didn't believe in as he gently massaged the trigger. The weapon bucked again, and then his attention was pulled from the image in the scope to a federal police sniper running towards him at flat out speed, the business end of his weapon pointed in his direction.

❧❦

It seemed as though the mayor's enthusiastic oration was drawing to a close, and the Chinese leader smiled broadly, this time with genuine happiness at the thought of getting on with the signing. The mayor's wife, who stood beside him like a pig that had fought its way out of a Chanel factory outlet store by putting on clothes, beamed at him like he was dessert, and he heard the clicking of shutters as the grouped media memorialized the moment for posterity.

His eyes burned like hellfire from the smog, and he was wondering about whether one of his people could get him drops when a tickle began deep in his septum, making his eyes water, and then, in spite of his iron will, his lids automatically squeezed shut, and he sneezed.

"Salud!" the mayor exploded, as his wife laughed and clapped her hands together, and then everyone had a chuckle as the Chinese leader grinned again, a slightly sheepish look on his face, and then pointed up at the sky and uttered the single word that would endear him to an entire generation of Mexicans, the R sound admittedly coming out sounding more like an L, but other than that, remarkably sincere.

"Gracias."

❧❦

This time the bullet flew straight and true, unhampered by stray atmospheric anomalies, and had it not been for the random interceding of an allergic purging of nasal airways, would have turned the leader's frontal lobes into pudding. But in spite of the best efforts of the artisans who had carefully milled the rifle barrel, the countless hours spent on ballistic improvements that would enable a fingernail-sized projectile to cut through the air at near miraculous levels of accuracy, and hundreds of dedicated

241

hours at firing ranges honing the highly specialized skill of long-range shooting, despite breakthroughs in optics that made distant objects appear to be no farther away than across the room, the most deadly working assassin in the world...missed.

Not once.

But twice.

CHAPTER 48

Rauschenbach jerked the Sig Sauer free from its holster and fired at the approaching sniper through the gap in the grill, both rounds catching him squarely in the chest. He didn't stop to confirm whether or not the officer was dead or had been saved by his Kevlar body armor, and instead pushed himself away from the opening, his mind now on only one thing: escape. Nothing mattered besides getting away clean – he would read about whether or not his last shot had struck home in the evening paper, but now his imperative was thinking faster than his pursuers.

That someone had spotted him was obvious, and it didn't really matter how – whether it was the crack from his silenced rifle heard by one of the snipers, or the ricochet alerting them to his presence, or the tiny muzzle flash, the damage had been done, and he couldn't turn back the clock.

At the end of the shaft he spun and pushed himself around a bend in the ducting, and then his hands gripped the familiar shape of the mountain climbing rope he'd fastened to a protruding bolt. He didn't even bother to listen for the other snipers arriving at the ventilation structure – he knew he would have at least twenty to thirty seconds before they got there, and then another ten to fifteen as they decided how to grapple with the darkened shaft, their foolhardy colleague lying shot only a dozen yards away. Those forty-five seconds would be enough, and would stretch longer as they timidly followed him into the shaft – by which time he would be gone.

He briefly considered donning the light again and then dismissed the idea – might as well put an illuminated bull's eye on his head. No, he would need to do it by touch, which he was prepared for. He took a deep breath and lowered himself down the shaft. The line vibrated as it took his weight, and then he dropped a story and a half to the next connecting duct, down which he knew he would have to crawl two dozen yards before he came to another junction that would lead him further into the bowels of the airport, to the oversized fans that turned tirelessly at the end of a chute, beyond which was the equipment room, and ultimately, freedom.

෨๏৶

Briones stomped on the cruiser's accelerator, tearing the wrong way down the perimeter road, the speedometer soaring through the digits as he pushed the big V-8 to its limits, sirens shrieking like a jilted bride, and Cruz groped for a hold in the passenger seat as he listened while the reports came in.

They had a man down on the roof, and the other officers were demanding instruction – the shooter was inside the ventilation housing, but they didn't want to endanger themselves further with a reckless pursuit. He listened as Lopez ordered them to go in after him, and then nothing but static came over the channel.

"Lopez. Is the Chinese leader safe?" Cruz barked as they slalomed around the gentle curve at the end of the runway, half the distance to the other terminal covered.

"Yes. He's on the bird. Everything's calm there. Nobody's the wiser." The captain's voice sounded strained, but under control.

"We're going to be at the terminal in another thirty seconds. Have all available units seal it off. He's in there somewhere. Let's not let him get away. If he went down the ventilation ducts, we need a plan of the system, stat," Cruz warned.

"10-4. I'll get everyone there immediately. And I'm already pulling up plans."

"Fine. Let me know when you have them – if you can, send them to my phone. And keep some security at Terminal Two, just in case, so the area is still secure. But I could really use some serious muscle backing us up here."

"You got it."

The engine throbbed as Briones goosed the car around the final bend and then raced for the front entrance in a screeching roar of rubber and brakes.

"How do you want to do this?" Briones asked as they skidded to a stop.

"We'll spread out. He's in the ventilation system. There can't be too many places he can get out. Dammit. I wish we had the plans," Cruz complained. "Briones, you stay out here and watch for anyone suspicious.

I'll radio to have the parking level shut off. That way, when he tries to get out, he'll have to come through here."

Briones gazed down the long expanse, temporarily empty of cars except for police vehicles and a few army trucks. "It's a lot of ground to cover. What is it, almost a kilometer?"

"He was on this end, so the likelihood is he's still here. That's where we'll start. Damn. Why didn't Godoy let me circulate the bastard's picture?" Cruz stabbed at his phone's speed dial and then ordered his assistant to get the photo transmitted to all federal police personnel. "It's a little late now for worrying about letting the cat out of the bag. But this won't be instant. We're going to need to rely on you as our last line of defense," Cruz told Briones.

"I'll keep an eye out, sir, and do the best I can."

El Rey and Cruz got out of the car, and *El Rey* leaned in to address Briones. "I need a weapon. Give me your sidearm. You have the shotgun. Divide and conquer."

Briones glanced at Cruz, who nodded impatiently. Briones un-holstered his Glock and handed it to the assassin. "It's a .40 caliber. Glock 22. Fifteen round magazine."

"I know it well," *El Rey* said, then hesitated. "Good luck."

"Thanks. You too. Good catch on the muzzle flash."

El Rey tried to contain a smirk, and then turned to Cruz. "You take one section, I take the other? Or stay together?"

"What do you think?"

"Sticking together hasn't hurt our chances very much so far, unless you consider the German getting within a hair of killing the target a bad thing."

"So split up?"

"Probably doesn't matter at this point. And I need to be with you to get through security with a gun. Just keep your eyes open. He's got to be around here somewhere. Order all the passengers to be held and screened. It'll play hell with traffic, but that's not our problem. If we continue to allow passengers to enter and exit, we're screwed."

"What about departing flights?"

"Get a one hour delay while we have your people check all manifests. And put a couple of men on each gate. You don't want him getting on a plane."

Cruz relayed the order to Lopez.

"All right. Now he can't get out. We've got him," Cruz said.

"No, we don't. This guy is good. Expect the unexpected."

"Good advice. Based on experience again?"

"I saw it in a movie."

❧

Rauschenbach peeked around the basement corner and then climbed the stairs to the arrivals level. The hall was crowded, thousands of people spreading through the terminal, and the overhead announcement that nobody was going to be permitted to exit had sent everyone into a tailspin, a good portion of the crowd alarmed and the rest angry at being detained. He eased a maintenance access door open and peered out, and then pulled the baseball cap down as far as it would go over his eyes and strode purposefully across the terminal, moving towards the center, away from the side of the building where the ventilation shaft was located.

Everyone got out of his way as he lifted his phone to his ear and pretended to be barking orders. Nobody wanted to cross the tall federal police officer, frowning and agitated, obviously engaged in some sort of crisis control. His footsteps sounded like small arms fire as he stormed along the line of shops, eyes roving over the glass exits for signs of a hole in the gauntlet he knew would be closing around him.

His skin was four shades darker, thanks to a tint he had used on his face and hands, and his hair was now dyed black and he had affixed a mustache that further created an impression of his being Mexican. It wouldn't pass close scrutiny by a trained eye, but all he needed it to do was get him out one of the doors so he could get to his waiting car, or steal one.

Rauschenbach's hand moved to his gun as he saw a dozen *Federales* deployed at the exits, stopping people from leaving, and then he forced himself to relax and dropped his hand, choosing instead to focus on finding an opportunity to escape rather than dying in a gunfight.

❧

"There are too many people. We're wasting our time," Cruz griped as he studied the sea of moving faces.

"Agreed. You stay here. I'll try over on the other end. You never know. Maybe one of us will get lucky."

"Kind of hard to believe based on how things have played so far, isn't it?"

"Hey, the target's alive. I'd take that as a win."

"Not because of anything we did."

"It still counts as a win," *El Rey* pronounced decisively, and then spun and made for the far section of the terminal.

Cruz tried to concentrate, but his mind instantly ran to the logistics involved of trying to catch the German in a crowd this size. Theoretically they would, eventually; but he suspected that sooner or later someone would make a call to a politically connected friend, and then favors would be called in, and soon there would be an outcry over the Gestapo tactics being used at the airport. He knew how the system worked, and if they were lucky, they would get an hour or two, tops. Then Godoy would be on the line, pointing out that everything had turned out fine, and that discretion would carry the day, the assassin having failed.

It was a crappy system sometimes, he knew.

All too well.

෴

El Rey began dividing the arrival hall into quadrants and methodically searching for something, anything, that might be a giveaway. He fully expected the German to have changed his appearance, and possibly be in disguise – a maintenance man or a service worker. Because that's what he would have done. Someone innocuous, whose presence wouldn't attract undue attention in the airport, who could move around unimpeded.

Movement caught his eye to his left, and then he dismissed it – a little girl had bolted from her mother and was running towards a candy display in one of the convenience stores. He knew the primitive reptilian brain was alert to unexpected movement, and he tried to relax and harness that power. The German would be anxious to get out before the building was completely sealed, and that might make him careless. It was really their only hope – that his nerves might give and he would make a mistake, draw attention to himself.

He registered another movement to his right and looked to see what had attracted his eye. An officer was stalking towards an exit, talking on his phone. But there was something about his gait that made the assassin take another look. He was covering a lot of ground, but seeming to not hurry.

That's what had caught his attention. He knew that rhythm. Like a predatory feline.

El Rey withdrew his phone and dialed Cruz as he began to walk in step with the man, who was about a hundred yards away.

"I think it may be him. He's making for one of the exits. Warn Briones. By the C section exit."

"Are you sure?"

"I'm closing in on him. Get over here. And have Briones pull up. We can get him in a pincer."

"A pincer?"

"Never mind. How far away are you?"

"I'll be there in sixty seconds."

"Try to make it thirty."

He picked up his pace as he watched the putative officer approach the two men guarding the exit, and then a strong grip locked on his arm.

"Sir. Slow down. Where are you going in such a hurry? The exits are sealed. Let's see some identification. Now." The soldier was eyeing him suspiciously, his partner holding his gun at the ready. *El Rey* reached to pull the lanyard out from under his shirt, where he'd slid it out of sight so he wouldn't arouse suspicion, and then the soldier with the rifle yelled a nervous warning.

"Look out. He's got a gun!" The soldier had spotted the Glock stuck in his waistband at the base of his spine.

"Easy, corporal. I'm with the *Federales*. I'm now going to pull my badge out and show it to you, all right? Don't get crazy with the rifle. Everyone just calm down," *El Rey* said in his calmest, most reasonable tone.

"No fast moves or you're dead," the soldier warned, his expression betraying that he could shoot for almost any reason, his nerves too near the surface for this duty.

"Nice and easy. Here, see? A badge. And an ID. Take a look, and lower your weapon, corporal. Show's over. We're on the same side."

The soldier leaned forward and inspected the badge as his partner fingered the trigger guard of his weapon, and *El Rey* considered how easy it would be to disable them both before they even realized what had happened, and then stopped that line of thinking. He waited patiently for them to verify his identity, and then both soldiers relaxed.

"Sorry, sir. We're on high alert. They told us to trust no one. And when I saw the gun..."

"No harm done. Now, I've got something to attend to. If you'll excuse me..."

Cruz came puffing up just then. "Where is he?"

El Rey pointed. "Over by that door. Then Mutt and Jeff here stopped me, and by the time I sorted them out, he was gone."

"Shit."

They both jogged to the door, and Cruz moved to the two *Federales* framing it. "What happened to the man who was just here?"

"Sir? You mean the other officer?"

"Where is he?"

"He was in a hurry. Talking to headquarters. He went that way." The policeman gestured to the right, out on the sidewalk.

Cruz called Briones and started talking when he heard the line connect.

"He's outside. By C. We're coming out. He's dressed as a federal police officer. Tall. Mustache. Hat."

"Damn. I think I see—"

Briones was interrupted by the screech of tires as one of the waiting police cruisers wheeled from the curb and accelerated.

"He's in the car that just took off," *El Rey* said, and then they both ran outside to Briones' cruiser and jumped in.

"Don't let him get away," Cruz ordered, buckling up, and Briones floored the Dodge, which leapt forward and took off like a scared rabbit.

CHAPTER 49

They watched as Rauschenbach tore towards a security checkpoint, where two police cars were parked, blocking the road, hood to hood, lights flashing. A passel of officers standing in front of them watched with puzzlement and growing alarm as the cruiser hurtled towards the checkpoint. Cruz grabbed for the radio to send a warning, but as he pressed the transmit button the German's vehicle blew through the blockade, knocking the cars aside and crushing his front fenders in the process. Sparks flew from beneath the front tires, but the cruiser was still drivable, judging by its minimal reduction in speed.

"He's headed for Sonora Street. If he can lose us, he'll be in the clear," Briones shouted as they slammed over scattered wreckage in the road, running the newly formed gauntlet between the two cars without hesitation.

"You can take him," *El Rey* said from the back seat.

"Try to get closer. I'll shoot out his back tires. That'll slow him down," Cruz commanded, and then lowered his window and pulled his Glock. Briones jammed the accelerator to the floor and they gained a few car lengths. A piece of Rauschenbach's fender tore off and skittered against the pavement. Briones reacted too late, and the errant piece of metal shattered the windshield, starbursting the safety glass and making it almost impossible to see out of it.

"Damn," Briones swore, leaning his head out the driver's side window so as not to lose the German.

"Hold it steady," Cruz yelled over the wind noise, and leaned halfway out of the car, gun trained on Rauschenbach's rear bumper. The range was iffy, at least sixty to seventy yards, but he wasn't trying to split a mouse hair. He was only looking for one hit, and he had a full clip to gamble with.

The boom of his pistol sounded, then again and again and again, as he rapid fired in a rough pattern, his aim thrown off by the car's bouncing on the uneven pavement.

"Pull to the left. Let me try," *El Rey* screamed, and Cruz slid back into his seat and re-clipped his safety belt as the assassin rolled down his window and brandished Briones' pistol. Briones veered left as instructed, providing a better angle for *El Rey*, who fired off ten shots in two seconds, the concussion of the gunfire deafening in the car.

Rauschenbach's vehicle swerved as the rear tires flattened. He lost control and the Dodge skewed sideways, doing at least eighty, and then it clipped the far curb and flipped, twisting end over end in an eerily graceful somersault before rolling three, four, five times and crashing to a halt on its roof. Pieces of the vehicle flew everywhere as Briones swerved to avoid the worst of it. A heavy wheel rim smashed into the front of the cruiser as he locked up the brakes and drifted into a slow motion skid, which was abruptly terminated when he slammed into a concrete support beam. The airbags deployed, saving Briones and Cruz's lives, but *El Rey* slammed into the back of the rear seat, his neck whiplashing before his head careened into the rear door panel.

Steam hissed from under the ruined hood as Cruz and Briones pawed at the airbags, blood pouring freely from the younger man's nose and staining the front of his shirt. A small cut over Cruz's left eye trickled a stream of crimson down the side of his face. Sirens wailed from behind them as Cruz fumbled with the door handle before releasing his belt and stepping unsteadily onto the pavement.

He slowly approached the mangled wreck, gun held by his side, and saw furtive movement from inside the twisted carcass, the lone remaining front wheel slowly spinning in the air seemingly of its own accord like a ghostly weaver's loom. He caught a flash of the German, hanging upside down by his safety belt, the shoulder harness holding him in place, and then gunfire erupted from inside. Cruz kept walking with a measured pace as ricochets chipped chunks out of the street next to him, and then he raised his Glock and drew a bead on Rauschenbach, squinting, one eye closed, brushing sweat and blood from his forehead as his gaze connected for a brief eternity with the German's.

The pistol bucked twice. Both rounds hit Rauschenbach in the upper torso. His gun fell from his hand with a clatter, and then he hung suspended, his arms limp, blood coursing down them onto the smashed interior panel of the roof. Cruz slowly lowered his Glock and took in the scene – gas trickling in a pool beneath the car, the assassin dead or dying, flames beginning to lick from beneath the hood. He sighed, suddenly exhausted, the adrenaline rush abruptly dropping off an internal cliff, and without a word, pivoted to return to the car to help Briones and *El Rey*.

Cruz didn't even wince when the German's car exploded, searing the air behind him, nor did he glance back as pieces of Dodge rocketed into the sky before the inexorable force of gravity exercised its pull and brought them plummeting back to earth. A part of a door landed a few feet to his left and he turned to regard it, his gaze devoid of interest, and then he realized he was still gripping his pistol so hard that his knuckles were white. He flipped open the holster with his thumb, slipped it back into place with a trembling hand, and mechanically refastened the safety strap.

He needed to get his men help. It was over.

He had done his job.

And he felt old.

CHAPTER 50

The helicopter set down on the parking lot of the Congress building, squarely in the center of the large yellow H painted on the black pavement, and a contingent of Chinese bodyguards rushed beneath the still circling blades and formed a protective shield around the door. After a brief pause it slid open with a crash, and two more security men stepped onto the ground before the Chinese leader poked his head out, and then was assisted from the aircraft as still more bodyguards, these Mexican, lined the area.

Grim-countenanced soldiers stood in their gray camouflage uniforms brandishing assault rifles as he paused to wave at the crowd across the street, some cheering, some toting protest signs, many unsure what all the fuss was about but caught up in the excitement. The delegation moved up the steps to the hulking edifice's oversized iron and glass doors, where an honor guard waited at stiff attention, in full dress ceremonial splendor, swords held rigidly in time-honored salute, their shoes so highly polished they were blinding in the morning sun.

And then the Chinese delegation was in the building. The hubbub outside lost steam, the show over for at least a time, and the excitement level visibly faded. Once in the assembly hall, the Mexican President stood in greeting from his position at the podium, behind a large rectangular hand-crafted mesquite table with only two chairs, and the room broke into cheering applause as the lawmakers welcomed their honored guest.

Speeches were made, commitments heralded, cameras whirred, and eventually the two men sat down, as fate had destined them to, beneath the iron sculpture of an eagle gripping a snake, and affixed their signatures to the groundbreaking accord that would change the future of Mexico forever. Hands were clasped in symbolic handshakes and yet more speeches were made, and then the procession moved back out of the building, retracing its steps to the waiting helicopter, and within ninety seconds of their reaching it the chopper was lifting into the hazy sky, the party over, the only thing remaining the clean-up.

⇛⇝

"Damn it. How could this happen? You assured us this was taken care of. Explain yourself. Make it very simple, so even a stupid old man like me can understand." The speaker was in his mid-sixties, balding, his face creased with the heavy lines of stress and time. He was staring across a conference table in Langley, Virginia, at the headquarters of the Central Intelligence Agency, where he directed the group until God or the president decided that his time had passed. Five somber men sat along either side of the table, all eyes fixed on a younger man in his early forties, standing at the far end like a student being dressed down by the headmaster.

The younger man cleared his throat, aware that his career was effectively over, his high-stakes gambit having failed. And the price for failure would be high. He had known that part of the risk of playing at the big table with the adults was that something would go wrong, and he would be the one held accountable. It was the way things had always worked, and always would. Didn't matter that he'd had twenty years of successes – one epic failure and he'd be running the bureau that dealt with Latvian militants, banished to servitude in a kind of purgatory. That was his future following this fiasco, after a brilliant run of triumphant operations. One bad one, and he was dog chow.

"Obviously, the contractor failed. The agreement was signed. There's not a lot else to say, is there? Something went wrong. We don't know exactly what. We hired the best in the world, and he wasn't good enough. The end." The younger man's tone was conciliatory and apologetic, but also no-nonsense. He knew the drill, and he knew that he would be tarred and feathered by these men, the upper echelon of the intelligence community, who had placed their faith in him. Mistakenly, as it turned out.

"Is it, though? The end? Is there any way anyone could trace even a hint of this back to us?"

"Negative. The German was hired using a cut-out, and the money came from operational accounts that had been left in place from Exodus." Exodus was one of the operations involving the transportation of heroin from Afghanistan into Russia and the former Soviet satellite countries.

The director nodded. "You know the ramifications. I now have a lot of explaining to do," he groused, unhappy at the prospect of the meeting that had been scheduled for an hour later with the president – who was not thrilled with the result of the operation, which he officially had no knowledge of, but had been following closely.

"This is completely my fault. One hundred percent. I'm trying to get some intelligence so we understand why it failed, but what's important is that it did. I take full responsibility, and will accept the consequences, which I'm sure will be severe."

"John, that's all well and good, but it doesn't really save me from getting an ass reaming from the Commander in Chief, does it? And it doesn't solve our problem. Your throwing yourself on your sword is duly noted, but I need some solutions here, not *mea culpas* or self-flagellation. This is a disaster, and the president's associates are not going to be pleased. It changes the balance of power for the oil industry moving forward. The Chinese will now be the entrenched players in Mexico, which will lead other countries to view them as legitimate contenders in the region. A lot of money is going to be lost as a result. Do I need to spell this out?" the director spat.

"I suppose we can always invade. Worked when we annexed California and Texas," one of the other men joked – the director's oldest friend, and an assistant director.

"Yeah, and look how that turned out," the director said, deadpan.

The gathering laughed, the tension broken, and the younger man saw a glimmer of hope for his prospects.

"It's never over till it's over. They still have to execute. And playing in Latin America can be difficult. Especially in a country that's riddled with corruption and cartel violence. I could envision chronic sabotage. Pipelines blown up. Profits siphoned off. Refineries destroyed. It's a rough world," he suggested.

"That's true. But it's a longer term play. We were all hoping for a quicker fix."

"Why didn't we just shoot the bastard's plane out of the sky? Do a TWA on his ass?" the assistant director demanded.

"We looked at that, but the risks were too great. It sets a bad precedent to eliminate a head of state in that public a manner," the younger man explained reasonably. "This was deemed to be our best option."

"And tell me again why we couldn't get our first choice? The Mexican contractor?"

"He's out of the business. No longer accepting contract work. He's now CISEN's asset, and we couldn't very well go to them for this, now could we? I mean, they're as broad-minded as any of us, but sanctioning a hit that runs directly against their national interests...that wasn't an option. Frankly, that's a shame, because his abilities were as good as anything we've seen. They don't build them like that every day. Made Carlos the Jackal look like a piker. But the German was always a reliable and skilled operator for us."

"Until he wasn't. Your report says he's dead?"

"Correct. At the airport. Fireball. Not much left but some dental records, and barely enough to fit in an ashtray."

"On the sabotage end, can we use our cartel partner there to help with it?" the director asked in a thoughtful tone.

"There are positives and negatives to that. I'd recommend that we farm it out, create a new 'insurgent' movement that's anti-Chinese or pro-Mexican or whatever the hell plays best. Keep the trafficking thing completely separate. Besides which, our man has lost ground this year against a rival. Los Zetas."

"Why the hell aren't we dealing with them, then? If they're kicking his ass, aren't we betting on the wrong horse?" the assistant director asked.

"They're too volatile. Our man is old school, and he's stable. These guys are cowboys. Way too violent. And we're not sure they'd even be willing to play ball. Frankly, they don't need us. They're expanding all over the world and doing just fine without our help."

"I hear what you're saying. But maybe there's a play there. Maybe they can be used against the Chinese. Think about it. I want creativity on this. We need to scramble and put something in place – at least something tentative I can float today so I don't get corn-holed by our glorious leader. His buddies are going to be righteously pissed – he made promises. And you don't want them angry. They're large supporters. Significant players."

The meeting went on for another half hour, and by the time it ended they'd cobbled together a rough plan. It needed refinement, but it was as good as any they'd fielded, and the agency had certainly backed worse ones. The Chavez screw-up was still fresh in many of their minds. They'd backed the leaders of the failed Venezuelan *coup d'état*, and the president had jumped the shark and come out supporting the new government before it had actually taken power – a mistake, given that Chavez repelled the attempt and emerged victorious, proving to the international community that the U.S. was still meddling in Latin America's affairs through government overthrows and assassinations. It had been a classic blunder, and no matter how much spin the U.S. had put on it and how compliant the media had been in spinning the story, most everyone other than the American public had seen the operation for what it was.

The younger man breathed a sigh of relief when the meeting broke up and the attendees rose and hurried off to issue instructions to their staffs. He wasn't out of the woods yet by any means, and it might take years to live this one down, but everyone seemed willing to let him have another inning; and with that, he was still in the game and could turn it around.

He closed the red file marked Top Secret and stood at the foot of the table, studying the walls for a few moments, considering his next move, and then nodded to himself.

Time to put together a good destabilization plan for our neighbors to the south.

It had worked before elsewhere, and it could certainly work again.

Now he just needed to tweak it and sell it.

His specialty.

CHAPTER 51

The nurse dabbed at Cruz's cut with an antibiotic pad and he winced from the sting, his legs swinging as he sat on the exam table. A knock sounded from the door and a doctor entered, sporting crisp physician whites and carrying a clipboard, trailed by Briones, who looked like he'd been mule-kicked in the head.

"Well, *Capitan*, you'll live. Just a few bruises and that cut. Cosmetic. Your associate here will have a slightly harder time of it. Couple of black eyes and a sniffer that might need some work down the road."

"Why is it that I always get it in the face?" Briones griped good-naturedly.

"The universe trying to tell you something? Maybe about keeping your nose out of other people's business?" Cruz opined. "This time around you got off light. No bullet wounds. Just a nosebleed from your reckless driving. The insurance company is going to get it worse than you."

The nurse finished her ministrations and offered a perfunctory smile to both men, and then she and the doctor left, leaving them alone.

"I think she liked you best," Cruz offered.

"But she was tending to you, sir."

"That's probably why she liked you best."

Briones rolled his eyes, then held his hand to his head. "Ow. Damn. I think I just hurt myself."

"That's what cynicism will do to you. It eats at your well-being like a cancer," Cruz intoned.

"Yes, sir. I've heard that."

Cruz's demeanor grew serious. "And how about everybody's favorite assassin? How did he pull through?"

"Concussion. But he's gone. Disappeared. They did a CT scan, and once he saw the results, he vanished while they were preparing to do a more thorough workup. Typical. Always about the drama. But he did leave this for you," Briones said, and then offered Cruz a sealed hospital envelope with his name neatly printed on the front.

Cruz took it from him, and after glancing at it, stuffed it into the breast pocket of his shirt. "How's the sniper who got shot on the roof?"

"He'll be okay. Vest saved him."

"He's very lucky. He could have gotten it in the head."

"I heard on the radio that the signing ceremony took place, and the Chinese leader is now back in the air," Briones said.

"So at least in that respect, this was a success."

"Sure doesn't feel like one, does it, sir?"

"No. It doesn't."

Both men sat contemplating their circumstances, and then Cruz's phone rang.

"Hello."

Godoy's voice boomed with effusive good cheer. "Congratulations, *Capitan*! He made it without getting killed! Good for you. I heard that you stopped the attempt!"

Cruz debated correcting the moron, then decided that it didn't warrant his effort. "All's well that ends well, right?" he said noncommittally.

"Yes, well, that's right. When can you be in my office?" Godoy asked, cutting to the chase.

"Some point this afternoon. I'm still at the hospital."

Godoy didn't ask whether he was okay, Cruz noticed.

"Fine. I'll leave instructions with my girl to put you through when you arrive."

"That's very kind of you."

Godoy's tone changed back to one that Cruz was sure he imagined to be camaraderie. "Nonsense. You're practically a hero. Although I don't have to remind you that this is all hush hush."

Cruz considered whether it would have been so secret if the Chinese leader had been executed on his watch. He was willing to bet money that his name would have been plastered all over the evening papers as the man who failed Mexico.

"You made that abundantly clear."

"Well, then, there it is." Godoy had run out of things to say, and like a car on an empty tank, had sputtered to a stop. Cruz considered softening the awkward moment, and then chose to let the egomaniac hang. Not that his superior would care whether anyone thought that he was a dolt. Godoy seemed singularly immune to self-awareness or introspection.

Instead, he simply hung up.

"Godoy?" Briones asked, brows raised.

"Yes. He was very concerned about you and the downed officer."

"I picked that up on the call."

"I'm reading between the lines."

"He probably figured that you would have told him if anything was seriously wrong."

"Right. No point in asking. Inefficient."

Cruz rose from the table and studied Briones. "You can put in a requisition for a new shirt. I doubt you'll get the blood out. You should be more careful."

"I intend to. I also bought some coffee while on assignment, as I recall."

"Have an expense report on my desk this afternoon. I'll sign it."

"Are you going back in today, sir?"

"I want to move some of my files back to headquarters. I have to see Godoy anyway. Might as well make that a useful trip."

"I'm going to take a few days off, at least until the swelling goes down."

"Not a bad idea. Do you want me to notify the shrink? Are you traumatized by your experience?"

"I'm hungry. Could that be a sign of post-traumatic stress?"

"I think so. I prescribe tequila. Three times a day for four days."

Briones saluted smartly. "Yes, sir. Whatever you say, sir!"

Cruz's face cracked as a smile forced its way to the surface. "It's about time I got some respect. Carry on, then. You up for lunch? I'm buying."

Briones thought about it, evaluating how he felt, considering his blood-soaked shirt and the cotton stuffed up his nose. "Lead the way. I could eat a horse, sir."

"Which is probably what it will be, if they're out of dog."

The pair trundled out of the room, Cruz weary and limping a little from where his knee had collided with the dashboard, Briones taking it slow because his head hurt with every step, as sad-looking a pair as had ever worn a uniform.

❧

"Ah, *Capitan*. Good to see you. Again, congratulations!" Godoy rose from behind his desk and actually came around it to shake his hand. Cruz couldn't remember a time when he'd ever exhibited the slightest interest in civility, or treated him as anything more than a servant. "Please, sit. May I offer you a refreshment? Water? Soda? Something with a little more kick?"

Did Godoy just wink at him as he returned to his plush executive chair? Cruz hoped it was the onset of some sort of devastating nervous disorder. Preferably painful. And embarrassing.

"No, thanks. I'm good."

"Well, then. Thank you for coming in. I just wanted to tell you how pleased I am that this was resolved without becoming an international crisis. The German is dead, the accord is signed, and the Chinese are none the wiser. I was told to express the president's gratitude, as well," Godoy gushed.

Ah. So that was it. The president had congratulated Godoy, and told him to pass it down.

"How?" Cruz asked.

Godoy's mullet-stare drifted to the cut on Cruz's head, as though noticing it for the first time, and then back to his eyes. "I...I'm sorry, *Capitan*. Come again?"

"I asked how? *How* is the president going to express his gratitude?"

"Why...I should think that his thanks for a job well done would be good enough," Godoy stammered. The conversation was taking an unexpected turn.

"Well, it isn't."

Both men stared at each other for a few slow moments.

"*Capitan*, I'm not sure where you're going with this, but I don't like your tone..."

"I don't really care what you like."

The words had the effect of a slap.

"Now see here—"

Cruz cut him off, the rage that had been building coming out in a glacial, tightly-controlled tone.

"No, *you* see here. You blackmailed me into taking a job that I didn't want. You forced me to work with the man who killed my wife's father, as well as my men. You threatened to withhold the pension I earned with my blood and my loyalty. You're a despicable fecal stain and a disgrace to Mexico, and those are your positive qualities. And I feel ill just being in the same room with you. So listen carefully. I want my pension. All of it. No strings. And I want a security team assigned to me, under my direction, for the next five years. I'll keep my gun, and you'll issue a permit for a concealed carry for both myself and my wife. The department will continue to pay for my accommodations for that period, as well. I'm in constant danger, due to the service I rendered for my country, and I *will* be treated fairly."

Godoy sat, speechless, his mouth hanging open like a bass. Cruz had a momentary vision of him reaching over and stuffing a dirty sock into it, or maybe his underwear, and then shrugged it off.

"Now for the part you'll probably be most interested in: If you don't do as I say, I'll break the true story of what happened to every media outlet in the world, starting with the Chinese. Mexico, lying, cheating and stealing, endangering a world leader, acting like a third world backwater, withholding information any other country would have immediately divulged. And I'll further highlight the role that *El Rey*, the world-famous cartel assassin, played in it – you know, the valued asset of the Mexican government."

Cruz stood, the blood rushing to his face as his anger simmered, and then he removed his badge and flipped it onto Godoy's desk.

"I quit. Effective immediately. So now *you* run the cartel task force. You become the most endangered, underappreciated police official in Mexico. You have your wife kidnapped, your life threatened, and finally, your financial future threatened by your own people. I'm done. And if I hear even a hint of anything but glowing recommendations from your office when asked about me, I will make your life miserable and break the story of your treacherous blackmail. I'm sure the Mexican people will enjoy knowing what kind of government they have. I'll ruin you, and the president, and the next time his party has a chance of winning an election for anything more than town drunk will be in another century. Now, I know you're not very smart, so I'll send you an e-mail so that you have my conditions in writing. Someone can explain them to you. But the takeaway from this meeting is that I quit, you can bite me, and you'd better do exactly as I say or you'll regret the day you ever heard my name."

Cruz turned and walked to the door, and then turned to the speechless bureaucrat as he reached for the knob. "You're an empty suit, an arrogant little man in a big office. If you don't think that I can crush you like a bug, just try me. You do not want to test me, because you'll be the very first on my list. I trust that's clear enough so even you can grasp it."

The sound of the door slamming was so loud it reverberated down the marble corridor. Cruz smiled to himself as he stalked from the offices, the image of Godoy fresh in his mind – mouth frozen in rictus, eyes betraying fear for the first time since he'd met the man. He wished he'd taken a photo, but knew that for the rest of his life he would be able to recall the memory in full living color.

For the first time in a long while, he felt truly good, like he could run a marathon or climb a peak.

Maybe it would finish up a pretty good day after all.

☙❧

Cruz stepped into the condo foyer, set his briefcase down next to the wall, and moved quietly down the hall to the bedroom. Dinah was in bed, sitting up, reading a magazine. She started when he opened the door, fear crossing her face for an instant, and then relief flooded her and she put down her tabloid.

"*Amor*. You're home early! Oh my God...what happened to your face? Are you all right?" she asked, her voice rising in pitch as she spoke.

"Everything's fine, my love. It's just a scratch. Really. It's nothing. How are you feeling? Any better?" he asked, concerned that she had still not worked up the enthusiasm to get out of bed for any length of time. The bruising had largely faded, but not the psychological damage. That would take considerably longer, he knew. Sometimes people experienced more than they could safely handle, and their psyches couldn't process it. Dinah was one of those. She had seen too much.

The memory of the three words on the note in *El Rey*'s envelope tugged at him as his eyes caressed her face, but he pushed them aside. *Remember your promise*. There would be time enough to consider the implications later. All the time in the world. But not now. This moment belonged to them.

"Oh, you know. Don't worry about me. I'll be fine. Tell me what happened! I saw on television that the accord was signed, and the Chinese leader is still breathing," Dinah said, waving him over.

Cruz moved to the bed and sat down on the edge, and then took her hand, staring deep into her eyes – eyes that he could escape into forever.

"It's not important. None of it is. But it's over. It's really over. And it's all good."

She looked at him uncomprehendingly, and he squeezed her hand, a mild electric current running between them, an energy that had never faded since they'd first met. She took in his cut face and his gentle, warm eyes, the unambiguous love that pulsed from him like a magnetic field strong enough to power a small city, and a single tear rolled down her cheek.

"Everything's fine. I promise. And it will be from now on," Cruz said.

Then he pulled Dinah to him and held her, the only thing of any real, lasting value in his world, and inhaled the rich scent of her skin as they rocked together, a single organism that would need time to heal. She sobbed quietly into his shirt, whether from hurt or sadness or relief, he couldn't be sure; and then he closed his eyes and offered up silent thanks to fate for giving him one last chance, in the end, to make everything right.

ABOUT THE AUTHOR

Russell Blake lives full time on the Pacific coast of Mexico. He is the acclaimed author of the thrillers: *Fatal Exchange, The Geronimo Breach, Zero Sum, The Delphi Chronicle* trilogy (*The Manuscript, The Tortoise and the Hare,* and *Phoenix Rising*), *King of Swords, Night of the Assassin, The Voynich Cypher, Revenge of the Assassin, Return of the Assassin, Blood of the Assassin, Silver Justice, JET, JET II – Betrayal, JET III – Vengeance, JET IV – Reckoning, JET V - Legacy, Upon a Pale Horse, BLACK,* and *BLACK is Back.*

Non-fiction novels include the international bestseller *An Angel With Fur* (animal biography) and *How To Sell A Gazillion eBooks (while drunk, high or incarcerated)* – a joyfully vicious parody of all things writing and self-publishing related.

"Capt." Russell enjoys writing, fishing, playing with his dogs, collecting and sampling tequila, and waging an ongoing battle against world domination by clowns.

Sign up for e-mail updates about new Russell Blake releases

http://russellblake.com/contact/mailing-list

Made in the USA
Lexington, KY
02 December 2014